A BLACK HEARTS
STILL BEAT TRILOGY

RAFE

l. a. cotton

USA TODAY AND WALL STREET JOURNAL BESTSELLING AUTHOR

RAFE

A Black Hearts Still Beat Trilogy

L A COTTON

Published by Delesty Books

RAFE
A Black Heart Still Beats Trilogy

Edited by Andie M Long Editing Services
Cover by Opulent Designs

RUSH

CHAPTER ONE

"WELL, don't just stand there, open it," my best friend Molly stared at me expectantly, a glint of excitement in her eyes.

"What did you do?" I asked, turning the envelope over in my hands.

"Just open it already, the anticipation is killin' me."

Trepidation swam in my veins. Molly meant well, but she was always trying to push me to live. To step out of my comfort zone and *try new things*. The only problem was I didn't like leaving my bubble, and my parents hated it even more. Especially Mom. She preferred me safe; tucked away at home where they could keep an eye on me. It was suffocating at times, but there was something strangely comforting about it too.

Hands planted on her hips, with a scowl not even old Mrs. West, our third-grade teacher, could rival, Molly groaned, "Oh for Pete's sake, Evangeline Star Walker, will you just open the damn letter already?"

With a heavy sigh, I picked the corner loose and slid my finger underneath, tearing it open. "Dear Miss Walker," I started. "We are pleased to acknowledge your entry into the 2019 Jamesboro Talent Showdown..." My eyes flew to Molly's. "Tell me this isn't what I think it is."

"Oh it is," she clapped, unable to hide her excitement, "it so is."

"No way. I can't..." The words got stuck, my throat suddenly dry. "I'm not ready."

"I think you'll find that letter says otherwise."

"But how...?" I scanned the letter again. "Don't you have to audition?"

The bi-annual Jamesboro Talent Showdown was a big deal around these parts. Probably because it had scouted some of country's biggest stars over the last three decades. What our county lacked in size it apparently made up for in talent.

"They accept video auditions."

"So you sent them a video of me, without my permission?" I gawked at her.

"Eva, you were born to perform, the way Michaela Farrow was born to suck dick." We both snickered at that. Michaela was the Queen Bee of our high school and made *Regina George* look angelic.

"It's been too damn long since you played and you know it."

"I don't know, Mol. Mom and Dad won't—"

"Actually, they think it's a great idea."

"They do?" My brows pinched as I tried to process the bomb she'd just dropped.

She nodded eagerly. "Helped me pick out which video to submit and everythin'."

"Sneaky, very sneaky." I clutched the letter in one hand, hardly able to believe my eyes. I'd attended every showdown I could; watched with stars in my eyes and hope in my heart as performers from all over our small corner of Tennessee came to compete for the coveted title of Jamesboro Talent of the Year, not to mention the twenty-five-thousand-dollar prize check.

"So, what do you say?" Molly could barely contain herself now. A wide grin split her heart-shaped face, anticipation dancing in her hazel eyes.

"I'll need to practice." Something stirred inside me. Performing had once been my passion, my life. I'd been singing and playing the guitar for as long as I could remember. But I hadn't played for an audience in over two years.

"You have time. The regional shows aren't for another month."

"A month?" I grumbled. Of course, it was only a month away, held the weekend after July fourth, with the final a couple weeks after.

"Just imagine if you win... twenty-five-*thousand*-dollars."

"Let's not get carried away just yet. I'm out of practice." *And confidence.* But I didn't want to tell her that, not when she looked so happy, and when she and my parents had gone to so much trouble submitting my video.

"You're a natural, Eva. You could be ten years out of practice and still hold your own against any country star out there right now."

"I don't know about that." Strained laughter spilled out of me, my stomach twisting into a string of knots.

"I do. I believe in you, babe. You should too."

I gave my best friend a tight smile. My guitar had once brought me happiness. Moving my fingers over the frets, tapping my foot to riffs created in my head; I'd felt free. But where music had once been my escape, it was now my burden. A heavy weight settling in my chest every time I slid the strap of my cherry red Gibson around my neck. A reminder of dreams lost, never to be found again.

"Hey, don't cry," Molly's voice jerked me from my reverie. "I didn't mean to upset you." Her slender arms enveloped me. "You know me. I act first, think later. I'm sorry."

"It's fine." I swiped the rogue tears away, sniffling. "You did a nice thing. A good thing. I just—"

"Yeah, I know."

Silence descended over us. It wasn't uncomfortable silence with Molly, my best friend in the entire world. It never was. But it was heavy with the pain of my past. Tainted with the uncertainty of my future.

"I still think you should do it, Eva. It's all you ever wanted when we were kids... *before*."

"I still want it," I whispered, the knots in my stomach tightening, as longing edged into the corner of my thoughts. "I'm just not the same girl I was back then."

"No," a slight smile played on her lips, "you're stronger."

"You're a good friend, Molly Steinberg."

"The best." She was grinning again.

"You are." When so many of my friends had forgotten about me, Molly had been there every step of the way. Through every treatment and hospital admission. Every good day and bad. And there were plenty. Molly was the definition of best friend and my heart swelled that she'd done this for me.

For the *old* me.

"I'll do it." The words slipped from my lips before I could consider their meaning.

Molly blinked, her eyes widening with surprise. Then she was pulling me into her arms, shrieking with delight. "This is a good thing, Eva, the best. You'll see."

It was just a talent contest. Hundreds of other singers and musicians from all across Jamesboro County would be attending.

The best of the best.

Competing would give me a focus; help me forget real life for a while. The one where I had to return to school soon and learn how to live my life again. It was just what I needed.

A little fun.

A big distraction.

Besides, it wasn't like I actually stood a chance of winning.

———

Molly couldn't stay long. She had to help her mom with her younger twin brothers, Silas and Tim. So I'd picked up my guitar and started playing. Letting myself imagine what it would be like to perform at the Talent Showdown. To stand up there in front of the crowds and pour my heart out on stage.

"Sweetheart, you in there?"

I smiled to myself, placing my guitar down against the bed. "Sure, Mom."

"I've missed that sound." She slipped into my room, tipping her head to my Gibson.

"Just playin' around." I shrugged as if it was no big deal.

We both knew it was.

"Figured I'd better brush up my skills before the showdown," I added when she didn't say anything.

Surprise lit up her face but was quickly washed away with tears. "Oh, Eva, that is..." She swallowed hard, moving to the edge of the bed. I reached for her the same time as she reached for me, our hands linking together the way they had so many times over the last eighteen months.

"I'm so proud of you, sweetheart. This is a good thing. Darn good. You have such a gift. Your daddy and I always hoped you'd play again."

"It feels good," I whispered, blinking back my own tears. The familiar feel of the strings underneath my fingers was like home. But I couldn't deny I was out of practice. That a deep ache had spread through my muscles as I cradled the guitar against my body.

There had once been a time it was like an extension of me, another limb, but that was *before*.

Before chemo wrecked my body and cancer infected my soul.

But strumming, that was second nature. I didn't even need to think about it. I simply ran my fingers up the fretboard and let them work their magic.

"The Ploughton show is in a month?" she asked, and I nodded. "And the final is a couple of weeks after school starts?"

"Yeah, but come on, Mom, it isn't like I'll actually make it."

"You always were modest, even as a child. But you have a rare gift, baby. You just need to find your spirit again."

I was pretty sure my spirit was back in Jamesboro General Hospital. Chemo and surgery might have saved my life, but it had also stolen something from me.

Something I wasn't ever sure I'd get back.

Mom squeezed my hand again. "You have so much to live for, Eva." Tears threatened to fall again, clinging to the corners of her eyes.

"I know, Mom. I'll get there. I will."

"Okay, it's almost time for church. Are you—"

I shook my head, feeling panic claw its way up my throat. "I'm not ready."

She nodded, disappointment washing over her. "If you need us for anythin', I'll leave my cell phone on vibrate. Just don't tell Pastor Branneth."

We shared a smile and she left me to it. I sank back into the pillows, letting out a heavy sigh, and my hands found their way to my stomach—my battle scar as Molly liked to call it. Two years ago, I'd been a teenager living life to the full. A tenth grader, I was popular and had good grades.

I had my whole life ahead of me.

I'd wanted to pursue a career in music. Everyone said I had what it took. Said that one day, it'd be my name in lights. But then I got sick and everything changed.

Cancer had taken away so much from me. I knew I had to do this. If not for myself, then for them.

I should have died.

Only I'd lived.

I'd been granted a second chance—a miracle, they'd all called it. But even now, even as every day passed and I got healthier, I knew I wasn't really living. I was hiding. This was my chance to step out of the shadows and into the light again.

I just had to find the courage to take it.

CHAPTER TWO

Leaning over, I grabbed a pencil and struck out the last couple of words, replacing them with the new ones. "Woke up this morning, with tears on my pillow," I sang the words softly, strumming a basic riff, "And I cried. Went through the motions, the questions and anger."

"Eva?" A knock sounded on the door.

"You can come in, Mol," I answered, and she slipped into my bedroom, closing the door behind her.

"Sorry, I didn't want to disturb you."

"How long were you out there for?" I raised a brow.

"Who, me?" She winked, coming over to the bed. "It's soundin' good."

I shrugged, closing my notebook. "It's a work in progress."

"So you won't play it for me?"

"Not yet, no." The words were too personal.

Too painful.

When Molly had informed me she'd entered me in the Talent Showdown, I'd been flooded with ideas. As if deciding to do it had torn open the floodgate I'd kept closed for so long. Creating an original song wasn't the problem; the thought of standing on stage, in front of the judges, of hundreds of spectators was.

"You're writin' again." She eyed my notebook.

"I never stopped." I had book after book filled with song words: some articulate, beautiful lyrics spilled straight from the heart; others jumbled irrational ramblings that made little sense to me, let alone anyone else.

But all were important to me.

A part of my soul.

"If I get to the final—"

"Which you will."

"*If* I do, I'll play it for you. But until then," I snatched the book toward me, "No peekin'."

"Spoilsport." Molly stuck her tongue out at me. "Have you decided on a song for the Ploughton Regional?"

"I think I'm goin' to go with 'Look for Me'."

"No freakin' way." Her eyes grew to saucers. "You're goin' to sing our song?"

"Your song, Mol. You know you were the inspiration for it."

Launching herself across the bed, our laughter filled the air as Molly tackled me to the mattress, smothering me with appreciation and love. "Thank you, thank you, thank you," she breathed the words, rolling away to lie shoulder to shoulder beside me.

"I take it I have your approval then?"

"Hells yeah." Molly grabbed my hand. "Whenever the road gets hard, and things look impossible..." she sang the bridge.

"Whenever thunder rumbles overhead, and you think you can't survive the storm," I joined in.

"Just remember, all you have to do is look for me."

"Look for me," I echoed. "Cos I'll be there, I'll always be there. And there isn't a single thing I wouldn't do for you." I held the note, letting it drift off until silence lingered between us.

After a beat, Molly whispered, "You can do this, Eva. I know you can." She squeezed my hand. "I know you're probably terrified, and I know it isn't easy playin' again. But I wouldn't have entered you if I didn't think you could do it."

"Molly, I..." The words died on my tongue. I couldn't tell her the truth. Tell her how I didn't doubt I could do it, but how, deep down, I wasn't sure I wanted to. Tell her how I wasn't done being angry, so angry at life, at the universe, and at God.

I'd spent almost nine months of my life in Jamesboro General, another six months before that in and out of appointments. Not to mention months before that not feeling myself. I'd seen kids like me, kids with cancer, come and go. Some came and left healthy, granted the same second chance I'd been given. But some didn't. Some were there one day and gone the next. They would never get to return to school, to their friends and families; they would never get the chance to chase their dreams.

And I didn't know how to deal with that.

I didn't know how to deal with the fact that I was still here and they weren't.

It felt like no amount of therapy would change that.

So yeah, I could enter the Talent Showdown and play my heart out, but I didn't know how to do that without feeling guilty. The kind of guilt that paralyzed you, that buried itself so deep inside your soul you weren't ever sure you'd get rid of it.

"What?" Molly sat up, staring down at me with concern. "What is it?"

"I'm..."

She'll understand, won't she?

But if she doesn't...

"I'm really lucky to have you," I said, swallowing down the truth. Molly might have understood, but the truth would change things. It always did. So for now, I would pretend. I would paste on a smile and practice for the contest and let them all see what they wanted.

A girl who had survived the odds and been granted a second chance at life.

Even if she wasn't yet sure how to live it.

———

"This is nice," Mom said.

"It's just the store, Mom." We'd driven into Ploughton to do some grocery shopping.

"Yeah, but I've missed this." She smiled at me. "Spendin' time with you."

"We spend time together." My brows furrowed.

"We do, but I don't know, sweetheart. Lately, it's been, different. You're different." Her voice cracked and she let out a long sigh, no doubt collecting her thoughts. "It finally feels like we're gettin' you back, Eva. The old you."

I don't know if she realized, but her hands had tightened around the shopping cart as we wandered up the aisle.

"Mom." I laid a hand on her arm, causing her to jerk to a stop. "I'm okay."

"Oh, Eva." She swiped her eyes, inhaling deeply. "I'm sorry, baby, I didn't mean—"

"It's fine, Mom. Let's just get the groceries and maybe on the way home we can stop at Minty's for sweet tea?"

"That sounds like a fine idea, sweetheart. You can tell me all about your song for the regional."

I could give her that—sweet tea and idle talk about my song choice.

"Okay, Mom." I smiled. "It's a deal."

We turned the corner to start down the next aisle but came to a stop when I saw Jenson Blaufield.

"Oh look, there's Jenson and his sweet old grandma." Mom was already moving toward them before I could stop her.

"Juliette," she said warmly, "how lovely to see you."

"Jesse Walker, is that you?" Jenson's grandma hobbled around on her stick, offering us a shaky smile. "It's been a while, darlin'."

"Oh you know how it is, Jules."

"And would you look at you, Evangeline Star. Aren't you a sight for sore eyes? Get over here and give me some sugar." She opened her arms and I went grudgingly. It wasn't that I didn't like her, I did, but I didn't want to be anywhere near her cheating dirtbag of a grandson.

"Eva," the dirtbag finally spoke, "it's good to see you."

"Jenson."

"Mrs. Walker, it's good to see you too." He leaned in to kiss Mom's cheek, causing her to blush. She always did have a soft spot for my ex-boyfriend. A soft spot that would've turned to a black hole of wrath if I'd have told her the truth. But Mom had enough to worry about, so I'd made up a story about us ending things amicably.

"Eva, can we talk?"

"Go, sweetheart." Mom offered me a reassuring smile, not even giving me chance to protest. "I'll finish up here and help Jules at the checkout. I'm sure you two have lots to catch up on."

We really didn't.

But Jenson gave me puppy dog eyes, motioning for me to follow him. There had been a time those eyes would make me weak at the knees, now they only made a storm swell inside me.

We walked to the front of the store in thick silence. "You look good, E," he said as we stepped outside. "How are you?"

"Alive," I bit out without thinking.

"Shit, Eva, that isn't..." He almost choked on the words, and I felt smug watching him squirm. "I mean, I wasn't... fuck, I'm so fuckin' sorry."

It lasted all of a minute and then I felt overcome with guilt.

"No, I'm sorry. I shouldn't have said that." Things might have ended badly between us, but he didn't deserve dying jokes, no one did.

I wrapped my arms around my waist, holding myself together. It was one thing to come face to face with people you were friends with *before*, but it was another to come face to face with the boy you thought would be by your side through it all.

"I tried to come and visit, when you were in the hospital. I sent flowers."

"I don't even know what to say to that." My voice rose as I fought back tears. I was lying in hospital alone and scared, my heart broken for more reason than one and he… sent flowers.

"Shit, Eva, don't cry. I'm not worth it."

Incredulous laughter gushed out of me. "You think these tears are for you?" I got all up in his face, jabbing my finger at his chest. "I was done cryin' tears over you when you cheated on me three weeks into my treatment."

"It was a mistake, bab—" I leveled him with a hard look and the term of endearment died on his tongue. "I was scared and confused and—"

"And Sheridan Black just fell on your dick?"

I don't know who was more surprised at my outburst, but I was just so angry.

"Jesus, Eva…" Jenson raked a hand through his tousled hair, the tips lightened by the summer sun.

"I needed you, Jenson. I was scared and confused and I needed you." The dam broke and I sobbed violently into my hands, anger coursing through my veins like wildfire.

Overwhelmed with the tsunami of emotions raging inside me, I barely had the energy to fight off Jenson when he pulled me into his strong arms. He felt so familiar, so safe and warm. And although I hated him, I couldn't deny part of me missed him. Missed his touch.

"I'm so glad you're okay, E," he whispered against my hair.

"Let me go," I ground out, slamming my hands into his chest. He staggered back, surprised, and shook his head with shame. "You don't get to do this. You don't get to comfort me. Not now, not ever, Jenson. I don't need you."

I was already backing away, putting space between us. A couple of people slipped around us to enter the store, pretending not to watch. But I didn't care. I'd been through worse than a few nosy bypassers.

Survived worse.

"E, come on." He reached for me, but I ducked away and made a run for Mom's car. I didn't want to do this; not today, not ever. I'd filed Jenson Blaufield away with all the other things in my life I'd rather forget.

"You can't hide forever, E," he called after me. "It's a small town and school starts again soon."

As if I needed reminding.

In a little over a month, I had to return to Ploughton High School for senior year. After the surgery and my recovery, there had only been a few months left of eleventh grade, and my parents, along with my doctor, decided it was probably for the best to keep me out of school. Just in case. But I'd officially been given the all clear in March. My stage four Non-Hodgkin's Lymphoma was in remission. Which meant, for better or for worse, I had to return to class come August. Back to my friends who had forgotten about me; friends who had moved on when they realized I wasn't coming back anytime soon. Back to an ex-boyfriend who couldn't keep it in his pants, and to classes which no longer seemed important.

I guess that was another part of my survivor's guilt. I was alive. I'd beaten cancer. Yet, I couldn't seem to find it in me to be thankful or grateful or any of those things the doctors, my family, and Molly talked about.

Because I didn't get it.

I didn't get why I was still here and why all those other kids weren't.

Mom said it meant it was God's will, that he still had a plan for me. She genuinely believed I still had to make my mark on the world. But I wasn't special. I wasn't going to be the next First Lady, or campaign for world peace, or develop a cure for cancer.

So *why* was I still here?

It was a question I asked myself every second of every day.

A question I wasn't sure I'd ever find the answer to.

CHAPTER THREE

"Holy freakin' cow," Molly burst into my bedroom. "You'll never guess who they just announced as a guest judge for the Talent Showdown."

"Hmm, Blake Shelton?"

"Think bigger." Excitement rippled off her in infectious waves.

Too bad I was immune.

"Bigger than Blake?"

She rolled her eyes at that. "You're such a dork. Two words. Hudson Ryker."

"Never heard of him."

"Of course you have." Molly flounced down on my desk chair, spinning a three-sixty. "Drummer for Black Hearts Still Beat, only the hottest rock band on the planet right now."

"Rock band?" I scoffed. "They picked a *rock star* to judge a country music contest? That makes a whole bunch of sense said no one ever."

"Really, Eva, sometimes it's like you've been livin' under a rock. Black Hearts are huge. They're already being hailed as the next Rolling Stones. They asked Hudson to sit on the judge's panel because he was born in Klineville."

That got my attention.

"He was? I don't ever remember hearin' his name." Klineville was the next town over.

"That's because he moved before the band was founded, but his family still lives there. I guess they're pullin' him in to boost the status of the contest. And the band could do with some positive PR, they're not exactly angels."

"Let me guess, sex, drugs and rock and roll?" My brow quirked up, teasing.

"You really haven't heard of them?"

"I've been kinda preoccupied, Mol." Guilt flashed over her face, and I instantly regretted saying the words. "Listen, I didn't mean…"

"I know." She smiled, but it was strained. "Besides, music is a great distraction so don't try to pull the, 'I've been busy fightin' cancer card' with me."

And that's why I loved her. Because even when things got heavy or awkward, Molly could lighten the mood. She wasn't one to tiptoe around the C-word like most people. It was also partly why I'd agreed to do the Talent Showdown in the first place. To thank her for the way she'd stood by me through everything.

Not that it would ever be enough.

Pulling out her cell phone, Molly tapped the screen a few times before thrusting it at me. "Here."

I took it from her, watching the video come to life. A single figure was illuminated by candlelight, a low rumble of drums building in the background, the haunting voice of the singer rising over the top.

"That's Levi Hunter, the lead singer. He's a lyrical genius."

"It's…" I didn't know how to describe the somber melody, the bone-chilling tone of his voice. "Dark."

"Straight out of the bowels of Hell, as my mom likes to say. She caught me listenin' to their latest album the other week and almost had a conniption."

"He sounds in pain."

"He *is* in pain. The whole band has *issues*."

"Yeah, must be really hard bein' *rock's next big thing*." I mocked, studying the band's front man as he stalked across the screen. Slow and precise, he reminded me of a predator. A vampire maybe. Or some otherworldly creature.

"He's delicious, right?" Lust thickened her words.

"That's not exactly the first word that sprang to mind."

"Prude," Molly smothered her laughter.

"Am not. I just… he's not my type."

I preferred my guys softer around the edges. Probably why I'd had a huge crush on Blake Shelton since I was just a kid.

"Levi Hunter is everyone's type. Elusive. Ethereal. Dark and dangerous. I bet he's a total freak between the—"

"Enough." I launched a pillow at her.

"See, case in point." She gave me a pointed look. "It's been too long, babe. We need to get you out there, get you back on the horse."

"I was never on the horse," I groaned the words.

"But Jenson was—"

"A mistake." A giant mistake I wish I'd never have made. I'd given him the one part of me I could never get back. Because I foolishly thought he was the one.

My forever love.

It sounded so stupid now. I didn't love Jenson. I loved the idea of him. I wanted what my parents had. The southern dream. Childhood sweethearts who were still going strong.

Or, at least, I'd thought I did.

"Hey, where'd you go?" Molly's voice pulled me back into the room.

"Nowhere." I managed a weak smile.

"You know, you should probably be practicin'. There's not long until the regional."

"Maybe if you didn't keep comin' over here to distract me with videos of bad boy rock stars," I smirked, "I'd get more done."

"So," she snatched her cell phone and dropped it on the desk, "how's it comin'?"

"It's... coming."

"Can I hear—"

"No and no. I told you already, no early performance unless I make the final."

"Which you will."

"Yes, well, we'll see. I'm just surprised I let you talk me into this." The words came out light, but a heaviness descended over us.

Molly's brows furrowed. "You're not ready." She looked so disappointed my heart cracked.

"Honestly? I don't think I'll ever be ready. It's why I know I have to do this."

"I'm so freakin' proud of you, and I know you don't feel ready yet, but you're going to kick ass at the showdown. Oh my god," realization dawned over her face, "you're goin' to meet Hudson Ryker. Like actually *meet* him."

"Hmm, I guess."

"You have to let me be your person," she rushed out.

"My person?"

"Yeah, backstage. I can hold your soda and fluff your hair and make sure you're ready."

"Fluff my—"

"And maybe we'll bump into Hudson and you can introduce me and we'll fall madly deeply in love and—"

"Molly."

"Y- yeah?" Her eyes had clouded over.

"Come back from fantasy land."

Her cheeks flamed. "Oopsie. It's just so excitin'. I've never met a famous person before."

With a little shake of my head, I grinned at her. "You know you are though." Molly frowned. "Oh, don't play dumb with me," I added, "You're my person, Molly Steinberg, and of course I want you there when I perform." Something told me I wouldn't just want her there, I'd need her.

She let out a little squeal of excitement. "For real? I'm your person?"

"I thought about askin' Kayleigh Magdiver but realized she probably wouldn't know who Hudson Ryker is and well, I *need* that information." I fought another smirk.

"Bitch." She threw the pillow back at me.

"Hussy."

"For Hudson Ryker? Hells yeah!"

We fell about in fits of laughter, and for the first time in a long time, I felt lighter. I felt like maybe I could do this.

Like maybe I could find myself again in the darkness.

Maybe.

———

FOR THE NEXT THREE WEEKS, I PRACTICED AND PRACTICED SOME more. I practiced until my fingers were sore and my arms felt heavy. I practiced until I went to sleep dreaming of chords and woke up humming lyrics. It was borderline obsessive. But I couldn't seem to stop. The more I played, the more immersed I became with my music. Until slowly, riff by riff, note by note, the pieces of my broken soul were being glued back together.

I knew it was only temporary fix though.

A Band-Aid on a wound that needed stitches. It would hold for a little while, but eventually it would require something stronger.

Something *more*.

But for now, it was enough.

Music had always been my escape. A way to forget all the other stuff and just be in the moment. And I welcomed the reprieve. Even if I knew that once the showdown was over, reality would come crashing back down around me.

Exhaling the final note, I stilled my hand over the strings.

"Soundin' great, sweetheart." Dad entered the living room.

"Uh, hi." I smiled, caught off guard by his early return home from his job at ST Holdings, a local agricultural company. "I wasn't expectin' you back yet."

He gave me an easy smile. "Still feeling a little shy at performin'? You need to shake off those nerves soon, the regionals in less than a week."

"I know, Dad." My lips pulled into a tight line. "I just..." I'd been practicing my original song. The one I still hadn't let anyone hear.

"Juice?" He disappeared through the archway dividing the living room with the kitchen.

"Please," I replied, stowing my guitar behind the couch.

"Here you go." Dad came over and handed me the glass. "I'm sorry if I surprised you," he said, his expression hardening.

"Dad?"

"It's bad news, sweetheart." He dragged a hand down his face, worry lines crinkling his eyes.

"They're lettin' you go?" My heart sank.

"No, no. But they're makin' cuts and can't offer me full-time hours anymore."

"I'm sorry, Dad." Guilt coiled around my heart.

"Now, now, Eva, none of that. We've been over this. None of this is your fault."

But it was.

If I hadn't gotten sick, Dad wouldn't have lost his job at the Soya Corp, one of the area's largest soybean producers, and ended up working a much less paid job at ST Holdings.

"Somethin' new will come up, it always does." He yanked open the newspaper and began reading it as if he hadn't just dropped a bomb.

It was another reason I'd become so obsessed about the showdown. The more I practiced, the more I realized that maybe I did have a shot at the final. Winning that prize check would pay Mom and Dad back twice over.

I knew they wouldn't want it. But if I did win, I'd already decided I wanted them to have it. I wanted to make life easier for them.

After everything, they deserved it.

"No Molly today?" Dad asked over the top of his newspaper.

"She's on twin duty."

"Ahh, I see. She's a good egg that one."

"She's the best."

"You know if you wanted to get out of the house and spend some time with her, me and your mom would be okay with that."

"I know, Dad."

He let out a heavy sigh, shaking out the pages and folding them neatly. "It's just... you got the all clear almost six months ago and you barely leave the house—"

"I leave the house."

"Grocery shopping with Mom does not count. You're almost eighteen, Eva. You should be out there with your friends, gettin' into mischief."

"Mischief? Really, Dad? Mom would loooove that."

He smiled but it didn't quite reach his eyes, and that made my chest deflate. "You have so much to live for, sweetheart. So much. But I can't help but feel like you're..." he hesitated, his face saying everything he didn't want to.

"I know, Dad. I'm trying, I am. I'm doin' the showdown." I perked up, trying to reassure him.

Gavin Walker was a strong man. Solid and supportive, there was nothing more he treasured than providing a home and good life for me and Mom. But he was different since my diagnosis. The fire in his eyes had dimmed.

It was just another thing I'd lost to cancer.

"And don't you worry about your mom. She means well but we both know she projects." He leaned forward and shifted his eyes from side to side, as if he was about to share some guarded secret with me. "She called my boss twice last week because I was late home. I know she worries after... it's hard for her, but I'm a grown man." His tone was playful, but it didn't match the sadness in his eyes.

"She's just extra protective now."

"And we love her for it," Dad exaggerated the words as if he expected her to walk in at any second. When she didn't, he added, "It might take you to make the first move, sweetheart. Show her you're ready to be a normal seventeen-year-old kid again. Get out there and live a little."

If only it were that easy. Mom might have agreed with me entering the Talent Showdown. That was safe. Structured and predictable. She could prepare. Not to mention the fact she was going to be there. But me being a regular teenager, that was something she couldn't control, and Mom was all about being in control these days.

Not that I blamed her. She'd watched her only daughter try to outrun Death for the best part of a year.

"I don't know, Dad," I said. "I think I should probably start small."

"I hear you, kiddo. But just remember, you can't make your mark on the world hidin' up in that bedroom of yours." He got up and came over to me to touch my head. "I'm going to make a sandwich, I'm starved. Want anythin'?"

"I'm good, thanks, Dad." Eating was a chore these days, just another side effect of chemo apparently. I usually made myself eat a wholesome breakfast and Mom watched over me like a hawk at dinner, but I preferred to graze.

Besides, with the weight of his words—*Mom's words*—pressing down on me, I couldn't have eaten.

Even if I wanted to.

CHAPTER FOUR

"WELL WOULD y'all take a look at that." Molly let out a low whistle beside me, squeezing my hand a little tighter.

She wasn't wrong.

The Ploughton Convention Center was a hive of activity; lines of spectators already winding into the building. We followed the signs marked 'contestants', bypassing the crowd, and slipped inside.

"Contestant?" A stern-faced woman asked Molly who thumbed to me. "She is."

"Check in is over there." She waved us through. Molly burrowed close into my side and whispered, "Someone really loves their job."

"Ssh," I scolded.

"Oh come on, Eva, she had a stick the size of Tennessee shoved up her—" My hand clamped over her mouth.

"I'm not sure I can do this." The words spilled out, the knot in my stomach twisting and tightening. My hand found my guitar strap, squeezing, as my eyes darted wildly around the room.

"Eva, look at me." Molly's face filled my vision. "Breathe, okay? Just take a deep breath."

Sucking in greedily, I let the recycled air fill my lungs, slowing my racing pulse. "I'm okay." I forced a smile.

"Eva..." Molly didn't look convinced, but I shook my head a little, inhaling another deep breath.

"Promise," I added. "Come on, I should probably get checked in."

Mom and Dad had wanted to come in with me, but I hadn't wanted an entourage, and honestly, it was bad enough being around Molly with her overzealous excitement. So we'd compromised. Molly would accompany me backstage, and Mom and Dad would wait until my fate was decided. Mom had wanted to protest, to insist she came, but Dad offered to take her across the street to the local mall. That way she was close by, but she wasn't breathing down my neck.

The desk came into view, but I ground to an abrupt halt when a blur of denim and flannel blocked my path. "Rude much," Molly muttered, letting out an exasperated breath.

The guy chuckled, his eyes dancing with amusement. "I could talk dirty to you all day darlin'."

"Ugh, could you be any lamer?"

"You're here for the showdown?" He eyed the Gibson strapped to my back.

"Aren't we all?" I quipped.

"Guess I walked right into that one." He raked a hand through unruly sandy-blond hair. "I'm Josiah Golden." His expression held a certain kind of expectation, as if we should know his name.

"That's... nice for you." I nudged Molly, shooting her a 'play nice' glare. "I'm Molly. This is Evangeline Walker, my best friend and your stiff competition."

"Mol," I whisper-hissed, feeling myself flush.

"Oh, it's that like, is it?" Josiah grinned. "You think you got what it takes to win this thing?"

"Oh, I know she does," Molly answered, oblivious to the fact I was slowly shrinking in on myself, silently praying the ground would open up and swallow me whole.

Josiah's gaze lasered in on me as if he was sizing up the competition, searching for any signs of weakness.

It occurred to me he probably was.

"I do the competition circuit a lot and I've never heard of you before."

"I..." I froze, but right on cue, before he could even notice my hesitation, Molly added, "Yeah, well, Josiah, you know what they say, actions speak louder than words."

I smothered a smile. Molly was fierce and I was both relieved and pleased to have her in my corner. Even if she didn't know when to quit it.

"Now, if you don't mind," her brow rose, "I think the back of the line is right behind us." She winked at him and pulled me around him.

"I can't believe you just did that," I whispered.

"Babe, if you're goin' to survive this thing, you need to learn to play the game."

"Game?" I blinked, confused.

"People like Goldenboy," she said his name loud enough that Josiah had to have heard her, "are a dime a dozen. They think they're the bees knees. But don't let his bravado fool you. Your talent comes from in here, Eva, babe." She pointed right at my heart. "Don't ever forget it."

I glanced back at Josiah. His lips quirked up, a wicked glint in his eye as he let his gaze slide down my body and slowly back up. Quickly, I turned back around, a violent shudder rolling through me.

"Hey, you okay?" Molly asked as we reached the front of the line.

"Yeah." Doubt edged into my voice.

"Next." The woman beckoned me over.

"You've got this." Molly gave me a thumbs up, tipping her head in a 'go on' motion.

"Next!" The woman sounded impatient and Josiah snickered behind me.

Rolling back my shoulders, I hitched my guitar higher. "You can do this," I whispered. All I had to do was put one foot in front of the other and walk.

———

"Okay, Group A, we're ready for you," the stocky production director, Colton Manners, wafted his clipboard in the air.

"Eeek," Molly clapped, "this is it."

I wiped my clammy hands down my jeans before picking up my guitar. Since arriving at the Ploughton Conference Center, I'd been a big ol' ball of nerves. The morning had been a blur of rehearsals and briefings. Molly had been glued to my side the whole time, doing her best to shield me from the competition; the overwhelming hustle and bustle. She'd even stepped in after Josiah tried to strike up a conversation again. I didn't like him; his leering gaze and sly smirk. But I wanted to avoid a confrontation.

People from all walks of life huddled close to listen to Colton. I found myself wondering about their stories, the path they'd walked to get to this point. Some of them seemed completely at ease among the chaos, taking it all in their stride. But a few people, me included, were on edge. Strained smiles and trembling hands, we stood out against the sea of semi-professional competitors. Much to my irritation, Josiah Golden fit in the first category.

Even more annoying, he was assigned to my group.

"Listen up, because I'm only going to say this once." Colton stared out at us. "You hear your name announced, you get out on stage. First round y'all get two minutes apiece. We have backing tracks prepped and ready. Those of you playing your own instruments should have already been briefed on the do's and don'ts. Any questions so far?"

One hand went up, and Colton tipped his chin in acknowledgement. "Do I have time to take a leak?" A tall thin guy wearing a Stetson and flannel shirt asked.

"Do I look like your mother? As long as you're back here in time to hear your name, I don't care what you do or where you do it."

"Apparently Colton also loves his job," Molly whispered, smothering a snicker. I elbowed her in the ribs. The last thing I wanted was to be singled out by the production director. My stomach was already awash with nerves.

"Ten minutes to curtains up," someone yelled, causing a burst of anticipation to ripple around our group.

Colton didn't look pleased though. His expression was pissed as he touched his earpiece and listened to whoever was on the other end.

"Problem, Colt?" That was Josiah. He'd been nothing but a kiss ass all morning, reveling in the fact he knew most of the production staff.

"Just running a little behind schedule."

"Let me guess," my competitor replied. "One of your judges is late?"

Molly stilled beside me.

"Do you think he means Hudson?" I asked her quietly.

She shrugged. "I haven't seen him yet." And it wasn't for lack of trying. Molly was one hundred percent here for me, but I knew she also desperately wanted to catch a glimpse of the Black Hearts Still Beat's drummer.

"That's what you get for askin' a rock star to judge a country music talent contest," Josiah said out of Colton's earshot, and to no one in particular.

"Do I detect a hint of jealousy, Goldenboy?" Molly's brow rose.

"Jealous... of *them*? Not likely, darlin'."

Colton was paying us no attention now. He'd stepped away to continue his two-way radio conversation.

"Molly," I warned, not wanting her to make a scene.

"Sorry, babe, but I've listened to him go on all mornin'." She swung around to face Josiah again. "If he's that talented, *that good*, how come he's still here, enterin' talent contests? Enlighten us, Goldenboy, please."

"Perfection is a long time in the makin', sweetheart." He stepped closer, his smirk growing. "But mark my words, one day, it'll be my name on your lips."

"Okay, okay, this is just gettin'... weird." I ducked in between them, everyone else watching on with amusement. Josiah clearly had a reputation here and people either lapped up his antics or observed him like he was a science project. Either way, he wasn't someone I wanted to encourage.

Neither of them backed down, eyes locked on the other.

"Mol—"

A commotion behind us caught my attention and I turned just as Molly shrieked, "It's him! It's Hudson Ryker."

Everyone stopped what they were doing, all heads turning to watch Hudson Ryker as he cut across the room toward Colton, whose expression turned from pissed to relieved to awe all in the space of a second, just like the rest of the room.

Except unlike everyone else, I wasn't sure I was awed by him, so much as everyone else's reaction to him. Like Levi Hunter, Hudson emanated darkness. It shrouded him like a black thundercloud. But unlike his bandmate, when he stopped near our small group and smiled, his whole demeanor shifted.

"Sorry I'm late, y'all," he drawled, giving Colton a small nod. "I got... held up. You know how it is." His easy smile grew, and Molly grabbed my arm, squeezing so tight I was sure she'd cut off the circulation. When I glanced over at her, I realized she was barely holding on. My best friend wasn't just awed, she was completely starstruck. It was an odd thing to watch her, a girl full of words and opinions, rendered speechless.

"Anyway, I suppose I'd better get out there."

"What, no words of encouragement for us?" Josiah called after him, stopping Hudson in his tracks. The drummer turned slowly, the light hitting his brow piercing, and smiled again. But this time it held an edge of annoyance.

"Good luck out there today. I'm excited to see what y'all have for us." And with that very short, very underwhelming proclamation, he disappeared through the thick curtain.

"Are you okay?" I immediately checked on Molly who was deathly still beside me. "Molly?"

"I think I'm in love." She clutched her chest.

At least it wasn't my hand.

"Love, really?" I joked. "If that's all it takes to win you over, I'm surprised you—"

"Oh, hush. You're ruinin' the moment."

"Moment? There was a moment just now? Because from where I was standin', it looked like—"

But there was no time to finish my sentence because Colton yelled, "First up is Kelly Inkin, you're on in five. Evangeline Walker, get ready because you're up second."

"I don't think I can do this," I rushed out.

Molly snapped into action, grabbing my hand and yanking me away from the group. "Eva, breathe."

I inhaled deeply. "It's not workin'," I confessed, panic crashing over me like a stormy sea.

"Go to the restroom and splash some water on your face. You have time. I'll stay here and stall if necessary, okay?"

"I—"

"Eva," Molly narrowed her eyes at me, "you can do this. You *have* to do this."

Glancing toward the door I knew led to the restrooms, I weighed up my options. It would have been easy, so easy to leave... and never come back. To flee the showdown and go back to hiding away in my bedroom, trying to shut out life. But deep down, I knew it couldn't go on for much longer. School was right around the corner. If I wanted to graduate with my class, I needed to complete senior year.

"Eva—"

"I got it, I got it." The words spilled out in a rush of breath. I could do this.

All I needed was a little faith.

And while my faith had recently been tested to the point of wavering, I knew Molly, Mom, and Dad had enough to get me through.

CHAPTER FIVE

I STARED out at the judges; my Gibson cradled in front of me like a shield.

"Evangeline Walker?"

"Y- yes, Sir," I answered the judge.

"Don't look so worried," he smiled warmly. "We don't bite."

"We might not, Garth," a petite woman with gray-blonde curly hair said, "But we can't speak for the young 'uns among us." She slid her heavily made up eyes to the other judges on the panel: Hudson Ryker and an emerging country star I recognized as a finalist from last season's *Nashville's Star*.

"No bitin' here. I'm Sara Lou, and you look real pretty." She seemed genuine and her reassuring smile made the knot in my stomach loosen somewhat. Until my eyes found Hudson. He was studying me. Giving nothing away. Running his eyes over every inch of my outfit of worn denim jeans, thong sandals, and my favorite pale blue blouse over a white tank, tied at the midriff.

Molly had given me the lowdown on him during the ride here. He was nineteen. Barely two years older than us. But he sat there, behind his judge's name placard, as though he was so much older and wiser. And maybe he was. Maybe being a rock star on the brink of world fame made you grow up quicker.

Whatever it was, there was something about him that made me feel uncomfortable.

"I only bite when provoked," he said in a way I didn't quite understand. Did he mean it as a threat? Or a general statement? The smile tugging his lips suggested it was a joke, but there was something in his eyes. Something darker.

A violent shiver rolled up my spine.

"Are y'all ready to wow us?" Sarah Lou asked.

"I hope so," I barely choked out the words.

During my preparation for today, I'd assumed the worst part would be performing for the live audience in the final round, if I made it there. But now I was here, standing in front of four judges with nothing but the guitar over my shoulder and trepidation in my veins, I knew I'd underestimated just how hard this would be.

"Take your time, sweetheart," Garth said with nothing but warmth and understanding.

I adjusted the strap of my Gibson and ran my fingers over the fret board, finding a comfortable position. "This is called, 'Look for Me'."

Eyes closed, heart in my throat, I inhaled a calming breath and strummed the first chord letting my words follow.

A thunderstorm rolls in today. Clouds so black they make me cry.
I feel it all inside my heart. A vision of things to come.
But then you call, I hear your voice. It keeps the storm away somehow.
You say you've got me, you always do. Because that is what friends are for.
Yeah, that is what friends are for.

To pull you up when you fall down. Or wipe away the tears that fall.
To share the burden of a thousand secrets. Or tell you what you want to hear.
To hold your hand when things get tough. Or give you hope when you need it most.
To share your successes, failures too. Or raise you up when you're feeling down.

Whenever thunder rumbles overhead, and you think you can't survive the storm,
Just remember, all you have to do is look for me.
Look for me, cos I'll be there. I'll always be there. And there isn't a single thing I wouldn't do for you.

A rainbow shimmers in the sunlight. Lighting my soul up so bright it hurts.

I feel it all inside my heart. The hope that things can be okay.
Because you're here right by my side. And I know together we can walk in the
light.
You say you've got me, you always do. Because that is what friends are for.
Yeah, that is what friends are for.

Just remember, all you have to do is look for me.
Look for me, cos I'll be there. I'll always be there. And there isn't a single thing I
wouldn't do for you.

SILENCE ENVELOPED ME AS MY EYES FLUTTERED OPEN.

Oppressive.

Unpredictable.

Suffocating silence.

My lungs ached with it. But I found the courage to meet the judges faces, waiting for their verdict. Colton had explained earlier, during the arrival briefing, that the first round was instant elimination. If the judges didn't find you up to par, you didn't progress to the live audience show this evening. The bar was high and places were limited. Even if you did make it to the final round later, if they put too many contestants through, they would have to verbally deliberate. Which meant, you could receive a pass now and still be eliminated.

Nausea washed deep in my stomach as I clutched my guitar.

"You wrote that?" Sarah Lou broke the silence, and I nodded, unable to find my voice. "It was beautiful. Can I ask, is it about someone special?"

Another nod. "My best friend."

"Beautiful," she uttered again, her eyes sparkling with admiration. "Well done."

"Thank you." Slowly, my confidence tamped down the nervous energy radiating through me. I'd given it my all. Hit every note, played every chord to perfection. It couldn't have gone any better.

But it still didn't mean it was good enough.

"You have a beautiful tone to your voice, darlin'," the older lady added. "So controlled with great range. It's not your first rodeo, is it?

"No, Ma'am." I'd performed a lot when I was younger. When I was a young girl unafraid of the world.

"Well, I'm certain it won't be your last." She gave me a wink.

"Hudson? Anything to add," Garth prompted, and I understood

now, he was the judge the others took the lead from.

"It was... good."

He couldn't sound more disinterested if he tried.

My heart sank.

Sarah Lou shot him a questioning look while my fingers tightened around the neck of my guitar. He didn't want to be here, that much was obvious. It shouldn't have bothered me he didn't have something nicer to say. He was no one to me. But I couldn't deny his impassiveness stung.

"It was better than good, Evangeline," Garth said. "You should be very proud of yourself. You have a pass from me. Betsy?"

"Pass."

He looked to Sarah Lou next. "It's a pass from me."

"Hudson?" he asked the indifferent guy on the end.

"Pass, I guess."

"Four passes, congratulations. We look forward to seein' you later."

An assistant ushered me off stage before I could process what was happening. It wasn't until Molly reached me, I finally snapped out of my reverie. "Well?" she asked.

"I did it," I gawked at her. "I'm through, I got—"

Molly launched herself at me, squeezing me tight, shrieking, "I knew it. I knew you could do it." She finally let me up for air. "So what did they say? What did Hudson say? Tell me everythin'?" Looping her arm through mine, she led me back toward the holding area.

Because I was still stunned.

I'd done it.

I was through.

I could still be eliminated, but I'd gotten four passes. It was as good as it could get at this point in the contest.

"So..." Molly prompted again.

"Hudson was... not impressed." I grimaced.

"Impossible," she scoffed. "I heard you, we all heard you. You killed it, babe."

"You heard me?" Of course they did.

"I'm so damn proud of you." Molly guided me to a chair, and we sat down. "How did it feel? Playin' again like that?"

"I... I don't really know. I kind of zoned out." Carried away with the music, the familiar feel of the strings beneath my fingers.

"You'd better call your parents. Your mom has been blowin' up my cell."

"In a minute. I need to let it sink in for a second." I screwed my eyes shut, trying to remember how it had felt playing to them. It felt good.

It felt like home.

"You're smilin'," Molly said, and I peeked up at her. "I am?"

She nodded. "I always used to wonder what your mom meant when she said music is in your soul, but I get it now. Seeing you like this, hearin' you... music will heal you, Eva. If you give it a chance, I truly believe it can help you."

"H- help me?" I didn't like where this conversation was headed.

"Oh come on, you think I don't know you by now? Almost six months in remission, babe. Six months and you've barely stepped foot outside."

"Molly, I go—"

"To the store with your mom. To the store with me. For dinner with your parents. To the coffee shop with me. That's not living, babe. It's barely survivin'. But what I can't quite figure out is if you're just scared the cancer will come back, or if it's somethin' else?"

Relief sank into me.

She didn't know.

Molly didn't know the truth.

She suspected something, but she hadn't worked it out, not yet.

"You're right. I'm just scared."

Her eyes narrowed. "But the doctor said—"

"I know what the doctor said, Mol." I was in complete remission. "But that doesn't mean it won't come back. It doesn't mean I'm home free."

"But you can't let fear shackle you. Not when you have so much to live for."

"You're startin' to sound like Pastor Branneth and Mom."

"I'm sorry," she chuckled, "I just worry about you. It's senior year. The year of big decisions and even bigger mistakes." Her brows waggled.

"Oh no you don't." My hands flew up. "I'll leave the mistake makin' to you, thank you very much."

Molly nudged my shoulder. "You mean you won't be my wing woman this year?"

"Do I get a costume?" I grinned.

"Do you *want* a costume?" She grinned back.

Laughter filled our quiet corner of the holding area. It felt good to laugh. To pretend I was normal. Just a normal girl at a talent contest with her best friend. But there was nothing normal about me.

Not anymore.

And that was just something I was going to have to learn to live with.

CHAPTER SIX

"Seriously, Mom, again?" I groaned, watching as she dabbed her eyes with a handkerchief.

"It's the hot sauce, it was very... hot."

We all exploded with laughter. The production team hadn't wanted us to leave the building, so Mom and Dad had brought lunch to us. We'd managed to find a quiet area where we could sit and eat until I had to return to the holding area. But already it was almost time for the final. In less than five minutes, Colton would pull the remaining contestants into a room and deliver our fate. Whether we got to perform again, or whether our journey ended here.

"Well, can you please stop? It's makin' me—"

"Oh, hush now, and get over here and give me a hug." Mom came for me, pulling me into her arms. "Whatever happens next, I am so proud of you, Eva. So darn proud."

"Okay," Molly said pulling me away from Mom, "it's time."

"Good luck, sweetheart," Dad added, his eyes glistening with unshed tears. The way the two of them were acting, anyone would think I was about to perform for the Artist of the Year. But I knew what this meant to them.

What it meant to all of us.

I was slowly realizing, maybe Molly was right. Maybe music could help me heal. If I only gave it a chance.

"Evangeline Walker," someone shouted, and we all turned to find one of Colton's minions beckoning for me.

"Okay, I'll see you soon. But hopefully not too soon," I added, feeling a swell of nervous anticipation in my stomach.

Dad slipped his arm around Mom's shoulder, and she hugged Molly into her side. The three of them were my rock, my family, and now that I was here, I wanted nothing more than to do this for them.

"Evangeli—"

"Coming, I'm comin'," I shouted across the room, grabbing my guitar and hitching it over my shoulder.

"We meet again," Josiah fell into step beside me. I'd managed to avoid him most of the day. But like an infection that wouldn't go away, here he was, burying himself under my skin.

"So it would seem."

"Nervous?" I heard the smirk in his voice.

"Nope."

"You should be." He moved ahead of me but not before shooting me a victorious wink.

Ugh. He was such a smug jerk. If I didn't have to see him ever again, it would be too soon.

One by one, the remaining contestants filed into a small room. It was a damn sight quieter than this morning. The excitement and chaos of the first round was replaced with quiet contemplation and a gentle hum of apprehension that made my hairs stand on end.

"Okay, listen up," Colton said. He stood at the front of the room, every bit the man with the power. "We have a full house out there. Three thousand of Ploughton's finest. And they want a show so let's give them one. Some of you will know the routine by now. One song apiece. Each judge will choose one contestant to advance to the final show in Camdena, two weeks from now."

Twelve contestants.

Four finalists.

And at least twenty people standing alongside me waiting to know their fate.

"Okay. If I call your name, unfortunately, your journey ends here. Please gather up your things and leave the room through that door." He pointed to a door on the far side wall. "There'll be someone waiting to give you your official contestant goodie bag."

"Mackensie Salida, Clay Brown, and Martha Lockstock."

People started filing out of the room. A low rumble of commiserations filling the air as other contestants offered their sympathies. Not me though. I was too busy trying to breathe; my heart crashing so violently against my chest I felt lightheaded.

"Peter Summers and Liza Lowell."

A thickset guy grumbled his disapproval, storming from the room, the door slamming behind him.

"Always one," Colton deadpanned, as if it was business as usual.

"Okay, I have two names left. Trevor McGee and…" the room seemed to inhale a collective breath. "Tamara Miller."

He waited for them to leave before adding, "Congratulations everyone. You are this year's Ploughton Regional Finalists."

Everyone exploded with excitement. Even Josiah managed to hug a couple of other contestants. I was grabbed and shook and high-fived. But I hardly registered a thing.

"Guess your friend wasn't blowin' smoke then." Josiah sought me out. "But you know, you're going to need to bring somethin' special for the final."

"Why don't you worry about your own performance, instead of mine?" I arched a brow, growing tired of his crap.

"Ignore him, honey," a woman who reminded me of a young Dolly Parton joined us. "He's just afraid of a little fresh competition."

"Keep out of it, Delilah," he spat before skulking off.

"What's his problem?" I asked.

"Josiah is harmless enough. He just takes himself, and these contests, too darn serious. Just keep doing what you're doin', hon, and don't let him get under your skin."

I wanted to tell her it was easier said than done but Colton returned and announced, "Okay, everyone, it's showtime."

———

I was to perform third.

Relief had washed over me when Colton informed me I only had to wait a short time until my performance. But then a young girl called Gina hit the open notes of a country version of *Eastside* by Benny Blanko and I completely froze. She was good. Really good. I couldn't see the audience from the wings, but I knew she held them in the palm of her hand, felt the collective intake of breaths as she strummed her guitar.

Damn.

It was good enough to be a hit on the Country Radio Music Chart.

"Evangeline," a production assistant whispered to me. "You have five minutes, okay?"

I gave her a tight smile, my pulse spiking. Then before I knew what I was doing, I inched away from the wings, weaving my way through the people milling about.

"Restrooms?" a woman asked me and I nodded. She pointed toward a door. "Down that hall." An understanding smile broke over her face.

I must have looked as bad as I felt.

Bursting through the door, I moved quicker, desperate to find refuge before I completely lost it.

I didn't end up in the restrooms. Instead, I found a dimly lit alcove to hide in. Leaning against the wall, I tipped my head back and squeezed my eyes shut, sucking in big greedy breaths. "You can do this," I repeated, over and over, until the words bled together.

"Evangeline Walker," my name echoed through the building, lurching my heart into my throat.

Crap, that was quick.

Had it really been five minutes?

The roar of the crowd was a like a rumble of thunder in the distance. Far enough away not to be a threat, but with a lingering warning that things could get worse at any second.

Molly was out there. Mom and Dad too. They were waiting for me. For my big comeback. But I was back here, hiding in a darkened hall, trying to tamp down the fear coursing through my veins.

"You can do—"

"I'm guessing you should be on stage?"

My head snapped over to the figure blanketed in shadows. "I... they told me to get ready and I choked."

"It's happens to the best of us." He stepped into the stream of light and I sucked in another breath. But it wasn't because of my impending panic attack this time. He was... gorgeous. No, that didn't accurately describe him. He was something else. Cloaked in black: dark jeans ripped at the knee, a faded Ramones t-shirt, scuffed military boots, and a thick black leather rope banding his wrist. He looked familiar, but it was impossible. I didn't know anyone here except Molly and my parents.

"Are you a contestant?" I asked already knowing the answer. He wasn't, I'd met them all. But the words had just spilled out, because I was suddenly more interested in him than the fact I was supposed to be out on stage giving the performance of my life.

"Nice guitar." He flicked his head to my Gibson, ignoring my question. "Is it a Hummingbird?"

"Montana," I corrected him, my eyes tracing the full sleeve of tattoos covering his left arm.

"Cool. I know my way around their EB range but have limited experience with acoustics." The faintest of smiles tipped his mouth. "So am I going to get to hear you play it?"

"I..."

"Last call for Evangeline Walker."

Crap.

I glanced down the hall leading back to the stage.

"You should probably go," he said.

"I should?"

Nodding, he thumbed the piercing in his bottom lip. "It could be the big break you're looking for. You'd be a fool to pass it up."

Disappointment tugged my stomach. For a second, I'd thought we'd shared a connection. But he thought I was just another kid looking for their ticket to bigger things.

A bitter laugh spilled out before I could smother it.

"Something funny?" His eyes narrowed, and I was struck by how gray they were. Like two pools of molten silver.

"It doesn't matter." I pushed off the wall and grabbed my guitar. "You're right; it only takes a second."

Confusion edged into his intense gaze. "A second?"

"Yeah, for everything to change."

I knew that better than most.

Without another word I walked past him, but his voice stopped me just before I made for the stage. "Hey, Evangeline, good luck out there."

But I didn't need luck anymore. Something about my brief introduction with the mysterious guy lurking in the shadows had calmed my nerves.

Or maybe it was because he was so gorgeous your brain short-circuited? I shook the intrusive thoughts from my head and made a beeline for the production assistant.

"Evangeline?" I nodded, and she let out a huff. "You're late."

"Sorry, I needed a minute."

"Don't we all, sweetheart. Now get out there, it's showtime."

CHAPTER SEVEN

"Congratulations." The guy from earlier approached me. I'd come off stage and fled straight into the darkened hall, too overwhelmed to go and sit with the other contestants. Emotion bubbled up inside me like a volcano, threatening to spill over and burn me alive.

There was no denying I'd come to life out there, lost to the music and lyrics, under the harsh glare of the lights. But as soon as I'd finished, guilt had snaked through me. Twisting and tightening and taking hold until I could barely breathe. I didn't know if I wanted to make a run for it, puke, or confess my sins.

I guess part of the healing process was acceptance. But it was painful and hard and still ignited too much confusion and anger inside me.

"I, uh, thanks." I swiped at my eyes, trying to hide any evidence I'd been crying.

"Hey, are you okay? If you need some time I can...."

He went to double back, but I said, "No. Stay, please."

"Want to talk about it?"

"No, I really don't." I pulled at the hem of my blouse. "But thanks anyway."

He jammed his hands in his pockets, lifting his shoulders in a small shrug. "You were great out there."

"You listened?" I found his eyes, instantly lost in their intensity.

"It was kind of hard not to." He lowered his head, staring at the ground, his boot kicking nothing but thin air. "Have you always wanted to be a country singer?"

"Why do I feel like that's a loaded question?" I smiled.

Talking about music was safe. Easy. The guy in front of me was a musician, that much was obvious, but he didn't look like your typical country singer.

"No reason." His mouth curved. "I just... well, you sounded great, don't get me wrong. But it almost sounded too rock to be country."

"Is that a compliment?" My brow rose. I'd chosen to sing an upbeat cover version of *Believer* by Imagine Dragons. It had always been a favorite of mine but since everything, there was something even more poignant about the lyrics.

"I'm not sure." The guy—I realized I still didn't know his name because he hadn't offered it—ran a hand through his dark, tousled hair. "Anyway, I should probably go."

"You should?" the words spilled out.

"Yeah, I need to..." He hesitated.

"Yeah, of course." A strange sensation tugged deep in my stomach. I didn't want him to leave. Which made zero sense considering I barely knew him from Adam.

"Good luck with the next round. Although something tells me you won't need it." His lip kicked up at the corner, and then he was gone. Walking down the hall as if nothing had happened.

And it hadn't.

Except I couldn't shake the feeling something *had* happened.

"Hey," I called out after him. He spun around but continued walking backwards. "Yeah?" he replied.

"I never got your name."

"That's because I never gave it to you." I couldn't be sure, but I thought I caught a smirk in his expression. Soft laughter escaped me, replaced with a sinking feeling when he offered me nothing more.

No explanation.

And still no name.

———

"THERE YOU ARE," MOLLY SPOTTED ME AS I MADE MY WAY backstage. "I've been lookin' everywhere for you."

"Do I even want to know how you got back here?"

"As if they could stop me." Mischief twinkled in her eyes. "How are you feelin'?"

"Like I'm on the Tilt-A-Whirl and it's getting faster by the second."

"You did so good. Like seriously, Eva, the crowd went wild. I thought your mom was going to pee her pants."

"I hope for your sake she didn't." We shared a smile.

"Where have you been anyway? I asked a couple of people after you, but they said they hadn't seen you since you came off stage."

"I needed a minute..." I let the words hang.

"Gosh, babe," she roped an arm around my shoulder and pulled me into her, "I can't even imagine how crazy this must all be for you. And overwhelmin'. But you've got this. There's no way the judges won't pick you after that performance. I had chills, Eva. Honest-to-God chills."

"Now I know you're just blowin' smoke."

She pulled back to look me in the eye. "I swear on Jesus. You know, I heard some of the other contestants talkin'. Apparently, there's always a party after—"

"No. No way. I signed up for the contest. I didn't agree to any parties."

Molly pouted. "Please, for me? We could blow off your mom and dad and hang out with the other contestants. I spied a couple of guys I wouldn't mind—"

"What happened to Hudson, huh?"

"A girl has to keep her options open. Besides, I can't imagine he'll want to party with us mere mortals."

"Will Josiah be there?" I couldn't believe I was even contemplating this. But Molly looked so hopeful, so excited. Going for a couple of hours couldn't hurt.

Could it?

"I guess so." She shrugged. "But we can surround ourselves with much nicer, much *cuter* guys."

"You're insufferable."

"But you love me."

I did. More than she would ever know.

"Fine. Maybe we can check it out... *if* I make the final four."

"If you don't, and you will, a party might be exactly what you need. A little pick me up."

"Oh no, that won't work with me. If I don't get through, I'm headin' home to break out the ice cream and Blake Shelton albums."

"You really need to expand your musical repertoire." She exaggerated the words.

"My repertoire, huh? And what do you know about musical repertoire?"

"I know that you need to move on from the likes of Blake Shelton and listen to some rock for a new era."

"Let me guess, the kind of rock Black Hearts play?"

"Annnd she gets it." Molly fake cheered, barely containing her laughter.

"Go ahead, mock me, mock me all you—" I spotted the guy from earlier darting into the hall.

"Eva?"

"Y- yeah?"

Molly frowned as I met her inquisitive gaze. "Is everythin' okay?"

"I just thought I saw someone."

"Who?"

"Hmm, no one. It doesn't matter." A bolt of guilt shot through me. But it wasn't like there was anything to tell her. He was just a guy.

A guy I knew nothing about.

I didn't even know his name.

So why did I feel like I was lying to my best friend?

———

THE LIGHTS BEAT DOWN ON ME, THE GLARE ALMOST BLINDING. I knew the audience were out there, a sea of faceless people beyond the judges table, but I couldn't focus. Anticipation flooded every cell making my skin tingle and my vision blur.

"Judges," the announcer said, "It is now time to choose your finalist to advance to the Final Showdown in Camdena. Garth, let's start with you."

"Firstly, Gabe, I have to say the bar was very high this year. Y'all did an amazing job." He let his eyes run over each of us. "But one act stood out for me in both rounds today and that was Scott Roscoe."

Applause broke out throughout the vast room, and Scott, a twenty-something guy from the next town over, stepped to the side, waiting for his competition to join him.

"Okay," Gabe ushered the crowd to silence, "let's move to you, Sarah Lou."

"Well, Gabe, I'm fixin' to agree with Garth. The talent this year has blown me away. I had my eye on one or two contestants, but this young lady really upped her game in the last round." The judge's eyes landed on me and my breath caught. Surely, she didn't mean—

"Gina Denby."

My shoulders sank, disappointment clinging to my insides as the crowd once again erupted. Gina bounced over to Scott and the two of them hugged.

"Congratulations, Gina; if you'll join Scott." He gave her a minute before moving on. "Now we're onto the lovely Miss Betsy."

"Well thank you, Gabe." Betsy Miller winked at Gabe and then looked out at the remaining nine of us. "I didn't need to think about this because let me tell you somethin' about my finalist. They've got what it takes to go all the way. Give it up for country's newest sweetheart, Miss Evangeline Walker."

The world fell away as the roar of the audience stunned me into complete paralysis.

I did it.

I was through to the Final Showdown, and one step closer to a place in the final at Camdena in two weeks time.

I could hear people chanting my name. Mom, Dad, and Molly, maybe? No, it sounded louder—too loud to just be my loved ones. Slowly, I broke free from my trance, like a butterfly emerging from its chrysalis.

"Your third finalist everyone," Gabe said over the noise which showed no signs of abating. "Miss Evangeline Walker."

That's all for you Eva.

Betsy smiled knowingly at me. As if she saw it, right there in my eyes. Saw the second I transformed from a contestant doing it for her best friend and parents, to a girl who *needed* it.

Heart fit to burst, I joined the others. Gina and Scott were quick to congratulate me but then Gabe was ushering everyone into silence again. I looked over at the remaining contestants. A couple had their eyes closed, mumbling, as if in prayer. Josiah's gaze met mine, narrowing, his jaw set. "And finally," Gabe said. "Our new guest judge to this year's showdown. Hudson, my man, who's it going to be?"

The drummer scrubbed his jaw, making a point of looking everyone up and down, as if he were judging a beauty pageant, not a singing contest.

"Josiah Golden," he said with little emotion.

"Yes!" Josiah mouthed, discreetly punching the air at his side.

"Anything you'd like to say to Josiah, Hudson?"

"Yeah," a slow smirk lifted the corner of his lips, "Nice hat."

The crowd's cheers turned to rumbles of amusement. Even I couldn't help but snicker as Josiah strutted over to us, obviously immune to Hudson's dismissal. I guess for some people a win was a win no matter how you earned it.

"Well, okay then." Gabe frowned. "Give it up for the Ploughton Regional 2019 Finalists."

Of course Josiah had nothing nice to say as he joined us, the crowd's applause drowning out his words.

"Don't get too comfortable, little lady," he mouthed out the side of his lips. "This is a cakewalk compared to the final at Camdena."

Rolling my eyes, I paid him no attention. The final was two weeks away. I'd worry about that later. Right now, I wanted to soak up the atmosphere, let it wash over me and purify my soul. Because up here, on stage in front of three thousand people, I could almost believe this is what I was destined to do. That this was why I'd been given a second chance.

And I wanted to cling onto the feeling for as long as possible.

CHAPTER EIGHT

"I'M NOT SURE ABOUT THIS." I grabbed Molly's hand, yanking her backward. She spun around and gave me her best Mom-look.

"Eva, we *are* doing this. You need this. Hell, I need this." A heavy sigh slipped from her lips. "One night of normal. Of good ol' fashioned fun. Besides, your parents already left and your dad paid for the room upfront."

"I still can't believe he did that."

"Believe it." Molly smirked. "This is a good thing, babe. It means your mom is finally loosenin' the strings."

I wasn't so sure about that. When Molly had slipped it out that we wanted to stay to the party, Mom had made it perfectly clear she didn't mind... as long as she and Dad stayed with us. Imagine her horror when Dad offered to check us into the hotel where most of the contestants and judges were staying overnight; the same hotel where the party was happening.

The same hotel I knew had cost him more than we could afford.

But that was my dad, always trying to put a smile on my face.

"By the time we get home tomorrow," I went on, "I'm sure she'll have initiated divorce proceedings." Mom was furious. But instead of making a scene in front of everyone, she'd given me and Molly a lecture about being responsible young adults, before shooting Dad her 'we'll talk about this later' stare.

Dad was in big trouble, and I was just relieved it was one argument I wouldn't be home to witness.

"So we're stayin'?" Molly's eyes lit up.

"Staying, yes." I was excited about a night in a plush hotel room with my best friend. "The party though... I'm not sure, Mol."

"Please?" She interlinked her fingers with mine and pouted. "We'll just stay an hour. Two, tops. I won't leave your side, promise. I think it would be good for you to go, put yourself out there a little."

"I don't need a babysitter Molly." Irritation rolled up my spine.

"I know that, silly." She flicked her brown waves off her shoulder. We were still in our clothes from the day, not having brought an overnight bag with us. But Molly being Molly had packed an emergency make up kit, just in case.

"Ready?"

"As I'll ever be," I mumbled half-heartedly, letting her take the lead and pull me towards the tenth-floor suite. My eyes widened as we stepped inside, my heart fluttering wildly in my chest. The huge suite was crammed with production staff and contestants.

"Okay?" Molly asked me as I tried to take it all in. I'd been to parties before, but I'd missed out on the ones where cups of soda were replaced with questionably acquired liquor. Where risqué games of seven minutes of heaven were replaced with couples getting lucky in darkened bedrooms. And morning after lie ins were replaced with hangovers from hell.

"I'll take one of those." Molly scooped up a glass of what I could only presume was champagne from a passing server. I half-expected him to card her but of course, he didn't. This was a private event.

"You didn't want one?" I gave her a bemused look, and she quickly added, "Your meds—"

"It's fine." I was still on a cocktail of post-chemo drugs. Would be for some time yet. "You drink enough for both of us."

"I do not." She smiled deviously. "Don't look now, but Scott Roscoe is comin'—"

"I was wonderin' if you'd show up," he said around a smirk. The kind of smirk I figured got girls like Molly to eat out the palm of their hand.

"Eva," he craned around my best friend to greet me, "you killed it out there today."

"Likewise." I tipped my chin, internally cringing at how brisk I sounded. It wasn't intentional, I'd just forgotten how to do this. How to be a seventeen-year-old girl at a party.

Probably because I'd never been a seventeen-year-old girl at a party. Much less a party like this one.

"Not much of a talker?" he asked, nothing but gentle curiosity in his gaze. "I dig that."

"Don't mind Eva," Molly intervened. "She's just..." I held my breath, silently praying she didn't reveal the truth. "A little overwhelmed."

"Happens to the best of us. But trust me when I say this is nothin' but a warm-up for the real party after the final show in Camdena. Colton might have a stick the size of Tennessee up his ass but him and his team sure know how to throw a party."

"We look forward to it." Molly flashed me a wink, and I managed a smile.

"Well, I should probably..." He flickered his head over to a huddle of people. I spotted Gina and another couple of contestants who had performed in the final round.

"Isn't this a bit... unnecessary?" I remarked in a hushed voice.

"Babe," Molly's brow shot up, "you really need to get out more. This is a taste of what it's like."

"What *it's* like?" I frowned.

"Yeah. Making it. Being someone in country musiclandia. You heard Josiah; he travels all over the state doin' these things."

"Yeah, but that's not what I want to do." This was a one-time deal. I couldn't deny today had ignited my passion for performing again, but I didn't want to spend my life chasing talent contest crowns.

"But you looked so good out there."

"If I'm destined to have a career in performin', Mol,"—which I didn't believe right now I was—"It'll happen when the time's right. But I'm not sure this is the path for me. One day maybe, but I'm not sure I want to regularly compete at these things."

The corner of her mouth lifted, a twinkle in her eye. "What?" I asked.

"It's just, I wish you could see what I see, babe. What everyone out there saw. You are born to be on the stage, Eva."

"It takes more than raw talent to make it these days." Josiah strutted up to us. "You need the whole package. You need to give the fans what they want."

"And what exactly is that?" Molly humored him.

"You've got to let them in on the journey with you. Let them get to know you, your story." He knocked back the rest of his drink. "So, Walker, I have to ask, what exactly *is* your story? Because from what I'm hearin', you're a closed book."

"Who said that?" I pressed my lips together, glowering at him.

He shrugged. "Just idle backstage talk."

"You don't know anythin' about me or my story," I ground out. "I'd like to keep it that way."

"Oh, it's like that, huh?" It only made him smirk.

"It's like that, Goldenboy," Molly said. "Now why don't you run along and annoy someone else?"

His easy laughter grated on me like nails down a blackboard, but thankfully he took the hint. "Sweet baby Jesus, he's annoyin'." Molly's nose scrunched in disgust as we watched him melt into the sea of people. "Shall we mingle?"

My expression must have said it all, because my best friend hooked her arm through mine with a chuckle. "I've got you, Eva," she leaned in, "I've got you."

———

THE PARTY TURNED OUT TO BE A BUST. EVEN MOLLY GREW BORED of the mindless conversation, all the industry talk. She'd hoped Scott would improve the situation, but he turned out to be a persistent flirt, working his way around the room like an old pro.

"This is not how I saw the night goin'." She flopped down beside me on the velveteen loveseat situated in a darkened corner of the suite.

"Aww, I'm sorry, Mol. I know how much you wanted to have fun."

"It's fine." Her eyes slid to mine. "At least you came. That's huge, Eva. Shall we call it a night? It's still pretty early so it doesn't have to be a complete washout. We can order room service and rent a movie?"

"You read my mind." I stood up and offered her my hand.

"I think Colton needs a lesson in party plannin'," she grumbled as we left the suite. It was only a little walk to the elevator, but before we'd made it even a few steps, I felt someone move up behind. Half expecting to see Josiah, my breath caught when I saw Hudson Ryker standing there.

"Leaving already?" he asked.

"I, uh... excuse me?"

A slow grin pulled at his lips. "Do you always get this tongue-tied around people or is it just—"

"Hud," a deep voice said from behind him, and the guy from earlier smiled in my direction.

"Hey."

"Holy cow," Molly breathed, standing beside me. "You're..." She swallowed, and slowly the missing pieces clicked into place.

"The band," I sighed, feeling stupid I hadn't realized sooner, "you're with the band."

The guy lowered his eyes, rubbing the back of his neck. Hudson chuckled quietly. "I take it the two of you have already met?"

Mystery guy cut his friend with a hard look I didn't understand.

"I'm sorry, did you need somethin'?" My question was for Hudson despite not being able to tear my eyes off his friend and the torn expression he wore.

"Actually, we wondered if you wanted to come and hang out?"

"You want us to what?" I shrieked.

"Hang out, chill, kick back..." Hudson stared at me like I'd grown a second head.

"Excuse us a minute," Molly grabbed my hand, "me and my friend need to clear up some things." She pulled me away, not stopping until we were out of earshot of the guys.

"Hey," I protested, "is there any—"

"Do you have any idea who that is?" She gawked at me.

"He's with the band?"

"He's not just with the band Eva. He's *in* the band. That is Black Hearts' bassist Rafe Hunter."

"Rafe Hunter." His name rolled off my tongue as I glanced over to where he stood watching us.

"We have to go with them."

"What?" I whisper-shrieked. "No! Absolutely not. Hudson is an ass, and Rafe is..." I had no idea how to answer that. But we couldn't go with them. They were rock stars. Actual living breathing rock stars. Rock stars we were—

"Evangeline Star Walker, listen up and listen good." Molly leaned closer, practically pushing her head against mine. "That is Hudson Ryker and Rafe Hunter, one half of Black Hearts Still Beat. Do you realize how many girls would kill to be in our shoes right now?"

"I guess," I grumbled. "But I'm not sure—" Molly pressed her fingers to my lips.

"I know, and I would never ask you to do anythin' you didn't want to. But this is Hudson Ryker and Rafe Hunter, babe. If we don't do this, we will regret it. For the rest of our lives."

"Molly, I'm not sure..." I was breaking. But she was giving me her puppy dog eyes, silently begging me to say yes. To give her this one thing. And I couldn't deny part of me did want to talk to Rafe again.

"They probably expect us to sleep with them."

"Please, I'm not goin' to sleep with him." She rolled her eyes as if the idea was preposterous. I wanted to believe it was, but there was something in her gaze. That dreamy sparkle girls got around guys they like. "But I wouldn't say no to a heavy make-out session."

"Molly!"

"Oh come on, babe. Like you wouldn't kiss Rafe. I saw the way you looked at him. What did Hudson mean, you two have already met? How did I not know about this?" Hurt flashed across her face.

Choosing to ignore that, I mumbled, "I can't believe I'm doin' this," under my breath. Molly squeaked with excitement, forgetting all about my earlier transgression. Before I could change my mind, she grabbed my hand again and pulled me toward the two brooding guys.

"So," she flashed Hudson a seductive smile, hardly fazed by the fact she was talking to music royalty. "What did you have in mind?"

"We've got the penthouse suite. The view is pretty incredible. You want to come check it out?" Hudson swiped his thumb along his bottom lip, brazenly checking my best friend out.

"It sounds amazin'."

"There's just one small catch."

"Go on..."

"You'll need to sign a non-disclosure agreement." Hudson flicked his eyes to Rafe who was silent and still beside him.

Molly gave a dismissive shrug. "It's no biggie for me. Eva?"

"The show already made us—"

"This is different." Hudson cleared his throat. "This means you can't talk to anyone... about us."

"You think we're goin' to run back and tattle to our friends?" Molly sounded genuinely hurt.

"It wouldn't be the first time," he grumbled. "But it's just the way it has to be."

"Fine, lead the way." She grinned as if she wasn't giving up the chance to hang out with them for anything.

I rolled my eyes, and Rafe snorted under his breath, lingering behind to walk with me.

"I guess we're signin' the NDA," it came out barely a whisper.

"Hey," he said. "If you don't want to do it, then don't. But believe when I say my intentions are pure. You were only headed back to your room and Hud is right, the view is pretty incredible." His eyes fixed right on me, pulling me in.

"The view... right."

"Eva, you don't have to come—"

"Too late." I flicked my head to where Hudson was leading Molly down the hall, flanked by a burly bodyguard. It was then I realized there was another one behind us.

"Don't mind Lennox and Jake." Rafe said, noticing my expression.

"Are they... comin' with us?"

"They'll be close by, but no, they won't be hanging out if that's what you mean."

"Yo, you guys coming?" Hudson called out from the elevator, but I was frozen in place.

Was I really about to do this?

Go up to the penthouse suite of two rock stars? One of whom was clearly into my best friend and another who I'd shared two intimate conversations with today.

"There's no pressure," Rafe's voice startled me. "If you want to head to your own room, I can have Lennox walk you."

"I..." I glanced back at Molly and she gave me her pleading eyes again. Taking a deep breath, I steeled myself and said, "Let's go."

CHAPTER NINE

"Eva, you have to see this," Molly said the second I followed Rafe into the penthouse.

It was a vast open plan room with a long oatmeal sectional dividing the living area and the kitchen. Huge windows ran along the far wall, and the décor was warm but modern. Splashes of burned orange and browns complemented the dark varnished wood counters and coffee table. It was a far cry from our small craftsman house back in Lyme.

"Drink?" Rafe asked me and I smiled.

"Just a water please."

"Eva, babe, get over here." Excitement radiated from Molly as I approached her and Hudson. He watched her, leaning casually against the wall, as her wide eyes took in the view. "I've never seen anythin' like it."

"You get used to it," Hudson murmured.

"I guess being a famous rock star has its perks." The words spilled from my lips, and Hudson's brow quirked up, his eyes narrowing on me. Molly looked mortified as she mouthed, "what the hell?"

"Different city, same view," he added, his expression softening. "After a while, it all looks the same."

"I don't believe that for a second," I said quietly.

During the show, I'd written Hudson off a spoiled arrogant musician. But there was something different about him tonight, something beneath his hungry gaze as he watched Molly take it all in.

Rafe came over and handed me my water. "Thank you," I said.

"Guess I'll get our drinks," Hudson grumbled. "Molly, drink?"

"I'll take a beer."

"How old are you exactly?"

"Old enough." She smirked.

"So long as you're legal it's all good."

My eyes flew to Molly who snickered into her hand. Rafe stalked after Hudson, leaving me alone with my best friend. "What the hell are you doin'?" I hissed.

"Havin' fun. Relax, babe. Besides, he's only nineteen."

"But their lives aren't like ours, Mol. They're…" I glanced over at the guys who were huddled close, expressions strained as they argued about something. Most probably us.

"Rock stars." She grinned. "It's like every girl's fantasy."

My brows crinkled as I let out an exasperated breath. "Just promise me you won't do anythin' reckless."

"Only if you promise me, you'll try to enjoy yourself. Rafe seems… nice." Molly's grin grew.

"*Molly!*" I warned.

"What? I'm just sayin' he's… oh, hey, Rafe. We were just—"

"Can I borrow Eva for a second?" he asked.

"Borrow away." Molly gave me a little shove and I stumbled into him. My hands went to his chest, as I steadied myself.

"I'm sorry." My cheeks flamed.

"Don't worry about it." His soft chuckle made my stomach clench. "Come on, I want to show you something."

"I… okay." I followed Rafe to the other end of the room, nervous energy swimming in my veins.

"Don't look so worried," he said, his gray eyes sliding to mine. "I just thought you might like to check this out."

I immediately saw the source of his interest. "Holy crap, is that a—"

"A '62 Zemaitis 'Heart Hole' Bass."

I moved closer, itching to get a better look. "It's beautiful." The classic handcrafted guitar was a rare beauty; mahogany neck, fretless rosewood fingerboard, and mahogany back and sides. "This must have cost a pretty penny." I'd heard of guitars such as this one going for upward of twenty thousand dollars.

"I won it in a bet."

"Shut up," I gasped. "You did not win a '62 Zemaitis in a bet."

"True story." Rafe's lip curved as he perched on the edge of the back of the sideboard. "Maybe I'll tell it to you one day."

"I'd like that, very much."

"Want to play it?"

My heart almost leaped into my mouth. "Oh no, I couldn't," I stuttered over the words, already imagining what it would feel like in my hands, how it would feel to move my fingers across the strings.

"Go on, it's an instrument. It's supposed to be played."

"But it's a '62—"

"Zemaitis, yeah, so you keep reminding me." His eyes twinkled with amusement, but I didn't feel like he was laughing at me. It felt like we were sharing an intimate joke.

It felt... disarming.

"I'm just... wow, for real?"

"Go ahead." He tipped his head. "Just be gentle with her."

Lifting her off the stand, I cradled the guitar against my body, finding a comfortable position. "It's surprisingly light," I observed, testing an A chord followed by a C minor.

"Nice," Rafe said, watching me intently. "Play something for me?"

"I, uh... sure."

It wasn't like this night could get any weirder.

Closing my eyes, I strummed the opening notes to a song I'd written a long time ago. It was a simple melody, given a dreamy sound by the alternating chords. The sound washed over me, and it didn't take long for the lyrics to spill from my lips.

"And what I'd really like, is for you to see me. See the girl behind these eyes. But you don't see and you don't know, what's lies beneath or where I go..."

My body swayed gently, my foot tapping softly against the plush carpet. Until I was no longer a girl standing in a penthouse suite playing a song for Rafe Hunter. Until I was no longer riddled with guilt and anger and fear.

Until I was free.

"That was..." Rafe's voice yanked me crashing back to the room. I hadn't even realized I'd finished until his words hit me. "Just wow," he added.

"Sorry, I kinda got lost in the moment."

"Don't apologize. You have a beautiful voice, Eva."

"Thanks." I gently placed the guitar back on its stand. "And thanks for lettin' me play."

"Anytime."

Why did that sound like a promise?

Shaking the crazy thoughts from my head, I glanced around his tall frame, frowning when I saw we were all alone. "Where'd Molly and Hudson go?"

"I, uh," Rafe grimaced, "I think he's giving her a tour of the place."

"Let me guess, the bedroom?" My brow rose.

"He's not a bad guy, Eva."

"I never said he was, but you're..." Shaking my head, I swallowed the words. "It doesn't matter."

"No, go on. Say whatever's on your mind. I have thick skin; I can take it." Rafe looked disappointed, and I felt a pinch of guilt.

"I didn't mean..." I sighed. "It's just we all know how this ends. Your friend will take whatever he wants from my friend and she'll..."

"She'll what?"

"It doesn't matter." I moved over to the window, needing space. Needing to be away from his intense stare. His questioning eyes.

"Molly seems like a girl who knows what she wants." Rafe came up beside me. "Is it so bad if they enjoy the moment?"

"No," I breathed out, lifting my eyes to his. "I just... that isn't what I'm looking for." I don't know why I said the words. He'd given me no reason to assume he was the same as Hudson, that he wanted the same thing.

But the words were out there now, hanging between us like a sheet of ice.

"And you think that I am?" His tone wasn't cold, but chills ran up my spine, nonetheless, making me shudder. "Are you cold?" he added.

"I'm fine, thank you."

"Hungry? Thirsty?"

Fighting a smile, I shook my head. "I'm good."

"So, Evangeline Walker, how long have you been playing?" Rafe wandered to the sectional and I followed. We sat down, keeping a safe distance between us. But I didn't miss the way he angled his body toward me, completely at ease sitting with a girl he barely knew.

"I can't remember a time when I didn't play. Mom says I was born hummin' a tune."

Something flickered over his expression. "Was she like those crazy pageant moms? The ones who have their daughters on stage before they can string together a sentence?"

I laughed. "Not really. I always loved performing but I never needed a big audience. I was just as happy playing in my yard to the birds and the neighbor's cat as I was performin' to the whole town at the annual hoedown."

"Your town has an annual hoedown? Now that is something I'd pay to see."

"It's about as excitin' as it gets where I live."

"And where is home?"

I hesitated, hardly able to believe Rafe wanted to know all of this. But there was nothing in his eyes to suggest he was just humoring me, so I answered, "Lyme. A small town ten miles out of Ploughton. What about you?"

"I hail from Atlanta, but it hasn't been home for a long time." His eyes darted to the floor, just for a second, but enough I knew there was a story there.

"I've never been," I said. "To Atlanta, I mean. In fact, I've never been out of state. But I've always wanted to travel."

"We were on the road until June. Six months of touring across the country."

"I bet that was fun."

"It was in the beginning; being in a different city every night. The sights and sounds, even the smells. But being on a tour bus with three other guys can get... cramped." The corner of Rafe's mouth kicked up wistfully. "It doesn't take long for the days to blur into one."

"You're really sellin' it to me." Strained laughter vibrated in my chest.

"Don't get me wrong, I love what I do. I love the fans, the music, getting to stand up on stage and play but..." he hesitated.

"It gets lonely."

His eyes widened on mine, as if I'd just uncovered his darkest secret.

"Yeah, it does." The air thickened around us and Rafe leaned closer, his eyes pinning me to the spot. "I can't remember the last time I just sat with someone and talked," he admitted. "People always want something from me. Selfies, autographs, just one quick song before I leave."

"I guess that's the price of fame."

"Yeah, well, sometimes it feels too high of a price to pay." Rafe flinched. "Shit," he raked a hand down his face, "I'm saying too much and you're probably thinking I sound like an ungrateful bastard."

"Not at all. I appreciate your honesty. It's... refreshin'." I'd leaned in now, erasing the space between us. Rafe was tall, much taller than my five-six. And he was nothing like the guys at school. Nothing like boys you could take home to meet your parents. But he looked down at me, with gray eyes that were so expressive and honest, it made my heart flutter wildly in my chest.

He wanted to kiss me.

I felt it in my bones.

Even more surprising, I wanted him to kiss me. I wanted to feel his mouth on mine, feel his lip piercing cool against my skin. I'd only ever kissed Jenson and two other boys before. We'd been young and inexperienced and clumsy; all tongues and teeth and giggles as we tried to figure out a natural rhythm. But something told me kissing Rafe would be the total opposite.

"What is it about you, Eva?" His voice drifted over me like a blanket, soft and warm and comforting, as he plucked one of my blonde curls between his fingers. Our faces were closer now. Just another fraction and our lips would be—

The bedroom door flung open and Molly dashed through it, giggling and gasping for breath. Rafe flopped back against the couch, letting out a small sigh, the almost-moment between us gone.

"It's mine now, buddy," Molly shrieked, "I'm goin' to sell that shit on eBay, make myself a small fortune." She hurried past us, Hudson hot on her heels.

"We should probably get the two of you back," Rafe said, "before that becomes an all-out war." He flicked his head to where Hudson had tackled Molly to the floor, the two of them wrestling for whatever it was my best friend had stolen.

"You're probably right," I let out a little sigh of my own. "You grab Hudson and I'll deal with Molly?"

Rafe stood up and offered me his hand. "Deal." His fingers curled around mine, his touch like wildfire. Heat crept up my neck and into my cheeks and a slow smirk tugged at his mouth, as if he knew exactly what I was thinking. Exactly how he was affecting me.

His gray eyes dropped to my lips and he swallowed, making no effort to move. "We should, uh..."

"Yep." I yanked my hand away and fluffed my hair, trying to think about anything but how much I wanted Rafe Hunter to kiss me.

And how much I didn't deserve it.

CHAPTER TEN

"W HAT ARE YOU DOING?" I ask Cody, peering over his shoulder, watching as his pencil brushes over the sketch pad in large sweeping arcs. The black swirls are a stark contrast to his usual portraits. Nurses. Patients. Doctors. Even the hospital porters. Cody has drawn them all at some point. He's only ten, but his talent is endless; his sketches somewhat of a talking point on Ward 10 at Jamesboro County.

"It's bad news, Eva." His voice is flat, and my heart aches at his words.

"No," I breathe. "They said it was looking good, that the surgery—"

"They were wrong." He finally gives me his eyes and my heart cracks a little more.

Cody is my one of my favorite people here. A ray of sunshine in a place that can feel so cold and clinical and downright depressing. But today he's a storm cloud, sucking the slither of hope I have into his black void.

"It's okay," I say, sliding into the seat beside him. "They'll have a plan. There'll be other treatments they can—"

"It's the end, Eva."

"The end?" My voice wobbles. "It's not the end, silly". I laugh but it comes out strangled and wrong. "You have your whole life ahead of you."

"Evangeline," he stops drawing and places his hand atop of mine, "it's okay."

But it's not.

Nothing about this is okay.

I've known Cody since the first day I walked in Jamesboro County Hospital. That was almost eight months ago. And despite our age difference, Cody gets it. He gets me. He understands what it's like to find out you're sick. To fight day in, day out, the cancer poisoning your body. Slowing killing you. He *knows the pain of being a human pin cushion. The grim side effects of intense chemotherapy. Cody knows things no ten-year-old should ever know.*

He starts sketching again, the black scrawl slowly morphing into faces. Eyes, noses, smiles of the kids we've seen come and go.

"Cody, what are you..." my voice trails off as the faces begin to shift and melt, the black masses stretching and shifting until four gravestones sit there.

My heart hammers against my rib cage, my skin growing clammy as I press my hands against my thighs, fighting the tears building. "Why are you doin' that, Cody?" I ask shakily.

"You can't fight Death, Eva. I can feel him coming for me."

"It's not fair," my resolve breaks, tears spilling my down my cheeks. "You've fought so hard, Cody. It can't be the end."

He keeps drawing, filling the page with more and more gravestones. Gray and black shadows filling the spaces between them like lingering souls.

"There was so much I wanted to do. To see and experience." His voice isn't sad, only resigned. But it splits me wide open until I can barely see through my ugly sobs.

"Eva." He turns to look at me, his face ashen, skin withered.

"Cody?" I cry. "What is happenin'?"

"It's time." His eyes sink into their sockets leaving behind two black holes.

"Cody!"

"Eva?"

"Cody, stay. You have to stay. I can't do this without you."

"But it's time."

"I'll go," I rush out. "Let me take your place."

His smiles, a big wide smile revealing a mouthful of rotting teeth. "It's not your time. You're one of the lucky ones, Eva. Remember that."

Cody begins to evaporate into wisps of smoke and air.

"No, no, no..." I repeat over and over, hoping this nightmare will end. That I'll wake up and Cody will be okay. That his cancer will be gone, and he'll be able to live a long happy healthy life.

But when I glance down at his sketch, the biggest gravestone reveals his name.

Cody Larkin.

I woke with a start, drenched in sweat. My heart almost beating out of my chest as Cody's wretched face lingered in my mind.

It was a dream.

But it wasn't just a dream; it was my memories and guilt swirled together in some harrowing messed-up nightmare.

"Eva?" Molly's whisper pierced the darkness. "Did you say something?"

"N- nothing," I croaked, sinking back into the pillows. "It was just a bad dream. Go back to sleep."

A couple of beats passed, my heart rate finally returning to a normal pace, the memories forced back down to where they couldn't touch me.

But Molly wasn't done. "Eva?" she said.

"Yeah?" I sighed.

I heard a shuffle then a muffled giggle. "I still can't believe it. I made out with Hudson f'ing Ryker."

"You're still maintainin' that's all you did?" They'd been locked away in the bedroom for far longer than seven minutes in heaven.

"There was some groping. Clothed gropin'," she added quickly.

"Did you touch his...?" My lips snapped closed, but I smiled to myself in the dark. This was a good distraction from the nightmare.

Normal.

"Dick, it's called a dick. You can say it, Eva." Molly snorted. "And yes, I touched it. I mean, it's Hudson f'in Ryker. Are you telling me you didn't even look at what Rafe was packin'?"

"Oh my gosh, stop. I didn't..." Who was I kidding, I totally looked. It was impossible not to look at him, to let my eyes sweep down his lean body.

"Haha, knew it." Molly chuckled. "What a night. I think if I never see another dick in my life, I'll die a happy... oh shit, Eva, I didn't mean. Jesus, I'm so insensitive at times."

"It's fine, you're excited. I get it. It was Hudson f'in Ryker, after all," I teased, rolling onto my back. Staring up at the ceiling, I chased shadows across the room, refusing to let my mind sink back into the dream because Molly mentioned dying. Instead, I focused on thoughts of last night.

We'd finally left their suite just before midnight when Rafe and I managed to prize Molly and Hudson apart and convince her to hand back the t-shirt. I was surprised Molly left at all, the way she was hanging off Hudson. Part of me envied her; envied how free she was. How easily she found it to live in the moment.

That should have been me, especially after everything I'd been through. But I still couldn't switch off the little voice in my head constantly whispering, 'why me, why me, why me?'

A couple of beats of silence passed. Molly was no doubt dreaming of all things Hudson and I was now thinking about eyes so gray I'd found myself rendered speechless more than once.

"So..."

"Yeah?" I replied.

"What do you think about Rafe?"

"He seems... nice."

"Nice? Come on, Eva. Even you can do better than nice."

"Honestly, I don't know what to say."

"You like him."

"I don't... maybe," I breathed, "yeah, okay, I like him. But it doesn't matter. He's this huge rock star and I'm no one."

"You're not no one, Eva. Don't ever let me hear you say that again. And I'm not askin' because I think you should fall in love and marry the guy. But Hudson let it slip Rafe will be in Camdena with him, and I thought—"

"Eva, what did you do?"

"Do?" She snorted. "Relax, I didn't do anythin'. But Hudson seemed up for hanging out again in Camdena, and if Rafe is there maybe we can all hang out? Together."

"I'm not sure I'm supposed to be cavortin' with one of the judges."

"It's hardly cavorting, babe. Besides, somethin' tells me Hudson does what he wants when he wants."

She wasn't wrong there.

"Anyway, I think we should hang out with them again. Tonight was fun."

I murmured a non-committal reply. I didn't have the heart to tell Molly, Hudson probably had a different girl in every town he visited. Maybe she knew that. Maybe she just didn't care.

Me on the other hand, I cared.

I couldn't deny I'd felt something talking music with Rafe, watching him play the guitar, listening as he confessed his feelings about being on tour.

But it would never be enough.

If I ever let a guy into my heart, I wanted them completely. I didn't want to share.

And I definitely didn't want to share with a bunch of fangirls who dreamed of one day being the girl to tame the rock star.

———

AFTER THE PLOUGHTON REGIONAL, THERE HAD BEEN NO MORE nightmares, and everything had returned to normal. Well, as normal as they could for a girl who hadn't attended school in almost a year. I don't know who was more stressed out—me or Mom. She'd gotten used to having me at home, helping me study or just keeping me company. But it was finally time for me to reintegrate at school.

Time to conquer senior year.

"Are you ready, sweetheart? I think Molly just got here."

"Comin', Mom." I checked my reflection one more time, taking a deep breath at the girl in the mirror.

She was different. Slightly thinner in the face, hair shorter than the kids at school would remember. When I'd found out I needed chemo, I'd asked Mom to cut it all off. I couldn't bear the thought of losing my silky blonde curls. Turned out I was one of the lucky ones. My hair had thinned during my treatment and I'd experienced some mild loss, but it had already grown back. Physically, to the outside world, it was impossible to know what I'd been through, but my scars ran deep.

Grabbing my cell phone, I couldn't resist opening my most recently downloaded app, Rock Review. I didn't even need to scroll down the list of entries to find Rafe's name. He was right there in a grainy photo, alongside his bandmates, a hoard of scantily clad girls surrounding them as they signed autographs. They weren't even old enough to legally buy liquor yet and already had the fairer sex falling at their feet.

A pang of jealousy shot through me, which was ridiculous. So we'd spent a few hours getting to know one another? Rafe hadn't offered me his number that night, and he hadn't asked for mine. I tried not to over-analyze it. It was easy now, with time and distance, to remind myself that Rafe and I came from different worlds. Even if we did see each other again in Camdena, it was only one weekend. Nothing more would ever come of it.

Yet, every day, I felt myself searching for articles on him and the band. Trying to learn everything I could about the mysterious bassist for one of the biggest breakout bands in the country. Trying to understand the complicated, guarded guy who had let me play his very expensive, very rare guitar.

But most of all, trying to figure out why, of all the people at the talent contest, Rafe Hunter had wanted to spend time with me.

CHAPTER ELEVEN

"Looking good, Eva," Charlie Fincham, one of Jenson's buddies, tipped his chin as I walked past him to my locker.

"Everyone's staring," I ground out to Molly who had been glued to my side ever since we stepped foot out of her car.

"They're just curious."

"Curious that I almost died but didn't? Because that's kind of sick." Frustration swelled up inside me, tears pricking the corners of my eyes.

I was an emotional wreck.

And it wasn't even first period yet.

"Eva, babe, breathe," she said. "You missed most of eleventh grade. You dropped off the face of the plan—"

"I was sick."

"I know that and you know that. Deep down they all know that." She flicked her head toward the group of kids watching us from across the hall. "It'll wear off. Once people get used to seeing you again, it'll be like nothin' ever changed."

But things had changed.

And deep down, I knew there was no going back.

At least, not for me.

"Hey, E." Jenson approached us. "Molly."

"Blaufield." The air around us chilled. There was no love lost between my best friend and ex-boyfriend.

"It's good to see you back at school." He ignored the daggers Molly was drilling into the side of his head and focused on me.

"Thanks." I pressed my lips together and gave him a strained smile. "Did you need somethin' because we need to get to class?"

"I, uh... I was hoping we could talk."

"I said everythin' I had to say last time I saw you."

"Eva, come on, please..."

Just then, Sheridan Black sauntered down the hall veering right past us. Time seemed to slow down as her eyes landed on me. "Eva," she said with a saccharine sweet smirk. "You look... *better*. Jenson, it's been a while, call me."

Molly let out a low growl, and I grabbed her hand, not wanting her to do anything stupid. But thankfully Sheridan was already gone, her smug laughter drifting back to me.

"Shit, E, I didn't... that wasn't... fuck." Jenson paled, guilt shining in his eyes.

"And that," I slammed my locker a little too hard, "is why I want nothin' to do with you. Ever. Again." Without looking back, I marched away from him. Molly jogged up beside me, letting out a low whistle. "Holy cow, babe, I didn't know you had it in you."

"Honestly, I don't know what came over me. I just can't believe he really thought that after everything, things between us would be okay. I just feel so... so..."

Angry.

Sad and frustrated.

But I also felt irrationally hopeless.

I'd only been in the building ten minutes, and I could already feel the walls closing in around me.

"I'm not sure I can do this," I said to Molly, aware of the eyes following me, the whispers dancing on the air as we moved further down the hall.

"It's not like you really have a choice though, babe. It's senior year. If you want to graduate—"

"I know." I didn't need a reminder.

"Just stick to the plan."

"The plan, right." I grimaced. "And what exactly is the plan again?"

Molly rolled her eyes. "Keep your head down and ignore them. And if all else fails, tell everyone you made out with Rafe Hunter over the weekend. That'll give them all somethin' to talk—"

"Molly!" Grabbing her hand, I yanked her beneath the stairwell. "One, you can't say stuff like that here. We signed an NDA. Secondly, I didn't make out with Rafe." I lowered my voice, but it didn't disguise the hitch in my breath when I said his name.

"Oh, babe, you've got it worse than I thought." She smiled knowingly.

"I haven't got anythin'. Just promise me you won't start spreading some ridiculous rumor, Mol, please?" The NDA was a legally binding contract. If either of us leaked anything about the guys, we'd both be in deep trouble.

"Fine, spoil all my fun. So if you can't tell them anything then at least ignore them and imagine Rafe swoopin' in to save you. In all his naked tattooed glor—"

"I'm goin' to class," I snapped. "I'll see you later."

Her laughter followed me all the way down the hall.

It wasn't until I got to class, I realized I was blushing profusely.

———

"Eva, could you come in here please?"

I kicked off my sneakers and wandered into the kitchen to find my parents seated at our small table. "Hey, what's up?"

"Take a seat, sweetheart."

Dread pooled in my stomach. "Is everythin' okay?" I sat down, not liking the grim expressions they were both wearing.

"Now that you're back at school and things are on the up, your daddy and I talked and decided it's probably best I go back to work."

"Because we need the money." My gut twisted.

"There's no denying things have been hard the last few months but this is a good thing, Eva. I'm ready to get back to the office and Mr. Delaware has been so good about everything. I'll only be working a few hours a day, while you're settlin' into senior year."

Slumping back in the chair, I let out a heavy sigh. "I'm sorry." The words came out raw.

"Now, now, baby, none of that. We did what we needed to do and we'd do it all again in a heartbeat. You are our priority, Eva, always. But with things lookin' unstable at ST Holdings this makes sense."

Dad's eyes slid to Mom's and she shook her head. But it was too late, I'd caught their silent conversation. "There's more?" I asked, a heavy weight settling on my chest.

"Your daddy has been asked to work some overtime—"

"That's great." I perked up but my hope was quickly dashed when his expression darkened.

"It's at their Landry depot. I'll be away for a few weekends." His eyes crinkled with regret. "It means I won't be able to make the final show, sweetheart."

"Oh." Disappointment edged into my voice, but I pushed it down. Being able to pay the bills was more important. "It's okay, Dad," I said forcing a smile. "We need the money and it isn't like you haven't seen me perform a hundred times already."

"You know I'd be there if I could, Eva. But this is too good an opportunity to pass up. The good news is though, I can drive up with you girls to Camdena on Friday night, then I'll head onto Landry."

Mom's lips pursed and I frowned. "You're still comin' right, Mom?" I couldn't believe a scenario where she'd readily send me off by myself. Not after everything.

But surprising me, she said, "Your daddy seems to think I'd only cramp your style. And since you turn eighteen next week, he thought,"—Dad nudged her gently and she corrected herself—"*we* thought, it would be nice if you and Molly spent some time together."

"For real?" I gawked. "You're lettin' me and Molly go alone?" For the whole weekend.

My best friend was going to freak—in a good way.

Dad nodded around a grin. "I already spoke to the Steinbergs and they agreed to let Molly drive you both since I'll follow you up and make sure you get there okay." The show was putting contestants up in the Camdena Royal Hotel where the event was being held.

At least I could rest easy, knowing it wouldn't cost Mom and Dad money they didn't have this time.

"And you'll check in with me every couple of hours," Mom added.

Dad chuckled at that, patting her hand. "You're a good girl, Eva, and we want you to know that we trust you. You're a young adult now, it's time we gave you some space to figure out your way in the world."

"Just not too much space, Gavin." Mom glowered at him, and I fought a smile. They had such a solid relationship: the way Dad knew exactly how to temper Mom's overbearingness; the way she melted into soft putty whenever he touched her.

"Thank you, *both* of you." It kind of sucked they weren't going to be there, cheering me on, but the local television station would air the live final. I couldn't deny though that a tiny part of me was relieved they were treating me like an adult.

"Just promise us you'll go out there and enjoy it." Dad gave me a pointed look.

"I will, promise."

"That's all we ask."

Just then, my cell phone started ringing. "I bet that's Molly," Dad said. "Her parents probably just told her the excitin' news."

Mom looked fit to burst, probably with all the rules she wanted to instill on me and Molly for our weekend of freedom. Leaping to my feet, I clutched my cell in my hand and flashed them an appreciative smile. "I'd better answer. Love you both, bye." I hurried out of the kitchen.

"Holycrapballs did you hear the good news?" Molly didn't even greet me.

"Blake Shelton is makin' new music?" I teased.

"Evangeline Star Walker, you'd better get serious. This is huge; freakin' huge, girl."

"It's just a weekend away, Mol. No big deal."

"No big deal? Are you kiddin' me right now? Not only is it a weekend in an all-expenses paid room in one of Camdena's swankiest establishments, it is also an entire weekend with Hudson and Rafe and no f'in parentals in sight."

My pulse spiked at the mention of his name.

"Eva, are you still there?"

"I'm here," I said quietly.

"It's going to be epic."

"Epic, gotcha."

"I swear, babe, sometimes I just want to—"

"Mol?" I urged, cutting her off.

"Yeah, Eva?"

"Love you."

She chuckled. "Love you too. Now do me a favor and check your wardrobe."

"My wardrobe?"

"Yes," she huffed and I could imagine her rolling her eyes at me. "For a suitable outfit."

"Outfit for what exactly...?"

"Seducing a rock star of course." I sucked in a shaky breath and it was her turn to chuckle. "You can deny it all you want, babe, but I know what I saw and you want Rafe Hunter almost as much as I suspect he wants you."

"I don't know what you're talkin' about," I mumbled.

"We'll see."

Which is exactly what worried me.

I couldn't get into classes. It was impossible with the looming final show; the possibility of seeing Rafe again. I'd followed him on social media, watched his life charted in a montage of grainy images and second-hand rumors. But no matter how hard I tried; it was hard to ignore the headlines.

Hunter brothers spotted on double date with runway models.

Rafe Hunter saves Levi from making a huge mistake.
Black Hearts Still Beat cause chaos at Knoxville mall.

No matter where they went or what they did, everyone wanted a piece of the band. And if you believed everything you read online; *a lot* of girls were getting their fair share of the Hunter brothers.

I felt torn. After everything I'd been through, I couldn't help but think Rafe and Hudson and the other guys in the band had it right. They were living the life they had been gifted, making every single day, every moment count. Sure, there was an element of shirking responsibility and becoming too detached from reality. But part of me wanted to commend them. You never knew what was around the corner. At least they seemed to be living without regret.

The other part though, the girl who had once been confident in her faith, in a deep sense of moral rightness, read the latest headlines and felt angry. Disappointed that these four young men were squandering the opportunity to be the role model so many young boys and girls needed. That they were being reckless with life—theirs and those around them.

Then there was the part of me who felt sorry for them. Because living life under the spotlight like they were was unsustainable. You only had to read the entertainment news to hear about the latest actor or singer or model to fall prey to the many vices of fame.

I'd seen something in Rafe when we talked that night. It was the same darkness that shrouded Hudson. And from what I'd heard of their music, I couldn't help but wonder about their story. The one beneath the hit records and sell out shows.

"Eva, he's ready for you," Mrs. Creedy's voice pulled me from my thoughts and I offered the school secretary a polite smile. "Thank you." I grabbed my bag and entered the counsellor's room.

"Ah, Eva, come in," Mr. Jefferies smiled warmly, relaxing back in his chair as I got situated. "It's good to see you. How are you settlin' in?"

"It's okay, I guess."

"I imagine it must be hard. But everyone is thrilled to have you back with us for senior year."

I wasn't so sure about that, but I let it go. He—or anyone else for that matter—didn't want to hear my complaints, not really.

"Your teachers all inform me they're happy with your reintegration." Shifting forward, Mr. Jefferies flattened his hands on the desk. "I'm not going to sugarcoat things, Eva. If you want to graduate with your friends next year, it's going to mean givin' it your all."

"I understand, Sir."

"Do you?" His brow went up. "Because you barely passed eleventh grade. When I spoke with your parents, I advised them the best course of action might be for you to stay back the ye—"

"I don't want to retake the year." Cancer had stolen too much from me already; it wasn't taking my senior year with Molly too.

"I get that, Eva. I do. And while I'd usually be in complete support of extracurricular activity, I really think you should be focused on school right now, not talent contests." His words were laced with concern. "Performing is great, Eva, but the bottom line is it's going to be difficult reintegratin' this semester."

"With all due respect, Sir, what I do outside of school is none of your concern."

"Actually, it is." His expression morphed to one of concern. "College applications are right around the corner, and I think you would stand a better chance if you—"

"I haven't even decided if I'm applyin' for college this year." I hadn't really thought about much beyond graduation.

Mr. Jefferies expelled a heavy breath. "Okay, how about this? It's early days still. I appreciate you have a lot to get your head around. Let's review where you're at in a month and make some decisions then."

I offered him a non-committal "okay." He didn't get it. No one did. They couldn't unless they had walked a day in my shoes; unless they knew what it felt like to have life snatched away from you in one hand and handed back in the other.

School was important; he didn't need to tell me that. But it no longer felt like the most important thing. Nothing Mr. Jefferies said right now would change my mind.

I needed time.

Something I didn't have since the senior year clock was ticking.

"I'll see you in a month then," he said, breaking the tense silence.

I rose from the chair and made my way to the door, but Mr. Jefferies' voice gave me pause. "And Eva?"

"Yes, Sir?"

"If you ever want to talk about what happened, I'm here."

"Thanks, Sir," I said, although I think we both knew I would never take him up on the offer.

CHAPTER TWELVE

THE CAMDENA ROYAL was an extravagant five-star hotel overlooking the Tennessee river.

"Now this is what I'm talkin' about." A bell hop approached us, gathering up our luggage. Molly slid her arm through mine and pulled me toward the door. "This weekend is going to be the best," she sang, so full of excitement I thought she might burst.

I, on the other hand, felt a little green.

"Walker, over here." Josiah Golden beckoned us over as we entered the lavish foyer.

"I see Goldenboy has already found his feet," Molly leaned in, whispering, "let's hope he gets eliminated in the first round."

"Molly." I shot her a bemused look.

"All set for the big day?" he wasted no time getting down to business.

"I'm ready. Are you?"

"Ready?" he snorted. "I was born for this. The title is mine this year. I can feel it in my bones." Josiah lifted his shoulders and stuck out his neck a little. "Rumor has it there's some big competition out of Klineville and Brescone."

"This has been enlightenin' and all," Molly said, "but we have to check-in." She dragged me toward the desk where we were greeted by a friendly woman.

"Welcome to the Camdena Royal. Are y'all here for the Jamesboro Talent Showdown?" I nodded. "Great, what was the name?"

"Evangeline Walker."

"Ooh my daughter has been talkin' about y'all. Her daddy takes her to all the regionals. She loved your performance of Believer."

"Wow, that's..." Emotion swelled inside me. "That's incredible, thank you."

"Okay, here we are." She handed us two keycards and an envelope. "This is your welcome packet and your room key. You're on the eighth floor in one of our superior twin rooms."

"Thank you." Molly accepted the room keys with a wide smile. She was enjoying every second of this. It almost made me think she should have been the one performing tomorrow given at how easily she fit into this world.

"I'm Sandy and if you need anythin' during your stay, don't hesitate to shout, okay?"

We thanked her again and made our way to the elevators, the bellhop hovering behind us. "Should we—"

"No way, babe. We're takin' full advantage of this." She shot the bellhop a sultry smile, all too happy to let him carry our luggage. "Besides, it's his job."

Rolling my eyes, I stepped inside the elevator and inhaled a deep breath. It was still hard to believe I was here. Ready to compete in the final of Jamesboro Talent Showdown. Out of the twenty-four contestants, only eight would compete in the final. The prize checks of five-thousand dollars, ten-thousand dollars, and twenty-five thousand dollars were incentive enough to give it my all, but with Mom back at work and Dad working his ass off to keep us above water, winning would mean so much more to us than just earning the title of Artist of the Year.

"Hey." Molly touched my arm. "Feelin' okay?"

"I'm fine."

I had to be because if I stood any chance of getting to the final tomorrow, I was going to have to sing my heart out.

―――――

"WELL, WOULD YOU TAKE A LOOK AT THAT." MOLLY FOLLOWED ME into the hotel room. "This is freakin' amazing. Talk about celebrating your eighteenth in style. All I got was a gift certificate for American Eagle." She brushed past me to check out the view of Camdena, the city thinning out toward the river.

"It's somethin', all right," I murmured, lingering by the door to tip the bellhop. When the door closed behind him, I finally moved deeper into the room.

"Let's just stay here, forever." Leaping onto one of the queen beds,

Molly began star-fishing, the sweet sound of laughter spilling from her lips.

The hotel in Ploughton had been nice, but this was on another level. I placed my guitar down in the corner of the room and spun around, taking in all the small details. The chrome finishings and pale green and navy accents. And my favorite touch; the black and white portraits hanging on the wall, each of a famous country singer from the last century. But one stood out from all the rest.

"Is that Patsy Cline?" Molly came up beside me, leaning her head on my shoulder.

"It is."

"It's an omen." She clutched my hand. "What are the chances that we'd end up in a room with a portrait of one of your favorite singers of all time hangin' on the wall?"

She had a point. But I didn't want to get ahead of myself. While I liked the idea Patsy was a good luck omen, after Josiah's warning about how good the competition was, I knew I needed more than superstition to get me through to the final round.

Molly left me staring at one of my idols and began unpacking her suitcase. Glancing at the growing pile of clothes on her bed, I said, "You do realize we're only here for two nights, right?"

"A girl can never have too many outfits. Besides, if I want to seduce Hudson, I need to look my best."

"I don't want to be the one to burst your bubble, but the chances of Hudson textin' are—" Her cell started vibrating and she shot me a 'you were saying?' look.

"That could be anyone," I grumbled.

"But, oh look," she smiled devilishly, "it's Hudson Ryker." Molly flashed me the screen. "He wants to know if we want to hang out with him and Rafe again later?"

"Are you sure I won't get into trouble? There are probably rules about that kind of thing."

"Rules smules," my best friend snorted. "Besides, no one will know. The hotel is pretty much on lockdown for the show."

"I don't know..."

But she was already texting back. "Molly," I cried. "What are you doin'?"

"Uh, tellin' him yes, obviously."

"But I thought... never mind." Once her mind was made up about something there was little use trying to change it. And not that I'd ever admit it to her, but a small part of me did want to see Rafe again, to see if the connection between us was still there or whether I'd fabricated the whole thing in my head.

Molly was still texting, completely oblivious to my internal dilemma. Finally, she gave me her full attention, her eyes alight with excitement. "Jake will be down for us at eight."

"They're sending the bodyguard to fetch us, how romantic." I gawked. This wasn't real life. Small town girls like Molly and me didn't hang out with famous rock stars.

No matter how easy to get my friend acted.

"Don't be such a Debbie Downer. It's different here. Ploughton is like the ass crack of nowhere compared to Camdena. I bet they have to be a lot more careful here. You saw the fangirls outside with the banners and face paints."

They were hard to miss, screaming for Hudson and Rafe until they were red-faced and breathless.

"We could stay here, take advantage of room service?" I suggested.

"And give up the opportunity to hang out with Hudson and Rafe? Not happenin'." She glowered at me. "You have less than two hours, babe. Get freshened up, choose an outfit, and get ready. Because tonight, Evangeline Walker, you are going to make out with a rock star."

———

JAKE WAS SEVEN MINUTES EARLY.

"Mr. Ryker has requested your presence," he said flatly. "Please follow me."

Molly smothered a laugh. "So fancy," she mouthed at me as we filed out of our room. "So, Jake," my best friend was relentless, and I rolled my eyes. "Nice weather we're havin'."

The bodyguard suppressed a smile, humoring her. "The weather has been very good."

The elevator doors pinged open and we all stepped inside. Jake pressed the button for floor twenty. As we rose higher so did my heart rate. The thought of seeing Rafe again was a lot to process.

Molly reached out and squeezed my hand. "Eeek, I'm so excited," she whisper-shrieked.

"We come together, we leave together," I said, determined to make sure she didn't do anything she would regret. It was one thing to make out with a rock star, but I didn't believe for a second she wanted to be just another notch on Hudson Ryker's drumsticks.

"Yes, Mom. I won't keep you out past midnight. I don't want you to turn into a pumpkin the night before your big show."

Jake was still and silent beside us, dressed sharply in a charcoal suit and white dress shirt. He fit in with the opulence of the hotel, but I doubted he got any downtime protecting Hudson and Rafe. If it wasn't for the occasional breath I heard him take, I would have assumed he was a statue.

Finally, the elevator came to a stop and the doors sprung open. "This way please," Jake said, completely devoid of emotion, as if chaperoning two young girls to the penthouse suite of a famous rock band was just business as usual.

It occurred to me, maybe it was.

"What?" Molly asked noticing my frown.

"Are you sure about this?"

"Eva," she groaned before checking her reflection in the mirror as we stepped out behind the stoic bodyguard.

Clutching my hand in hers, Molly flashed me a reassuring smile. "You have nothin' to worry about. Besides," she lowered her voice, "I know for a fact there is a certain bassist in there who can't wait to see you again."

"Oh yeah, and how do you know that?" I gave my best friend a pointed look and she smirked.

"I have my sources."

I didn't respond to that.

I couldn't.

The very idea Rafe was looking forward to seeing me again... it was too much to process.

Too much of everything.

But before I had chance to second guess her words, Molly pulled me toward the door which Jake had now pushed open. Heart crashing violently against my chest, I tucked my wild curls behind my ear, sucked in a shaky breath, and stepped inside the penthouse.

CHAPTER THIRTEEN

"There she is," Hudson said with an amused lilt. If Molly noticed it, she didn't react, practically throwing herself into his arms.

"Eva," Rafe said, rising from one of the stools at a sparkling marble counter. "It's good to see you again."

"Hey." I smiled and it wasn't forced because I was happy to see him.

Crap, I was so in over my head.

"Do you guys always travel like this?" Molly asked once we were all settled on the two huge soft leather couches, her wide eyes taking in our lavish surroundings.

"What, in style?" Hudson smirked. "The production team are putting us up."

"And how come you're doin' the show but Rafe isn't?"

"Do you always ask so many questions?" His brows crinkled. "If I'd wanted to spend the night playing twenty questions, I would have invited my mom."

Molly blushed, folding her hands into her lap nervously. I don't think I'd ever seen my best friend embarrassed but then it hit me.

She liked him.

Molly didn't just want her five minutes with the Black Hearts drummer... she *wanted* him.

Crap.

This wasn't going to end well.

For either of us.

Because the second I'd stepped inside the suite and my eyes found his, I knew my heart wasn't just reacting to Rafe Hunter, the bassist for a rock band.

It was him.

The guy beneath the rock star. The guy I'd seen glimpses of in Ploughton.

And when he'd taken my hand and led me to the couch, I knew I was in deep trouble.

"Hud, come on, man. Be nice," Rafe said, sending him a narrowed look. Hudson shuffled closer to Molly, leaning in and whispering something in her ear. Her eyes flared, heavy with lust, as he worked his magic on her.

"So how are you feeling about tomorrow?" Rafe turned his attention on me, ignoring our friends who looked awfully close to making out.

"It wasn't supposed to matter so much, but now I'm here..." my voice trailed off and I couldn't help but look over at Molly and Hudson, immediately regretting it.

"Come on." Rafe stood up, startling me. He held out his hand, his expression softening as he waited for me to decide. I slid my hand into his, enjoying the feel of his calloused skin against mine. "Another hotel, another view," he said around a smile. "But this time, there's a balcony."

Leading me over to the sliding doors, we stepped out onto the wide balcony, the balmy city air washing over me. He made a beeline for the edge to get a better look, but I was frozen to the spot, suddenly feeling out of my depth.

"Eva?" he glanced back.

"It's very high."

"You're not scared of heights, are you?" His words were teasing.

"Not usually." But then, I didn't make a habit of standing on twentieth-floor balconies.

"Come here." He held out his hand again, and I went to him, slowly. Instantly calmed by his touch. His brows furrowed as he stared at where our fingers linked, and I wondered if he felt the electricity simmering between us.

"Rafe?" His name fell from my lips in a gentle caress.

"Come on." Gently, he guided me to the balcony edge, the city lights twinkling below us. "Worth it, right?" he asked, and I nodded, words lodged in my throat as he caged me against the railing, curving his tall lean body around mine until I felt his chest pushed up against my back.

"It's beautiful." His lips were at my ear, his warm breath skating over me. And for a second, I let myself believe he wasn't talking about the view at all.

"I feel weightless up here," I admitted, comfortable silence settling over us. Nothing but the blare of horns and the rumble of traffic in the distance.

My hands curled around the polished railing, leaning forward a little. "Easy there, tiger," Rafe let out a quiet laugh. Deep. Gravelly. His voice wrapped around the deepest parts of me. Sliding one of his hands around to my waist, he held me tight.

"Don't worry," I breathed, "I'm not about to jump."

In an instant, Rafe had spun me around, his eyes pinning me to the spot. He didn't say anything but his body seemed to radiate with anger.

"Rafe?" I asked, confused at what was happening.

"Why did you say that?" The muscle in his jaw clenched, his eyes hard and cold.

"It was a joke. I was jokin'."

"Fuck, I'm sorry, I just…" The fury in his expression melted away replaced with shame.

"It's okay."

"No, it's not. I should have known…" he trailed off again, as if he was stopping himself from telling me something.

Without thinking, I slid my hand to his face, gently pressing it against his cheek. "We all have our demons to bear," I whispered, sensing that whatever was going on with Rafe was something big.

Something important.

"Yeah, and what demons does a girl like you possibly have to bear?"

Slave to eyes so dark and intense I could barely breathe, I choked out, "I lived."

His eyes widened, his sharp inhale of breath a visceral reaction to my confession. But before he could ask me what I meant, Molly spilled out onto the balcony. "There you two are." Her brows waggled suggestively. "We were just about to order room service. You two want anythin' or are you—"

"I could eat," Rafe said, inching away from me, leaving me cold. "Is there pizza?" he asked.

"I'm sure for you two rock gods there's always pizza." Molly winked, her eyes sliding to mine, brimming with questions.

I shook my head discreetly, aware of Rafe watching our interaction.

"Come on, I'm starving," she said, lightening the heavy mood.

Rafe kept my hand in his as he pulled me toward the door. "Hudson sure works fast," he mused.

"What's that supposed to mean?" I quirked my brow, looking up at him.

"What do you think they were doing to work up an appetite?"

"I... working out?" I deadpanned.

"Oh, I'm sure they were *working out*." He roped his arm around my neck, drawing me into his side. It was such an intimate move. So easy and comfortable, as if we'd been doing it forever.

As if he heard my thoughts, Rafe gazed down at me. His eyes dropping to my lips.

"Yo, Rafe, you want olives or not?" Hudson's voice was like a bucket of ice water.

Rafe grimaced, mumbling something under his breath about his bandmate's shitty timing. My cheeks flaming, I ducked out of his hold and went to join Molly on the couch. I needed a second to catch my breath.

To ground myself.

Because every second I spent with Rafe, the more I felt myself fall.

And I was terrified he wouldn't be there to catch me.

———

AFTER STUFFING OUR FACES WITH PIZZA, HUDSON DRAGGED MOLLY away again. This time to show her something on his iPad. As if they were fooling anyone. The two of them couldn't keep their hands off each other and despite being worried for my best friend, I couldn't help the pang of jealousy I felt watching them together.

Molly had insisted on wearing short denim cut-off shorts, a cropped tank top, and her favorite boots. Her hair hung down her back in soft effortless waves, and she had just enough make-up on to look stunning without it being overdone.

Ignoring her advice to wear something seductive, I'd stuck with my trusty old jeans and a plain striped tee. But I was beginning to think she had a point. Hudson had barely been able to keep his hands off her all evening. Whereas, aside from the hand holding and intimate position we'd stood in out on the balcony, Rafe had kept his hands firmly to himself.

I'd always felt like a plain Jane next to Molly. She was so comfortable in her own skin, so confident and sure of herself. And I'd always been okay with that. Some stars were supposed to shine brighter than others. But tonight, I wanted Rafe to see me.

I wanted him to *want* me.

Just for once, I wanted to be the girl who got the fairytale moment with the prince.

Which only compounded the guilt slowly gnawing at my soul. Here I was, granted a second chance, and I was preoccupied with whether a famous rock star, who could offer me nothing more than here and now, liked me or not.

But I couldn't walk away. Just as I couldn't explain the inexplicable pull I felt toward him.

"Is he always like that?" I asked.

"Hudson is... yeah, I'm not going to lie to you, Eva. He is." Rafe scrubbed his jaw. "But for what it's worth, I think he's really into Molly."

"Until the day after tomorrow when you're whisked away to a new city and he finds a new girl." It wasn't a question and Rafe didn't insult me with an answer. Instead, we stared at each other, the questions mounting on the tip of my tongue. He must have sensed it because he asked, "Go on, ask me."

"Ask you what?" I played dumb.

"Eva, I know you want to ask me something, I can see it in your eyes."

With a small sigh, I said, "I wanted to ask you if you're the same, but then I realized I don't want to know." Because I was pretty sure hearing him tell me I was just another in a long line of girls would be too much to bear.

And something told me Rafe wouldn't lie to me.

"This is... different. *You're* different." His eyes spoke the words he didn't say, and I didn't know whether to be relieved or disappointed. Of course there had been other girls. I'd read the headlines, seen the photos.

"I've never met anyone like you before, Eva. I hardly know you," he shifted closer, "and yet, I feel as if I've known you forever."

Our eyes collided. His hard with intent, mine soft with anticipation. I could feel him everywhere, even though he hadn't touched me yet.

"I've been wanting to do this since that day I found you crying in the hall." Rafe's hand glided to my neck, his thumb brushing over my skin sending shivers rippling up my spine.

"You noticed that, huh?"

"I notice a lot of things Eva," he breathed.

Then he kissed me.

Softly at first, his mouth tracing the shape of mine. His tongue darted out, swiping across the seam of my lips before slipping between them. The subtle sting of his lip piercing as he kissed me made me gasp but Rafe only used my surprise to his advantage, threading his fingers into my hair, angling my face closer. Kissing me deeper.

Harder. Kissing me until I was panting for breath and desperate for more.

"Rafe..." His name was a prayer on my lips, a cry for mercy, as my fingers curled into his black tee, anchoring us together. He pushed me back against the cushions, covering me with his body.

"The things I want to do with you," he peppered kisses over my jaw, running his tongue down the slope of my neck. Sucking and nipping. My arms slid over his shoulders as I swallowed another moan. He felt good, *too good*, pressed up against me.

My lower body was half off the couch, his too, but it didn't stop him from grinding into me, showing me just how much I affected him. A thrill shot through me despite the nervous shiver that spread through me.

I hitched my leg around his hip but before I could rub against him, his hand shot out, steadying my thigh. "Eva, stop," he said breathlessly, dropping his forehead to mine.

"You don't want me?" I choked out, hardly able to believe I'd said the words.

"Does it feel like I don't want you?" His eyes were hooded, glittering with lust. "I want you. So fucking much. But not here, not like this."

I wanted to argue, to tell him that I didn't care if he took me right there on the couch with Molly and Hudson just beyond the bedroom door and Jake and Lennox standing guard outside.

But I did care.

"Thank you," I said as he eased back, his brows pinched. "For stoppin', I mean."

He sat up, pulling me with him, and the two of us straightened our clothes. I smoothed my unruly curls. "You're something else, Eva Walker." His smile had my stomach clenching so tight I felt a little giddy.

"Is that a good thing?" I asked.

"Oh, it's good." His smile turned wicked. "It's a very good thing."

My mouth curved. It was impossible to not give in to my baser feelings around Rafe. My body lit up around him, my emotions going haywire.

And my heart... my stupid reckless heart galloped like a band of wild horses. Rafe Hunter was breathing life back into me, and I was quickly becoming addicted. But our time was finite, and I couldn't help but wonder what happened after the show ended.

When the high was over and we came crashing back down to Earth.

What then?

CHAPTER FOURTEEN

"CAN I SUGGEST SOMETHING?" Rafe asked me as we sat on the floor of the penthouse, his guitar cradled in my lap.

"Of course."

We'd been like this for over an hour, after Rafe asked to see the piece I had prepared for tomorrow's first round. I'd hesitated at first but as he'd so smugly pointed out, it wasn't every day you got an offer of help from one of America's rising guitarists. And since Molly and Hudson were showing no signs of coming up for air, I'd hurried down to my room under Jake's watchful eye, grabbed my notebook, and plucked up the courage to show Rafe my country rendition of *Zombie* by The Cranberries.

"It sounds great," he went on, "but I think it'd sound even better if you tweaked the chords a little. Can I?" He motioned for his guitar and I handed it over, watching raptly as he slid his fingers up the neck. "Okay, so on the change from E Minor to C, if you leave off your first finger and then add it back on the next change, it'll deaden the sixth string for when you go into G then D." He played the chords, repeating them a couple of times to let me hear the difference. "See?"

I nodded and Rafe grinned.

"Then if you stick with your strumming pattern for the first verse and chorus but switch it to a down strum only for the second verse and chorus, I think it'll build that second half better."

"I like it. I like it a lot." He handed the Zemaitis back to me and I tested it out, hardly surprised that his subtle suggestions gave the song something extra.

"The judges won't know what's hit them." I lowered my eyes, his compliment washing over me. "Eva, come on," his voice coaxed me to look at him. "You must know how good you are."

"The competition is really strong," I said weakly.

"You've got this. You had it before I offered my expertise, but now it's sure to win them over."

"Oh, it's like that is it?" I smirked. "I guess if I do win, I can expect you on stage to take full credit?"

"And cause a security breach?" The corner of his mouth kicked up. "I think I'll stick to watching you from the wings." His gaze flickered to my lips.

Rafe hadn't kissed me again, but I'd caught him looking a lot, and strangely it was enough.

"Can I ask you something?"

"Sure." I lifted the guitar off my lap and propped it against the couch carefully. As far as I was concerned, the guitar was an antique and I didn't want to be responsible for damaging it.

"What you said earlier about having demons to bear, what did you mean exactly?"

"I..." The words lodged in my throat. I hadn't meant to reveal so much to him earlier. Rafe was just easy to talk to and I found myself wanting to open up to him.

But I wasn't ready to bare my soul; not yet.

"I had some stuff going on last year but it's all good now." I glazed over the truth, pasting on my best smile. "Play something for me? It only seems fair that I get to hear you since you already heard me."

I was deflecting. We both knew it, but Rafe humored me anyway, picking up his guitar. "Any requests?"

"So, I umm, have a confession to make." Heat blazed up my neck and into my cheeks. "I'm not exactly a huge fan."

Rafe gasped, clutching his heart. "That's impossible."

"Don't worry, I looked you up after Ploughton." I let the words hang. "I like what I've heard so far." We shared a mutual smile, and I added, "Play me something from the band. Your favorite song or one that means something to you."

Songs could tell you so much about a person, and I wanted to know all the Black Hearts bassist's deepest, darkest secrets.

Something passed over Rafe's face, but it didn't linger. "You know my brother usually sings lead?" I nodded. We hadn't talked much about his brother, but I'd noticed Rafe got this dark look whenever he came up. "Well, there's a reason for that so bear with me."

He strummed the opening chords and I was entranced, watching as his fingers moved expertly over the strings. But it was nothing compared to the way his voice affected me as he rasped out the first verse.

The way you used to do your hair, the perfume that you wore
A song that plays or a stranger's face in the crowd
It's the little things that remind me of you
But then I remember you're gone and the light fades

Here in the darkness the truth sets me free
From a place I don't wanna be
Here in the darkness blood runs free
Washing away the pain that lives in me

The way you wore your hair, the softness of your voice
A familiar smell or a simple touch
It's the little things that remind me of you
But then I remember you're gone and the light fades

Here in the darkness the truth sets me free
From a place I don't wanna be
Here in the darkness blood runs free
Washing away the pain that lives in me

By the time he sang the last lyrics, I had tears brimming in my eyes. "Shit, Eva, I didn't..."

"That was beautiful," I sniffled, "and you said you couldn't sing. Who is it about?"

"What?" He seemed taken aback by my question.

"The song," I added. "Who is it about?" Because there was no way a song so painful yet passionate wasn't about *someone*. There had been a split-second, during the second chorus, I'd felt a sting of jealousy. I was envious of whoever the song was about. Because who didn't want that kind of love? The infatuation. The pure unadulterated yearning that was bound to leave a mark.

"I, uh," he ran a hand through his hair and down his neck, rubbing vigorously, "we all have our demons, right?" Rafe's shoulders lifted in a dismissive shrug, and I knew it was the only answer I was getting tonight.

I didn't know whether to be relieved or disappointed. Relieved because I wasn't the only one keeping secrets, or disappointed because he didn't want to share the truth with me.

"Rafe, I want to—"

My phone blared to life, startling me. There were only two people who would be calling me this late, and one was currently locked away with Hudson Ryker doing things I didn't want to think about.

"Sorry," I said glancing down at Mom's name flashing across the screen. "I need to take this."

"Sure, I'll make a start cleaning up."

Surprise must have registered on my face because Rafe rolled his eyes. "I'm quite capable of cleaning up after myself."

"I didn't—" My ringtone grew louder and I groaned beneath my breath.

"Go," he mouthed. "I got this."

I moved to the sliding door and stepped out onto the balcony. "Mom?"

"Hi, sweetheart," she sounded lost and my heart cracked wide open. "How is everything there?"

"Everything is..." Glancing back into the suite, I saw Rafe standing over by the kitchen counter, watching me. "Great, Mom." I swallowed the lie. "Are you okay? You sound—"

"I'm okay, sweetheart. It's just... well, the house feels so lonely without both of you." Because Dad was gone too. Guilt snaked through my chest.

"You could have come with me and Molly."

"No, no, baby. Your daddy's right. I have to do this; to give you space. I just..." she gulped audibly.

"I know, Mom. I know." It was hard for her to let the people she loved most out of her sight. "But I'll be home before you know it, and you'll get to see me on TV tomorrow."

"Oh gosh, Eva. I'm so excited. I don't think I'll be able to sleep. I always loved watchin' you up on stage."

"Try to sleep. You should have a cup of sweet tea; it might help."

"I will. I'm sorry for calling so late, baby. It's hard for me but I'm trying. I'm really tryin'."

We said goodbye and I clutched my cell phone to me. "Everything okay?" Rafe's voice drifted over to me and I looked over my shoulder.

"It will be," I said, giving nothing away.

"I made you some hot chocolate." He offered me the mug and I took a sip, the smooth rich liquid warming my insides.

"How very rock star of you."

"I try." His gray eyes twinkled with laughter. "Come here."

I went to Rafe, and he eased the mug out of my hand, placing it on the ledge. His long fingers brushed my jaw, moving along my neck and into my hair as he tilted my face up to his. "I've wanted to do this again all night."

My hands wound around his neck as he kissed me, his lips brushing over mine with a heated desperation I felt right down to my toes. We stumbled back as Rafe's hand slipped to the small of my back pushing me closer as he pressed me against the wall.

"Rafe…" I panted and he broke the kiss.

"You want me to stop?" His eyes searched mine, his pupils blown with lust.

"N- no."

"Thank fuck." He dived for me again, attacking my mouth with fervent need. One of his hands slid to my throat, stroking the skin there, his lips chasing his fingers. Sucking and biting, sending shocks of pleasure zinging through me.

"Where have you been all my life?" Rafe whispered into my neck, his words so low I wasn't sure they were for me. But I'd heard them. Like a gunshot to the heart they'd impacted me.

It was crazy.

We didn't know each other. We didn't know any of the important stuff. But I was falling. Hurtling towards the ground hoping, *praying*, he'd be there to catch me.

"Eva, tell me what you want." He lifted his face, eyes dark and stormy and so full of need. I swallowed hard.

"This." I pulled his face to mine, kissing him deeply, rubbing myself against him shamelessly. His mouth curved, and he pushed his head to mine, forcing me further against the wall. My hands pressed at my sides, steadying myself as he hooked one of his hands under my thigh, hitching my leg around his hip. I could feel him thick and hard beneath his jeans, but I wasn't ready for that.

As if he sensed my hesitation, Rafe made no move to undress me or continue his exploration of my body. Instead he rocked gently into me at the perfect angle. I clung to his body, my breaths growing shallow and choppy.

"Imagine I'm inside you." He whispered against the corner of my mouth, his dirty words making me shudder with pleasure. "Your tight little body gripping me. You're so fucking wet, Eva, I can hardly stop myself." Rafe pulled me closer, grinding my body over his jeans. It was clumsy and messy and the most erotic thing I'd ever experienced. And he hadn't even touched me, not really.

Waves of intense pleasure began to build inside me, but he didn't let me catch my breath. He stole my thoughts as he kissed me deeply, letting his tongue tangle with mine in slow, lazy licks. Devouring me. My shoulders began to ache, the wall pinching my muscles, but I didn't complain.

I didn't want him to ever stop.

"More," I cried, pushing up on my tiptoes, trying to reach the place I needed him most.

"Jesus, Eva." Rafe's voice was ragged as he continued to rock into me. The fact he still hadn't tried to touch me, to slip his hands down my jeans or up my tee wasn't lost on me. But in a strange way, it only made him more attractive. He might have wanted more than I was willing to give him right now, but he wasn't going to push me for it.

And that meant something.

I just had to figure out *what*.

"I'm going to…" The words came out breathy as my body began to tremble. Rafe slowed his movements, drawing out the pleasure crashing over me. Then I felt him tense, a low groan rumbling in his chest as he found his own release.

The weight of the moment hit me and a strangled laugh spilled from my lips.

"Something funny?" he asked, eyes alight with awe.

"That was…" How did I even begin to explain it to him? So I chose deflection instead. "I bet you haven't done that in a long time Mr. Rock Star."

Rafe stared at me for a second, let out a chuckle of his own, then buried one of his hands into my hair, kissing me softly. When he finally released me, I was flushed all over again. "We should probably go back inside and clean up, before they come looking." Embarrassment flamed my cheeks, and he chuckled. "Now she goes shy."

I swatted his chest but Rafe caught my wrist, tugging me into him. "Want to know a secret, Eva?"

"Yes?"

"I've *never* done that before." He watched me, gauging my reaction. But I had nothing, gawking up at him with utter confusion and reverence. "Come on." Rafe pulled me toward the doors. At least, Molly and Hudson were still doing whatever they were doing in the bedroom. I wouldn't have to face her inquisition just yet.

But the second we stepped inside, I realized I was wrong.

Molly stood there, arms folded over her shoulders, glancing

between me and Rafe. "Evangeline Star Walker, why do you look like you just—"

"*Molly!*" I hissed, my eyes wide with mortification. Hudson smirked, raising an eyebrow at Rafe who scratched his chin with his middle finger.

"We should, hmm, go. We should go," I announced, wanting nothing more than the ground to open up and swallow me whole. Molly opened her mouth to protest, but I hurried over to her, grabbed her hand and yanked her toward the door.

CHAPTER FIFTEEN

The second we stepped into the elevator, Molly shrieked "You have some explainin' to do." Her eyes twinkled with amusement and what looked a lot like pride.

Trust Molly to be proud of my moment of madness out on the balcony with Rafe.

I pressed my lips together, refusing to answer. Desperately trying to focus on something—*anything*—other than the memory of his touch, how his piercing felt against the soft flesh of my lip.

"Please tell me what I think happened out on the balcony happened?" My eyes flew to hers, heat bursting into my cheeks. "Eva, babe," she chuckled. "It's written all over your face."

"I didn't have sex with him," I rushed out.

"Third base then?" She waggled her brows.

"Hmm, not exactly." My cheeks flushed five shades deeper.

"Okay, you're going to have to work with me here because from where I was standin' it sure looked a lot like the two of you were—"

"He made me... you know..."

"Come?" She said matter of fact, and I nodded, burying my face in my hands. "Babe, that is a good thing. A very good thing indeed. Did he..." She motioned with her head.

"I think so. We were... we didn't actually touch each other."

A frown pinched her brows but quickly morphed to amusement. "You dry-fucked."

"Molly, seriously. Do you have to be so crass?"

"It is what it is." Her shoulders shook with a soft chuckle. "No wonder you looked like a deer caught in the headlights when you came back inside. That's very old-school. I dig it."

I buried my face again, but Molly was there in an instant, pulling my fingers away. "You need to lighten up." It was my turn to frown, keeping my eyes on the floor. "Listen," she said. "Did you want it?"

I nodded. Because I had.

I'd wanted it so much.

"And did it feel good?"

Another nod as my eyes slowly lifted to hers.

"And did Rafe enjoy it?"

"I think so."

"So what's the problem? I should be commending you for not givin' it up to him." Worry flashed over her face.

"Molly, tell me you didn't...?" But of course she had. "Oh, Molly." I wrapped my arm around her. "You promised."

"I know, I know. But I'm a weak woman and he's... holy shiitake, Eva, does the guy know what he's doin'. It's okay though." Resolve slammed down over her expression. "I know this is all it is. One weekend with a rock star. A very hot, very talented rock star. And I plan on enjoyin' every damn second of it."

Her words didn't fill me with hope though. Because while she might have been okay with walking away after the show and filing her time with Hudson away as a fun story to tell her future grandchildren, I already knew I couldn't do the same.

Rafe had stolen a part of me. Taken it without me realizing. I didn't want it back though. I wanted him to have it; to cherish and protect it, keeping it with him as a reminder of our time together.

But I knew better.

I knew we didn't always get what we wanted.

"Eva?" Molly brushed my arm, pulling my attention. "What is it?"

"Nothin'." I choked out the word, forcing a weak smile.

"Oh no... no, no, no. You weren't supposed to fall for him, babe."

"Fall? I'm not fall—" She gave me a pointed look, letting out an exasperated breath.

"I didn't mean to; it just happened," I admitted.

"One weekend, Eva. That's all this was supposed to be."

"I know." My smile widened despite the sadness clinging to my words. "It's fine. I'm fine."

"Good because this life, their life... it's great and all, but we wouldn't last two minutes in their world. You know that, right?" I couldn't help but think she didn't mean us at all.

She meant me.

I wouldn't last.

The thought sat heavy in my chest.

"Rafe's different." The argument sounded pitiful on my tongue, and I don't know why I'd said it.

"He might be different now, here, away from the band and the spotlight. But did you know they're goin' on tour again soon?" Molly looked right at me and I looked at the elevator buttons, counting off each floor as we passed it on the way down, hating how much her honest words affected me.

"Guys like them, guys with the entire world at their feet, don't want to be shackled to a girl."

"Okay, I get it," I finally snapped. "It's doomed. I'll focus on the contest."

"Eva, come on." She came to me and hugged me tight. "I'm not saying don't enjoy it while it lasts. I'm just sayin' be careful. I'm so happy you're finally taking risks and livin' life, but I don't want you to get hurt. Not any more than you have been already."

There it was again.

Cancer.

Lingering in the background.

Even though I was in remission, technically cancer-free, I would always be bound to it and it to me. It should have been a small price to pay for being granted a second chance.

But it didn't feel like it.

Molly hugged me tighter, refusing to let me go. Eventually, I managed to wriggle free, but she was pouting at me. "Do you hate me?"

"I could never hate you, Mol. I just don't know what to say either."

"So don't say anythin'. It's the contest tomorrow, you need to focus on that right now. We can worry about the rest after."

I gave her a half-hearted nod, relieved when the elevator doors pinged open to our floor. It was late and I was tired. All I wanted was to climb into bed and forget all about what happened earlier.

Well, maybe not all of it.

Some things were better saved for sweet dreams...

Or beautiful nightmares.

I WOKE WITH A START, MY EYES DARTING AROUND THE ROOM, straining against the darkness. Panic flooded me when I didn't recognize my surroundings.

Where was I?

The hotel in Camdena. I was in the hotel with Molly, who was currently lying on her stomach, snoring softly.

Sitting up, I ran a hand down my face, trying to figure out what had woken me.

Tap. Tap. Tap.

I pushed back the covers, sliding my feet to the floor.

Tap. Tap. Tap.

Moving silently across the room, I checked the peephole and gasped, quickly fumbling with the lock to open the door ajar. "Rafe?" I whispered, "what are you—"

He pushed me back into the room, closing the door behind me. "What is it, what's wrong?" I asked, my heart racing.

His eyes glittered in the darkness, running over every inch of me. I had pajamas on, but they left little to the imagination. A low groan rumbled in his throat as he scrubbed a hand over his face. "I had to see you."

"You did?" Warmth pooled inside me at his words.

"Yeah, you left so quickly. I couldn't just leave things like that. Besides, I needed to wish you good luck for later."

I frowned. "You came down here, at one in the mornin', to wish me good luck?"

His mouth kicked up at one side. "I don't need a lot of sleep. Hazard of the job. But it wasn't the only reason I came." Rafe crowded me against the wall, pressing one hand right next to my head. He leaned in, ghosting his lips over mine. "I can't stop thinking about you."

"Rafe, I..."

"Ssh." His finger moved to my lips, silencing me. "I know what you're going to say and I know it's complicated, but who knows where the road might take us? I like you, Evangeline Star Walker. I like you a whole lot."

My head whirled at his words. He sounded so honest.

So real.

But Molly's words from earlier rang in my head.

"I don't like that look," he whispered, brushing his thumb along my jaw. A shiver worked through me, breath catching in my throat.

"You caught that, huh?"

"I did, Starshine."

"Starshine?" My brow rose. When he didn't answer, I added, "What would you have done if Molly had answered the door instead of me?"

"It was a chance I was willing to take."

My breath caught. "What are we doin', Rafe?" Because though I knew I needed to heed Molly's warning, this thing between me and Rafe didn't feel temporary.

"Right now, I'm going to kiss you. Then you're going to go back to bed and dream of me."

"Is that—" His mouth came down on mine, stealing the words from my lips and sending my heart into freefall. One of his hands went to my hair, sliding through the strands to give him control over me. Rafe teased me, licking the inside of my mouth, running his tongue over the seam of my lips.

"Rafe," his name came out a half-moan. But before I could ask for more, he pulled away, touching his head to mine once more.

"We should stop unless we want to give your friend something to really lose her shit over." He smiled, leaning in to steal another quick kiss. "I'll see you tomorrow, okay?"

"You'll be at the show?"

"I wouldn't miss hearing you sing again for anything," he said taking my breath away, his eyes so honest and intense. "Remember what I said, Eva... dream of me." Rafe slipped out of the room and I slumped against the wall, completely overwhelmed by him.

And almost certain I was on a one-way street to Heartbreak City.

———

LIKE THE SHOW AT PLOUGHTON, THE MORNING PASSED IN A BLUR OF rehearsals and briefings. Only this time, anticipation was replaced with tension as we waited around for the audience to fill the hotel's impressive auditorium. Unlike the regional shows where there was a conveyor belt of performances ranging from the good, the bad, and the downright ugly, all twenty-four of us here today had earned our spot. Now we had to survive the first round of judges eliminations to advance to the aired show this evening, where the remaining finalists would compete for a spot in the top three.

"Gather round everyone," Colton wafted his clipboard above his head, waiting for everyone to gather in. "We're about thirty minutes out to curtains up. You should all have the running order memorized. It's going to be a long day, so sit tight, take a few deep breaths, and most of all, enjoy it out there. Any questions?"

"What happens if we forget our words?" Josiah called out, earning him a few snickers.

"No second chances. The judges know the deal. Six minutes per performer. Not a minute longer. You screw up your lyrics, that's on you."

"Jeez, it was a joke," Josiah grumbled under his breath.

"Okay, before we get this show on the road, I just want to take this opportunity, on behalf of the production team, judges, and the people at Jamesboro County Productions, to congratulate you all on making it this far. Today is your chance to shine." Colton's hand went to his earpiece and he hurried off.

"I don't know about anyone else, but I really felt his—"

"Do you ever quit talkin', Golden?" Scott smirked. "You should focus less on making wisecracks and more on preparing for the show."

"I'm ready, Scott. Been ready my whole goddamn life." Josiah stiffened his collar before slinking away.

"He never learns." Scott came up beside me. "Hey, where's your friend?"

"Molly? She's gettin' coffee."

His eyes twinkled. "You'll be at the party tonight?"

"I, uh, I'm not sure what we're doin' yet."

"You have to come."

"Maybe." I highly doubted Rafe and Hunter would be at the wrap party.

"Oh hey, Scott." Molly strolled up to us. "Sorry it took me so long. It's gettin' pretty crazy out there."

"It's a sellout, always is. But with Hudson Ryker on the panel things have been even crazier."

"Yeah, well, some of those fan girls are vicious. I almost got into a fight with two girls in the line."

I fought a chuckle. "Maybe you should stay back here where it's safe," Scott said, his eyes slowly raking down my best friend's body. To my surprise—or not, given her current thing with Hudson—Molly didn't seem to notice. She pulled out her cell and checked the screen, frowning. I shot her a questioning look, but my best friend didn't take the bait. Instead, she slid it back in her pocket and pasted on a fake smile.

"It's almost showtime," she said. "Are you all set?"

"As I'll ever be." Nervous energy danced in my stomach. It had been the same all morning; a flight of butterflies fluttering wildly, causing havoc to my insides.

"Just remember, babe, all you can do is your best."

I looked at her and forced a smile. She was right, of course. But now I was here, so close to the final, all I could think was what if my best wasn't good enough?

"Betsy called her the new sweetheart of country. Welcome on-stage Miss Evangeline Walker."

The production assistant gave me a little nudge, forcing me out of the wings. The glare of the stage lights hit me first, then the rumble of the audience, the force of their roar knocking me back like a tsunami.

"And what have you prepared for us today, Eva?" Garth asked, cool and collected, unaffected by the sea of people behind him.

"I'll be singing *Zombie* by The Cranberries."

He gave a sharp nod. "Good luck, the stage is all yours."

Silence fell over the auditorium, like the eerie calm before the storm. I strummed the opening chords, and it only took a split-second for the rush to hit me. All the anticipation, the nerves and fear dissipating, melting into nothing as the first lyrics left my lips.

I'd enjoyed performing at Ploughton, found my love of playing again somewhere between Molly handing me the entry letter and stepping out in front of the judges for the first time. But it was here, in Camdena, I found my reason.

This wasn't just a contest of vanity; of proving you were the best. It wasn't just a platform to launch your music career.

It was more.

To me, it was *so* much more.

It was a step toward healing; to finding my path again. But more than that, it was a chance to ease the burden on my parents. If I could win that prize check, I could give Mom and Dad back everything they lost from watching me almost die.

As my fingers moved over the frets, as I sang each haunting lyric, I felt my resolve harden. I'd always been modest, always played down my talent. But maybe it was time I started listening to everyone around me.

It was time to start listening to myself.

I could do this.

I *needed* to do it.

I needed to believe I'd been given a second chance to make a difference.

Because otherwise, the burden of getting a second chance at life was one I wasn't sure I'd survive.

———

"And the crowd goes wild." Molly punched her fist in the air, beaming with delight as I weaved my way backstage. "You were sensational," she added.

"You think?"

"Oh hush now; you know you rocked it." Her eyes flicked to a darkened corner of the room. "You should probably... go."

"Go?" My brows furrowed, and she rolled her eyes. Leaning in, she whispered, "A certain guitarist is waitin' for you."

"He is?" The butterflies were back.

Molly let out an exasperated breath. "Will you just go already? Before I do." She smiled but there was a tightness in her words. I didn't need to ask to know something bad happened between her and Hudson, or maybe nothing had and that was the problem. Molly liked him. It was right there in her eyes every time they were together. But now she'd slept with him, and everyone knew sex changed things. People either usually caught feelings or they didn't.

Molly had caught feelings. But Hudson... something told me he *never* caught them.

"Eva, babe, go." Her words pulled me from my thoughts.

"What happened to 'we can't live in their world'?"

"We can't." She smiled sadly. "But I think you deserve to share the spotlight for a little while. Now go." My best friend held out her hand and I slipped off my guitar strap and gave it to her. I didn't want to be that girl, the girl chasing after a guy she liked, but the second Molly hinted that Rafe was waiting for me, the invisible rope in my stomach tightened, pulling me toward him.

Discreetly, I crossed the room, smiling at a couple of contestants who caught my eye. Josiah looked ready to stop me in my tracks but thankfully Scott intercepted him. By the time I reached the door, my heart was pounding so hard I felt lightheaded. This wasn't real life, sneaking into dark hallways to meet famous rock stars. But it was real.

And right now, it was my life.

I gripped the door handle and pushed, slipping inside. Rafe was on me in a second, pulling me further into the darkness. "You were amazing," he whispered, his hands cupping my face, lips brushing over mine.

My hands went to his tee, curling into the soft material. "You listened?"

"I could listen to you all day, every day." He kissed me again. the cool sting of his piercing sending a delicious shiver skittering up my spine.

His words softened something inside me and I melted against him. Rafe kissed me like he felt it. Felt the simmering need between us, the growing bond.

Molly's warning lingered in the back of my mind, but every stroke of his tongue, every time his teeth teased my skin, it got pushed further and further away, until I could barely remember why this was a bad idea.

When Rafe finally broke the kiss, my knees were weak and my mind was mush. "Hi." He gazed down at me, his eyes more black than gray now.

"Hi." I smiled, aware of how easy he pulled me in. Made me forget all the other stuff going on around me.

"I probably shouldn't have done that, but I couldn't wait."

"I'm glad you did it." My hands curled tighter as I leaned up to kiss the corner of his mouth. His taste was addictive, his touch like wildfire, setting my body alight.

"The things I want to do with you," he murmured. It was the same thing he'd said to me before. At first, the words had struck me as odd. The things he wanted to do *with* me. Not *to* me. But now I liked them.

I liked them a whole lot.

Until the reality of our situation edged into the corner of my thoughts. I stepped back, putting some space between us. But it only gave more room for Molly's warning to slam into me.

"Eva?" Rafe frowned.

I tucked some stray curls behind my ear and forced a smile. "I should probably get back, the production team will wonder where I am."

Jamming his hands in his pockets, Rafe rocked forward. "I meant what I said last night, Starshine. I know it's complicated, but you never know where this might lead. You just have to give it a chance."

Panic welled up inside me. He wanted this.

He wanted me.

I didn't doubt that.

But what happened when tomorrow came and he had to return to the band and I had to go back to trying to figure out how to live again?

"I'll see you later, okay?" I started for the door.

"I won't let you run, Eva. Not yet." His words rolled off me as I hurried back to the backstage area. No one seemed to notice me, too preoccupied with their preparations.

Molly was watching out for me though. She rushed straight over, her brows crinkled with concern. "What happened?"

"What am I doing?" I whisper-cried. "This isn't me."

"Oh, babe, come here." Molly wrapped me into a hug, letting me have my moment of despair. Then, after a couple of beats of silence, she said the words that shook me to my core. "Maybe there's a reason you're both here, at this exact same time. Maybe he's supposed to help you heal."

Her words sank into me.

Was she right?

Was Rafe really part of my healing?

Or would he be my downfall?

———

"You're shaking, darlin'," a woman from the Klineville regional took my hand in hers as we waited for Colton. Two hours later, after the last contestant performed, the judges had disappeared into one of the hotel's conference rooms to deliberate over who would be commencing to the final eight. Molly had kept me company, supplying me with soda and candy while we waited for the callback.

I didn't see Rafe again.

It was a good thing too, because I wasn't ready to deal with him or how I felt about him. Not yet, at least. Not when I had the show to think about.

The door finally opened and Colton entered the room, the four judges filing in behind him. My eyes immediately went to Hudson. If my fellow contestants knew I'd hung out with him, they might have had something to say about it. But the fact was, I still wasn't entirely sure he liked me, and I expected no preferential treatment just because he'd slept with my best friend.

"Okay," Colton said, "this is it, the moment you've all been waiting for. Some of you know the routine by now and some of you don't. If I call your name, please step forward. Gina Denby, Jet Ollerton, Josiah Golden, Mary Sue Kinley, Evangeline Walker, Joelene Proctor, Davy

Larson, and Tiffany Meriah..." I glanced down the line, trying to place each contestant and their performance. Gina had been pitch-perfect again and was shaping up to be a firm audience favorite. But I couldn't remember at least three of the performers. Not to mention the fact, I couldn't believe a scenario where the judges chose Josiah to progress to the final.

So when Colton said, "Congratulations, you're our 2019 finalists," I almost didn't believe it.

Cheers broke out around me, a deafening rumble that reverberated deep in my chest. Colton was quick to usher the room into quiet. "It's never easy saying goodbye to contestants at this stage but the judges would like to say a few words. Garth, over to you."

He stepped forward, offering the twenty-four of us a warm smile. "This year's talent has been unbelievable. The level at which y'all are playing and singin' has really blown us away. It's never easy being told it's the end of the road, but it's all part of auditioning and tryin' to make it in this business. We've all gotten our fair share of rejections but keep doing what you're doin' and one day, you'll get there."

"Thank you for that, Garth." Colton checked his clipboard. "We wish you all the best and hope you'll stick around to celebrate with the winners tonight. I have it on good authority there's a free bar and copious amounts of fried chicken." He chuckled. "Winners stick around as production want to run over a few things with y'all. Everyone else, if you please follow Shelby, she'll get you debriefed."

One by one the contestants who had not gone through filed out of the room, but the judges lingered. Colton and Garth were deep in conversation while Sarah Lou chatted to Gina and a couple of the other finalists. I remained by myself, letting the news soak in.

"We meet again," Josiah said.

My eyes slid to his, silently pleading for him to leave. "Congratulations," I replied.

"I'd say the same to you but at this point in the contest the time for playin' nice is over."

"It's just a contest, Josiah."

"Just a contest?" His eyes narrowed with vehemence. "Do you know how many people would kill to be here?" He stepped closer to me and I craned my neck around him to try to catch someone's attention.

"You think you're somethin' special" he sneered, "because Ryker took a—"

"Eva," Hudson's voice was hard. "Production needs you."

Josiah turned on his heel and dropped the intimidating asshat routine. "Hudson, my man. I was just giving Eva some tips, if you know what I'm sayin'."

Hudson looked right past him and said, "Eva, now." He almost barked the words, but his sights were set firmly on Josiah. I slipped around him and moved behind the Black Hearts drummer. He was slightly shorter than Rafe but broader, his biceps bulging out beneath his tight black tee. I imagined it was from all the hours spent practicing.

"Go," Hudson clipped out. "I want to talk to Goldenboy a second."

I smothered a snicker at the fact Hudson had used Molly's nickname for him. Josiah's jaw clenched, but he didn't argue, waiting for me to leave. Eventually, I inched away, making a beeline for the door. I needed air. Or better yet, a shower to wash away the feel of Josiah's unnerving gaze.

As I grabbed the handle, I glanced back to where Hudson had Josiah cornered. It looked anything less than friendly, but I couldn't work out if Hudson was simply being a good human being, helping a girl in need, or whether he was looking out for me for a certain gray-eyed bassist.

CHAPTER SEVENTEEN

THERE HAD BEEN no time to dwell on Josiah and Hunter; backstage was becoming a flurry of activity as the production team prepared for the final eight performances. I was primped and polished within an inch of my life. The make-up felt heavy on my skin, but we all had to wear it for the cameras; something about lighting and sheen reduction. But as I stood center stage, the lights beating down on me, it seemed pointless, and I was convinced I would look like a melting waxwork to the viewers at home.

"Welcome back, Evangeline." Garth asked, folding his arms on the table. "What'll you be singin' for us?"

"This is a song I wrote called, 'All it takes is a second'."

"Whenever you're ready." He gave me a little nod.

Closing my eyes, I moved my fingers into position, inhaled a deep breath, and started strumming.

Woke up this morning, with tears on my pillow.
And I cried.
Went through the motions, the questions and anger.
And I tried.
Told myself I'd make it, would fight 'til the end.
And I lied.

Because all it takes is a second for everything to change.

You never saw it coming, never expected the storm 'til it arrived
With nowhere to run to and nowhere to hide
All you can do is hope that passes without too much wreckage
Because all it takes is a second for everything to change.

Woke up this morning, with barely a whisper.
And I cried.
Fell down again, then picked myself back up.
And I tried.
Held onto hope, then let it slip through my fingers.
And I lied.

Because all it takes is a second for everything to change.
You never saw it coming, never expected the storm 'til it arrived
With nowhere to run to and nowhere to hide
All you can do is hope that it passes without too much wreckage
Because all it takes is a second for everything to change

And I cry, and try, and I lie, over and over
Because all it takes is a second for everything to change
And I cry, and try, and I lie, over and over
Because all it takes is a second for everything to change

ADRENALINE HUMMED THROUGH MY BODY AS I STARED AT THE judges, the roar of the crowd barely drowning out the pound of blood between my ears. I'd experienced a lot of medically induced highs in the last year. Fentanyl, oxycodone, hydromorphone; you name it, I'd felt it coursing through my bloodstream. But no synthetic drug could ever replace this. The sound of two thousand people applauding you.

Applauding your words. Your music. Your story.

"Phew," Gabe pretended to dab his eyes. "I'll think you'll all agree that hit us right in the feels. Give it up for Miss Evangeline Walker."

I walked off stage, head held high, and heart on my sleeve. It was the first time I'd performed the song, and in that moment, I knew it was the right decision. My performance had a raw vulnerability that came from singing the lyrics to an audience for the first time. The air had crackled with pain as I'd shared something so personal, so profound and difficult, with them. Inviting every one of them to walk a day in my shoes, even if they didn't realize it.

My fellow contestants swamped me the second I reached the holding area. "Christ on a cracker, you really raised the stakes with that." Joelene Proctor, a thirty-something woman out of Brescone, said. "I damn near ruined my shirt." She made a show of dabbing her heavily made-up eyes.

"You did good, Eva," Gina added, "Real good."

Everyone seemed to have something nice to say.

Everyone except Josiah, who stood off to the side, glowering at me as if I'd just ruined his favorite toy.

"There she is." Molly jostled through the crowd, pulling me into her arms. "I just want you to know, no matter what happens later, you're the winner in my eyes." She held me at arm's length. "That was... I don't even have any words. No wonder you didn't want to play it for me before."

Cheeks burning, I offered everyone a smile, and inched away slowly until Molly and I had some space. "The rush was..." My breath caught. "I can't explain it. It felt transformational."

"I'll say. I almost cried me a river watchin' you. If you don't place in the top three, I'll—"

"Ssh." I grabbed her hand, aware we still had an audience. "There's still a long way to go." Over half the finalists had yet to perform.

"Have you seen Rafe?"

I shook my head. "But Josiah looks pissed."

"He's just cryin' over the fact Hudson put him straight." When I'd told her about what Hudson had done, Molly had, of course, swooned.

I still didn't understand what had happened between the two of them earlier. But something told me I was better off not knowing. Besides, if it meant Josiah stayed away from me, I really didn't care what Hudson had said to him.

Just then, my cell phone vibrated. Molly dug around in her bag and handed it to me. "It's probably your mom." She was smirking which seemed odd until I read the message.

UNKNOWN: YOU WERE AMAZING.

I GASPED SOFTLY. RAFE HADN'T ASKED FOR MY NUMBER, AND I hadn't offered it which meant there was only one person...

"Molly," I gawked at her. "What did you do?"

"Hudson can be very persuasive." Her eyes twinkled with suggestion.

"But I thought—"

"That I wasn't done cryin' over the fact after tomorrow I'll probably never see him again?" She shrugged. "Life's too short and Hudson Ryker is too damn good with his tongue."

"Molly!"

"What?" She grinned. "Like you don't want to find out how good Rafe's lip piercin' feels pressed up against your—"

I clamped my hand down over her mouth, spinning us away from prying eyes and ears. "You're crazy."

"And you're so gettin' some tonight. Forget what I said before. Forget it all. If you don't do this, you will regret it. It's better to have loved and lost a rock star than to never have loved one at all, right?"

"And by loved you mean..."

"Do you really want me to spell it out for you?" A quiet chuckle spilled from her lips. "Regardless of what happens in the final, tonight we make all our dreams come true."

Molly's change of heart didn't really surprise me. My best friend liked to straddle the thin line between responsibility and recklessness. And I had no doubts her plan to *make all our dreams come true* would be in full effect by the time we hit the party tonight.

Only I was pretty sure her dreams and mine looked very different.

"Well, don't just stand there," she leaned over me as I stared at Rafe's message, "text him back."

ME: THANK YOU.

"THANK YOU?" SHE GROANED. "THAT'S THE BEST YOU CAN DO? GIVE me the damn phone."

"Mol—" Snatching it from me, she began typing. When she was done, she handed it back to me, a sly grin tugging at her mouth.

"Were you listenin', Mr. Rock Star? I'm starting to think I might have a stalker." I read her words. "Oh my—" My cell vibrated with an incoming text.

UNKNOWN: MOLLY, IS THAT YOU?

. . .

I EXPLODED WITH LAUGHTER, ONLY LAUGHING HARDER WHEN I SAW Molly's frown. "Fine," she grumbled. "Have it your way."

After saving Rafe's number, I texted him back.

ME: SORRY ABOUT THAT. SHE WANTED TO HELP.

RAFE: HELP? WITH WHAT EXACTLY?

ME: HONESTLY? I HAVE NO IDEA. SO YOU HEARD MY performance... does that mean you're close by?

RAFE: I'M... AROUND.

THAT MADE ME SMILE. HE WAS SO MYSTERIOUS. AN ENIGMA I WANTED to crack wide open. Before I could reply, another message came through.

RAFE: I'LL SEE YOU TONIGHT... AT THE PARTY?

MY HEART ALMOST LEAPT INTO MY THROAT. "HE'S COMIN' TO THE party," I whispered, while typing a quick reply that I looked forward to seeing him later.

"Well, yeah. I figured Hudson would have to make an appearance since it's in his contract."

"But..."

"Don't look so worried." Molly gave me an easy smile. "Rafe Hunter likes you, Eva. Enjoy it, remember?"

Her change of attitude almost gave me whiplash, but I knew she only wanted to help me embrace the moment.

Even if we were trying to fool ourselves into thinking it wouldn't hurt when tomorrow rolled around.

―――

"YOUR MOM JUST TEXTED AGAIN."

"Again?"

Molly smiled. "She's proud, give her that at least. Want to text her back?" She held out the cell phone, but I shook my head.

"Can you do it?" My hands were trembling too much. "Put somethin' nice."

Her fingers flew over the screen and then she said, "All done." Sliding my cell back into her pocket, Molly reached out and clutched my hand.

"This is it," she grinned. She was supposed to be out front, sitting alongside the other two thousand people ready to watch the results announcement. But Molly had sweet-talked one of the production assistants into letting her backstage.

"Whatever happens from here on out, just remember you did it. You got up on stage and rocked the hell out of the judges."

"I think I might puke." I groaned, pressing a hand to my stomach. "The money would mean so much to them."

"Your daddy would blow a gasket if he knew you were doin' all this to pay them back. As if there's a price on you bein' healthy." She scoffed, as if I'd lost my ever-loving mind.

And maybe I had.

Maybe all the chemo had burned away my brain cells.

It would explain my out of character behavior of late.

"We need the money, Mol. *They* need the money."

"I know, I know. But this was never supposed to be about the money. It was supposed to be about you findin'—"

"I have." I cut her off. I didn't want another lecture on how I needed to find myself and start living again. Since meeting Rafe, everything had changed. I was still weighed down by the guilt; but being with Rafe was like being in a bubble. A vacuum separating reality with fantasy. Your problems were still there, waiting for you... they just couldn't reach you inside the bubble.

But it wasn't lost on me, the one who made it all go quiet, was the one person I could never truly have.

Not unless I was willing to share him with the entire country.

"They're callin' you." Molly tapped my arm. "Remember, I love you and you got this."

We hugged quickly, before I grabbed my guitar and joined the remaining contestants as we made our way backstage. We were going to perform one more song, together, before the judges crowned their winners.

"How are you feelin'?" Gina asked me.

"Like havin' tacos for lunch was a mistake."

Her laughter eased the tight knot in my stomach. "Just picture them all naked, that's what I do. Although this year my vision has been pretty tunneled."

"Let me guess, Black Hearts fan?"

"They're just so... raw. The lead singer is in a league of his own. I saw them play earlier this year and the whole thing was just..." She let out a heavy sigh.

"Hudson is a closed book though, huh?"

"They're all the same. A publicist's worst nightmare." A smirk tugged at her lips. "That's half the appeal though. They're so broken, you can't help but want to put them back together."

I wanted to ask what she meant about them being broken, but Colton appeared, barking orders at us like we were children. "It's showtime people," he yelled. "Just like we practiced earlier. Gina, Jet, and Mary; followed by Josiah and Davy; with Evangeline, Tiffany, and Joelene rounding out the performance."

"Good luck," Gina whispered as she slipped away, making a beeline for Jet and Mary who were already waiting by Colton. Josiah glanced over his shoulder, our eyes connecting for just a second. Contempt flashed in his gaze, but there was no time to decipher his intent because Gabe's voice rang out loud and clear, and we were being ushered on stage.

CHAPTER EIGHTEEN

"Judges, have you come to a final decision?" Gabe asked, anticipation rippling around the room.

"We have," Betsy answered. "It wasn't an easy one, but we've made it."

"Kind of the point of the show, Miss Betsy," he teased, moving to the judges table to pluck the envelope from her fingers. "Okay, moment of truth..." There was a dramatic pause, kicking my pulse into overdrive. "And the third-place prize of five-thousand dollars goes to... Miss Evangeline Walker."

Someone nudged my shoulder, and I blinked, straining against the lights.

"Eva, honey, it's you," a voice said, "you won."

"I..." Stumbling forward, I barely managed to make it to Gabe. A production assistant appeared beside him with one of those over-sized checks written out to me for the amount of five-thousand dollars.

I wanted to be ecstatic. To revel in all the things I would do with the money. But the truth was, it wasn't enough. Five thousand dollars wouldn't even make a dent in Mom and Dad's debt.

My stomach twisted as I accepted the cardboard check and posed for the camera alongside Gabe. He asked me some questions, but I couldn't focus. I couldn't get past how I was so close... and yet, so far away.

Before I knew it, the production assistant ushered me to the side and Gabe launched into announcing the second and first prizes. Josiah looked almost as disappointed as I felt as he was announced the second runner up to Joelene, who took first place. That was a small mercy as I wasn't sure I would have stomached someone like Josiah winning the contest.

"Congratulations, hon," Joelene said as we posed together for a winner's photo. "Young thing like you has a long and successful career ahead of her."

But this didn't feel like the beginning, it felt like the end.

Closure on a part of my life I would never truly get back.

I'd done this for Molly, for my parents and our situation. And while I'd loved performing, had found myself completely lost in the music, I couldn't do this month in month out. I didn't want to be another Josiah, chasing a dream that would never come true. I wouldn't stop playing because, if anything, the contest had showed me singing and playing was a part of who I was. But I didn't want this to be my legacy. Talent shows and third place prize checks.

It didn't seem enough.

Not for a girl who had outrun Death.

Music was a part of my soul, something I would never give up, but I needed to believe I was here for something more.

Something worthy.

———

"Third place is amazing, babe. You should be so proud."

"I am." The words came out muffled as I slipped the blouse over my head. "It's just not enough."

"Eva, I'm telling you, you're bein' too hard on yourself. It was your first contest."

First and last, but I didn't have the heart to tell Molly that. Not yet.

"To place third in the entire county is somethin'—"

"I don't mean to sound ungrateful, I don't. But we needed that money, Mol, and I guess the more I performed, the more I began to believe I could do it. That I could actually win."

"You could have easily won," she gave me a pointed look, "but the competition was tough."

"Josiah placed second." I frowned back.

"Yeah, well, the guy might be a total asshat off stage but there's no denyin' Goldenboy can sing. He's been workin' the circuit for years now."

She wasn't wrong, and it only made it me feel even more bitter.

"Look," Molly came over to me, "What's done is done. You can go back home with your head held high. You did somethin' amazing here. I know you're disappointed. I know five grand isn't going to change your life, but it's about so much more than the money, babe."

I wanted to believe her, I did. But since being told I was going to make it—that the cancer which should have killed me was in remission —it was like I was wired wrong. Things that should have made sense no longer did.

"Come on, we still have tonight. Whether you want to or not, we are celebratin'."

"Has Hudson texted you?"

"No. Why has Rafe texted you?" Her brows pinched.

"No." The knot in my stomach tightened. He'd been so playful earlier, texting me back and forth. But there had been nothing but crickets since they announced the winners.

"I'm sure they're just busy with post-production stuff. Hudson was moaning about how much Colton was ridin' him to do publicity and interviews."

"Yeah, I'm sure that's it." My smile was tight, but I continued getting ready, applying a light layer of make up to my face. Molly had gone all out for the wrap party; dressed in a killer black dress that hit her knee and cinched at her waist. She looked older than her barely eighteen years. I'd played it safe with a pair of jean shorts and sheer blouse over a black tank top.

"Ready?" she asked.

"As I'll ever be." I joined Molly near the door and she grabbed my hand.

"One night, Eva." Her eyes sparkled with anticipation. "Let's make the most of it."

THE WRAP PARTY WAS HELD ON THE SECOND FLOOR OF THE HOTEL, in the Camdena Royal Suite. My first thought as we stepped inside was that we were in the wrong place. It was gaudy and brash and Colton hadn't been lying when he said there was fried chicken. The smell permeated the air, but no one else seemed bothered as they drank and chatted and mingled.

"Well, this is... not quite what I had in mind." Molly glanced down at her dress. "Good thing, I stuck with my boots. Come on, let's get a drink."

We weaved our way through the sea of people; some I recognized as production team members. People stopped us to congratulate me. But it was when a thick set man in a flashy suit stopped me, holding out a business card, and said, "Give me a call sometime, I think I can take you to the next level," the weight of the contest began to truly settle in.

Molly was right. Coming third might not have been enough for me, but for these people it meant something.

"I don't see them," Molly said, her eyes scanning the room, disappointment leaking from her.

"Maybe they got held up." I silently ordered myself not to look for him. Telling myself that Rafe would seek me out if he wanted to, and if he didn't... well, it would just be another disappointment to add to the weekend.

"Yeah, maybe." Molly's expression was crestfallen.

"Hey, now," I said, "What happened to makin' our dreams come true tonight?"

Seeing my strong, funny, beautiful best friend so deflated left a sour taste in my mouth. So Molly Steinberg occasionally ran away with herself, daydreaming of rock stars and cute guys who she hoped would sweep her off her feet. It didn't mean she didn't have feelings like the rest of us. As my mom liked to say, "the bigger the heart, the more it hurt". Something told me Hudson Ryker was going to leave a mark she wouldn't erase anytime soon.

Just like Rafe, a little voice whispered, but I ignored it, focusing on Molly and the party in full swing around us.

"Walker," Josiah strolled up to us, standing that little bit taller and smugger. "Bad luck today."

"Go f' yourself, Goldenboy." Anger blazed in Molly's eyes as she stepped forward, glaring up at him. He looked like the typical cowboy; jeans and flannel shirt, Stetson propped proudly on his head, worn snakeskin boots. But what he had in looks, he lacked in Southern charm.

"Easy, tiger," he chuckled, taking a long pull of his drink. His eyes looked a little glazed, his smile easy, in that liquor-buzzed kind of way.

"Just go, Josiah. It's a party; you should celebrate."

He advanced toward me, taking the air clean with him. I gawked up at him; Molly scowling over his shoulder. "We could celebrate, darlin'."

"Josiah, I really think you should go."

He kept coming until my back hit the wall, panic seeping into every cell of my body. "Don't be such a spoilsport, we're just talking, havin' some fun."

"I'm not—"

"Relax, little lady." He reached out, plucking a curl between his fingers. "I've been watching you. The way you've got them all wrapped around your finger. But you're not foolin' me, Angel," he drawled the word. "I know your game."

"I think she said leave." A hand came down on Josiah's shoulder, yanking him back sharply.

"What the hell, man?" Goldenboy protested to Hudson, who glared at him, a murderous expression on his face. Molly watched on, a mix of desire and concern swirling in her eyes.

She wasn't the only one.

"Hey, hey, what's going on here?" Colton appeared, forcing himself between the two men, although Hudson was six year's Josiah's junior.

"You need to control your judges." Josiah scrubbed his jaw.

"Hudson?" Colton gave the drummer his attention.

"It's not the first time I've caught him harassing Miss Walker."

"Harassin'?" Josiah seethed. "Now let's not be hasty. It's nothin' but a little friendly—"

"Josiah, go wait over there. I'll deal with you later."

He shot Colton a look of disbelief but stalked away without argument.

"Evangeline?" The production manager was looking at me now. "Is what Hudson said true?"

"He... he makes me uncomfortable." I wrapped my arms around my waist. "But I didn't want to make trouble, so I tried to avoid him."

"I see." Colton's jaw ticked. "We don't tolerate any kind of harassment at Jamesboro County Productions. You should have come to me with this."

"I really didn't think—"

"The guy is a complete douche," Hudson interrupted me.

"He's also the douche *you* put through to the final." Colton reminded him.

"Yeah, well, I'm beginning to realize what a huge fuck-up I made." Hudson never missed a beat as his eyes slid to mine, shining apology and regret.

"I'll deal with Golden, if you promise to stay away from him. You're supposed to be making us look good, not dragging us through the mud."

Hudson tensed. "I fulfilled the terms of my contract."

"I know, and we're grateful. But the show is effectively over, and I know how you guys like to... never mind." Colton shook his head a little. Their whole interaction was intriguing. Colton was a grown adult, a manager heading up a huge show, and yet he talked to Hudson as if he held all the chips. I couldn't imagine having that kind of power at the tender age of nineteen.

It wasn't any wonder the band had a colorful reputation.

We'd already drawn an audience. Everyone watching to see what was happening; no doubt wondering if they were witnessing the next Black Hearts scandal. I figured everyone was tied into an NDA like me and Molly though.

"You don't need to worry, I'm done." Hudson's whole demeanor had changed. His eyes narrowed and brows pinched. This was the Hudson Ryker I'd first met back in Ploughton.

"Hudson, come on, man, I didn't mean—"

"It's all good, Manners. I have somewhere to be anyway." His eyes grazed over me and landed on Molly who was as still as a statue at my side.

"Thanks, for everything," Colton grumbled, as we all watched Hudson walk away. As if he hadn't just pulled the rug out from under the show's production manager.

CHAPTER NINETEEN

"It's Hudson," Molly said, checking her cell. "He wants us to meet them." She pulled her bottom lip between her teeth as she scanned the room.

After Hudson's, and subsequently, Colton's, intervention, Josiah had disappeared and the rest of the night had gone without a hitch. I'd only stayed for Molly after it was clear Rafe would not be coming. But my best friend had seemed preoccupied most of the evening.

I didn't need to ask to know why.

"You want to go?"

"Don't you?" She pouted.

Did I?

Rafe hadn't texted me again and Hudson hadn't mentioned him. It was almost as if he'd disappeared off the face of the Earth.

My stomach knotted.

I wanted to see him again, I did. But I also knew it was probably a bad idea.

When I didn't answer, Molly said, "I'll tell him no." She stared at her cell longingly. "We can go back to the room and order room service—"

"Tell him yes."

I'd officially become *that* girl. But I couldn't leave Camdena without seeing Rafe one last time.

The knot tightened.

"Okay." Molly fluffed her hair, a mischievous grin painted on her lips. "Let's do this."

We left the party with little fanfare. Joelene had collared me, insisting on swapping numbers, certain she could help me, 'figure out a plan'; whatever that meant. I'd politely smiled and mumbled something about exchanging numbers before we left and then gotten the heck out of there.

"I think it's this way," Molly grabbed my hand and pulled me down the quiet hall.

"Boo," Hudson jumped out from around the corner startling me. Molly simply rolled her eyes, unaffected by his surprise appearance. Rafe lingered behind him, offering me a weak smile.

My heart sank.

"Wondered if you'd come," Hudson mused, letting his gaze rake down my best friend's body again.

"So where are we going?" Molly ignored his blatant appraisal of her and started down the opulent hall.

"Is she always this hard work?"

"Molly is—"

"Already bored of waitin'," she called out. "I thought you guys were supposed to know how to party?"

Hudson smirked at her. "Don't wish for things you can't handle."

I frowned at his cryptic response, but then Rafe finally spoke. "Hud, man, maybe this isn't such a good idea."

Hudson slung his arm over my best friend's shoulder, glancing back at us. "Lighten up, Hunter. Besides, Molly and Eva are cool chicks, right? You can keep a little secret?"

Secret?

I internally analyzed his strange choice of words while Molly practically flamed at the mouth. "Of course we can." She stared up at him with stars in her eyes.

"Should we go?" I asked Rafe, who looked visibly uncomfortable at the fact Hudson was leading us toward the elevator.

"Eva, I..." his gray eyes slid to mine. "Fuck." he grumbled under his breath.

"Maybe this isn't such a good idea." I went, ready to move away, to tell him goodbye, but his hand circled my wrist, his touch sending a thousand bolts of electricity shooting through me. My gaze dropped to where he held me, before slowly lifting back to his. Rafe looked down at me through thick black lashes and smiled.

"You should come. I'm not ready to say goodbye yet." His voice reverberated deep inside me.

Truth was, I wasn't ready to say goodbye either. I liked Rafe. Liked that he knew music. Like that he didn't push me to do anything I didn't want to do.

But most of all, he seemed to see the real me. And I liked that he liked me for me. Not because I twirled my hair and batted my eyes or spewed Black Hearts facts and stats at him. He seemed to like me because I *didn't* know all those things.

Because I was different.

"Okay," I said quietly, walking a little closer beside him, our hands dangling between us, almost touching.

"Aww look," Hudson shouted over, uncaring that we were in a hotel hall where anyone could see or hear. "They're almost holding hands."

"Fuck off," Rafe mouthed at him and I smothered a laugh. "Sorry about him. He really doesn't know when to—"

"Rafe?"

"Yeah, Eva?"

"It's fine." Our eyes locked, understanding and a million other things passing between us.

We had almost reached the elevator when Rafe grabbed my hand and stopped me. "Before we go up there, I just want you to know..." he hesitated.

A beat passed.

And another.

Tension descended between us.

He blew out an exasperated breath. "I'm sorry, okay? I wanted to be there for you today, to tell you how amazing you were. That song was... wow, Eva. The way you laid it all out, it was amazing. But something came up, and I had to..." He ran a hand through his hair. "Well, you'll see."

Something was wrong, that much was obvious. It was written all over his face. But I didn't have time to ask because their bodyguards ushered us all inside the elevator and doors pinged closed, taking the air with them.

Minutes later, we arrived at Rafe and Levi's suite. It was the same one we'd hung out in last night, except now it was full of people. People I didn't recognize. Guys with piercings and tattoos and faux hawks, and girls scantily dressed in leather and latex, denim and silk. I stalled in the doorway, Rafe bumping into me. "Sorry," I threw over my shoulder.

"Listen, if you want to get out of here and—"

"Rafe, bro, get over here," a voice boomed over the music, "Kendall has a party trick she wants to show us."

Rafe's expression darkened, flitting from me to the room and back again. "I'll be right back, okay?"

"I—" but Rafe was already moving around me, melting into the sea of people.

"Molly…" I called, but Hudson was already guiding her towards the kitchen counter, the one lined with bottle after bottle of liquor.

I moved deeper into the room, my eyes adjusting to the dim light, cutting through the smoky haze lingering in the air. People were sprawled over the huge sectional, laughing and drinking. But the guy Rafe approached held court.

I saw the resemblance immediately.

Levi Hunter looked even more devastating in person. I knew he was one year older than Rafe, but from the way he howled at something the guy beside him said, the way they high-fived and fell back in fits of laughter, he seemed younger. Almost childlike.

Rafe leaned down to whisper something to his brother and Levi's eyes narrowed, his head shaking in disagreement. Then his black eyes drifted out over the room… landing on me. "You," he barked. "You the chick who has my brother tied up in knots?"

Rafe shot me an apologetic look, but it did little to quell my racing pulse. Everyone had stopped to see what—*or who*—had caught Levi Hunter's attention, the rumble of laughter and chatter drowned out by heavy silence.

"What's up? You a mute or something?"

"Leave her al—" Hudson pulled Molly into his side and whispered something in her ear, silencing her.

Everyone kept staring.

Kept waiting.

I wanted to disappear, to evaporate into smoke and shadows.

But Levi's assessing glare pinned me in place.

"Well?"

Stepping forward, I sucked in a shaky breath. "I'm Evangeline Walker. It's nice to meet you."

You could hear a pin drop. Everyone waiting on tenterhooks to see how the rock god from Philadelphia would respond to the small-town girl from Lyme.

"Is that right, *Angel?*" He glanced up at Rafe. "I like her, bro. She's got… charm."

Laughter exploded around me as Levi and his friends mocked me. Indignation burned through me, tears welling behind my eyes. Rafe threw his brother a murderous look before making a beeline for me, but I hurried away, going straight for the balcony door.

"Eva," he called after me as I spilled out into the balmy night. "Fuck, I'm sorry about Levi. He's…"

"An ass?" My eyes slid to his.

"Among other things. Shit," he dragged a hand down his face. "I knew it wasn't a good idea to bring you here."

"So why did you?"

I didn't belong here. It was exactly what I'd known and refused to believe. This was their world and I didn't fit in here.

I never would.

"I wanted to see you again." Rafe stepped closer to me. He went to reach out for me but hesitated, jamming his hand in his jean pocket. "But it isn't like I could ask you out on a date like a normal guy."

"You want to take me on a *date*?"

He lowered his eyes, looking up at me shyly. It made him appear so angelic. *A dark dangerous angel more like.*

"You caught that, huh?"

"And where would you have taken me?" I moved an inch closer. "On this hypothetical date?"

"I—"

"Everything okay out here?" Hudson and Molly appeared. She came over, her big hazel eyes silently asking me if I was okay. I offered her a small nod.

"Sorry about Levi, Eva," Hudson added, surprising me. "He can be a real asshole."

"Hudson assures me he won't upset you again." Molly grabbed my hand, levelling him with a hard look. "But we can leave if you want to?"

"Aww, come on, babe. Don't be like that. I said sorry. Don't leave. Not yet. It's your last night in Camdena," he said. "You should make it a memorable one." Hudson winked at her and she practically melted into a puddle.

"We can stay," I said, wondering if I'd completely lost my mind. But it was a big suite. Staying out of Levi's way wouldn't be too difficult.

"Excellent, I'll get us all some drinks. Molly..." Hudson flicked his head as if she should join him, a knowing smirk on his lips.

When they left, Rafe let out a soft chuckle. "Is it me or did you get the impression they were giving us some space?"

"Hudson definitely needs to work on the art of being discreet." I smiled weakly. "So who are all those people?" I glanced back at the suite. The party was raging on inside, the heavy bass of the music drifting out to us.

"Groupies... roadies... stragglers my brother picked up on the ride here."

"Is it always like this?"

Rafe's brow furrowed as he swiped his tongue over the silver ball in his bottom lip. "Levi likes the spotlight. I know it sounds strange, but he needs the attention. It helps him..." He let out a heavy sigh. "Do you really want to spend what limited time we have left talking about Levi?"

Rafe was in front of me now, his eyes gazing down at me with such adoration it knocked the air right out of my lungs.

"I want to know about you," I said with complete honesty. "And Levi is a big part of who you are."

Pain flashed across his features and Rafe inhaled a sharp breath, his eyes shuttering. When they opened again, fixing on my face, his torment had been replaced with a note of sadness. "I wish we had more time."

"We have all night," I whispered, the words full of promise and intent.

Even if I wasn't entirely sure what I was offering him.

CHAPTER TWENTY

IF SOMEONE HAD TOLD me a month ago, that tonight I'd be sitting in Rafe Hunter's penthouse suite, partying with the rest of Black Hearts Still Beat, I probably would have asked who the hell they were talking about.

But like an unforgiving storm, Rafe Hunter had swept into my life and obliterated all my walls. Walls I thought were so strong, so reinforced from my battle with cancer, that I never saw him coming.

"Go again," Damon Donnelley, electric guitarist and one fourth of Black Hearts, lined up his quarter. "Shit," he rasped as he missed.

Smirking, I lined up my own penny and flipped. It hit the rim of the cup and promptly fell inside. "And that's how it's done."

"Who are you and what have you done with my best friend?" Molly plopped down beside me, her drink sloshing over her cup. I eyed her and she groaned. "It's my third. Maybe fourth."

"Are you sure I can't persuade you to celebrate with something a little harder than soda?" Damon asked me for the fifth time since we'd joined him and another guy called Jack, who I'd learned was a roadie on their tours, playing quarters.

"I'm good, thanks."

"How'd you get so good at this game?" Rafe's warm breath danced over my neck. He wasn't kissing me, but I could imagine his lips brushing my skin, the cool sting of his piercing there. My breath shallowed and he chuckled. "Eva?"

"Y- yeah?"

His hand slid over my knee. "Come back to me," he whispered.

I shook my head, trying to focus. Damon caught my eye, giving me a knowing smile. He was so different to the others. Like sunshine on a rainy day, he was warm and kind and so easy to be around. He also seemed to be pissed at Levi which earned him extra brownie points with me.

The Black Hearts front man was busy on the other side of the room, entertaining a rapt audience, and knocking back shots of liquor as if it was going out of fashion. With every shot, every clink of a glass, Rafe's expression grew more and more uneasy, but when I'd asked him if everything was okay, he'd simply deflected by touching me. A slight brush of his hand against my thigh; a ghost of his lips over my forehead. Despite his unease about his brother's behavior, he seemed completely at ease being with me in front of everyone. And although I didn't know any of these people, I knew that through their eyes, it looked like me and Rafe were together.

At least, for now.

No one questioned it, no one dared to mock or tease. No one except Hudson, but as I was quickly learning, that was Hudson's MO; to make jokes, usually inappropriate ones filled with sexual innuendo. Much to my surprise, he also had no problem being intimate with Molly in front of his bandmates and the rest of the people crammed into the penthouse. I didn't want to think about how often he did this, picked a girl to bring into their inner circle, because every time the thoughts infiltrated my mind, I couldn't help but ask the same of Rafe. I wanted to believe things were different with us, but after seeing a glimpse of their world, how easily the girls offered themselves up to guy after guy, it was difficult to trust my instincts.

"Hey," he squeezed my knee, "You okay?"

"Fine." I nodded, averting my eyes when a girl and guy started making out against the wall, uncaring they had an audience. "I thought it would be awkward being here, but surprisingly, it's not."

At first glance the party had looked crazy, and to a certain extent it was, over in Levi's end of the room at least. But we'd managed to carve ourselves a little pocket of calm in among the chaos.

"So, Eva," Damon asked, "what are your plans now you're a Jamesboro County Talent Showdown winner?"

"Oh, you know... complete senior year and graduate." I kept my voice light despite the gnawing in the pit of my stomach.

"You're a senior? No shit." He threw Rafe a questioning look.

"What? She's barely two years younger than us."

"Yeah, but—"

The sound of glass smashing echoed through the room and we all whipped our heads around to where Levi was.

"Fuck," Rafe muttered, shifting beside me. He slipped his arm from around my shoulder and got up. "I'll be back."

I sank back against the cushions. Molly gave me a reassuring smile, but it was Hudson who spoke. "Don't worry about Lev, he can be a handful after a few drinks."

"Why do it then?"

Liquor was flowing freely despite the band being under twenty-one, and more than one person already looked smashed, swaying on their feet, eyes glassy, and smiles uninhibited.

Hudson and Damon shared a look and Jack cleared his throat. "I heard you killed a version of *Zombie* by The Cranberries. It's like one of my all-time favorites. I'd love to hear it."

"That's a great idea, Eva." Molly nudged my shoulder. "I bet Rafe wouldn't mind you playin' his guitar."

"The Zemaitis." Damon reared back. "Rafe let you play the Zemaitis? No fucking way?" Heat creeped into my cheeks, but the guitarist wasn't done. "He never lets anyone play that damn thing. Not even me." Shock flashed in his green eyes.

"I... it was really only for a minute."

"Interesting." His brow quirked up. "But yeah, you should play. Maybe we could jam together?"

Loud voices cut through the air. "Back the fuck off, Rafe. I got it," Levi yelled, eyes frantic as his brother tried to help him clean up the mess. Hudson leaped to his feet, Damon too, both of them swerving through the bodies to get to their bandmates.

"Chill out, man," Hudson said, his voice easy.

"Yeah, and who the fuck asked you, Ryker? Why don't you go back over there and fuck your latest piece of ass?"

Molly gasped beside me, shrinking into the couch. I reached for her hand, watching with horror as Black Hearts unraveled in front of my eyes.

"Fuck you, man. We didn't ask you to show up here." The two of them were up in each other's face now, anger radiating off them in heavy waves.

"Hud, not here, man." Damon pressed his hand against Hudson's chest trying to force him backward. He budged a couple of inches, giving Rafe room to slip between them. He kept his eyes on Levi, saying something I couldn't make out from our position on the other side of the room.

"Should we do somethin'?" Molly's voice was cracked with pain.

"Like what?"

"Yeah?" Hudson yelled at Damon. "Well, he can take a fucking——"

Levi tried to lunge for him, but Rafe caught him, grappling him like a bear.

"Do something," Molly cried, burying herself into my side, "You have to do somethin'."

Before I knew it, I'd moved off the couch and found Rafe's guitar in the corner of the room where we'd left it the night before. Slipping the strap over my neck, I strummed an E Minor. A couple of people glanced in my direction, confusion marring their faces. Jack caught my eye and gave me a little nod of encouragement, so I strummed again, moving into the C Minor.

"What the fuck do you think you're doing playing my brother's guitar?" Levi had shrugged out of Rafe's hold, stalking toward me. He stopped in the middle of the room. If looks could have killed, I was pretty sure I'd be dead. But I had his attention.

I had the attention of the whole room.

"I heard you're supposed to be a big deal or somethin'."

So help me, Jesus. What was I saying?

But there was no backing down now. If Levi was focused on me, he wasn't focused on Hudson or Rafe.

"Like you don't know who I am," he said smugly, running his thumb over his snake bite piercings. "Everyone knows who the fuck I am."

"Until a month ago, I'd never even heard of Black Hearts Still Beat."

"Bullshit." He inched closer, his eyes a strange mix of fury and fascination. "Now tell me why the fuck you're holding my brother's guitar like it belongs to you."

Offering him a half-hearted shrug, I plucked the strings again, playing the opening chords of *Zombie*. "I figured I'd like to see what all the fuss is about. You know the lyrics?"

"Do I know the fucking lyrics?" Levi glanced around challenge sparking in his eyes. "Who the fuck is this chick?"

A rumble of laughter cut through the tension. But I saw people's uncertainty, the looks of pity and dread and everything in between. All while Rafe, Hudson, and Damon watched me with what looked a lot like awe.

My mouth was dry, my hands clammy as they cradled wood and string.

Levi smirked, like a shark circling its prey. "What's the matter, Angel?" he said. "Don't you want to play with the devil?"

No one intervened. Molly didn't run to my rescue and Rafe made no move to stand beside me, to protect me from his big, bad brother. I was all alone. But something told me I held the power. What I did next would determine how the rest of the night played out.

"I'm game, if you think you can keep up?" Sweat beaded along my neck, trickling between the valley of my breasts, and down my back.

"Let's see what you've got, *Country*." It was meant to be an insult, but if there was one thing I wasn't ashamed about, it was where I came from.

As I went into the opening chords again, I risked a glance at Rafe, wondering what he thought about all this. But he wasn't looking at me. He was watching Levi.

Watching Levi watch me.

As Levi's raspy voice dropped the first lyric, I was certain I caught a flash of jealousy in his brother's eyes. Which was ridiculous. I didn't like Levi; I was scared of him. I'd just wanted to do something to stop the anger bleeding into the room. Felt an overwhelming need to help.

Now I was here, playing guitar while Levi Hunter growled the words, intensity rippling off him. It was visceral. A physical transformation. Levi didn't just come alive as he sang, he flew. Elevating to some higher level. I almost stumbled over the chords a couple times just watching him.

We fell into an easy rhythm, and somewhere during the second chorus I started singing along with him. My eyes found Rafe again, and this time, he was looking back at me. His eyes full of so much emotion, I didn't know what to pick out first. But quickly, I realized he didn't look relieved or thankful or even appreciative.

He looked sad.

He looked like he thought I'd just made a huge mistake.

CHAPTER TWENTY-ONE

THE SECOND THE MUSIC STOPPED, people swarmed us. Molly lunged for me and I barely managed to slip the guitar strap off and hand it to Jack before she reached me.

"Holy cow that was f'in amazin'." She pulled me into her arms, my laughter strained as I searched for Rafe across the room. But another face filled my vision.

"Not bad, *Country*," Levi said around a playful smirk. "I like what you did with the chords."

"I had a good teacher." I looked for Rafe again but couldn't see him.

Disappointment flooded me.

"Shit, Eva, Rafe and Hudson said you were good," Damon added, "But that was, well you fucking rocked it. Are you sure you want to be a country singer?"

I shrugged, not at all comfortable with all their stares and questions and compliments.

"I'd like to make a toast." Levi announced, grabbing a beer from the closest person to him. "To Eva for playing like a fucking pro and bringing a little fun to this dull as fuck party."

There were a few grumbles at that, but no one complained. I sensed no one would dare. Levi Hunter was king among these people and his word was law.

"And to my band," he spun around to face Hudson and Damon, "we might have our ups and downs but I fucking love you guys."

Molly nudged me discreetly, her brows furrowed as we watched

Levi. He was like a yo-yo swinging back and forth. Low then high. Angry then elated.

"And Rafe, bro, where the fuck are you?" He stood taller, searching over the heads. "Rafe?"

"I think he went to take a piss," someone answered.

"Oh well, to Rafe. The best guy I know and the only guy I trust." Levi capped the bottle with his thumb and shook it rapidly before releasing it, thrusting it high, and letting the spray rain down on everyone.

Girls shrieked and guys howled and Levi looked punch drunk as he rejoined his loyal servants.

"That was f'ed up, right?" Molly whispered as Hudson and Damon discussed something out of earshot. "Maybe we should go?" Concern shone in her eyes. "Before things really get out of control?"

"I'll be right back, okay?" I rushed out, unable to get the image of Rafe, the hurt in his eyes, out of my head.

"But—"

"Hudson," I tapped his shoulder and he whirled around. "Can you keep Molly company for a little while. I need to go find..."

"Go," he said as if he knew exactly what I was thinking. "I'll look out for her, promise."

This time, I believed him. Hudson Ryker was a lot of things—player; brooding, hot-headed, impulsive drummer for one of the country's hottest bands—but something told me I could trust him.

At least, I hoped I could. Because I wasn't leaving here until I'd found Rafe.

Until I understood what the hell had just happened.

———

It didn't take much to find Rafe out on the balcony. As I stepped outside, the couple of people making out on one of the chairs got up and went inside, giving us privacy.

"Hey," I said, gingerly joining him by the railing. "What are you doin' out here?"

"Just thinking." His boot scuffed against the tiles.

"Rafe, did I do something wrong just now? I was only tryin' to help."

His eyes shifted to mine, glittering under the moonlight. "You didn't do anything, Eva," he let out a heavy sigh, "it's just... Levi is—"

"Complicated?" I repeated the word he'd used about his brother before.

"He's my older brother, but it's always felt like I'm the one looking out for him."

"Is it the band? The lifestyle?" They were so young to be thrust into a world of fame and fortune. I couldn't ever imagine walking into a room and have people fall over themselves to appease me.

"Music is in his soul. It's all he knows." He said the words as if they explained everything, when really, they explained nothing.

"I only wanted to help," I said the things again, unable to shake the feeling Rafe wasn't telling me everything.

"I know." He reached out for me, tucking a stray curl behind my ear. His hand lingered and I turned into his touch, unable to resist the pull. "I didn't want tonight to end like this. But that's Levi, always fucking things up." There was no anger in his words, just a resigned acceptance that made my heart ache. Whatever existed between these two brothers was soul deep.

"Yo, Rafe," a voice called, and he let out another sigh, "We've got a problem."

He cussed under his breath, shooting me an apologetic look.

"Go," I said. "I'll be fine."

Even if was a lie.

Rafe hesitated, his eyes shuttering. Without warning, he dropped a kiss on my head before disappearing inside. I stared out at the city, my thoughts running a hundred miles a minute. There was so much I wanted to know about Rafe, questions I wanted to ask. But my time was almost up and part of me resented Levi for stealing what little time we had left away from us. But part of me also felt conflicted about him. He'd sparked something in me: anger, frustration, fear... protectiveness. It didn't really make any sense, but Levi brought out a side of me I hadn't felt since being in hospital, watching the kids younger than me try to make sense of it all.

Overwhelmed, I tilted my face to the night's sky and closed my eyes, letting the cool air wash over me. I didn't hear Rafe until I felt his body behind me, his arms sliding around my waist. "Hi," he whispered, his lips brushing the shell of my ear.

"Hi," I replied, warmth spreading through, memories of last night flooding my mind.

"Levi and his entourage just left."

"They did?" I whirled in his arms. "Is that okay? I mean, where will they go?" The concern in my voice surprised me.

"They're heading downtown to the warehouse district for a private party."

"You didn't want to go?"

"And give up my last night with you?" Rafe leaned in, ghosting his lips over mine, sending shivers up my spine.

"But don't you need to... go and look out for him?"

"Jake and his guys have it covered. Besides, Damon went with them."

"So you stayed... for me?"

He cupped my face. "Is it so hard to believe?"

I gulped, trying to give myself a second to process the fact Rafe had decided to stay.

With me.

For me.

"Molly and Hudson?" I asked,

"Are... inside. But I'm not sure they will be for much longer."

"Let me guess, Molly already forgave him?"

Laughter crinkled Rafe's eyes. "She told you about earlier?"

I frowned. "You mean you know why she was acting all weird?"

"I, uh, shit. She didn't tell you, did she?" He let out an exasperated breath, and I tensed.

"What did he do, Rafe?"

Guilt bled into his expression. "Molly caught him flirting with a couple of girls."

"I see."

"You don't sound surprised?"

Shrugging, I replied, "I figured it was somethin' like that."

"Hudson is..."

"Hudson." I shrugged.

"Let them have their fun." Rafe's expression turned serious. "I'm only interested in one thing. You, Starshine. Ready to tell me what you meant before?"

"About?" I was confused, letting him grip the rail either side of my body, caging me in.

"I want to know you, Eva. The good, bad, all the dark and deep bits in between. I know you're hiding something."

"I..." The words were right there on the tip of my tongue.

But I couldn't do it.

I couldn't tell him the truth. I couldn't see the pity in his eyes.

So I did the only thing I could think of. I pressed my lips to his. Rafe slid a hand into my hair, kissing me back, his tongue teasing and playful. "Are you trying to distract me, Starshine?"

"Is it workin'?" I asked breathlessly, loving how easily his nickname for me came out.

"I'm not sure." His thumb stroked the skin beneath my ear. "You should probably do it again."

Soft laughter filled the air as our lips met again in a slow caress.

"What time is it?" I whispered, finally coming up for air.

"Still early."

Easing back, I arched a brow.

"Fine." He chuckled. "It's a little past eleven."

"Already?" We'd promised our parents to be home tomorrow before church; not that I would be attending.

"Stay," Rafe said.

"Rafe, I'm not sure that's a good idea."

"I'm only asking you for what you're willing to give me, Eva." He brushed my lips again. "But stay, please."

"Okay," the word hung between us. One little word that held so much intention.

Rafe's face lit up, and I noticed how much younger he looked. Lighter somehow.

"What?" he asked.

"You. You're like no one I've ever met."

"Cut me open and I bleed, Eva. Just like everyone else." His words seeped into me, chilling me to the bone.

I shuddered and Rafe pulled me closer. "You're cold, let's go inside." He took my hand and led me back into the penthouse. I didn't tell him that I wasn't cold, that his kiss had ignited a firestorm in my tummy. I didn't confess that it was his words that had affected me, the darkness behind them.

Because I was slowly beginning to realize we were more alike that I first thought.

I had secrets.

But so did Rafe.

———

MOLLY NEVER SURFACED AGAIN. HUDSON DID MAKE A BRIEF appearance to grab snacks and drinks from their fully stocked refrigerator. I guess being famous had its perks. I'd quickly averted my eyes when I realized he was practically buck naked, save for a tiny towel secured around his waist.

"Did that seriously just happen?" I asked Rafe, eyes still wide, cheeks flaming with embarrassment.

"Hudson doesn't care. Now you know why signing the NDA was so important."

"You don't say," I grumbled, my eyes flicking to the closed bedroom door. "This feels weird. It's weird, right?" My friend was beyond that door, doing God only knew what with Hudson. If the muffled giggles coming from the other side were anything to go by, she was enjoying every second.

"Do you want to...?" Rafe pressed his lips together, swallowing whatever words he'd been about to say.

"What?" I asked.

He let out a small breath, reaching over to take my hand, sliding his fingers through mine. "I was going to say we could go to my room. But I don't want you to be uncomfortable."

A feminine moan drifted through the walls and I cringed. "More uncomfortable than sitting here listening to my best friend... nope," I shook my head, "not goin' there."

Laughter reverberated in Rafe's chest as he stood up, pulling me with him. "Come on. I'll keep my hands to myself, promise."

I gave him a small nod, not trusting myself to speak. Worried I would say something I couldn't take back. Because the truth was, I did want him to kiss me, to touch me, to feel his hands exploring my body.

But I was scared.

Fear lodged in my throat like jagged stones.

"This is it." Rafe pushed open the door and hit a switch on the wall. Like the rest of the penthouse, it was extravagant, a suite within a suite. A huge four poster bed sat proud against the pale walls, drenched in pale green sheets. I walked toward it and ran my fingers over the silky material. "It's beautiful," I said.

It was so ostentatious, I felt small standing there.

"What's wrong?" Rafe watched me from the door. He shouldn't have fit in a place like this either, but somehow, he did. Maybe it was the fact I knew *who* he was. Or maybe it was because he was impossibly gorgeous. But Rafe belonged here.

And I didn't.

"Do you always stay in the nicest hotels?"

"Usually it's the tour bus."

"Yeah, but when you're not on tour? When you're doin' all the other stuff?" Interviews and appearances and impromptu performances. From what I'd seen online and read on *Rock Review*, the band never stopped working.

"You don't like it, do you?" He moved closer, every step reverberating deep in my chest. Until he was right in front of me and my breath was caught in my throat.

"It's just a lot to take in."

"Most girls are impressed by all this."

I blanched, offering him a sad smile. "I'm not most girls."

"No, no you're not." Rafe ran the back of his knuckles down my cheek, his eyes fixed on mine. "Who are you, Evangeline Star Walker?" Intensity blazed in his gray eyes. "Because I have never wanted to know someone as much as I want to know you."

CHAPTER TWENTY-TWO

"Let's play a game," the words came out before I knew what I was saying.

"What kind of game?" Rafe's eyes twinkled.

"Not *that* kind of game." I frowned, ducking around him to move to the love seat. He let out a low chuckle, dropping onto the edge of the bed.

"A question for a question."

It was Rafe's turn to frown.

"I'll ask you a question," I explained, "and if you answer, you get to ask me one."

"I know the game, Eva. I just don't understand why you want to play it."

"Because our time is almost up, and I want to know everythin' there is to know about you."

If he was surprised by my answer he didn't let on. "Are there any rules?"

"You can choose not to answer a question, but you forfeit a turn asking one."

"The floor is all yours." He made a grand gesture of sweeping his arms wide.

"Okay, favorite city?"

"Chicago," Rafe answered without even thinking.

"I've never been. Why do you like it so much?"

"That's two questions." He smirked.

"Humor me."

"No way. Wait your turn. Okay... first kiss?"

Of course he would have to ask *that* question. But in the spirit of the game, I answered, "Jenson Blaufield in eighth grade." Rafe's lips thinned, and I added, "What?"

"Was he your boyfriend?"

"That's two questions!"

"Humor me." he teased.

"Next question... my turn. What was Rafe Hunter like as a child?"

"Really?" His brows furrowed. "You want to know this shit?"

"Humor me." It was my turn to smirk.

"I was a quiet kid." The strain in his voice got my attention. "I guess the kids at school would have called me a loner. Kept myself to myself. But I was loyal to a fault."

"There's only fourteen months between you and Levi?" A fact Molly had all too easily known.

Rafe gave me a pointed look, slowly shaking his head. "My turn. You go to church every Sunday like a good Southern girl?"

"I did, yes."

"Did?" He sat straighter. "Give me one more question and you can have two in a row. No holds barred."

"Rafe..."

"Come on, Eva, it's your game."

"Fine." I let out an exasperated breath.

"What happened to you?"

The words echoed through my skull like a jackhammer.

Thud.

Thud.

Thud.

"Pass."

"Come on, Eva. We're sharing. Isn't that the point of the game? I know something happened; I just want to know what."

"Pass," I repeated, my expression hardening.

"You don't want to talk about it, I get it. But if you think avoiding the hard stuff makes it go away, it doesn't."

"What happened with Levi earlier before he sang with me?" I asked, deflecting the attention from me to him. "Why was he like that?"

"Not fair, Eva. Not fucking fair, and you know it."

"So I have to bare my soul, but you won't tell me anything about you? You're right, doesn't seem very fair, does it?" I was irate now, indignation burning through me.

"Eva, it's not like that. But my relationship with Levi is—"

"Complicated. Yeah, you already told me that."

A beat passed, and neither of us spoke.

But eventually Rafe broke the thick silence. "Come here." He crooked his finger, offering me a small smile. "Please."

Reluctantly, I got up and went to him, letting him slide my body between his parted legs, his hands resting on my hips. "I don't want to fight. Not when time is against us."

"I was sick." The words twisted my insides.

It wasn't much, but it was something.

"Are you better now?"

I nodded, not trusting myself to speak.

"It's only been Levi and me for a long time. We're all each other has, and I'm very protective of him. But he's... *it's* complicated."

I was beginning to hate that word.

"Do you regret not goin' with him, to the party?"

"He can survive one night without me, Eva. Besides, I wasn't going to give up this. Not for anything."

"What are we doin', Rafe?"

He stared up at me. "Falling," he whispered before pulling me onto his lap. His mouth crashed down on mine. Hard and unyielding. Our tongues tangled together, slow and searching, my heart pounding in my chest, building like a soft melody.

"You are so fucking beautiful." Rafe cupped my face, kissing me harder, alternating the rhythm. Our lips, our tongues, and kisses playing us our own personal song.

My body hummed with nervous anticipation as my hands ran down the front of his tee, desperate to feel his skin. I found the hem, tugging gently to slip my fingers beneath the material. His body was lean, the smooth planes of his stomach giving way to subtly defined abs. I explored and explored, drifting my fingers up and down; pulling away with surprise when I felt the ring of metal through his nipple.

"Do you have any more piercings I should know about?" My brow rose.

"Maybe you should find out for yourself." Rafe leaned back in, kissing me. Heat coursed through my veins, my stomach awash with desire.

"No," he whispered against the shell of my ear, "just the two piercings."

"And the tattoos?"

"Why don't you take a look?" He dropped back onto his elbows, staring up at me with a lazy smile.

Curious, I pushed the tee up his torso, running my eyes over his inked skin. There weren't as many as his arm, but it was still impressive. Tracing them with my fingers, I asked, "Do they all mean somethin'?"

"Some mean more than others." He shrugged. "Some just seemed like a good idea at the time."

I brushed over the barbed heart over his chest. It was the band's emblem. Their name inked inside a banner flowing across the bottom portion of the heart.

"How did the band start?"

"You really want to know?" I saw the question he wasn't asking, in his eyes.

"This isn't me... stoppin' things," I admitted, blushing deeply. "I just want to talk a little."

He sat up, brushing my neck, placing a tender kiss there. "Well, if we're going to talk, we might as well get comfortable." Tapping my thigh, he nudged me up, and pulled his tee clean off. Then he started unbuttoning his jeans. I couldn't move, transfixed on the way the tattoos seemed to come to life as his body flexed and tensed.

"Are you going to stand there all night?"

"What... I..." The words dried on my tongue as he closed the space between us. Rafe didn't take his eyes off me as his hands found the hem of my tee.

I nodded, swallowing hard. Giving him the silent permission he was asking for. He tugged gently and my arms went up, letting him slide it over my head. His gaze moved down my body, hungry and heated, lingering on my scar. Silence echoed around us as Rafe reached out, letting his fingers flutter over the slightly raised skin. My eyes closed, my breath caught in my throat, as his touch washed over me.

"One day, Starshine, I'm going to know all of your secrets." His other hand slid around my hip and pulled me flush against him. "Even the dark ones."

He saw it.

Rafe saw the darkness inside me.

And the only explanation for it was that he'd experienced something similar. Maybe not an illness but some other life-altering, faith-testing incident.

Our lips met again, this time softer, as I let him push my jeans off my hips until they were pooled at my feet. "Come on." Without another word, Rafe led me around to the side of the bed, yanking back the silky covers. "Get in."

This was not what I had in mind when I followed Rafe to his room earlier, but it was even more perfect. Once we were both snuggled beneath the covers, Rafe's arm around my shoulder; my head on his chest, fingers still exploring his tattoos; he finally started.

"When I was ten, Levi got into some trouble. He was barely twelve, but he was so angry at the world. Still is, I think." Rafe stroked my hair absentmindedly. "Anyway, the school signed him up for this music program. I'll never forget the first day he came home. He was pissed. Everyone got assigned an instrument, but nothing had come easy to Levi. Anyway, at the second session the instructor asked Levi to try singing a few lyrics. Levi wasn't interested. Said if he couldn't play guitar or drums, he didn't want to be in their stupid band."

"What happened?"

"He turned up every week for two months and refused to sing. Then one day he came home grinning so wide, I felt for sure the instructor had finally let him play an instrument. But he'd done it. He'd finally sung. And not only did he sing, he blew everyone away with his voice.

"From that day on, he became obsessed. Said I had to pick an instrument and learn it so we could form a band. Little did he know that ever since he'd started the project, I'd been sneaking into the music room at school, fooling around on the guitars."

"No," I gasped, and Rafe chuckled.

"He was my big brother. My idol. I didn't want him to become some huge star without me. I picked it up pretty quickly and then had lessons."

"How did you meet Hudson and Damon?"

"Hudson was in the program with Levi. After it ended, neither of them wanted to stop practicing so the instructor agreed to let them use the center a couple nights a week. I started going along with them, and then one night, Damon strolled in, asked us what we were doing, picked up the guitar and blew us away. The rest, as they say, is history."

I rolled onto my stomach to face Rafe. "You do realize you just told me a story without revealin' any important details?" He'd told me the *how* but not the *why*.

Why was Levi in trouble?

Why was Hudson at the program?

Why was Damon at the center?

I felt like I was still missing all the vital pieces of the puzzle. The pieces which made them the band they were today.

Rafe gazed at me intently, his gray eyes searching my face. "I can't remember the last time someone wanted to know all this stuff."

"What do people usually want to know?" I moved slightly, hyperaware of how our legs brushed against each other's.

"Am I single? How much money do I have in the bank? Will the band be releasing a new album anytime soon? The list goes on."

"What does this one mean?" I traced a different tattoo, changing the subject.

"That,"—he traced the artistic razor inked along his ribs—"was a drunken mistake after one too many shots with the guys. We'd just been signed to Razorsharp Records and Damon managed to score us some liquor to celebrate. I was only sixteen at the time. One drink led to one more and before I knew it, I was in the chair being inked."

"I can't imagine what that must be like... being thrust into this world so young."

"Eva?" His eyes darkened, homing in on my mouth.

"Yeah?" I breathed, a violent shiver running up my spine.

"It's time to stop talking now."

CHAPTER TWENTY-THREE

RAFE ROLLED me onto my back, hovering above me. "We go at your pace, okay?"

My heart skipped a beat at his words, my throat dry and skin tingling with nerves. Leaning down, he brushed my jaw with his fingers, fixing his mouth over mine. A soft moan slipped from my lips at his touch, the feel of the cool metal pressed against my flesh.

"Imagine me touching you, Eva; curling my finger inside you," his dirty words were like a bolt of lightning through my chest and I involuntarily arched into him, wanting more.

Needing more.

"I don't want to imagine," I whispered. Rafe eased back to look at me, his gray eyes hooded, smile lazy with lust.

"Yeah?" he asked.

I nodded, finding his hand with mine and gently guiding it to my lower stomach. "Touch me, Rafe. I want you to touch me." He needed the words, but I needed to say them too.

His hand splayed over my stomach as he kissed me harder, deeper. Then slowly he swept his hand down to my panties, dragging it over me, making me gasp. Rafe broke the kiss, watching me intently, as he dipped inside the damp material and worked a finger into me. My eyes fluttered closed, my breathing growing shallow as his thumb circled the sensitive bud of nerves. "Look at me, Starshine," he rasped, "Give me your eyes."

I opened them to find two pools of molten silver watching me as he worked me in slow, sensual strokes. My stomach coiled tight as waves of pleasure began to sweep over me. It started off gentle but quickly built into something powerful, crashing over me. Leaving me a breathless, quivering mess. But Rafe didn't give me chance to catch my breath, sealing his mouth against mine, kissing me as if he might never get to kiss me again.

"I want you," he whispered against my neck. "More than I've ever wanted anything."

My hands ran eagerly down his smooth inked body pausing at the waistband. "I want you too," I said shakily.

His body tensed, his eyes questioning as he looked at me.

"I want you, Rafe. Please?"

"You're sure? Because I meant what I said, Eva. I'll only take what you're willing to give me."

"I want you," I repeated with more conviction. "All of you."

He dropped a kiss on my forehead before scrambling off the bed. I watched as he kicked off his black boxers before rummaging around in his jean pocket. When he came back, he threw down the foil packet before kneeling between my legs. Slowly, Rafe inched my panties down until I was bare to him. Lust flashed in his eyes, making me feel beautiful.

Desired.

So alive I wanted to freeze-frame the moment.

He palmed himself a couple of times, and I watched transfixed on how comfortable he was in his own skin. How confident. His body was like a painted canvas, telling a story I hadn't yet pieced together.

But I wanted to.

I wanted to know everything about the deep and mysterious and loyal Black Hearts bassist.

Grabbing the foil packet, Rafe tore it open with his teeth and slowly rolled it over his hard length. Then he covered my body, kissing me once. Twice. Dragging his tongue up the slope of my neck, making my stomach clench and my heart pound.

"You're sure?" he asked, a trace of uncertainty in his words.

"I want you," I said.

So much it scared me.

One of his hands slipped underneath my thigh, hooking my leg around his hip as he gently guided himself inside me. My body trembled as Rafe stretched me, filled me, but his kisses helped me relax.

"Fuck, Eva, you feel..." The words left him in a long drawn out breath, as he dropped his head to the crook of my shoulder, sucking the skin, rocking into me. Slow, sure, measured strokes. I felt him everywhere. His weight pressed down on me, making me feel so small and protected. His lips on my skin, tasting and marking. His fingers gripping the fleshy skin of my thigh, biting harder with every rock of his hips.

It wasn't only physical though, it was emotional. The way he handled me with such tenderness, as if I was fragile and precious. Something he never wanted to hurt.

I felt myself spiraling. Giving over to the waves of pleasure. Letting myself fall further and further for him.

His free hand found mine, tangling our fingers together as he pressed it into the mattress beside my head. "I'm not sure I can..." His jaw clenched and I knew he needed more.

Because I needed it too.

"It's okay," I breathed, hardly able to form words.

Rafe thrust harder, burying himself deeper, and I cried out, clinging onto him. "Jesus, Eva," he groaned, his husky words only drenching me in more pleasure.

My eyes fluttered closed, too overwhelmed, too lost to sensation. It was intense, the way we fit together. Our bodies, moving as one to create the rhythm, our labored breaths becoming the melody, and the sounds of our moans producing the lyrics.

"Rafe... I..." I panted, the words choppy.

"I know," he rasped, pressing his forehead to mine. Our hair was damp and sticky between us. "This isn't the end, Eva," he rocked harder, hitching my leg higher, anchoring us as close as possible, "It can't be the end."

His words melted away as he reached some magical place inside me, the world shattering into bright white light before my very eyes.

Rafe came hard, his body shuddering above me as he traced letters of love on my skin. Painted promises of more.

Of this being the start, not the end.

"That was..." he swallowed, offering me an adorable smile.

Amazing.

Perfect.

Indescribable.

Right.

The words sat on the tip of my tongue as I fought the emotion rising inside me.

"Eva?" Concern flashed in Rafe's eyes. "Was it okay? I thought you wanted to—"

"I did, so much." I leaned up to kiss him. "It just felt..." How was I supposed to explain something I didn't fully understand myself?

Rafe didn't push though. It was as if he knew. As if he also felt the tether between us snapping into place the second he pushed inside me.

A soft yawn slipped from my lips and Rafe smiled. "Let me get cleaned up and then we can sleep, okay?"

I didn't want to sleep. I didn't want to miss a single minute with him. But my eyes were growing heavier by the second.

"Okay," I said, and he dropped a kiss on the end of my nose before clambering off the bed to take care of the condom. When he came back, Rafe slipped under the covers, pulling me into his chest, and whispered, "Promise me this won't be the last time I see you, Eva?"

A heavy feeling settled over me as sleep edged into my thoughts and I whispered, "I promise."

———

MY EYES FLUTTERED OPEN, A DELICIOUS ACHE RADIATING THROUGH me. A small sigh of contentment slipped through my lips as I rolled onto my back, stretching my hands. "Rafe," I asked, voice thick with sleep, "what time is it?"

Met with nothing but silence, I glanced over. But the space beside me was empty. The sheets cold to the touch.

Rafe was gone.

Disappointment sank into me, clinging to the edges of my memories of the night before. Of the way Rafe had loved me. Worshipped my body and played it to perfection.

Then I saw it. The note scrawled on hotel issued paper.

Eva,
Sorry I didn't get to say goodbye, but our manager called and needed us on the
road. I tried to wake you, but you were out cold and looked so peaceful.
But I'll call you, I promise.
Last night was... thank you.
I'll never forget it.
You're destined for great things, Starshine, don't ever forget that.
R xo

I CLUTCHED THE NOTE TO MY CHEST, A FEELING OF ELATION washing over me. Rafe hadn't abandoned me—he'd had to leave because the band needed him.

It was a dangerous thing to fall for a rock star, but despite the little voice of reason in my head, I knew I would count the days until he called.

Because Rafe Hunter was different.

We'd connected on a level I never had with anyone else. There was no pressure or expectation or fear around him, only gentle acceptance. And after last night, I didn't doubt he felt the fledgling spark between us.

"Eva?" Molly's voice drifted through the door. "Are you—"

"In here," I called out, hardly surprised when she burst into the room.

"Thank you, Jesus. I thought you'd been abducted by a very hot guitarist." She shot me a playful look, but it quickly melted away. "They left, didn't they?"

"Hudson didn't—"

"Leave me a note?" Her eyes went to the paper in my hand. "No." Sadness crept into her expression.

"I'm sorry."

"I knew exactly what I was gettin' myself into with Hudson. But what about you and Rafe?" She sat down on the loveseat. "Did you two..."

"We did." Heat flooded me.

"And?"

"It was perfect. Intense, sensual... it was everythin', Mol."

"I'm happy for you, truly." I didn't like the caution in her voice.

"But...?" I prompted.

"But I don't want to see you get hurt. You're my best friend and I love you."

"He said he'd call. He left a note." But as I said the words, my chest tightened.

"Then I'm sure he will."

Molly didn't believe it. I could see it in her eyes. She'd already written Rafe off as being the same as Hudson, and I guess I couldn't blame her.

"He will," I said defiantly. Confidently. Because I had faith in the gray-eyed bassist who had stolen a piece of my heart this weekend. "I don't know how we'll make it work or when I'll see him again, but last night meant somethin', Molly. I feel it in my bones."

———

"Where is she?" Dad's voice filtered into the house. "Where's my superstar?"

"Hey, Dad," I said as he entered the living room.

"Don't 'hey, Dad' me, young lady. Get over here and give me a hug."

With gentle laughter, I went to him, letting him pull me into his arms. "I'm so darn proud of you, kiddo. So proud."

"I hoped I could go all the way," I said, the words muffled as Dad held me close. His posture stiffened as he eased me away.

"What on Earth do you mean?"

Mom huffed in the background, still not over our earlier discussion. Dad's eyes flitted over my shoulder but then he was focused on me again, confusion pinching his brows.

"I thought if I won, I could give you the money and—"

"Stop right there," he sighed, his eyes crinkled with tension. "You did this... *for us?*"

"Of course I did. We need the money, Dad. I know we do. And I was so close." So damn close.

"Oh, Eva, we never wanted that. We wanted you to find your passion again, sweetheart. Music has always been such a big part of who you are. We hoped the contest would help you realize that."

"I did, Dad. But I wanted to win so much." Tears burned the backs of my eyes as I swallowed down the emotion. "I wanted to be able to fix everythin'."

"Eva, baby," that was Mom. Her arms slid around me and she pressed her cheek against my shoulder. "You think we care about the money, about the house? Sweetheart, all we care about is you. About havin' you here with us still."

"Your mom is right," Dad added, roping his arm around us both, pulling us against his chest until I sandwiched in between them. "As long as we have each other, we have everythin' we need."

I wanted to believe him, I did. But I saw their stress lines, heard their hushed conversations after I went to bed. Something had to give, and I'd really thought the contest could be the answer.

But it wasn't.

And it was just another thing I had to live with.

———

"Hey, it's me." Molly's head peered around the door. "Your mom said I could come up."

"Hey." I sat up, hugging the pillow to my chest.

"Is everythin'... shit, babe, why didn't you call me?" She came over to the bed and sat down.

"I just needed some space. Things got a little intense with Mom and Dad. I got upset, they got upset." After we'd hugged it out, Dad had insisted we sit down and talk. But talking had only led to more tears. Eventually, I'd retreated to my bedroom.

"Did they agree to take the money?"

"What do you think?" My teeth ground together. Dad had vehemently refused to take the money. He wanted me to keep it for college, for my future. But I didn't want it. I wanted them to have it. It was the least I could do.

He wouldn't hear of it though. Insisted we'd manage, that he'd find more work. Something more secure.

"Oh, Eva, I don't know what to say."

"There isn't anythin' to say. He's a proud man, and I get it, I do. But I wanted to... I *needed* to do this for them." Swiping at the tears, I shook my head gently, forcing a smile. "We'll figure it out, I'm sure."

Now I was feeling healthier, I could look at getting a part-time job or something.

"Babe, you can't carry all this guilt around with you. You lived, and we're all so damn happy you did. Because losin' you would have..." My best friend couldn't even say the words. Instead, she pulled me into her arms and hugged me like it was the last time. "You can't leave me, okay? Promise."

The blare of my cell phone ended our moment and Molly gave me space to grab it.

RAFE: I MISS YOU ALREADY, STARSHINE XO

"IT'S HIM ISN'T IT?" THERE WAS A HINT OF JEALOUSY IN MOLLY'S words as she watched me staring at the screen, hardly able to believe he'd texted.

It shouldn't have mattered so much, but it did.

After such an emotionally exhausting day, seeing Rafe's name, reading his words, filled me with warmth.

With hope.

"Yeah, it's him," I whispered.

"Maybe I was wrong," Molly said. "Maybe he is different."

My eyes lifted to hers and I smiled weakly. Because while I wanted to heed her warning, I knew what I felt. What Rafe and I had shared was special.

It was worth the fight.

And I was prepared to find a way to make it work.

All I could do was hope he felt the same.

EPILOGUE

Rafe didn't call.

A week passed. Seven long days of waiting, of hoping. Molly told me to put myself out of my misery and text him since I had his number. But I didn't want to be *that* girl. I didn't want to be the girl who chased the guy.

He'd said he would text when he could.

He promised.

So I waited.

And waited.

I think part of me needed him to be the one to reach out, to keep his word. I needed a sign that he felt the same. That he thought we were worth the fight, despite the odds being stacked against us.

School kept me busy enough. Classes weren't the same as before. Kids didn't know how to act around me or what to say, and if they did talk to me it was only to get their five minutes of fame with a Talent Showdown winner. But I was over it. Despite not winning, the contest had given me that much. I was now able to walk into a room with my head held high. Let their whispers and stares roll off me. Being a cancer survivor would always be a huge part of who I was. But it didn't define me. Just like not winning the contest didn't define me.

I was still discovering myself. Who I was meant to be. And for the first time since leaving the hospital, I felt like maybe, just maybe, I could do this thing called life.

Two weeks later...

Rafe still hadn't called. I told myself he would though. We had shared something special that night at the hotel. Something impossible to forget. It was imprinted on my soul like the ink on his skin. I refused to believe he could just cast that aside. Cast any chance of *us* aside.

He was busy with the band, recording new material for their upcoming arena tour. It had been announced just last week, selling out tickets at record breaking speed. I wouldn't admit it to Molly, but I'd been keeping tabs on their progress; official fansite updates only after I'd deleted the *Rock Review* app from my phone. The constant headlines and news articles were enough to drive me crazy. Everyone knew the media was toxic, the way they made up stories and spread rumors to sell copies. But I knew Rafe, the *real* Rafe Hunter. The guy underneath the tattoos and piercings. The guy fiercely protective of his brother and loyal to his bandmates. The guy who had kissed me so intensely, held me as if he never wanted to let go. That guy wouldn't just ghost me.

Not without good reason.

So I would have faith.

I would have patience.

I would wait.

One month later...

I deleted Rafe's number today.

I finally broke and drunk dialed him a week ago, after I let Molly talk me into going to Homecoming. She'd managed to sneak out some of her daddy's hooch and we'd sat under the stars, allowing ourselves to remember our weekend with one half of Black Hearts Still Beat.

Rafe didn't answer and I didn't know what to say, so I went with a very honest, very desperate, 'please call me'.

He didn't.

I guess Molly was right all along. You couldn't trust people like Hudson. Like Rafe. Their lives were too hectic, too wild. And I was just another warm and willing body who fell for the bassist's charm.

Knowing he'd fooled me only made my heart ache more. Because it meant everything I thought we'd shared that weekend had been a lie. It sucked that the person I chose to put myself out there with used me.

But I couldn't change the past and I was done reliving every second of every minute spent with him that night.

Rafe Hunter was nothing but a liar I wanted to forget.

Three months later...

Levi Hunter was splashed all over the front-page news again. It was hard to escape Black Hearts, to escape Rafe, when they were everywhere I looked. I tried not to read the articles but sometimes it was impossible to avoid the headlines.

Reckless and unpredictable. Hunter trashes hotel during stay.

The prince of rock falls in nasty clash with paparazzi.

Hunter forced into rehab?

The Black Hearts lead singer was on downward spiral no one could seem to stop. Not even his brother Rafe.

I tried to tell myself they deserved one another. That I didn't care.

But the truth was, I did care.

I cared too damn much.

And I hated it.

Four months later...

"I am so ready for the holidays." Molly yanked her jacket around her, burying herself into the thick material. "No school, no homework, just endless reruns of holiday movies, candy, and my mom's infamous eggnog."

"Sounds... awfully like a broken heart."

"Don't be ridiculous. I knew Troy Mackenna was a disaster waitin' to happen." Troy was on the football team. He and Molly had casually dated for the last six weeks. Until she found out he was also casually dating a girl from the next town over.

"I'm beginnin' to think all guys are—"

"Sorry." I dug around in my bag to find my vibrating cell, my brows pinching at the out-of-state number.

"Who is it?" Molly asked.

"I have no idea."

"Maybe it's a talent manager?"

I'd had a couple of calls since the Talent Showdown, but my answer was always the same.

"I'll be right back." I stepped away from Molly and answered the call.

"Hello?"

"Is this Miss Evangeline Walker?" An unfamiliar male voice asked.

"It is, can I help you?"

"This is Alistair Portman from Razorsharp Records."

"I know who you are, Mr. Portman," I bit out. "What can I do for you?"

"Actually, it's more like what I can do for you." There was a smug arrogance in his voice that stiffened my spine. "How would you like to come on tour with one of America's biggest bands?"

The ground dropped away from under me as I choked out, "I'm sorry, I don't understand what you're—"

"I'm sure you've seen the headlines, Eva. Can I call you Eva?" He didn't wait for me to answer. "Levi has had some... issues of late. The damage to the band's reputation has been extensive. The Blood Runs Thicker tour hopes to fix all that."

"So why do you need me?"

"You made a good impression at the Talent Showdown. Our people inform me you had quite the positive impact on Levi."

His people... surely, he didn't mean Rafe?

"I..." I squeezed my eyes shut, desperately fighting the memories of that weekend. "I'm not sure what impact you think I can make, but I barely know him, and with all due respect Mr. Portman, I can't just go on tour. I have school. It's my senior year." Not to mention, I had no songs, no experience, and no record label.

"Eva, I'm offering you a once in a lifetime opportunity here, and Damon was quite insistent you were the girl for the job."

My heart withered in my chest.

Of course Rafe hadn't been the one to suggest me.

"What exactly do you expect me to do?" I asked. Levi was unstable, that much was obvious from the short time we spent together.

"Let's just say you'll be the light to Levi's dark. His reputation has taken hit after hit the last few months and he needs opportunities to be seen in a more positive light. Bringing in the small-town girl talent contest winner who dared challenge him to a sing-along is something my team can work with."

"So it'd be a publicity stunt?" I didn't know how to feel about that.

"It could launch your music career," Mr. Portman went on. "If I know anything, it's music talent. And you, Evangeline Walker, have it in spades. The people love you. They're already calling you the next sweetheart of country."

"I haven't performed publicly since the Talent Showdown and you want me to go on tour?"

"I know it's a lot to digest," his tone softened, "but this could be make-or-break for the band."

"Do the rest of them know?" The words spilled from my lips. "Rafe and Hudson, do they know you're inviting me on tour with them?"

"They are aware, yes."

"And they agreed to it?" Because I couldn't ever imagine a scenario where Hudson and Rafe would want me on tour with them.

"They understand what's at stake, Eva, yes."

It wasn't the answer I wanted. But I guess the band was the most important thing, and I already knew there wasn't much Rafe wouldn't do for his brother.

But will he really accept you going on tour with them?

"I don't know what to tell you, Mr. Portman, but I'm not sure I'm the right person for the job."

"Ahh, but see, I think you are. You're the perfect candidate. People loved the Talent Showdown, the blend of country and rock. It made waves, Eva. Waves that show no sign of slowing down. If we can get you playing something more upbeat, more in line with the band, I think it could really work well, for everything and everyone."

"You're serious, aren't you?"

"I'm sorry," he cleared his throat, "do I not sound serious?"

"Even if I wanted to do it, Mr. Portman,"—and I wasn't sure I did —"I can't just leave school... my parents..."

"How are your parents? Gavin and Jesse Walker, right?"

"Yes," I said coolly, unsure where he was going with this.

"It must be hard on them."

"If you have a point, Mr. Portman, I suggest you make it."

"Look, I know about your recent... *struggles*."

"Y- you... know?" I choked out the words. "About me?"

"It came up in the background check, yes."

"Background check? You ran a *background check* on me?"

"Standard procedure," he said. "But don't worry, Eva, only very few people have access to those records. If you don't want it out in the open, we can be very discreet."

"Wow, I don't even know what to say to that."

Discreet... they could be discreet.

"What if I told you the label are willing to sign a very big check to make this happen? Big enough to erase all your parent's financial concerns."

It was a low blow, using my parents as bait, but I fell for it hook, line, and sinker. Mom and Dad were barely keeping their heads above water. Bills were piling up, and Dad was having to take more and more jobs out of town. It was taking its toll, on all of us.

"How big are we talkin'?"

"They'll never need to worry again."

The air left my lungs in a sharp breath.

"Listen, Eva, I know I've dropped a huge thing on you, so how about you take some time to sleep on it?"

"I don't need to think about it," I said, brows pinched with resignation. "I'll do it."

If it meant being able to help Mom and Dad, it was the only option.

"That is fantastic news." Mr. Portman's voice held an air of victory. As if he'd won a great battle.

And maybe he had.

But I couldn't let a weekend of mistakes ruin what could be a life-changing opportunity for my family. Besides, it wasn't like I was going to be on their tour bus. Didn't support acts usually travel by much lower budget means?

"When does the tour commence?" I asked.

"February first. The first leg will run until spring break, with the second leg commencing April through June. But we'd need you in for rehearsals as soon as possible."

"That's less than two months away."

"It's tight, but not impossible. We envisage a twelve song set, but it's negotiable to some degree."

"I want to celebrate Christmas at home, with my family," I blurted out, focusing on the simplest part of all this.

"Done. But we'll need to pencil in a meeting between you and production as soon as possible."

I couldn't believe I was negotiating terms with the manager for one of America's hottest bands. I hadn't even spoken to my parents about it yet. But even if they disagreed—and I expected they would—it didn't matter. I was eighteen now. An adult. And this was something I had to do.

Something I *needed* to do.

"You'll need to meet with our legal team to go over the contracts and formalities. I can have someone out to Lyme this afternoon for a meeting tomorrow. I trust you can handle informing your school?"

Tomorrow?

This was happening tomorrow?

Nausea washed over me.

"Eva?"

"Yes, I'm here."

"For as much as we want you for this, you should go into this with your eyes wide open. Being on the road, performing night after night, it's a life most aren't cut out for."

"Why the sudden moral conscience, Mr. Portman?" I asked, and he gave a strained laugh.

"Because believe it or not, I do want the best for my clients—all of them."

Had he just referred to me as one of his clients?

Blood pounded between my ears, drowning out Mr. Portman's voice.

"Still with me?" His voice cut through the *thud thud thud* in my skull.

"Still here."

Barely.

"It's overwhelming, I know. But trust me when I say, this won't be anything compared to how you'll feel being thrown into the deep end with the band."

"I'm not some weak, impressionable girl, Mr. Portman."

But I had been. In Camdena with Rafe. It was okay though; the next time I saw him I had plans to treat him with the same respect he'd shown me.

"I meant no offense." Mr. Portman mumbled. "Oh, is that the time already? My two o'clock is almost here. I'll have the details sent out today." He was sounding more distracted by the second. "The sooner we get the meeting set up with legal, the better," he said goodbye and hung up.

I returned to Molly in a daze, barely able to process what had just happened. "Who was it?" she asked, frowning at my expression.

"Alistair Portman," his name was a whisper on my lips.

"Alistair Portman, who the heck is Ali..." her eyes widened. "Wait a minute, Alistair Portman. *The* Alistair Portman?"

I nodded slowly.

"Holy cow. What did he want?"

"He wants me to go on tour."

If Molly looked surprised before, she looked stunned now. "He wants you to *what*? But how... I don't... okay," she took a deep breath. "Tell me everything."

"With Black Hearts, Molly. He wants me to go on tour with Black Hearts."

RISE

You may shoot me with your words,
You may cut me with your eyes,
You may kill me with your hatefulness,
But still, like air, I'll rise.
- Maya Angelou

CHAPTER ONE

EVA

"Eva, sweetheart, we're here."

I blinked over at Mom, shaking myself out of it. Now was not the time to get cold feet.

"Are you okay? Do you feel sick, baby?" She frowned. "Gavin, maybe this isn't such a—"

"I'm fine, Mom. Just tired." The two-hour ride to Nashville had felt like ten, my mind working overtime. Alistair had wanted me to fly out to Atlanta to join the band, but my parents had set him straight at that suggestion. I was their daughter. Precious cargo. I might have been about to embark on a sold-out arena tour with the country's hottest rock band of the moment, but they still insisted on driving me to Razorsharp Records Nashville branch to meet Alistair so he could chaperone me.

"Jesse, you promised..." Dad's words were quiet.

"I know," she replied, glancing back at me and offering a sad smile. "But the money is not—"

"I signed the contract, Mom. I'm doin' this."

For the next six months, my life belonged to Alistair Portman and Razorsharp Records. They were paying me handsomely for my time and efforts. It was money we needed. Money my parents desperately needed.

Sure, I had reservations. Plenty of them. I was, after all, just a quiet girl from Lyme, Tennessee. I didn't flourish under the spotlight; I shrank into the shadows. Not to mention the fact that going on tour with Black Hearts Still Beat meant seeing *him* again.

Nope, not going there. That wasn't important—*he* wasn't important.

My family was.

Dad climbed out of the car and opened my door. "You've got this, sweetheart," he said as I got out. The frigid air hit me and I rubbed my hands together trying to ease the chill.

"I'm proud of you, Eva. We both are," Dad went on. "But remember, if it gets to be too much, if you need a break, all you have to do is call me and I'll come get you. Wherever you are." A wide smile cracked his face, but I saw the promise in his eyes.

Dad wanted me to do this, way more than I wanted to do it. Not because we needed the money, but because he wanted me to follow my dreams.

He wanted me to live.

"Did you pack your medication?" Mom came around the car to us.

"Yes, Mom."

"Scripts?"

"Yes."

"And you have the vitamins?"

I inhaled a deep breath and cast a quick look at my dad.

"Jesse... she's good." Dad chuckled. "Besides, Mr. Portman gave us his word that he'd—"

"Take extra special care of our sweetheart of country."

The nickname made me flinch, but I forced a smile at my new manager.

"Jesse, Gavin, it's good to see you again." Alistair extended his hand to Dad.

"We're trusting you to take good care of our girl."

"I've already briefed Eva's assistant of her medical... requirements."

My eyes widened but Alistair only smiled. "You have nothing to worry about, Eva. Letty has signed an NDA."

"Of course she has," I grumbled.

"However, I still think we should inform the band of your—"

"No!" I snapped, forgetting who I was talking to. "I don't want them to know. I don't want anyone to know." It was going to be hard enough being the unassuming girl on tour with Black Hearts without the media learning I was a cancer survivor too.

"Very well." Alistair gave me a curt nod. "I'll give you some time to say goodbye. Jesse, Gavin, I'll see you both soon." He pulled out his cell phone and strode off toward a sleek black SUV.

"Come here, sweetheart." Dad enveloped me in his arms. "You can do this, Eva. You were born to do this."

I clung to my father the way I had so many times before. He had always been my protector. My rock. He worked hard for me and Mom, and when I'd gotten sick, he'd given everything he could to make sure I'd had the best care available.

"I know why you're doin' this," he whispered. "But I want you to know, all I want is for you to follow your dreams, sweetheart. Don't ever forget that."

"Thanks, Dad." I eased away, swallowing down the tears burning my throat.

"Oh, Eva, baby." Mom launched herself at me, pulling me into a bone-crunching hug. "Promise me you'll take good care of yourself, promise."

"I promise, Mom. You heard Alistair; I have a babysitter."

Dad chuckled again.

"I'm not sure I can let you go." Mom tightened her grip on me. "On tour... with a rock band... it's..."

"All going to be fine." Untangling myself from her arms, I brushed the curls out of my face. "I need to do this, Mom." I needed to do it for them.

She shot Dad a worried look, but he only smiled, moving closer to take her hand. "She's eighteen, Jesse; a young woman. She's got this." The conviction in his words made the lump in my throat grow.

"I'll call as much as I can."

"Every day," Mom said. "You'll call every day."

"Mom..."

"Okay, every other day." She conceded, an uncertain smile tugging the corner of her mouth.

"I should go," I said, not wanting to drag it out any longer than necessary. "I'll call when we get to Atlanta."

"Okay, sweetheart. Be safe and have fun." Dad winked.

"Oh, Gavin, don't encourage her, please." We were all smiling now. It was nice. Something we hadn't done together in a really long time. It felt good. Hopeful. It felt like we were about to turn a corner and put all the pain, hurt, and financial worries behind us.

I was finally getting a chance to repay my parents for all the sacrifices they'd made for me. Even if it meant spending the next five months touring the country with the boy who'd made me believe in fairytales... and then reminded me of the age-old saying:

Never fall for a rock star.

———

THE FIRST THING I NOTICED WHEN WE STEPPED OUT OF ALISTAIR'S SUV almost four hours later, was the air no longer smelled like home. The second thing I noticed about the city was the noise. Tires screeching, horns honking, sirens wailing, and cars blaring music. Even the people here seemed to talk louder, barking into their cell phones as they went about their day. Atlanta was worlds away from my small hometown in Tennessee, and I suddenly felt the gravity of what I was about to do.

"Okay over there?" Alistair asked as he pulled out a packet of gum and shoved a stick into his mouth. Something he did a lot, I'd noticed, on the awkward ride here.

"How long since you quit?" His brow rose and I smiled. "You chew a lot of gum. I figure you're an ex-smoker?"

"Perceptive and talented; you're quite the package, aren't you?"

There was no time to answer as two burly men strode toward us. "Mr. Portman, good to see you."

"Travis, Grayson, meet Ms. Walker." They both nodded.

"Hey," I said quietly.

"Travis and Grayson are assigned to you, Eva. They'll be—"

"I'm sorry, assigned to me?" My brows furrowed.

"Yes, they're your bodyguards. We covered this in the meeting." His eyes narrowed.

"I, uh..." Between Alistair and the people from Razorsharp Records legal team and the many, *many* big words they'd used, I hadn't taken in much besides the fact that they wanted me to tour with the band. I was, according to them, the next sweetheart of country, and the perfect candidate to fix Black Hearts' tarnished reputation after Levi Hunter, lead vocalist and rock's latest bad boy, spiraled out of control and ended up in rehab some months earlier.

If you asked me, they were all freakin' crazy. I wasn't performance ready. I'd barely had any time to pull together a set list, let alone rehearse. But here I was. Standing outside Razorsharp Records HQ with nothing but the duffel bag on my shoulder and the promise of a check big enough to erase all my parents' financial worries.

"Ready?" Alistair's question pulled me from my thoughts.

"As I'll ever be," I half-heartedly mumbled, following him inside. Everyone looked our way. Some people greeted Alistair, some people simply watched. One girl, an intern I guessed since she didn't look much older than me, even greeted me. Because I wasn't a no one now.

I was *someone*.

Yet, I still didn't know how to feel about that.

Singing and playing my cherry red Gibson had once been everything to me. But that was before cancer. Before I realized how cruel and senseless things could be. I was one of the lucky ones though. A medical miracle who had lived to tell the tale. To make her mark on the world.

If only it was that simple.

There were days I didn't feel lucky though. Days when the guilt of surviving was almost too much to bear.

Things were better now—eased by the comfort of knowing I could fix things for Mom and Dad—but I still had my moments. I still woke up in the middle of the night, tangled in damp bed sheets calling out Cody's name. He'd deserved to live, but God had spared me and taken him. I knew that wasn't how it really worked; I knew it was the cancer that had taken him. But even after all this time, it still didn't seem fair that I got to live and he didn't.

"Alistair," a tall blonde strutted over to us, peering down at her clipboard.

"Riley, everything good to go?" he asked, ushering me into the elevator.

"Everything's set. Duke is doing a final check as we speak." She hesitated, and Alistair's jaw set in response.

"They're not here?"

"Rafe called. He said there was a... complication."

Alistair grumbled something inaudible beneath his breath. The air suddenly felt thick; too dense to breathe. I rubbed at my chest, trying to slow my racing pulse. If I was going to survive the next few months, I needed to be able to handle hearing Rafe's name. Heck, I needed to be able to handle much more than that.

I hadn't seen him yet. Not since the Jamesboro County Talent Showdown final in Camdena. He and the band were supposed to be at my rehearsals but they'd never showed, and Alistair never gave me much in the way of an explanation. Not that I needed one. Black Hearts were... well, they were, despite their young age, already rock star royalty, and I was a talent contest runner up offered the opportunity of a lifetime. They didn't owe me anything, just as I wanted nothing from them in return. It was a business transaction. Plain and simple. Part of me couldn't help but wonder though, if the lack of people present at my rehearsals was strategic on Alistair's part. The band was a lot to handle and I was only here because I didn't have any other choice.

It wasn't exactly a match made in heaven.

"Eva, this is Riley Panem, my PA."

"It's nice to meet you," I said.

"Likewise." Her perfectly lined eyes gave me the once over. Before I could try to read her assessment of me, the doors pinged open and we were on the move again. "Dowager called. He wanted reassurance Levi isn't going to cause problems."

"Levi knows the score." Alistair pulled at his tie. "He can't afford to screw this up."

Riley snorted. "Levi Hunter thrives on chaos. If you think for a second—"

"Riley," Alistair warned, his gaze flicking briefly to where I stood wedged between my new bodyguards.

"Don't mind me." I shrugged, pretending I could care less about their conversation, when deep down I wanted to know who Dowager was and why he was worried about Levi.

The sour-faced woman pursed her lips, making no effort to hide her disapproval toward me. I glared back, feeling a wrinkle of irritation travel up my spine. I'd been here less than two minutes, and yet I couldn't help but suspect she felt threatened by me. Which was crazy.

I'd done nothing wrong.

"Travis, escort Ms. Walker to the meeting room," Alistair checked his wristwatch, "Letty will be along shortly."

Ahh yes, Letty. My elusive assistant who had also been missing at my rehearsals. I'd never had an assistant before, but then I'd never gone on tour with a rock band before either. It was definitely a day of firsts.

Travis motioned for me to follow him down the hall, but I hesitated. "Eva," Alistair asked. "Is there a problem?"

"No problem," I muttered, hitching my bag up my shoulder.

Lies. All lies.

There were plenty of problems with this whole scenario. But something told me Alistair didn't want to hear them, so I bit my tongue and followed Travis. Framed gold and platinum records lined the walls, interspersed with photographs of some of the label's most successful artists. My skin tingled as I let my eyes run over each of them. When I was younger, I'd never wanted fame and fortune, not in the way most of these artists had it. But I'd always wanted to perform. Dreamed about a future of making music and writing lyrics; of pouring my heart and soul into song after song.

Music was everything to me, so to have the chance to go on tour— to perform to sell-out crowds in a different city every night—should have been a dream come true.

A commotion up ahead stopped me in my tracks. There was no mistaking the deep gravelly voice of Levi Hunter. "Country, is that you I spy hiding behind Travis?"

Sucking in a sharp breath, I stepped around my hulk of a bodyguard and lifted a hand in greeting. "Levi."

"*Ms. Walker.*" He smirked, his eyes dancing with mischief.

"Nice to see you again, Eva." Hudson Ryker, drummer and perpetual player, gave me a curt nod.

"Wish I could say the same." I smiled. It was a joke, but there was no denying the trace of bitterness in my voice. Damn, it had only been a second and these boys were already messing with my head.

"Get over here, Walker." Damon Donnelley opened his arms, but I remained still. The corner of his mouth lifted. "It's like that, huh?"

"How else would it be?" I shot back, fighting a smile, all while my insides quivered and shook.

"It's good to see you again," he added, his eyes flitting to Levi's who looked at Hudson. Tension crackled around us as they watched me.

Hating the awkward silence, and in an attempt to show them I wasn't going to let my very brief, very misguided history with the fourth member of their band affect me, I finally said, "Where's Rafe?"

"He's, ah—"

"Eva." My name spilled from his lips in a single breath, and the ground seemed to fall away from beneath me as Rafe Hunter stepped into view.

Same gray eyes and dark hair. Same worn leather jacket and holey jeans. Same tattoos disappearing beneath his t-shirt. My heart hammered against my ribcage, a frenetic symphony thrumming through me. But as I forced a weak smile, his expression grew dark, his eyes clouded with contempt.

"We should get this thing over with if we want to get on the road."

"Chill, man," Levi nudged his brother in the ribs oblivious to the icy stare Rafe had pinned me with. "We have time. Besides, they'll wait for us."

"Lev's right," Damon added. "We didn't make it to Eva's rehearsals. I'm sure she'd feel better if we—"

"Whatever. I need a soda. I'll be in the meeting room." Rafe barged past his band mates and disappeared through the doors, not sparing me a second glance.

"I'd better..." Hud thumbed to the meeting room before taking off after his friend.

"Did I miss something?" I asked, dread snaking through me.

"Don't mind Rafe," Levi said. "He's on his period."

"Levi," Damon scolded.

"What? He's been walking around like a bear with a sore head for weeks now. If he had a problem with her coming on tour with us, he should have—"

"*Levi!*"

"What? Eva's a big girl, she can handle it. Right, Country?" His eyes narrowed at me.

"I..." Words failed me. I didn't know what I'd expected when I finally saw the band again, but it wasn't this.

This felt like an ambush.

Or a hostile takeover.

I couldn't quite figure out which.

"You *can* handle it. Right, Walker? Because there's a lot riding on this tour, for all of us."

"Levi." Rafe appeared at the door, his lips pressed into a thin line.

"Yeah, yeah, I'm coming." He started to move toward the door. "I hope you're ready for this, Country, because you're not in Kansas anymore." His words were low, meant only for my ears as he passed me.

"You okay?" Damon's apologetic gaze burned into me as he remained in the hall with me.

"I'll be fine." I barely met his heavy gaze.

"Don't let him get to you." He squeezed my shoulder as he ducked inside the meeting room, leaving me standing there all alone.

I knew Damon meant Levi. But it wasn't the unpredictable Hunter brother I was worried about. It was the quiet, brooding one.

Rafe had once looked at me like I was everything he needed. But today he'd looked at me with hatred in his eyes.

Which made no sense since I'd done nothing wrong.

Unless Alistair had lied when he'd told me the band was okay with me coming on tour.

Unless Rafe really didn't want me here.

CHAPTER TWO

RAFE

"So much for playing it cool," Hudson whispered as we sat around the table waiting for Alistair and Riley to arrive.

I ignored my best friend, letting my eyes flick over to the door again. Eva still hadn't come inside. Maybe she'd decided this whole thing was the wrong decision. Maybe she was already on her way back to Lyme where she belonged.

She wasn't supposed to be here, coming on tour with us. Alistair and the label thought she was exactly what the band needed to rebuild the damage caused with our younger fans. Sex, drugs, and rock and roll might have been a big hit with our older fans but Levi's stint in rehab had done us no favors with the 10-14 demographic.

It was ironic really. We'd never set out to become a hit with the pigtail and bubblegum brigade, but Black Hearts fever had swept through junior high schools up and down the country. Parents hated us and their daughters worshipped us.

"Maybe I should go check on her," Damon suggested.

"Nah, leave her." Levi kicked up his legs, dropping his military style boots on the table. "She had to know what she was getting into when she agreed to do this thing."

I rose a brow and he said, "What?"

"Riley hates when you do that."

"Riley needs someone to fuck the sourpuss right out—"

"Don't mind me," Eva stepped into the room and sat in one of the empty chairs. I tried to ignore the fact she took the one furthest away from me. Even though it shouldn't have, it stung.

"I heard Ali is banging that." Hudson leaned back, stretching his hands behind his head.

"Ali and Riley?" Levi frowned. "No way. She needs it a little dirty in her life and Alistair is as straitlaced as they come."

"Not according to Susie."

"Oh yeah, and when did *Susie* tell you that?" Levi's brow shot up.

"When I was balls deep in her the other night." Hudson caught my eye and he blanched, running a hand over his face. "Shit, Eva, I didn't—"

"Don't worry about it. I can handle it."

"What's up, douchebags?" Letty, our old PA, breezed into the room and took the seat beside Eva. "Miss me?" she asked, earning a rumble of inaudible replies. "Shut up, you know you did. Hey, I'm Letty," her attention went to the quiet girl on her left. "You must be Eva."

"Hi."

"Don't look so worried. I don't bite. At least, I didn't until I toured last year with these four."

"I... have no idea what to say to that."

"S'all good." Letty grinned, sifting through a stack of papers in front of her. "I might be officially off your asses but don't think for a second I'll let you off the hook."

"Jesus," Levi groaned. "Is it me or did the power go straight to her head?"

"Hey, it could be worse... you could have had Riley riding your ass. But who knows, maybe you'll get lucky with your new PA." She smirked.

Hudson smothered a grin while Damon shook his head. He was the most sensible person in the room, excluding Eva, but she looked like a fish out of water, her eyes darting between my brother and Letty as if she expected one of them to throw down at any second.

"At least Riley isn't a frigid bitch."

Hudson hissed at the same time as me and Damon barked, "*Levi!*"

"You're only bitter because I wouldn't drop my panties for you. Newsflash, rock star," her words were saccharine-sweet but her smile was full of venom, "I prefer my men with a little less arrogance and more stamina between the sheets, if you know what I'm saying."

"Burn." Hudson couldn't contain his laughter this time, his cackle filling the meeting room.

"Fuck off, Let, you don't know shit."

"Oh, baby, we've all heard you... give it to me, Levi. Oh God, yeah, just like... is that... *it?*"

I pressed my lips together, stifling the laughter bubbling in my chest.

"Fuck you. It was one time and I was wasted."

"Yeah, yeah, that's what they all say." Letty waved him off, offering Eva a warm smile.

Before Levi could retaliate, the door swung open. "Ali, boy, all set?" Hudson grinned at our manager as he entered the meeting room with Riley.

"It's not me you need to worry about, Hudson." He gave each of us a serious look, lingering on Levi. "You ready for this?"

"Ready?" My brother scoffed. "I was born ready."

"It's a grueling schedule." Riley handed him a sheet of paper and began reeling off the first leg of concerts: Charlotte, Orlando, Houston, Dallas...

"We know the schedule, Ali."

"You mean *I* know the schedule," he countered. "I'd bet my bottom dollar you haven't even looked at the damn thing."

"Ali," I said quietly, really not wanting to pull my brother off our manager today.

"Exactly. Why do I need to know the schedule when I have people like you to do it for me?"

The air grew thick with tension. Levi liked to push Ali's buttons and our manager liked to push back, but the truth of the matter was we needed Ali as much as the band needed Levi. And he was one of the few people left willing to work with us.

"Well, this is entertaining and all," Letty slammed her hands on the table and grinned, "but if all you're going to do is argue like little old ladies, I'm stealing Eva away."

"Actually, I need her to stick around," Ali said. "This won't take long and then you can go."

Eva shifted uncomfortably. I didn't want to imagine what she thought about being dropped in at the deep end of all this, but I couldn't help it. Everything about her pulled me in. From her soft pink lips to her unruly blonde curls. I knew every blemish on her skin, every ticklish spot, every place that made her moan. But what we had shared in Camdena, the weekend of the Talent Showdown final, was finite. A moment in time we'd never get to experience again. I couldn't be who she needed and she sure as shit couldn't be who I needed. So here we were; two strangers who knew one another in ways no two strangers should.

Lyrics started forming in my head. A riff my fingers itched to play. I didn't sing vocals a lot for the band, but I did my fair share of songwriting. I'd always had an affinity for words; for the way they blended to tell a story... a memory... an emotion.

"Yo, Rafe, care to join us?" My brother smirked across the table at me.

"Uh, yeah, what were you saying?"

"Alistair was laying down the *rules*."

"Rules?" I balked. "Since when did we have rules?"

"Since we have Eva joining us." Alistair glared at me. "You are to treat Eva with nothing but professionalism and respect at all times. She isn't a groupie or a roadie... that means no cavorting—"

"Not an issue," she cut Alistair off. "I'm... not like *that*." Her eyes flicked to mine, hatred burning in their depths.

My stomach sank.

"You wouldn't be the first to fall for their charms, Eva." Ali regarded her.

In that moment, she seemed so young. Or maybe it was the other way around. Maybe fame had aged us. Fuck only knew I felt years older than my twenty.

"You don't need to worry about me," she said sharply.

"Ease off, Ali, yeah?" Damon said. "We know the deal. Eva is off-limits."

"I still don't see why she isn't riding on our bus." Levi huffed like a petulant child who had lost his favorite new shiny toy.

The thought made my insides twist.

"You want her to what?"

"While you were distracted..." Damon's brow quirked up as he said the words. "Levi suggested Eva could ride with us on our bus."

"No." No fucking way.

Eva sucked in a harsh breath. We all heard it. But I forced myself to remain focused on Damon. "She can't ride with us." The words echoed around my skull and I knew how they had to sound to her... but, fuck, it was bad enough having her here. But having her here and on our bus... hell no.

"*She* is sittin' right here, you know?" Eva scowled.

"Rafe's right," Alistair joined the conversation again. "Eva, Letty, and a few other vital staff will be on the smaller Van Hool. Everyone else is on the sleeper buses."

"Sorry, boys, looks like you're going to have to find someone else to attend to your every need this time around."

"When do we get to meet this replacement assistant you spoke so highly of anyway?"

"You're looking at her," Riley said.

"You?" Levi deadpanned. "You're putting her in charge of us? What happened to Cruz?"

Cruz was a good guy and a good friend. If Eva was getting Letty, we wanted someone we could trust, someone who had our best interests at heart. Someone like Cruz.

"As I said in the email which you obviously didn't bother to read, Cruz is attending to some urgent business. He hopes to join the tour for the second leg. Until then, Riley will be filling in."

"But Riley can't stand us," Hudson said.

"I..." she flushed. "That is not true. I am a huge fan of your music and no one knows the schedule better than me."

"We're not here to debate Riley's qualifications. Management already signed off on it. She's on the tour whether you like it or not."

Levi sank back in his chair, raking a hand through his messy hair, dragging his teeth against his snake bite piercings. Riley didn't shrink under his severe glare. She was used to boys like us playing at rock stars. But despite her cool exterior, I wondered if she had what it took to be on the road. She seemed like someone who preferred the finer things in life. But maybe Hudson was right? Maybe she was banging Ali and couldn't stand the thought of being separated from him for the next few months. Maybe she'd used her relationship with him to leverage herself onto the road with us. Whatever. Riley was just another person in a long line of people trying to bring us to heel and play puppets. But like everyone before her, she'd quickly realize while you could usually reason with me, Damon, even Hudson; my brother was a different matter entirely. If she wanted to try to pull his strings and earn herself a nice promotion or a pat on the back from boss man, then who was I to try to stop her?

"So does that mean *you'll* be staying on the bus with us?"

I didn't miss the look in Hudson's eyes as he blatantly checked Riley out, probably planning all the ways he could seduce her. He'd been going through women like they were a dying breed ever since Camdena. Ever since his weekend with Eva's best friend Molly. He swore it was only sex between them, but I knew Hudson, and I knew something was off.

I had my own shit to worry about though. Like how to survive the tour with Eva being there while making sure my brother didn't fall off the deep end again. Because although he was my big brother, I'd been taking care of him for as long as I could remember.

"I, umm, well, no," Riley tucked a strand of hair behind her ear, her eyes darting between Hudson and Ali. Jesus, she was already falling for the Ryker charm and he'd barely even spoken to her.

"Riley will be on the other bus," Ali replied. To anyone else he might have looked cool and collected, but I wasn't anyone. I saw the slight set to his jaw, heard the way his voice hitched just a fraction. He was jealous and pissed. And if that wasn't a shitshow waiting to happen, I didn't know what was.

"Brave move," Levi said, "leaving us to our own devices."

"The label wants to trust you, Levi, but you need to work with us. You need to prove to us you're in control... but until then, you're stuck with me."

"What do you mean, we're stuck with you?"

"I mean, I'll be on the bus. This bus."

"This is fucking bullshit." Levi's hand balled into a fist and slammed against the table. "We don't need a babysitter."

"Don't you?"

Levi shot up off his chair, but Damon threw his arm out. "This could cause problems, Ali, not help the situation."

"It isn't forever and trust me when I say I'd rather not be on the bus with you. Let's get the first couple of shows out of the way and we'll discuss this further. Until then, I'm taking one of the bedrooms."

Levi was practically foaming at the mouth, but thankfully, for all of us, he managed to bite his tongue and sit back down. I wondered if Damon was physically restraining him out of our sight.

"I'm going to check in with Duke. Do not leave this bus. I mean it. Stay put and we'll be out of here in no time."

"Yeah, yeah, Ali," Damon said. "Go do your thing. We've got this."

"Grab us a drink yeah, Riley? Make yourself useful." Levi gave her a wicked smirk that had Alistair straightening.

"Riley, with me, please." She nodded and took off. "Letty, Eva, you too."

"Guess that's our signal," Letty said. "Come on, Eva, I'll give you the tour." The two of them followed Alistair out of the room.

"You good?" I asked my brother as soon as they were gone.

"They're screwing us over, Rafe." He drummed the table with his fingers. "Treating us like kids who need babysitting."

"Riley can be my babysitter any day of the week."

"Dude, she's fucking Ali, you cannot go there." Damon levelled Hudson with a hard look.

"Says who?" He shrugged.

"It's your funeral," I replied, turning my attention to Levi. "We play by his rules. This tour could seal our future, but we have to play by the rules."

"They didn't sign us because we play by the rules. They signed us because they know we don't play by the rules."

"Two shows. We do the first two shows and prove to Ali we've got this, that you've got this, and then he'll back off."

"And if he doesn't?" Levi snapped. "Him and me on this tour bus is a fucking disaster waiting to happen. I know he holds the cards, but I can't have him breathing down my neck every second of the day."

"I'll talk to him."

"Fix it, Rafe. You need to fix it."

I'd been trying to fix it for the last ten years.

I let out a heavy sigh, "I'll talk to him, but you need to do your part too."

He gave me a weak nod. Levi had issues with authority. With people telling him what he could and couldn't do. To outsiders, he looked like an arrogant, selfish guy with entitlement issues, but they were wrong. They were all so fucking wrong.

"Okay, fuckers." His expression morphed in a second. Gone was the suspicious glint in his eye, the lines of frustration along his forehead. It was replaced with a mischievous grin. "It's time to celebrate."

"Now that I can get on board with." Hudson clapped his hands on the table. "This is the first day of the rest of our lives. This tour is going to change everything," he said. "I feel it in my bones, boys. It's going to change every-fucking-thing."

Hudson wasn't wrong. I felt it too. The shift in the air, the hint of things to come.

Only I wasn't sure if this tour would be the making of Black Hearts.

Or its downfall.

And I wasn't sure I wanted to find out.

CHAPTER THREE

EVA

"This is… wow."

"You've seen nothing yet." Letty led me deeper into the bus. "You think this is special, just wait, the other bus is going to blow your mind."

This one looked pretty special to me. It had a cleverly designed living space complete with table and bench running down one side and curving around to make a cozy seating area. On the other side was a fully functional kitchenette. Further down the bus I could make out several bunks lining either side and what I hoped was a private bathroom beyond that.

"If I were you, I'd choose your bunk now before the rest of them get here." She arched a thin brow.

"What's better, takin' the top or bottom?"

"Trust me, after a few days on the road you won't give a shit where you crash."

"That bad, huh?"

"We're all just living the dream." Letty winked before grabbing her bag and throwing it onto one of the bottom bunks. "Hey, listen. I'm sorry I didn't get to meet you at rehearsals. I had a family emergency."

"It's okay."

"It's not. I should have been there. I know this can't be easy, but I'm on your side, Eva, I promise."

Letty looked like exactly the kind of girl I'd usually avoid. Loud and brash with pink dipped tips; her skin was decorated with brightly inked tattoos and an array of piercings that made me feel a little queasy.

"We girls have got to stick together." she added, and I wondered if the fierce petite pixie could also read minds. There was a warmth in her eyes and a softness in her voice that made me want to trust her though. But I didn't want to let my guard down too quickly.

Letty knew the band. She worked with the band. They had a history that started long before I ever showed up.

"What's up with you and Rafe?" The question came out of left field. My eyes bugged, and laughter rumbled in her chest. "So I didn't see him watching you like a hawk during the meeting?"

"I..." The words dried on my tongue as I pressed my lips together.

He'd been watching me?

I thought I'd felt him but hadn't let my thoughts run away with me. Not after he made it perfectly clear he didn't want me there.

"You don't want to kiss and tell," Letty went on. "I can respect that. But friendly piece of advice; a girl like you doesn't want to get mixed up with the likes of that."

"What do you mean?"

She paused, her expression softening. "You'll see. Come on, I'll give you the grand tour."

But before the tour could commence, male laughter filled the bus, and Levi, Hudson, and Damon appeared. "Country," Levi said, pointing his finger at me. "On the other bus, now."

"I'm not sure that's a good—"

"Lighten up, Let, everyone gets initiated, you know that."

My wide gaze went to her. She gave me a weak smile. "You can try to resist but they'll only make it harder."

"Initiation?" I tried to sound calm. "I'm not sure I like the sound of that."

"You're not supposed to like it, new girl." Hudson grinned. "Let's do this thing so we can get this show on the road." Damon came over to me and whispered, "Humor him; it'll be easier for everyone."

Rolling my eyes, I motioned for him to lead the way. I didn't want to play Levi's games, but what choice did I have? He was volatile. A beast I most definitely didn't want to poke.

"Hey." Letty grabbed my hand, pulling me back as the guys filed off the bus. "Sorry I didn't give you a heads up. I didn't think he'd do it. Not with you."

"What's that supposed to mean?"

"Nothing... I just figured Ali would have told him to go easy on you since you're—"

"I'm fine." My eyes flicked over my shoulder, hoping no one could hear us.

"Shit, sorry. I know it's a need to know thing. I just meant I assumed he'd warn the band to behave where you're concerned."

"Does the band ever behave?" I'd read the headlines, seen the news reports. Black Hearts weren't only famous for their music, it was them. The way they'd swept onto the music scene as if they had always belonged there.

"You have a point," she chuckled. "But I should have given you a heads up."

"Don't worry about it. I can handle the band."

"Atta girl." Letty looked impressed. "I gotta say, I was a little worried when Alistair told me you were joining the tour. But something tells me I didn't need to be."

We exited our bus and boarded the much bigger, much flashier other bus. The guys were all seated around the table, all except Rafe. Letty shot me a knowing look as she barged past me and joined them. I lingered back, feeling very out of my depth.

"Get over here, new girl."

"Really?" I scowled at Hudson, folding my arms over my chest.

"Come on Eva," he smiled. "You're about to go on tour with the hottest band in the world right now. Would it hurt you to smile?"

"Hud," Damon warned, kicking him underneath the table.

"It's okay, Damon," I said, inching closer. "Hudson's right. I have to embrace the crazy." Sliding onto the bench, I nudged his shoulder. "So what was this about initiatin' me?"

"Think you've got what it takes to play with the big boys, Angel?" Levi drawled the words, his lazy smirk not half as alluring as it was irritating.

For whatever reason, he wasn't going to make this easy on me. Maybe he wanted me to prove I belonged here, or maybe it was just a stupid game to pass the time. Whatever it was, something told me that if I didn't play, we'd see a very different side to the reckless and impulsive Hunter brother.

"Drink," he said, producing a bottle of liquor from behind his back. "One shot."

"Just one?" I could handle one shot.

"Do you know what this is?" Levi inspected the bottle, running his finger over the label as if it was precious.

"Vodka? Tequila? I don't know, don't really care." The sooner I did his stupid little initiation, the sooner we could all move on with our lives.

"This is Devils Spring vodka, Country. It's 80% proof and I'm betting one shot will have you falling at my feet."

"Lev, come on, you didn't say anything about making her drink—"

"She wants to play, so we'll play." He slammed the bottle down. "Letty, do the honors."

Her eyes slid to mine, silently asking me if I was sure about this.

"Do it," I said without hesitation.

One shot.

It was just one shot.

Sure, I hadn't drunk alcohol in forever, but what harm could one shot do?

"You don't have to do this," Damon whispered. Not quiet enough though.

Levi glowered at his bandmate. "She's not a fucking baby. Are you, Angel?"

"I…"

Thankfully, Letty reappeared with two shot glasses. "You sure about this?"

I nodded, too overwhelmed to answer.

Levi smirked again as he withdrew a lighter from his pocket. My heart crashed beneath my rib cage, blood pounding between my ears.

"What are you—"

"You gotta take it flaming."

"No. No way. I'll drink it but you're not settin' me on fire."

"It's perfectly safe," Hudson added with a shrug.

"*Safe*? That's what they all say until they end up half on fire screamin' in agony. I'll drink it, but without the flame." My eyes narrowed at Levi. He glared right back. If I'd learned anything in my short time with Levi Hunter at Camdena a few months back, it was he didn't like to be challenged. I'd done it then to distract him and calm a tense situation, and I was doing it now to save my own hide.

"Fine," he bit out. "No flames. But don't think this means you're getting out of it. Me and you, Angel. It's on." He uncapped the bottle and poured two shots. The overpowering smell of liquor permeated the air making my stomach churn and my mouth water, and I hadn't even brought the damn thing to my lips yet.

"Ready?" His tone was teasing but there was something else in his expression.

Bringing the glass to my lips, I didn't dwell on what madness could possibly be running through his mind. Levi Hunter had demons. The kind that made you take risks and stick two fingers up to authority time and time again. The kind that gave little regard to consequence or self-preservation.

Levi lived recklessly and without abandon. And the fans loved him for it.

"Are you?" I threw back, surprised at how I responded to his arrogance.

He grinned, letting his tongue run over his snake bite piercings before mouthing, "On three. One... two..."

Without second guessing myself, I tipped the glass back and downed the cool liquor. Fiery heat exploded in my mouth, racing down my throat. "Holy crap," I murmured.

"Fuck, it gets me every time." Levi shook his head, taking his fingers through his hair as I tried to swallow down the acid rushing up my throat.

"Here, it'll help." Someone shoved a glass of water toward me, and I looked up to find Rafe staring down at me. Disappointment glittering in his eyes.

"Thanks," I mumbled, greedily lapping it down, trying to focus on anything but the way the vodka burned.

The guys all watched me as if they expected me to combust into flames, or tears, or worse, puke all over the plush bench. I dropped my gaze and gently smoothed a hand over my stomach, willing it to calm down. I felt okay—nauseous, but okay. One shot, even if the liquor was strong, wouldn't affect me.

I hoped.

"Well, this was a hoot and all, but we really should get back." Letty broke the thick silence. "Eva..."

"Uh, yeah, let's go."

I stood on shaky legs, trying to avoid eye contact with any of them. Rafe hovered over by the counter, his piercing gray eyes burning into me. But I didn't meet his gaze. I didn't want to see the bitter disappointment again. Besides, what right did he have to feel disappointed I was taking shots with his brother when he'd barely spoken two words to me since I arrived.

"Hey, Country," Levi's voice stopped me in my tracks.

"Yeah?" I glanced back, meeting his scrutinizing gaze.

He thumbed one of his piercings. "I didn't think you had it in you."

"There's a lot you don't know about me," I said before following after Letty.

"Yeah," he hesitated. "Welcome to our very fucked-up family." Levi raised his empty glass, a hundred things flashing in his murky eyes.

Unsure of what to say, I gave him a small nod before taking off after Letty. The second the air hit me, my stomach roiled. Pressing a hand against the side of the bus, I waited for the world to stop spinning.

"Shit, Eva, are you okay?"

"I don't drink much."

"Crap." She approached me. "I shouldn't have let him do that. It's Levi's thing. Has been from the start but he doesn't usually pull out the harder stuff."

"He's testing me."

Her brows furrowed. "Well, I think you passed with flying colors. Damn girl, even I can't stomach that stuff and there isn't much I haven't drunk, snorted, or swallowed."

"I... really don't know what to say to that."

"Made you forget the burn though, am I right?" She chuckled, squeezing my shoulder as I continued deep breathing. "Think you can make it back onto our bus?"

I nodded, feeling the warm liquor trickle through my veins. It was potent stuff. Much stronger than the couple of beers I'd had at a party once, before life became a never-ending cycle of hospital visits, treatments, and depleting hope.

Letty backed off, giving me some space. I took my time with small measured steps, certain I was only one wobble away from puking up my lunch. Just as I reached the bus, I had the strangest feeling of being watched.

Sure enough, when I turned back, Rafe stood at the door to their bus, his eyes fixed right on me. The liquor had taken my breath away, but it was nothing compared to how he looked at me.

Through me.

"Eva, coming?" Letty's voice yanked my attention and I nodded my head, shaking all thoughts of Rafe out of it.

"Comin'," I said, glancing back.

Only Rafe was gone.

And I was about to...

I took off at a sprint, darting up the stairs and down the galley straight into the small bathroom at the back of the bus. Falling to my knees, I clutched the bowl just in time.

"Fuck, fuck!" I could hear Letty in the background as I purged everything down the toilet except my soul. That was still intact for the most part. My dignity however was washed away in a swift press of the flush.

I sank back against the counter, accepting the wet towel off Letty.

"Is it ... you know?" she asked.

"It's the Devil's fault; you don't need to worry. I'm not exactly a seasoned drinker."

Letty breathed a sigh of relief as she leaned against the doorjamb. "I feel like this is all my fault and we haven't even made it to Charlotte yet.

"Stop," I said. "I didn't have to drink the shot, and I don't need a babysitter. But this all feels way out of my depth. The band, the tour..." *Rafe.* I swallowed his name.

"It's a lot, I get it. But please, don't think of me as your babysitter. Think of me as the best friend you never knew you had."

"I'm not sure what Molly would say about that."

"Molly?"

"Yeah, my best friend since forever. You remind me of her a little actually."

"She must be a great girl then." Letty winked. "You should invite her out to a show one time. We can all hangout."

"That would be amazin'." Just the thought of seeing Molly in the near future had me feeling a little better.

"Just say the word and we'll make it happen."

"So you're basically like my fairy godmother?" I teased.

"Among other things. Look," she dropped to a crouch, "Ali didn't want you to feel alone. The guys are... well, you know how they can be. I know how things work and I know how to look out for myself in a world where little boys want to play at rock star."

"Hmm, Letty, they kinda are rock stars."

"Yeah, but ssh," she leaned in and smiled, "don't tell them that. Come, new girl, let's get you cleaned up."

Letty helped me up before getting me a clean toothbrush. "Paste is in the cabinet. There are only ten minutes until we head out. Soon this place will be brimming with bodies and banter and you'll be grateful you got five minutes to yourself."

"Great, thanks," I mumbled as she disappeared. My hands went to the small sink basin, gripping on for dear life as I stared at the girl in the mirror.

This time last year, I was teetering on the edge of death, wishing I could close my eyes and just have it all be over.

But here I was.

Healthy and alive.

And about to start an adventure I wasn't sure I'd ever be ready for.

CHAPTER FOUR

RAFE

"Do you think she's okay?" Damon peered through the tinted windows as if he could see the other bus. He couldn't.

"Who, Country? She'll live." Levi stretched out his legs and pulled the ball cap down over his eyes. We'd been travelling for less than an hour and he was already crashing. I'd have to keep a careful eye on him. Despite his recent stint in rehab, I knew his thoughts were darker than ever, his mind a constant enemy. Levi thrived on chaos. On anything to distract him from the memories... the pain... the self-loathing. It wasn't that he loved the crowds or the attention or even the adoring fans, it was that he *needed* them. Levi needed the validation, the worship and praise.

The love.

Even if it was all fantasy.

"That was savage, man," Hud said. "Making her drink that shit." He eyed the vodka bottle on the table. Levi and vodka had history—bad history. It wasn't his poison of choice for more reasons than one, which was why I'd been really fucking surprised when he pulled out that particular brand. But that was my brother, an ever-evolving enigma.

"Where d'you even get it?" I asked from across the bus.

"Doesn't matter." Typical Levi response. "And before you start bitching me out, I had one shot. I didn't even plan on having that," he mumbled.

"So why d'you do it?" Hudson asked the question I already knew the answer to.

It was her.

Eva.

She got to him. The guy, at times, not even I could reach. It was one of the reasons she was here. We'd all seen how she'd handled Levi back in the summer, at the party after the showdown finale. Eva hadn't fallen at his feet like most girls, but she hadn't cowered either. No, she'd held her ground and challenged him to a singing contest of all the fucking things.

She'd broken through whatever hell he lived in and distracted him.

Bottom line, Eva intrigued him. Whether it was because she was so pure and innocent and good, and he wanted to find out all the ways he could dirty up her soul, I didn't know.

Thankfully, I wouldn't ever have to find out.

Eva was off-limits—here to help smooth things over with our younger fans and bridge the appeal between our music and hers. Levi couldn't make a move on her, the same way Hudson, Damon... or I couldn't.

Levi bolted upright and flung his arms out, stretching. "I'll be in the back bedroom. I need to sleep."

"Sleep in the other one," Hudson said.

My brother ignored him, padding down the bus like a zombie.

"Levi, come on, man, you know the deal. The back bedroom is for—"

He flipped Hudson off over his shoulder and disappeared into the bigger of two artists bedrooms on the bus.

"That's bullshit."

"Leave it, Hud." I let out a heavy sigh, my eyes fixed on the door now separating Levi and the rest of us.

"He seem unsettled to you?" Damon asked me.

"He's always fucking unsettled."

"Yeah, but there's something else."

"He'll be okay." He had to be. Our entire future was riding on this tour. Razorsharp Records had taken a risk signing a bunch of misfits like us. Between our group of four we had more skeletons in the closet than the paparazzi could handle. It's why Alistair and the label had worked hard to bury that shit. Yet, we all knew it would only take one nosy journalist to poke his nose where it didn't belong for our unstable kingdom to come crashing down around us.

"I don't know, Rafe, maybe having her here wasn't such a good idea."

"Yeah," I scrubbed my face, "well, it's too late now." Eva was here whether we wanted her to be or not.

Hudson got up, still grumbling to himself about Levi. "I'm going to take a piss and then I'm going to make some food."

"So," Damon said, the second Hudson was out of earshot, "how was it seeing her again?"

"I'm not doing this with you."

"Come on, humor me. I saw you watching her during the meeting, watching *both* of them. You still have feelings for her," he said as if it was the simplest thing in the world.

It wasn't.

"I have no idea what you're talking about."

"No?" His brow quirked up. "You're telling me that you—"

"That ship has sailed." It had sailed so far it was nothing but a grainy dot on the horizon. "You need to let it go," I said flatly.

Damon was the best of us. Compassionate and kind, he had this infectious energy about him. If Levi was the darkness, Damon was definitely the light, and he brought much needed balance to our little band of lost souls.

He let out a smooth chuckle. "I don't think it's me who needs to worry. Five months. That's a long time to be on the road with a girl you *don't* have feelings for."

My eyes shuttered as I inhaled a shaky breath. What Eva and I had shared that weekend in Camdena was unlike anything I'd ever experienced. We'd connected. Not only over music but with the pain that lived inside us both. I never did get her full story, but I knew enough to know she'd battled her own demons. She was the only thing I saw that weekend. Her smile, her laugh. The way she handled herself around my brother and my closest friends.

But it was all a fantasy.

A dream I could spend my life chasing and never quite grasp. Let alone make a reality.

"You don't always have to put him first," Damon lowered his voice.

"Yeah," I said grimly, feeling the truth of the words settle in my bones. "I do."

"Rafe, come on. It doesn't—"

"I'm going to check on Levi." I shot up, wanting nothing more than to make him stop talking. Stop pushing me for answers I didn't have. "Do me a favor though, yeah?" It came out exasperated. "Stop bringing up this shit with Eva. It's done." *It's over*, the words echoed through my skull. "We have to focus on the tour. That's all that matters."

"Yeah, sure, man." Guilt washed over his expression. "Listen, I didn't mean to push."

"It's cool. I just don't want anything else to cause problems between us."

Because fuck only knew, we already had enough to deal with.

———

A LITTLE OVER FOUR HOURS LATER, I STOOD IN THE VAST AND EMPTY space of the Spectrum Center. It was hard to believe that this time tomorrow seventeen thousand fans would be filling up the seats, waiting to see us perform.

"Do you feel it, bro?" Hudson clapped me on the back and my brows pinched.

"Should I know what the fuck you're talking about?"

"Don't tell me you don't feel it." The corner of his mouth curved as he looked out to where the roadies were setting up the equipment on the stage. "Tomorrow night, we'll be standing up there, listening to thousands of girls scream our names. That shit will never get old. This is it," he went on. "This is the game changer. I can feel it in my bones."

"You mean you can feel it in your dick?" My eyes dropped to his crotch.

"Are you kidding me? All that fresh puss—"

"Soundcheck," someone yelled, and an unfamiliar riff blasted out of the speakers.

"Well, would you get a look at that?" Hudson tapped his feet involuntarily, no doubt hearing a beat in his head. "She looks good up there."

He wasn't wrong. Eva came to life with her guitar in her hand. Her soft Southern accent was almost pitch perfect.

The music stopped and Letty ran on stage, the two of them studying her clipboard.

"Letty hasn't left her side since we got here. She was never that attentive with us," Hudson grumbled.

"Can you blame her? We didn't exactly make things easy on her."

"You mean Levi didn't." His eyes slid to mine.

"We all played our part."

Our first tour had been chaos, but what had the label expected? They'd plucked four guys out of a relentless cycle of dead-end jobs and shitty paid gigs and thrown them into the studio and then sent them on the road. No one could have predicted the way Black Hearts would have blown up. We'd dived head-first into a world of sex, drugs, and rock and roll. None of us had doting parents behind the scenes, warning us of the vices that came hand-in-hand with fame. We had Alistair and the label. Looking back, it was a miracle we'd survived our debut tour. Levi had been high or drunk for almost four months straight. Hudson had slept with enough fangirls that I was almost positive he'd have a whole football team of mini Hudsons up and down the East Coast. Damon and I hadn't indulged the way the two of them did, but we'd still partied too hard and pushed our bodies too far.

Eva's guitar strummed again, silencing the thoughts flooding my head. It was the first time I'd ever seen her play on stage. At the talent showdown I'd heard her, but I hadn't seen her, and even though she was only performing for a handful of roadies and staff, she still gave it her all. It was breathtaking.

She was breathtaking.

"You have a little drool," Hudson's hand shot out toward me, "right—"

"Fuck off," I growled, swatting him away.

"My bad. I can see it for what it is." He smirked. The fucker actually smirked at me. "One musician appreciating another musician's... *talent*."

"Hud," I warned. It had been months since I'd ghosted Eva, and yet, Damon and Hudson were treating me like I was the one ghosted by her.

His eyes burned into the side of my face as I watched her switch gears and play *Zombie* by The Cranberries in the arrangement I'd helped her with all those months ago. Fuck. That song was imprinted on my brain. I couldn't listen to the original version without seeing her face, hearing her voice.

"Holy shit," my friend breathed as she reached the bridge. "Your girl brought her A-game."

I didn't even correct his slip about Eva being my girl. I couldn't. She'd pulled me into her performance; taken me hostage with her words.

Hudson was wrong though.

Eva wasn't my girl, she never was.

And nothing I said or did was ever going to change that.

———

"Fuck, we sound good." Levi grabbed his t-shirt and pulled it up to wipe the sweat from his face. We were an hour into sound check and we'd never sounded better. Levi was killing it on vocals; giving me, Damon, and Hudson the energy we needed to nail song after song, even the newer ones we'd added to the set.

"Charlotte won't know what's hit 'em," Hudson said, resting one of his sticks behind his ear.

"Sounding good," Letty breezed up to the stage, Riley hot on her heels. "The new arrangement for *Darker Days* sounds freakin' awesome."

"Yeah?" I asked, still buzzing. We'd switched up a few things for the new set. Same songs from our debut album, but with some added twists here and there.

"I liked it," Riley added. "It sounded very... hip."

"*Hip*," Hudson mumbled beneath his breath as me and Damon stifled a laugh.

"Oh yeah, Riles," Levi stalked to the edge of the stage, crouching down. "Which part specifically did you like?"

Everyone stopped to watch their exchange; road crew, stagehands, even the cleaning staff watched the infamous Levi Hunter as he stared down at Riley like she was nothing more than dirt on his boot.

"Levi," I hissed. She was our PA now. We needed her, even if my brother thought otherwise. Not to mention the fact she was most likely banging our manager.

"It's only a question, Rafe, no need to get your panties in a bunch." He shot me an amused look before pinning Riley with another hard stare. "I'm waiting."

"Sweet baby Jesus," Letty breathed, shooting me a look that said, 'do something'. But he wouldn't back down, not until he had an answer.

Rolling back her shoulders, Riley met my brother's glare with a fierce one of her own. "I liked *Deep Waters*. It's great on the album but this had a darker edge to it. Rafe's solo really amped up the feeling of despair." Her eyes slid to mine, flashing with something I couldn't quite decipher.

Levi dragged his thumb across his bottom lip, twirling one of his piercings. "Interesting," was his only reply as he stood up again and nodded at Hudson, "Let's go over *Tomorrow's Just Another Day* again. I want to nail that second verse. It felt... off."

It wasn't off. It had been note-perfect. But my brother was his own worst critic at times.

"How are we looking?" Alistair approached Riley and Letty as we got into position.

"Great," Riley said, sounding a little smug. "They're looking great."

Clearly, she thought she'd won the war with my brother, but what she didn't realize was, Levi didn't quit. And he rarely lost.

"Everything okay?" Alistair's eyes asked her the words he didn't say. Riley offered him a small smile before folding her arms across her chest and waiting for us to start.

Hudson hit the opening beat and everything fell away to the music. I watched as my brother came alive. Eyes closed for most of the song, he sang the lyrics I had penned as if they were his own, as if they'd been forged on his very soul. I might have been able to hold a note or two, but Levi had the voice of an angel. A fact that both inspired and haunted him.

My eyes found Alistair and he nodded, approval etched into his serious expression. He saw it too. Levi was born to perform, to seduce an audience with nothing more than a microphone and lyrics and presence.

When the song ended, a moment of silence fell over us. My heart thudded, adrenaline coursing through my veins. It was nothing compared to how it would feel tomorrow with the cacophony of thousands of fans echoing throughout the arena. But there was something about performing to a small crowd that hit me right between the chest.

"Let's take five," the production manager yelled.

I slid the strap of my Zemaitis off and placed it in its stand before grabbing a bottle of water and chugging it down. "Right, I need to go take a leak," I said, heading for the backstage area.

I figured Eva had returned to the bus. I didn't expect to find her in the dimly lit hall with her head tipped back against the wall. Half-wondering if I should turn back around and find another bathroom, her voice caught me off guard. "You sounded good out there," she said, her eyes sliding slowly to mine.

"You weren't so bad yourself."

"Oh, I don't know about that." She gave me a wry smile. "I thought I was going to puke at one point."

"Wait until tomorrow."

The blood drained from her face and I found myself chuckling. "You'll be okay." Turning on my heel, I went to leave, but my name on her lips pierced the air.

"Rafe, wait." Steeling myself, I turned around and met her weary gaze. "I just wanted to say, whatever happened between us... well, I'm not here because of that."

Her words sliced through me, but I didn't flinch. "Your point?"

"I get the impression you don't want me here, and that's fine." Her eyes darted to the floor as if the words were hard to say. A sting of guilt shot through me, but this was our reality now.

"Look," Eva looked at me again, sadness radiating from her. "I'm here and I'm not goin' anywhere. I owe my parents that much at least. So I figured we should probably try to at least find a way to be around one another."

Parents? What the fuck was she talking about?

"Eva, I'm not—"

"Yo, dude, hurry the fuck up." Hudson burst into the hallway, sucking in a harsh breath when he realized Eva was standing right there. "Shit, my bad. I'll just be—"

"It's all good," I said. "Eva was just leaving."

The second the words left my lips I regretted them. She'd offered me a get out of jail free card. An olive branch toward peace. Yet here I was trampling all over her attempt at starting over. Because seeing her standing there reminded me too much of another time. A time when I'd been captivated by the girl with pain in her eyes.

Part of me wished things could be different, but when you'd grown up in a living nightmare, I knew better than to believe in fairy tales.

"It's okay, if you two need to—"

"Rafe's right," Eva said coolly. "I was just leavin'." She moved around Hudson.

"Okay," he said the second she was out of earshot, "what the hell was all that about?"

"Nothing."

"Rafe..."

"Hud..."

"Shit, man, this is why I always told you never to get in deep with a girl. It screws everything up."

I pressed my lips together, refusing to humor him. I wasn't in deep with Eva, I was in deep with life. Trying to hold together the fragile pieces of everything.

"Come on, lover boy." Hudson roped his arm around my neck. "Levi wants to go over a couple more songs."

Of course he did.

I didn't protest though, I knew the drill by now.

What Levi wanted, Levi usually got.

CHAPTER FIVE

"Now for the fun part." Letty waggled her brows as she stepped to one side, revealing a rack of outfits. "What do you think?"

"I... wow." I stepped closer, running my fingers over the denim and leather, plaid and lace. There were jackets and miniskirts, jeans and shirts, even a dress or two.

"It's awesome, right?" She could barely contain her excitement. "I mean, I had fun helping style the guys last year but I'm itching to get to work on you."

My eyes widened as Letty grabbed a denim shirt off the rack and held it up against my body. "It's not usually an assistant's role to help style an artist, but I told Alistair you'd probably feel more comfortable with me than a team of stylists."

"Thank you. I feel so out of my depth," I admitted.

"Get a couple of shows under your belt and you'll be fine. You sounded great out there during soundcheck."

"It's like a switch flips and the music takes over. But performin' to a few stage crew, and you and Riley, isn't a crowd of seventeen thousand people."

Seventeen. Thousand. People.

The words ricocheted around my head like gun fire. It seemed unquantifiable. Impossible. Too surreal for words. But tomorrow night, I'd perform my opening set for not a few hundred people, not even a few thousand. Seventeen. Thousand. People. Sure, they were coming to see Black Hearts. I was just the unknown special guest. But they would still be out there, listening to my songs, casting judgment on my performance, probably my worthiness to be on the same stage as their idols. The four guys they worshipped.

"Whoa, are you okay?" Letty touched my arm. "You've gone as white as a sheet."

"How am I supposed to do this?"

"Try on a few outfits?" She frowned.

"Perform, on stage, Letty, to all those people. People who paid good money to see them, not me."

"Listen to me, and listen good, Eva Star Walker. You really think you'd be stepping foot anywhere near that stage if Ali and the label didn't see something special in you?" Her brow rose. "Well, do you?"

"I... I guess not."

"Pfft," she muttered. "I can handle you being overwhelmed. I can even handle you denying there's anything between you and Rafe, but what I can't handle is you pretending you don't know how talented you are."

I smashed my lips together to stop myself from saying something that was only going to make Letty more irritated. She draped the shirt over the back of a chair and grabbed my shoulders. "This is your moment to shine, Eva. Do you know how many people would kill to be in your position right now? Don't go out there thinking you don't deserve it; go out there with something to prove."

"Has anyone ever told you you'd make a great motivational speaker?"

"It has been said before." She grinned, backing up to give me some space. "Feeling better?" I nodded. "Ready to pick out some killer outfits for the opening show?" Another nod. "Good. Because by the time I'm finished with you, the guys won't know what's hit them." Letty winked before snatching another outfit off the rack and ushering me behind the changing screen. "We should pick out something for tonight too."

"Tonight?" I asked as I shimmied out of my jeans.

"Yeah, for the launch party."

"Funny, my *assistant* never mentioned any party to me."

Letty's soft laughter filled the room. "You should ask Alistair for a better one."

"Oh, I don't know, she's growin' on me."

"You're not so bad yourself." Letty appeared around the screen and I scrambled to pull down the shirt.

Letty rolled her eyes. "You need to get used to having people in your space, Eva. Here let me." She unbuttoned the last two buttons of the shirt, grabbed the ends and tied them into a knot.

"Much better. It'll look as cute as hell with that leather jacket."

"So where is this launch party?"

"At a club downtown. It's very exclusive. There won't be a huge crowd but if the Die Hearts get wind of the location, it'll be a security nightmare."

"The Die Hearts?"

She snickered. "Yeah, it's what we call the rabid fans. The ones who would sell their left kidney to get up close and personal with the guys."

"They sound... delightful."

"They're ten shades of crazy is what they are." Her expression grew serious. "You should be prepared for them."

"Prepared how?"

"I know you're only here because the label asked you, but these girls think they have some kind of ownership over the band. They're very protective. You're going to be seen with the band, it's inevitable. There's already—" She dropped her gaze, and a bolt of dread shot through me.

"Already what, Letty?"

"There's been a lot of speculation about the mystery guest joining the tour in the press already."

"But they promised me anonymity until the first show." Which was less than a day away, but still, I wasn't quite ready to be outed.

"They shouldn't have," she said, her lips pressed into a thin line. "There's no such thing as anonymity in this world. But once it is out, you can get to work on winning them over with that huge Southern heart of yours."

I didn't share Letty's enthusiasm. Instead, a pit carved deep inside my stomach. I'd been foolish to think I'd stay anonymous forever. Of course people would learn it was me, Evangeline Star Walker, supporting Black Hearts Still Beat on tour. But ever since Alistair had called me all those weeks ago to offer me the gig, I hadn't allowed myself much time or space to think about the what ifs and maybes. All I knew was I needed the money and I had to do this. Regardless of the consequences, regardless of whether tomorrow my name became splashed over newspapers up and down Charlotte... and then Orlando... and Houston.

But I knew what Letty was saying. She was warning me about the darker side of the business. The side where girls vilified female artists and shamed their appearance... their talent... their personalities. I was supposed to be here to win over the band's alienated crowd. But I had a whole other crowd to contend with. A crowd that was possessive of their Black Hearts boys.

What the hell had I gotten myself into?

"I'll give you a minute," Letty announced, sensing my façade crumbling.

"Thanks."

She left me alone, and I snatched up my cell phone and dialed the one person who could talk me through this.

"Hey, girl. I was just—"

"Molly, what the hell am I doin'?"

"Hello to you too," she chuckled. "I'm guessin' it finally hit you that you're not in Kansas anymore?"

"You're not the only one who's said that. Hud… it doesn't matter."

"You can say his name, babe. I am so over that rock asshole I can barely remember what he looks like."

I wasn't sure about that, but I didn't argue. "Tell me I can do this," I said to my best friend in the whole world.

"You can do this."

"Tell me I'm not makin' a huge mistake."

"It's not a mistake."

"Tell me I'm not goin' to end up paparazzi fish food."

"That I can't tell you, babe. But you got this, Eva. You're one of the strongest people I know."

"You're right. I can do this. I can absolutely do this." If I kept telling myself that maybe it would come true.

"Atta girl. Now let's talk about Rafe. Did you kick him in the balls like I suggested?"

Laughter spilled out of me. "No, I didn't kick him in the balls, Mol."

"Darn it, babe, he deserves nothin' less."

"I tried to clear the air between us. He's been a complete jerk since I got here."

"Well, duh. He probably took one look at you and realized what a fine piece of ass he let slip through his fingers."

"I doubt that," I murmured remembering how cold he'd been with me. "But it doesn't matter. I have more important things to focus on." Like how I was going to survive the opening show tomorrow.

"Letty, my assistant, said we can arrange for you to come out to one of the shows."

"Oh, hell yes! Just name the time and place and I'm there." She hesitated. "Although I'll need to make sure I'm not on twin duty. Mom is away more and more and I'm stuck watching Thing One and Thing Two; it's tramplin' all over my sex life."

"You love those two kids more than anythin'."

"I know I do," her voice softened. "But I love getting' laid more."

"I miss you, Molly," I said, feeling my chest tighten.

"It's only been a couple of days, babe. We'll be reunited in no time, and by then you'll be a superstar."

Letty slipped back into the room, hesitating when she realized I was still on the phone.

"I should go. Apparently, I need to be styled."

Molly let out an ear-splitting shrill. "You get a stylist? Of course you get a stylist. Holy crap, Eva. I'm not sure our friendship will survive your newfound stardom. I'm turning green as we speak."

"Shut up, you love me."

"I do," she chuckled again. "I do. Text me photos of everythin'. I mean it, babe. I gotta get my kicks somehow."

"I will. I'll call soon."

We said goodbye and hung up. Letty approached, a cautious smile painted on her face. "All better?"

"I think so. Just promise me you won't drop me in at the deep end at the party."

"Deal," she said, excitement glittering in her eyes. "Now, let's turn you into a star."

———

I RAN MY FINGERS AROUND THE MOCKTAIL LETTY HAD LEFT ME WITH while she finished up getting ready. The label were putting us up in a hotel for the night before we started a grueling full week of shows.

"What time is it?" she yelled from her bedroom. Mine was on the other side of the suite. The bed was so soft, part of me didn't want to ever leave it. The other part didn't want to leave for other reasons. Mostly, the bright red lip gloss Letty had swiped over my mouth and the smoky eyes she'd insisted I needed. Tonight was about making a statement, she'd said. Secretly, I think she hoped the makeup, outfit, and brand new GANNI boots I was wearing would give me a confidence boost. But while I felt the part on the outside, inside I was a quivering mess.

"Okay, I'm ready." Letty emerged from her room dressed in skin-tight leather pants and a deep-pink halter top. It was daring and sexy and everything I wasn't.

"Too much?" She dropped her eyes down her body.

"No, you look amazin'. I love how the pink in your hair matches your halter."

She grinned. "I wasn't lying when I said I have experience. How was the mocktail?"

"I'm thinkin' I should have let you add some liquor."

"Nervous?"

"Terrified."

"Just remember, be yourself. Ignore the Die Hearts, and most of all, breathe. This is supposed to be fun, okay?"

With a small nod, I grabbed my purse and followed Letty out of our suite. Travis and Grayson were waiting for us. "Ms. Walker," he said.

"Eva," I replied. "Please call me Eva."

"Yes, Ms... Eva." I smothered a laugh as he and Grayson ushered us toward the elevator. "The car is waiting downstairs. The band went on ahead in the other car."

"That means we should be able to sneak in undetected." Letty grabbed my hand, giving it a reassuring squeeze.

"Ahh, there you both are." Riley slipped out of another door, looking elegant in a glittery pant suit and killer heels. "Travis, I'll be riding with Ms. Walker and Letty."

Letty shot me a bemused look, and I sensed there was no love lost between the two of them. We all piled into the elevator, Travis and Grayson standing up ahead like two statues.

"Eva, you look... nice." Riley's lips pursed. "Did you pick that out yourself?"

"Actually, Letty did, and I think she did an amazin' job. I love it."

"I bet you do."

I jerked back at that ready to give her a piece of my mind, but Letty shook her head discreetly, silently telling me to back down. I knew then I'd been right about Riley the second I'd met her. For some unknown reason she didn't like me, and if her snide comments were anything to go by, she liked Letty even less.

"Not riding with the band, Riley?"

"I had something to take care of. But don't worry, I'll be there to attend to their every need at the club."

"Oh, I bet you will." Letty's cough barely disguised the words.

Thankfully before Riley could respond, the elevator doors pinged open.

"Watch your back with that one," Letty whispered as Riley stuck close to Travis while Grayson tailed us.

"Is it true she's sleepin' with Alistair?"

"Him and anyone else who can advance her career. Believe it or not, we used to hang out when we were both just interns with the label. But when I got a break with the band, she turned on me. Told everyone I only got the job because I'd slept with one of the senior managers."

"That's..."

"All par for the course in this business. Everyone's your friend until you're standing in the way of career progression."

"I'll bear that in mind."

Travis led us out of the maintenance entrance at the back of the hotel and ushered us into a sleek black SUV. As he closed the door, I noticed him mumble something into his wrist, a hidden mic no doubt.

It was all so surreal. The hotel, the makeover, the close protection security, riding to an exclusive party downtown in a brand-new SUV.

Riley settled back in her seat, ignoring the two of us as she pulled out her cell and began texting someone. I strained through the tinted glass to watch the city roll by. I'd never left Tennessee before, and now I was about to see a different city every day.

"Shit," Riley mumbled, tapping the glass partition separating the front seats and ours.

It rolled down and Grayson peered back at us. "We have a problem. The location was leaked on a fansite."

He and Travis discussed something in hushed voices. "Change of plan. We're going to drive around back and enter through the emergency exit."

"How bad is it?" Riley asked.

"The band was mobbed but made it safely inside."

My gaze darted to Letty and she mouthed, "Relax, we knew this could happen."

It was easy for her to say. She wasn't about to become the center of attention for being the mystery girl on tour with Black Hearts Still Beat.

"I thought the location of the club was need to know only?" Letty directed her question at Riley.

"It was, but you know how these things go sometimes. A roadie overhears something and tells someone else and before you know it, you've got four hundred teenage girls camped outside the mall because someone posted online that they had heard the band was going to be there."

"Did that really happen?" I asked.

"Sweetheart, it happens all the time." Riley's cell blared to life and she answered it. "Hello... yeah. Yeah, we're okay... No, they're going to bring us around back... I don't know, she seems fine." Her eyes flicked to mine and she let out a little huff before looking out the window. "Okay, we're just pulling up now."

Two things happened at once. A camera smashed against the window flashing brightly, and the crowd erupted into high-pitched screams and shrieks of adoration.

"We love you, Levi."

"Rafe, I want your babies."

"Hudson Ryker can ruin me any day of the week."

The catcalls went on and on and on.

"They're following us," Letty said, keeping her eyes trained on the back window.

"We're going to do another loop of the block and see if we can shake them." But as the SUV picked up the pace, so did the horde of girls.

"This is crazy," I mumbled.

"This is nothing." Riley smoothed her hair out of her face before sending another text. "Local PD are on their way."

"That is not standard protocol," Travis responded.

"We have an army of teenage girls in pursuit of our vehicle and nowhere to go. What would you suggest?"

Travis didn't reply, but I caught his narrowed expression in the rear-view mirror. "It would help us to do our job, Ms. Panem, if you let us do our job. Gray, radio in for someone to meet us around the back of Muy Yungs."

"Chinese food? I really don't think this is time for—"

"They're not getting Chinese food, Riles," Letty smirked. "They're going to pull the old bait and switch, am I right, Trav?"

"You got it Letty. Johnson and Stalter will be waiting to escort you inside while we create a diversion."

"Is that... safe?" Riley balked, earning her a heavy eye-roll from Letty.

"Don't worry, now you're on tour with the band, you'll get used to it. There hasn't been a situation Travis and his guys haven't saved our asses from yet."

"Do I even want to know?" I asked her.

Letty smiled, a knowing glint in her eye. "Oh, you'll find out soon enough."

CHAPTER SIX

RAFE

"You look like you could use this." Damon thrust a beer at me. I took a long pull on it, wiping my mouth with the back of my hand.

"They should be here by now," I said.

"It's sweet you're so concerned about Riley." My eyes snapped to his, narrowing, but the fucker exploded with laughter. "If you could see your face right now. Chill, man, security can handle it."

I didn't doubt that; our guys were some of the best in the business. But the crowd gathered outside weren't the usual local fans, they were Die Hearts; a special brand of crazy. By the time the club manager had called Alistair to tell him, it was too late and our car was swarmed with teenage girls, and a few moms, all waiting to get their glimpse of the band. Thanks to Alistair's forward thinking, we'd managed to calm the crowd with promises of free merch and a few selfies, but now they knew we were inside, they would circle like piranhas for the rest of the night. And since Levi had evaded them altogether, thanks to his personal bodyguard and a ridiculous disguise, Alistair was worried they would assume he was coming in another car.

Like the one Riley, Letty, and Eva were currently riding in.

"It's okay to be worried about her," he added when I didn't reply.

My hand tightened around the bottle as my eyes fixed on the entrance to the club. "She's not cut out for this," I mumbled.

"Hey, don't be so quick to write her off. Eva's strong. She can handle herself."

"You don't understand..."

"So tell me, man. Talk to me." His eyes burned holes into the side of my face, but I couldn't look at him. I wasn't supposed to care.

I *couldn't* care.

But the second Alistair had announced the girls were riding in a separate car, a knot had formed in my stomach. A knot that only tripled in size when I saw the crowd of girls waiting outside the club.

"At least when we got thrown into this life, we had each other." My eyes finally slid to his. "She has no one."

"She has Letty."

But Letty wasn't always going to be there; she worked for the label, not for Eva. There would be times when things got crazy and Eva would have no one, and for as much as I tried not to care, I did.

"Who the fuck died?" Hudson swaggered over to us, already buzzed.

"I see you found the open bar."

He flipped me off around a wolfish grin. "It's a celebration. We're supposed to be celebrating."

"Where's Levi?"

"He's—" Hudson glanced around and let a long groan. "He was right behind me."

"I'll go find him," Damon offered. "You stay here and... brood."

"Thanks," I said.

He wandered off, leaving me with Hudson. "You need to get her out of your system, man. Find a cute little blond and fuck Angel right out of your—"

"Hud," I warned.

"What?" His smooth chuckle made me bristle. "I'm just saying. It worked for me."

"Looks like it did."

"What the fuck is that supposed to mean?" He ran a hand over his new shorter hair. The restyled hair he denied had anything to do with Eva's best friend.

"Nothing," I conceded, "it means nothing."

"Where are they anyway? Shouldn't they be here by now? We go on in fifteen."

Alistair had organized with the club manager for us to do an impromptu performance. It was supposed to be a surprise, but everyone knew we rarely showed up to a party and didn't perform. My heart wasn't in it though, not tonight.

"There was a problem getting past the Die Hearts. They think Levi is inside that car."

"Fuck." Hudson scrubbed his jaw. "Are security—"

"Already on it. They should be here any sec—" My eyes found her almost immediately.

"Holy fucking shit, is that Eva?" Hudson practically drooled beside me. I nudged him in the ribs, feeling possessiveness stir in my chest. She didn't belong to me, but if he thought for a second, I was going to tolerate him jonesing after her, he was sorely mistaken.

He wasn't wrong though. Eva looked as hot as sin. Every bit the star she was about to become.

"The leather jacket has Letty written all over it," Hudson remarked. I grumbled some reply, barely able to take my eyes off her. I knew I was staring but I couldn't help it.

"Yep, good luck with that." Hudson clapped me on the back, chuckling to himself as Riley spotted us and made her way over, the girls trailing behind.

"Ladies, looking good." His gaze swept over Eva and Letty, lingering a little too long on our support act. "Riley, I'm almost empty."

"It's an open bar, Hudson. I'm your assistant, not your gofer. You have hands, use them. Now if you'll excuse me, I need to find Alistair."

"Is she allowed to talk to us like that?"

"Maybe if you didn't insist on pushing her buttons it'd go smoother." I suggested.

"Nah, she's too easy to work up. Besides." his eyes followed her across the club, "it's all part of the irresistible charm."

"Please tell me you're not going to try and bed her." Letty sounded mildly disgusted.

"What?" Hudson gawked at her. "She's hot and I like a challenge."

Eva turned her attention to the dance floor, watching the hand selected audience—contest winners, industry types, friends of the label —fake it up.

"Yo," Hudson nudged me, "we're up." He pointed to where Damon and Levi were chatting to the club manager.

"Kill it," Letty said, holding up her fist.

"You know it." Hudson downed the remnants of his beer and slammed it on a nearby table before fist bumping her. "Laters, baby."

"You're performing?" Eva asked. "I didn't know." Her eyes slid to Letty's in question.

"I thought it would be a surprise." Guilt flashed across her face, but I didn't miss the conspiratorial look she shot me.

What the fuck was she up to?

Knowing Letty, it was nothing good.

"Are you okay?" I asked Eva before I could stop myself. "You know... with everything. It was pretty wild out there."

A couple of guys barreled past us, knocking Eva into me. My hands shot out, steadying her. "Hey, watch it," I yelled after them.

"Shit, sorry, Rafe, my man. I didn't see you there."

"It's not me you almost flattened."

"Fuck, my bad." The guy held up his hands to Eva. "Sorry."

"It's fine, really." She stepped back and I released her, jamming my hands in my jean pockets. I shouldn't have touched her. Because now it was all I could think about doing.

"I should..."

"Go, of course. Good luck up there." Eva flashed me a blinding smile. It was more than I deserved, but no less than I wanted.

Damon and Hudson were right. I wasn't sure I could do it—keep her at a distance, suppress my feelings for her. Especially not when she was standing there, looking at me like I was everything she wanted.

Everything she needed.

"Rafe," Letty's voice grounded me. "They're waiting."

"Uh, yeah... right." Tearing my eyes away from Eva, I made my way over to the guys, who were already on stage setting up.

"What took you so long?" Levi asked me, none the wiser, too amped up to notice.

Always too distracted to notice.

"I'm here, aren't I?" I grabbed the guitar—one of my back-ups since my favorite was back at the hotel safe and sound—and slid the strap over my neck. The familiar weight of the instrument settled me. Became an extension of me. A way to channel all the shit I had to shoulder. When my fingers ran over the frets, I was free.

"Welcome to Basement Vibes," Levi stepped closer to the mic, adjusting the stand the way he liked it. "For those of you who don't already know it, we're Black Hearts Still Beat, and Gary, the owner of this very fine establishment, asked us to stop by and play a few songs tonight." Actually, our label had brokered the performance, but Levi knew the routine. He knew how to work the crowd and tell the people what they wanted to hear.

The room exploded with applause, a much less raucous response than what we were used to. But these people weren't your average fans, so we had to work a little harder for their approval. Levi shot me an amused look, his lip curving into a devious grin. Shaking my head, I silently tried to tell him to abort whatever fucked-up plan I knew he was hatching.

"We've been warned to be on our best behavior tonight," he went on, "but we're about to go on tour. And if you have any idea what it's like to be cooped up with three other guys for months on end, then you'll probably know it's only healthy to blow off a little steam beforehand. So what d'ya say, Charlotte. Do you wanna help me fuck things up?"

Alistair caught my eye, dragging a single finger across his neck. Fucking Levi. He hadn't only gone off script, he'd ushered the room into near silence. A couple of people down by the front of the stage, probably contest winners, whooped, but everyone else stared wide-eyed, mortification etched in their expressions. Their disapproval only spurred my brother on. He gave Hudson the nod, mouthing something at him, and the intro beat of one of our darker songs, *Poison in My Veins*, filled the room. I cursed beneath my breath as I plucked the strings, building the opening bars. We were supposed to be sticking to our more mainstream material, but no, my self-sabotaging brother had decided to pick the one song he knew I had vocals on.

The one song he knew I wouldn't want to sing.

It stings, it burns, but the pain don't hurt
Cut me open and I will bleed, oh, you're poison...
Poison in my veins.

I CLUTCHED THE MIC, EYES CLOSED, STAGE LIGHTS BLAZING DOWN ON me as the words spilled from my lips. Beads of sweat rolled down my back, clung to the strands of hair falling over my face.

Cut me open and I will bleed, oh you're poison...
Poison in my veins.

You say you want to cleanse me, save me, purify my soul
But you're not the messiah, you're just the Devil in sheep's clothes
So cut me open and I will bleed, oh you're poison...
You're poison in my veins.

I LOOKED OVER AT LEVI. HE TOO WAS LOST IN THE LYRICS, IN THE meaning behind them. No one knew the truth, they never would. It was a secret that would die with us, but we knew.

We lived with the burden every single minute of every day.

Poison, poison in my veins...

OUR VOICES HELD THE LAST NOTE, MY GRAVELLY TONE WRAPPING around his raw screech. Even on stage, I couldn't help but want to protect him; to reassure him and hold him up. We weren't only brothers; we were all the other had. Sure, we had Damon and Hudson and the band and all that came with it, but nobody would ever know me the way Levi knew me. Or know my brother the way I knew him. What we shared transcended the bonds of family, of brothers. It was part of us, weaved inextricably into the fiber of our beings.

The music faded, the pain that always came with singing that song lingering deep in my soul. I wiped my brow with the back of my hand and looked out at the crowd. It was always the same; a sea of faceless people. But tonight, my eyes found solace in a pair of ocean eyes.

Eva stood with Letty right where I'd left them, and although I couldn't be certain, I was sure I saw the shimmer of tears in her eyes. The sudden applause from the crowd broke our connection though. Levi stalked toward me, slinging his arm over my shoulder.

"Thought you might appreciate something from our early days. Although my brother, here, might disagree." He grinned at me and I wanted nothing more than to knock his head off his shoulders. "I love this sonofabitch more than anything. He likes to stay hidden behind his guitar, but he's got a killer voice too. What do you say? Do you think my bro Rafe can sing?"

"Quit it," I gritted out, forcing a smile to our rapt audience. He'd done it. Levi had won over a room full of industry types; men with fat wallets and women with expensive habits.

Damon caught my eye and shook his head, hardly surprised. I rolled my eyes. Levi was a cocky motherfucker. The perpetual thorn in my side. But he was also my blood and despite our differences, I loved him something fierce.

Humoring him, I cupped the mic and said, "I appreciate the applause but don't get too used to it. I prefer the shadows not the spotlight."

Levi let out a hearty laugh. He seemed in a particularly good mood tonight; that or he was high. Which meant he was using, again. Moving to center stage again, he winked at me and then declared, "Good job for my brother, I fucking love the spotlight. Hud, I'm feeling kinda *Dirty*, give me a beat."

The sound of his drums rattled around my chest and for the next thirty minutes we played an intimate set for our audience. By the time we were done, my shirt was soaked and my throat was dry, but my skin tingled in the best possible fucking way. Unlike my brother, I'd never needed a synthetic high. This was enough.

The music.

The lyrics.

The adrenaline pumping through my veins.

It was enough to settle my demons and soothe my soul.

"I need a drink," I declared, running a hand through my damp hair.

"Drink? I need a good hard fuck."

"You ever considered getting help with that?" I teased Hudson.

"What like sex therapy? Nah, man, ain't a problem unless you make it one." He shot me a wink and then took off towards a group of waiting women.

"Hey," I grabbed Levi as he went to walk away, "what was that?" His brows bunched together as he stared at me. "Don't do that, Lev. Don't pretend like that wasn't something. We don't sing that song. We *never* sing that song."

He shrugged as if it was no big deal.

But we both knew it was a big fucking deal.

"It's nothing. Chill."

I searched his face for a clue he was lying. Levi was a master in deception. A chameleon when it came to hiding his true feelings or intentions. Sometimes he wore his mood for all to see: depressed, high, excited, angry. They were the things we were all used to, the things we could deal with. But it was the times he masked the truth that caught us off guard. The times he chalked up his wild behavior to boredom or restlessness, even our messed-up childhood. The times you didn't know whether he was high on drugs or high on the ride.

He cracked a smile, squeezing my shoulder. "Relax, little brother, I'm good. Everything is good."

Warning bells started sounding in my head, a distant jingle hinting that something wasn't right. But before I could push him for answers, we were swarmed by people. "Great set, Levi. I'd love to talk to you…" My brother and the man melted into the crowd, leaving me to deal with a group of women old enough to be my mother. The thought made bile burn my throat.

"Rafe, that voice, you've been holding out on us." One of them wrapped perfectly manicured nails around my arm. "So deep and sultry." She batted her heavily made up eyes at me.

"Excuse me, ladies." Riley appeared, flicking her hair off her shoulder. "But I need to borrow Rafe for a second."

The woman beside me pouted, her free hand dipping into her purse. Before I could step away, she pressed something into my hand.

"Call me," she mouthed, licking her bottom lip, hunger blazing in her eyes.

Jesus. Women like her were a dime a dozen. It didn't matter I was barely twenty and not legally old enough to buy them a drink. I was Rafe fucking Hunter and women all wanted their chance to bed a rock star.

"Going to keep that?" Riley dropped her gaze to my fist as we walked away from the women.

"Never do."

"Is it always like that?"

"What do you think?" She gave me a weak smile. "Thanks for the save, though. I appreciate it."

"Yeah, well, despite what your brother might think about me, I really do have your best interests at heart." Riley flagged down a bartender and ordered. "Margarita extra lime, please. Rafe?"

"Just a beer please." I slid onto the stool next to her, tapping my fingers against the black gloss counter.

"Your set was great."

"Thanks. It's not our usual crowd."

"Levi seemed to win them all over in the end. Alistair is in high demand." Her eyes flicked over to a booth where Alistair was seated with a group of suits, no doubt negotiating the band's future.

"He's never off the clock." The bartender pushed a beer my way and I snatched it up, taking a long pull.

"Are you?" Her eyes bored into mine, asking me things I didn't want to answer. Things she had no right to assume.

"Listen, I—"

"I'm probably going to get into a shit ton of trouble for this." My brother's voice echoed over the mic, and I glanced over at the stage to find him standing there again. "But I've never been one to follow the rules, and I'm not about to start now."

A rumble of laughter reverberated around me, but I wasn't laughing. "As most of you know, we've kept our special guest under wraps until now. But she's here with us tonight, and I thought what better way to introduce her than with a song, just for you guys. Country," he said, "get up here up and sing with me."

Anger shot up my spine as I snapped my gaze to Riley. "Did you know about this?" She shook her head, her expression as surprised as mine. "Ali?" I asked.

"If he did... he didn't breathe a word of it to me." An indignant sigh left her lips.

I searched the darkened room for Letty, hoping she would be there to intervene. I might have been nothing but a cold-hearted dick to Eva since she arrived, but I knew her better than anyone on this tour and I knew she wouldn't want to be ambushed like this, not where performing was concerned.

"I'm going to find—" The words dried on my tongue as the spotlight found Eva and she walked gracefully on stage.

"Ladies and gentlemen," my brother drawled, "our special guest and the new sweetheart of country, Miss Evangeline Walker." He held out his hand and she took it without missing a beat. It was so damn perfect it almost looked rehearsed, but I saw the tightness around her eyes, the thin press of her lips as she smiled.

Eva might have been fooling every single person in the room, but she wasn't fooling me.

Levi covered his mic and leaned in to whisper something to her. Her eyes widened as she shook her head, but then he spoke again and her expression softened giving way to a small nod. "She said yes, thank fuck," Levi said to the rest of us, "or that could have been all kinds of awkward."

Someone ran on stage and handed Eva an acoustic guitar. She slipped the strap over her shoulder and familiarized herself with the instrument while Levi had someone bring him a stool. My brother never sat down to sing. He liked to perform. To strut up and down the stage or prowl or even crawl. But here, in a small club in Charlotte, Levi Hunter sat and performed a cover version of *Running Up That Hill*, while Eva gave an almost note-perfect performance of her own. She even provided flawless backing vocals.

"They look good together up there," Riley said as they went into the last verse of the song. It was an innocent enough comment, but her words stung all the same.

Because she was right—they did look good together.

But that was the point, wasn't it?

To let Eva's light smother Levi's darkness. To soften his jagged edges and make him more relatable to our younger fans.

Eva was here to fix what Levi had broken. But as I watched them weave together a note-perfect rendition of one of Levi's most favorite songs ever, I couldn't help but think she might end up fixing more than just his reputation.

CHAPTER SEVEN

EVA

LEVI PROWLED TOWARD ME, slinging his arm around my shoulder and pulling me into his side. "How does it feel, Angel? That's all for you." He tipped his head to the crowd. There wasn't a single person in the club not clapping or cheering or whistling.

"I..." Words failed me. I'd been unimpressed when Levi ambushed me like that, but Letty had told me to embrace it for what it was: a chance to warm up before the opening show tomorrow. As she'd also pointed out, everyone would know who the Black Hearts special guest was come tomorrow night anyway. So I could either go along with the plan or I could surprise everyone and reveal myself on my terms.

So I'd done it.

I'd actually done it and the crowd had loved it. Not that it would have mattered much if they hadn't. Performing with Levi was like walking a tightrope. Dangerous and unpredictable, but a total rush.

I still felt like I was flying.

"Speechless looks good on you," he said around a wicked smirk. "What do we think ladies and gents?" Levi crooned into the mic. "Do we think she passes the Levi Hunter test?"

Test.

It was another damn test.

I rolled my eyes at him, too caught up in the moment to care, and he rewarded me with a dark chuckle. "Fuck yeah, she does." Levi's eyes locked on mine, the weight of his stare sending a confusing shiver up my spine.

"We'll need to keep an eye on you." Hudson jumped up onto the stage and handed Levi a bottle of water before passing one to me. "Or else you'll being stealing our front man right out from under us."

"Like I'd ever leave you bunch of misfits." Levi collared his friend in a headlock, ruffling his hair.

"That was freakin' awesome." Letty was waiting for me as I walked off stage. "Seriously, Eva, I've seen a lot of live music, but the way the two of you complimented each other... wow. It isn't any wonder Alistair wanted you on the tour."

Heat bloomed along my neck and into my cheeks. "I can't believe I just did that."

"Believe it, girl." She looped her arm through mine, guiding me toward the bar. Strangers called my name, congratulating me as we passed them, and a couple of important looking men tried to shove cards into my hands. I smiled politely, letting Letty do her thing and get us to the bar in one piece. Travis and Grayson hovered close by, moving in the shadows, their eyes permanently trained on me. I hadn't been certain when Alistair first introduced me to them, but now there was an odd kind of reassurance knowing they were there.

"What'll it be?" Letty asked me as she waved to the bartender.

"Just a soda please."

"No way. You just performed with Levi freakin' Hunter and you killed it. This deserves a drink. I'm talking straight up liquor."

"I'm not twenty-one."

"The same rules don't apply here as they do out there in the real world."

"You're saying this isn't real?" I half-teased, because it sure as hell didn't feel real. It felt like a dream. One I would surely wake up from any second.

"What'll it be, ladies?" The bartender asked.

"Two Cherry Pies, please. Extra cherries."

His eyes lingered on Letty's ample cleavage. When he disappeared to make our drinks, I leaned in close and said, "I think you have an admirer."

"I think he admires my boobs." She chuckled. "Having fun yet?"

"I am feelin' so many things right now I don't even know where to start."

"Feeling is good. Soak it up, Eva. That's all we can do. Live each moment and make memories." Letty gave me an easy smile before hopping up onto a stool and looking out over the crowd.

I liked Letty. I liked her a lot. It was a relief to have her in my corner. But even though having her by my side made me feel at ease, she wasn't Molly.

My chest tightened and I knew I needed a minute to catch my breath. "Hey," I said, "do you know where the restroom is?"

"Sure," Letty replied, pointing toward a neon sign hanging over a dark archway. "You want me to come with you?"

It would have been easy to say yes, to let her hold my hand and babysit me. But she was right, I had to embrace my newfound life. "No, I'm good. Wait for me here though?"

"You got it."

The second I got up and started moving, I felt Travis follow. Stopping, I turned around and said, "I'm only goin' to the bathroom." His brows furrowed and I clarified, "You can't follow me in there."

How was I supposed to catch my breath with him always two steps behind me?

"Didn't plan on it." The faintest of smiles broke his serious expression. "I'll wait right outside."

"Am I not safe here?" The words just poured out. It wasn't that I objected to having a bodyguard, I didn't, but I didn't exactly understand how these things worked either.

"You're perfectly safe, Ms. Walk... Eva." Travis's expression softened. "But I'm still coming with you."

"Because it's your job?"

He nodded. "And because your safety is my number one priority."

"Well, okay then, I guess. Thank you." I didn't know what I was thanking him for, but our exchange settled some of the nervous energy bouncing around my stomach.

I found the restroom without difficulty. After washing my hands and checking myself in the mirror, I slipped into the hallway connecting the restrooms to the main room, grinding to a halt when I saw Rafe and Riley at the smaller bar. She was laughing at something he said. Jealousy burned through me which was ridiculous. Rafe wasn't mine and they were only talking. But I couldn't deny it hurt seeing him with her. Just another thing I'd underestimated when I agreed to come on tour with the band. There would be girls, lots of them if the news stories were anything to go by. Levi and Hudson seemed to live the playboy life more than Rafe and Damon, but I wasn't a fool. I knew there would be other girls.

Girls who weren't me.

Knowing it and seeing it were two different things though.

"Eva, is there a problem?" I sensed Travis inch closer, but I couldn't make myself move. Riley was touching Rafe. Her hand was rested casually on his arm, as if it belonged there.

As if *she* belonged there with him.

"I... uh, what?" Forcing myself to meet his concerned gaze, I smiled. "No, I'm fine. Thank you for waitin'."

He gave me a sharp nod before stepping aside to let me pass. I made a beeline for Letty and my sugary drink. It was only supposed to be one, but after seeing Rafe and Riley, something told me I was going to need a couple more if I was going to survive the rest of the night.

———

"Eva, baby, come dance with me." Hudson crooked his finger, a wicked glint in his eye as he prowled toward me.

"Oh, hell no," I said, backing up. Letty cackled beside me, making no effort to protect me from the Black Hearts drummer.

"One dance," he drawled. "You've been sitting here like Debbie Downer all night."

"I have no—"

He reached me, pressing a single finger against my lips, stealing me of both my breath and my argument. "One dance, Angel. Let's go." Hudson curled his hand around mine and yanked me toward the dance floor.

"It'll go a lot easier if you don't resist," Letty yelled after me.

People smiled and laughed at us as Hudson pulled me right into the center of the dance floor. "Don't tell me a country girl as hot as you can't dance?" He cocked a brow.

"You're drunk," I remarked, letting him twirl me around the floor.

"It's a party, you're supposed to get drunk." Hudson beamed at me and I couldn't deny it was hard to stay mad at him. His excitement was infectious.

Just then, the music switched gears, the latest P!nk track blasting into the club. "Show me what you've got, Angel," he shouted over the music, rolling and popping his hips in a way I would never have imagined.

"You've got moves," I replied, fighting a smile.

"You haven't seen anything yet." Hudson closed the space between us, hooking his arm around my waist and pulling me flush to his chest. My body was pliant in his hold as he swayed and jerked us to the beat. "He's watching you know." Hudson's warm breath tickled my ear. He flattened his hand against my back as he swung us around so that I could see who he was talking about.

Rafe.

My breath caught.

His eyes were narrowed, intensity rolling off him as he watched one of his best friends dance with me. It was almost impossible to figure out what he was thinking; his expression clouded with so much emotion I felt a little winded.

"He's not fooling anyone," Hudson went on. "But the question is, what you gonna do about it?"

I reared back, startled. "You're lovin' this, aren't you?"

"Loving it? Rafe's been nothing but a miserable fuck since Camdena."

He had?

But that didn't make any sense.

"And what about you?" I asked, desperate to deflect the attention from me to him. I needed to clear my head, process what he was saying.

What he was implying.

I risked peeking over at Rafe again, but he was gone.

"What the fuck is that supposed to mean?" Hudson growled the words, but I saw the amusement in his eyes. Everything was a game to him. But what I couldn't quite figure out was if it was real or a front.

"Nothin'." My brow quirked suggestively but I kept my lips pressed together.

Hudson accepted my silence, refocusing his efforts on moving me around the dance floor like a rag doll. It was completely over the top, but by the time we were done, my sides hurt from laughing and I hadn't felt so alive in a really long time.

"Someone looks like they had fun out there," Damon said as I accepted a much-needed bottle of water from him.

"Best time of her life," Hudson winked at me before chugging down his beer.

I glanced around looking for the Hunter brothers. I spied Levi in the middle of a group of people, his hands moving maniacally as he told them something.

"Looking for someone?"

My eyes slowly lifted to Damon's. "No."

"If you say so."

"I do," I said defiantly, hopping up onto a stool and switching my water for a cocktail. Letty was busy flirting with the bartender from earlier. Riley and Alistair were entertaining a group of industry looking people. I couldn't help but notice if she sat any closer to him, she'd be in his lap. I snickered.

First Alistair. Then Rafe. And now Alistair again. Maybe Letty was right. Maybe Riley was only interested in working her way up the ladder.

"What's funny?" Damon asked, nursing his drink.

"This... everythin'." I let out a weary sigh. I'd only had a couple of drinks, but I felt the effects swimming in my veins. Or maybe it was the aftereffects of dancing with Hudson. Either way, I felt kind of weightless. Drifting in my own body.

"You're drunk."

"Am not," I grinned, spinning the stool, my head rolling on my shoulders.

Okay, so maybe I was a little tipsy.

Damon pulled out his cell phone and texted someone. The next thing I knew, Travis appeared. "Time to go, Eva." Damon doubled in front of my eyes and I blinked, grinning like an idiot.

"You look funny."

"Shit, how many did she drink?" Letty was here now.

"Two, maybe three. But she had a ton of water."

"She's not used to it."

"I am riiiight here you know? I can hear you." My words sounded slurred.

Whoa. Being drunk was weird. The room was spinning and my skin was vibrating in the best kind of way.

"I'll take her to the car," Travis said.

"I'm coming," Letty grabbed my hand.

"Actually, Letty, I might need your help with that." Damon pointed over to where Levi was. He looked funny too, his body shimmering and splitting into two.

"Fine, Travis can take Eva to the car and we'll round up the guys."

"There's still a big crowd out front."

"Then we'd better hope they don't see us," Damon grimaced before checking his cell. "Take care of her. Rafe will meet you at the car."

"Rafe, but I—"

"Go with Travis," Letty said, brushing the hair from my face. "We'll be right behind you."

Travis pressed his hand against the small of my back and started guiding me across the room. "How are you holding up?" he asked.

"I don't feel so good," I admitted, the small amount of liquor from the night sloshing in the pit of my stomach. That had escalated quickly.

"Nothing some water and a good night's sleep won't cure. Come on." No one paid us much attention as we slipped out of the back entrance. There were two more bodyguards waiting.

And Rafe.

Gosh, he looked so good in his usual dark jeans and tight-fitting t-shirt. He took one look at me and strode over. "What happened?" he asked Travis.

Not me.

My bodyguard.

"She drank a little too much."

"Three drinks. I had three measly drinks." I shrugged out of his hold but jerked too forcefully almost losing my balance.

"Easy there." Rafe caught me, his hands planting on my hips, steadying me. My eyes fluttered closed, his touch burning through me like wildfire. "The others?"

"Damon and Letty are rounding up Levi and Hudson as we speak."

My body melted into Rafe's side as he and Travis continued talking. The weightlessness I'd felt earlier began to shift, making my limbs heavy and my eyes sleepy.

"Come on," Rafe murmured, guiding me into one of the SUVs. He climbed in after me. "You need a bottle of water?"

"I... I think I'm okay." I sank into the plush leather seats. "Where were you?" The words spilled from my lips. "Earlier," I added at Rafe's confused expression. "I was dancing with Hudson and you were watchin' me... I mean us... you were watchin' us and then you were gone."

Like before, a little voice whispered. But I swallowed the words. I'd already said too much. Silence enveloped us. Rafe didn't answer and I drifted further into oblivion. His sudden cussing yanked me back into consciousness.

"Fuck, where are they?" he grumbled, checking his cell phone.

"We've got a group of Die Hearts heading this way," Travis said from upfront. "We need to leave, now. Before we're swarmed."

"Shit, yeah. Okay." His fingers flew across the screen, his hair falling over his eyes. I wanted to crawl forward and brush it away, to see his gray eyes I loved so much. But I could barely move.

"They're going to follow us in the other car as soon as it's clear for them to leave," Rafe told Travis. The passenger door swung open and another bodyguard climbed in and then we were moving, tires screeching, car lurching forward.

I pressed a hand to my stomach, deep breathing. "Here." A bottle of water appeared under my nose, a tattooed arm holding it.

"Thanks," I said, aware that we were now all alone, thanks to Travis rolling up the partition.

The water was cool as it sluiced down my throat. But it was nothing compared to the way Rafe watched me from across the SUV.

"Why do you hate me so much?"

"Hate you?" he sounded stunned. "I don't hate you, Eva."

"But you don't want me here?"

"I don't."

I was glad to be drunk. It numbed the pain I knew I would have otherwise felt at his honesty.

"Then I'm sorry to disappoint you."

Rafe shifted forward, his knees brushing mine. "You danced with Hudson, why?"

"Because he asked me. Because although he's a pain in the ass, he makes me laugh." Rafe's lips thinned and I was sure I caught a flash of jealousy in his murky eyes. "Riley wants you," I blurted out.

"Riley?"

"I saw the two of you talkin'. I might be a small-town girl, but I know how a girl looks at a guy when she wants somethin'."

He didn't flinch, didn't show an ounce of emotion. I don't know how he did it. Rafe had been so different in Camdena. Warm and tactile and gentle. He'd been everything I never knew I needed. But sitting here, even with the liquor swimming in my veins distorting things, it still felt like I was sitting opposite a different person.

Like my Rafe had been nothing more than a fantasy.

CHAPTER EIGHT

EVA LOOKED SO FUCKING CUTE. A sleeping angel sprawled out across the seat. I'd noticed her crashing when she was chewing me out about Riley. That shit would have been funny if it was anyone but Eva confronting me about it.

Fucking Riley.

I didn't like Riley and I certainly didn't want her. But Eva had noticed us talking, *watched* us talking, if her assessment of the situation was anything to go by. Her jealousy shouldn't have satisfied me as much as it did, but it made my heart fucking soar knowing that even after how I'd ghosted her, she still cared.

There hadn't been any chance to tell Eva I got weird vibes from Riley too, or that the band's new assistant had made me feel as uncomfortable as shit when she'd laid her hand on my arm as if we were old friends.

Or worse.

Lovers.

She had to be almost a decade my senior, maybe a couple years younger than that. Either way, it seemed skeezy that she was making it obvious I could have her if I wanted her. In fact, there were so many things wrong with that picture I didn't know where to start. But three stood out like huge fucking neon warning signs.

One: I was ninety-nine percent sure she was banging Alistair.

Two: She was our PA, and that shit was off-limits.

Three: I was completely and utterly hung up on Eva still.

There was no use denying it. Damon knew. Hudson knew. Even Letty suspected something. It didn't change anything—it couldn't—but at least I could admit it for what it was.

I cared for Eva.

I'd never stopped.

My eyes traced the planes of Eva's face, moving down over the soft curves of her body. Her chest rose and fell with deep breaths, hinting at what was underneath. I didn't need a visual reminder though. I remembered how she felt. How soft her skin was and how good it felt having her pressed up against me. Shit. I needed to get a grip. Running a hand through my hair, I let out an exasperated breath. Eva was my own personal version of hell, taunting me with everything I wanted and could never have.

I knew how good she tasted, how perfectly she fit against my body. I knew the little sounds she made when she came undone. I knew how addictive her touch was. How badly I'd burned for her that weekend of the Talent Showdown final.

But none of that mattered, because Eva was off-limits. A complication the band didn't need. Not now. Not ever.

"No... no," she cried in her sleep. "Cody, don't leave me. Don't go."

Cody? My spine straightened. Who the fuck was Cody?

I held my breath, waiting for more, but Eva didn't cry out again. Instead, she nestled into the seat, sighing softly. The partition lowered and Fenton, my bodyguard, stuck his head through the gap, "We're almost at the hotel."

"Thanks, man."

"How is she?" His eyes flicked past me to the sleeping girl opposite.

"She'll live."

He gave me a sharp nod. It didn't surprise me that Eva had already won over the bodyguards. The band was a handful to protect, but someone like Eva was a dream. Unassuming, humble, and so fucking beautiful it hurt.

Two minutes later, the SUV rolled to a stop and Travis and Fenton climbed out. The back door swung open and Eva's bodyguard peered inside. "We need to wake her," he said.

"Help me get her out," I said, cutting him off.

Travis's brow rose in question, but I ignored him, scooping Eva's ragdoll frame off the seat. Travis reached in to help me and between the two of us we got her out of the SUV in one piece.

"I'll carry her..."

"Let me." The words tumbled out before I could stop them.

Fenton had already gone ahead leaving just Travis. He glanced at Eva cradled in his arms and then looked at me.

"Should I be worried?"

"No, but I'd appreciate it if you kept this to yourself."

He gave me a stiff nod before gently placing Eva in my arms. I should have just let him take her, but I didn't want to let go, not yet. Not when being in the SUV with her, just the two of us, had been the first time in weeks I felt like I could breathe.

Travis led the way, waiting for me to enter the service elevator. Fenton shot Travis a questioning look, but he shook his head. Travis and his men could be discreet, it came hand in hand with protecting people like us. But this felt different. This felt like me making a statement.

A statement I had no right to make.

It was too late now though. Eva was out cold in my arms and I had no intention of letting her go until she was safely tucked up in her suite.

Seconds later, the elevator doors pinged open. Travis stepped out first, checking to make certain it was clear. "Okay," he said. "Fenton, you take point at the end of the hall. I'll help Rafe get Eva into her room."

My bodyguard nodded, bringing a hand to his ear. "The other car just left. Hudson took a hit though."

"What the fuck?" I balked.

"Don't worry. It was just a stiletto to the head. He'll live."

"Jesus," I mumbled. Same crazy shit, different fucking city.

"Let's move out." Travis ushered me down the empty hall. I knew the girls were sharing a suite. I also knew if Letty found me in there with Eva it would only fuel her suspicions.

I needed to get in, make sure Eva was okay, and then get the hell out of there.

Travis stopped at a door a few down from my own suite and let us inside. "Her room is on the right."

"Thanks." I padded across the room with Eva in my arms. Shouldering open the door, I slipped inside. It was similar to our suite, although smaller. I'd stayed in so many hotels up and down the country they all looked the same to me now.

Eva groaned, her eyes fluttering open. "R- Rafe?" she smiled up at me and fuck if it wasn't like a gunshot to my heart. "What's goin' on?"

Yanking back the covers, I laid her down gently, fighting the urge to brush her cheek. "We're back at the hotel. You fell asleep."

"I did?" She tried to sit up, her body failing her.

"It's late, you should get some rest. You have a big day tomorrow."

The grueling pace of the tour would keep us busy. I'd be able to avoid her, to avoid any more moments like this.

"Where is everyone?" Eva tried to shake off her leather jacket.

"They'll be here soon." I smothered a laugh, watching her struggle. "Here, let me." Barely touching her, I pulled the material free of her arms.

"Thanks. My head hurts."

"It was those three cocktails."

"Three? Ah, jeez, I'm never livin' this down, am I?"

I backed up, putting some much-needed space between us. "Your secret's safe with me." Eva's eyelids began to flutter, and I said, "I should go," as I began to inch toward the door.

"Rafe, wait..." The way she said my name stopped me dead in my tracks. "I don't know what I did wrong, but I'm sorry." She nestled into the pillow and was asleep within seconds.

I wanted to wake her and tell her the truth—that she'd done nothing, that this was just the way it had to be.

I didn't though.

Because her knowing the truth would only make it harder, and it wasn't fair to her. So I buried the words and forced myself to leave her lying there. The girl who owned my heart even if she didn't know it.

I'd moved closer, close enough to touch her. Leaning down, I ghosted my fingers over her face before pressing a single kiss to her forehead.

"My Eva," I whispered.

My Starshine.

———

"WHAT THE HELL HAPPENED TO YOU?" I SAID AS THE GUYS ALL PILED into the suite. Hudson had a wad of paper towels pressed up against his forehead.

"Crazy bitch almost took out my eye."

"Let me guess. Another Die Heart you promised to call and never did."

"Fuck off. You know I never promise to call." He sank down onto the couch. "Not how I saw the night ending."

"Why the fuck did we have to leave anyway?" Levi grunted, uncapping a soda.

"Eva wasn't feeling great," Damon replied.

"You mean Little Miss Lightweight couldn't handle her liquor?"

"Hud." I levelled him with a hard look.

"She's going to need to build some stamina if she's going to keep up with us."

My spine snapped straight. What the fuck did that mean?

"She's not *in* the band," Damon took the words right out of my mouth. "There's no reason she has to hang with us all the time."

"She should though," Levi said, a strange expression passing over his face. "She's... different."

"You mean you finally met your match?" Hudson cackled, wincing when Levi's bottle cap pinged off his head. "Not cool, fucker."

My brother flipped him off. "How'd you end up riding back with her?" he asked me.

"I was getting some air and Travis showed up with Eva. We had to scramble when the Die Hearts realized we were on the move."

"Fucking fangirls. Can't live with 'em, can't live without 'em." Hudson let out a heavy sigh.

"What was that anyway, back at the club when you pulled Eva up on stage?" I asked Levi. "Alistair put you up to that?"

"What do you think?"

"You did it to piss him off." Of course he had.

"He'll thank me tomorrow when our name is all over the papers."

But it wasn't just our names that would be everywhere, it was Eva's too. But as usual, my brother hadn't looked past his own selfish motivations.

"You think she realizes she's about to become the most envied girl in the country?" Hudson said.

"Envied... or hated." Damon grimaced.

"She can handle it." Levi sounded so certain, I wasn't sure I'd heard him right.

One song.

They'd sung one song together and he was acting like he had her all figured out.

Jealousy burned through me.

"Let's hope so." I stood up, needing to get away from him. "Or else the next five months are going to be a fucking disaster." Without another word, I headed for the room I was sharing with Damon. I knew he wouldn't follow though, not yet.

I needed some space. Chance to catch my breath after everything that had happened tonight. But in the quiet empty space of the room, I didn't find solace. I found nothing but regrets.

And the lingering feeling that I'd made a huge fucking mistake.

———

THE NEXT MORNING, I PADDED INTO THE SUITE TO FIND MY BAND mates all sitting around the table looking like someone had died. "Who died?" I asked.

It wasn't until I saw Alistair standing there, I knew that something had happened. Damon pushed a newspaper toward me. "It could have been worse."

My eyes drank in the headline. *Sweetheart of country parties with bad boy of rock.* The article brushed over Eva's impeccable performance, ignored the fact Levi had invited her up on stage to perform. Instead, they'd painted the entire night as some liquor-fueled party that ended with her being carted away by security.

"This is your idea of repairing our reputation," I seethed, forcing down the words I really wanted to say. But this couldn't only be about Eva, not with Alistair here.

He stepped forward, running a hand down his face. "I tried to bury the story, but you know how it goes. Sometimes we win, sometimes we lose. Damon's right, it could have been worse."

Yeah, at least no one had snapped a photo of me climbing into the SUV with her.

"You said everyone was vetted last night. NDA's, the whole nine yards."

Alistair grimaced. "We think it was a Die Heart. A couple of them slipped past club security and managed to get inside. We didn't find out until it was too late."

My fist clenched at my side. "Does she know?"

"She's still sleeping." At least Alistair had the decency to look concerned. "Letty will tell her when she wakes up. But let me make something very clear; Eva knew what she was signing up for. It's not your job to protect her from this." His eyes ran over each of us, but I felt the weight of his stare the most.

"After tonight's show, no one will give a flying fuck if she partied too hard." Levi's conviction was almost believable if it wasn't so naïve.

Fans were fickle. They could love and adore you one minute and want to burn you at the stake the next. We were lucky for the most part. But we were guys, a fact that came with a different set of standards. It was okay for us to sleep around and get drunk and verbally attack the paparazzi. The same could rarely be said for female artists.

"Look," Alistair went on, "we all knew it was going to present a different dynamic having Eva on the tour, but the PR team is handling it. Now that Eva's name is out there, we can get the ball rolling on her spinning her story."

Alistair talked as if keeping Eva's name out of the promotional campaign in the run up to the tour had been his idea all along. Thanks to Hudson's more than friendly relationship with Sally though, an intern at the label, we'd heard that Eva and her parents had walked into the meeting with legal with their own list of demands, one being that her name was kept out of the press until the first show. Part of me wondered if it was to ensure Eva could walk away anytime up until the first show and right back into her regular life without any consequence.

As it was, it didn't matter now. She was here and she wasn't going anywhere. Which meant once she woke up, her whole life was going to be flipped upside down. We'd all known it would happen. Whether it was tomorrow after our first show, or now after Levi's little stunt last night. But knowing it and watching it play out in front of your eyes were two different things entirely.

"You good?" Damon whispered as Alistair took a call.

Running a hand down my face, I inhaled a ragged breath. "Yeah, I'm good." The lie soured on my tongue.

But I was used to the lies. The half-truths and secrets. I was used to showing people what they wanted to see—what they needed to see.

"Okay," Alistair said, pocketing his cell, "I just spoke to PR and *The Rock Report* and *Country Music Weekly* are going to drop an exclusive press release about Eva. Once that hits, it'll drown out the story in the Charlotte Post and we can focus on the tour."

"Let's just hope you're right about this." I held his stare, wishing I could voice my concerns.

"Well, one thing's for sure," Hudson said, "there's no going back now."

He was right—we couldn't go back.

Having Eva here and not *having* her was one of the hardest things I'd ever done, but I still wouldn't have ever wanted to go back to a time when I didn't know her.

CHAPTER NINE

EVA

"Eva, baby, is that you? Oh, thank goodness. Gavin, it's Eva."

"Hey, Mom," I chuckled. "What's up?"

I'd finally plucked up the courage to call her back after a handful of missed calls. I knew why she was calling and I'd wanted to avoid her projecting any concerns on me before the opening show tonight.

"Don't 'what's up' me, young lady," she chided. "I read the newspapers, and I have to say Eva, I did not expect this."

"Mom, calm down, it's nothing."

"Nothin'? *Nothin'!*" Her shrill voice pierced my ears. "You were at a club, drunk. *Drunk,* Eva. And you've only been gone a couple of days."

"Mom we talked about this. The papers will say all kinds of things about me. You can't believe everything you read. You can't—"

"Eva, sweetheart," my dad's deep voice came over the line. "How's the head?" He chuckled.

"I'll live."

"I've got to say, I was a little surprised."

"You and me both. I can assure you it won't happen again in a hurry."

"I'm real glad to hear it." I heard his smile. "Just tell me one thing. Was it as bad as they made it sound?"

"No." I swallowed over the lump in my throat. "But please, reassure Mom for me. I don't want her thinking I'm being reckless. I'm not."

"Eva, we talked about this. You're eighteen. This is the opportunity of a lifetime. We want you to embrace it, sweetheart. Just keep your wits about you and be careful, okay?"

"I will, Dad. My assistant is great and my bodyguard doesn't leave my side. Everythin' is okay, I promise."

"Atta girl." Pride lingered in his voice.

"How'd you even hear about it anyway?" Alistair had reassured me the story had only broken locally.

"Mom set up a Google alert for your name."

"Of course she did," I grumbled, imagining her glued to the computer waiting for the alert to sound. "She can't do that."

"Try tellin' her that," Dad replied, and I heard the smile in his voice. "If it keeps her sane, leave her be. She knows you're sensible, sweetheart, and she knows you're in good hands. If you weren't, I wouldn't have let you get in that SUV with Mr. Portman. Now don't you have a show to prepare for?"

My gaze flicked to the wall clock. It was a little past five. I still had time before I had to be on stage. A shiver ran up my spine, imagining all the fans pouring into the arena. All seventeen thousand of them. Thanks to Alistair's press release, most of them would know who to expect tonight. They would know all about the *Sweetheart of Country*.

"Put Mom back on, please." Despite her over the top theatrics, I still needed her to know I was okay.

"Sure thing, sweetheart. Show them what you're made of out there tonight, my sweet girl. You got this."

"Thanks, Dad."

"Hi, baby," Mom sniffled, and I groaned.

"Mom, no waterworks, remember?" I'd made her promise she wouldn't cry every time we talked.

"I'm sorry, sweetheart. I'll do better, I promise."

"Mom, I had three drinks. I want you to know it wasn't like they said in the news article."

"Just be careful, Eva, please. Your body is still healin'."

"I know, Mom. I won't neglect my regimen, you have my word."

"So it's your big show tonight. I still can't believe my baby girl will be singin' for all those people." Her change of subject was a relief. I didn't want the whole 'you survived cancer' talk. Not now, not when I was waiting for the biggest moment of my life.

"The arena holds seventeen thousand people, Mom; it's crazy."

"It's really somethin'. I'm so proud of you, baby, you know that, right? I always knew you were destined for great things, Eva."

Letty slipped into the room and waved a bag of chips at me. My stomach grumbled. "Mom, I need to go and finish preparin', but I'll call you after, okay?"

"Gavin, she's goin'." There was a commotion and then both their voices came over the line. "Good luck, sweetheart, we're rootin' for you."

I hung up and took a deep breath. Talking to my mom was intense. She had this way of making me question everything. I knew she didn't mean it. It was just her protective mother bear instinct. But at times, it was stifling.

"Everything okay?" Letty asked, joining me on the couch. I'd been holed up in my changing room for the last hour. Letty had helped pick out my outfit, but a team of stylists had preened and primped me within an inch of my life. My hair was in curlers and I was wearing a big fluffy robe. The whole get-up made me snort; so much so, I'd sent Molly a selfie with the caption #divalife. Of course she didn't think it was diva at all. She thought it was fantastic and insisted I video call her to show her the entire room.

"Just my mom bein' her usual overbearing self, but I think for once, I probably deserved it."

"Better to have a mom who cares than one that don't."

"Crap, I'm sorry." Guilt coiled around my words. "I didn't mean to—"

"Oh, my mom cares just fine." Letty waved me off. "But in this biz most people have a story to tell and skeletons in their closet."

That was a strange thing to say. I wanted to ask her if she meant the band, but I didn't want to pry, and I didn't want to put her in an awkward position since she was friends with them as much as she was their ex-assistant.

"How are you feeling?"

"Okay, I think. I mean, I'm terrified but I also kinda want to get it over with."

"Understandable. Half the battle is the unknown. But after the press release, I think people will be excited to see what you bring to the show."

"So I shouldn't worry about bein' booed off stage or showered with eggs then?" My lip curved in a half-smile to match my half-serious words.

"When the Die Hearts are around, you always need to worry. Those bitches are crazy." Letty smirked. "Just worry about your set and leave everything else to other people."

Just then my cell phone vibrated. "It's probably Molly," I said, reaching to retrieve it off the table.

"What does it say?"

My brows pinched as I scanned the message from the unknown number.

. . .

GOOD LUCK OUT THERE, ANGEL.

"I THINK IT'S... LEVI," I CROAKED.

"Well, well, the fucker has a heart after all. How'd he get your number?"

"You didn't give it to him?"

"Me?" Letty blanched. "What the hell would I do that for?"

"Huh, weird." I typed a quick reply, keeping it to a simple 'thanks'. I'd seen the guys in passing today, at sound check and backstage, but there hadn't been much time to talk. Not that I knew what to say after last night.

I still cringed every time I pictured Travis having to practically carry me out of the club. Letty assured me it didn't quite go down like that, but it didn't ease the embarrassment that had burned through me most of the day. I could still remember the way Rafe had carried me to my suite, how safe and protected I'd felt in his arms. He'd been so kind and caring. So possessive. Part of me wanted to believe it—believe it meant he still cared—but I didn't trust the liquor-haze that had clouded my mind. And when I'd seen him earlier, he'd barely looked twice at me, let alone asked how I was feeling

It was confusing.

But there was no time to dwell. I had a show to prepare for, and seventeen thousand Black Hearts fans to win over.

The knot in my stomach tightened, my hands trembling.

"You need to find your pre-show ritual."

"Ritual?" I frowned at Letty.

"Yeah, like your way to get in the zone. You know like Weezer playing frisbee or the Foo's doing Jäger shots. I heard from a friend of a friend that Coldplay like to do this group hug thing before they go on stage."

"We could hug." I fought a smile as my shoulders lifted in a small shrug.

"You need to find your own thing." Letty tapped her lips with a single finger. "Like naked rain dancing."

"Naked... what?" Laughter rumbled in my chest. "You're jokin' with me."

"Of course I'm joking, but it took your mind off the show, didn't it?"

"Maybe that can be my ritual. You can make lame-ass jokes and distract me."

"Hey, my jokes aren't that bad." My brow rose, and she flipped me off. "What song are you most looking forward to playing tonight?"

"I haven't really let myself think about it. Since... well, since everythin' happened, it's like my brain is wired differently."

"What do you mean?" Letty swung around, crossing her legs in front of her.

"How much do you know?"

"Only what Alistair told me. You had Non-Hodgkin Lymphoma?"

I nodded. "It was bad, really bad. I spent all junior year and most of senior year in and out of hospital. I lost my friends, my boyfriend... *ex*-boyfriend. My music. It took everythin' from me. But I lived." The words stuck in my throat. "I lived and I should have been so relieved and thankful..."

"But you don't know why."

The fact it wasn't a question only confirmed what I already knew about Letty. She was perceptive and understanding and so darn easy to talk to. I found myself wanting to open up the floodgates and let it all out. Maybe it was because she was outside of it all. She hadn't watched me go through it. She hadn't seen me at my lowest. It gave her a perspective my parents and Molly didn't have the luxury of having.

"I know I should feel grateful. I'm here, I get to live. I get to do all the things I always dreamed of. But the things I saw in hospital... the things I lost. The kids, kids who became my friends, who weren't so lucky." The word tasted bitter on my tongue, my heart clenching.

Lucky.

It's how everyone thought I should feel, but I didn't feel lucky. There wasn't a single day that went by when I didn't feel guilty. I was here and some other kids, kids like Cody, weren't.

"And now I'm here, gettin' to live out this dream, and I know it sounds stupid, but it doesn't seem fair somehow."

"Something like that changes you, Eva. It makes you question everything you thought you knew." Letty gave me a warm smile. "And that's okay. Not everything in life has a bigger meaning or a higher purpose. You survived because it wasn't your time to go."

Silence filled the space between us. I wanted to heed Letty's words. I did. But it wasn't that simple.

"You should tell them, you know," Letty said quietly. "Before it comes out in the press."

"Alistair said they'll handle it if it does."

I wasn't ready to have my life plastered all over the press. I knew it was a risk, but Alistair had assured me and my parents that the PR team had some of the best staff in the country.

"I know what Alistair said, but all it takes is one journo looking to break the story of his career." She gave me a pointed look. "The guys should know, Eva, and it should come from you."

"I don't want them to pity me," I sighed. "I don't want them to look at me and see the girl who survived when she shouldn't have. Somethin' like what I went through doesn't only change the person, Letty, it changes how people see them."

"Well, I see you, and I think you're pretty damn awesome." Her lip curved. "Just think about it, okay?"

"Okay."

"They like you," Letty said. "It's hard not to."

"Is that your way of sayin' *you* like me?"

"You're growing on me, country girl." She stuck her tongue out at me. "Now, come on. No more distractions. You have a show to get ready for."

I inhaled a shaky breath.

I could do this.

I could totally do this.

———

THE NOISE OF THE CROWD REVERBERATED DEEP INSIDE MY CHEST AS I took my place on the darkened stage. Some chanted Black Hearts, some called their names. *Levi. Hudson. Damon... Rafe.* They were close by, watching. I knew because they had been right there when Letty finally ushered me out of the dressing room. It warmed my heart, knowing that they wanted to wish me luck, despite Hudson whispering for me to, 'break a leg'. Even Rafe had managed to offer me words of support.

I couldn't find the words to tell them I couldn't process anything they were saying. My heart was beating a little too hard, my palms were sweaty, and the roar of blood in my ears was like nothing I'd ever experienced. By the time one of the stage assistants pushed me out of the wings, I felt sure I would explode into a puddle of blood and guts.

The plan was simple. Me, my guitar, and my voice. Production had wanted something flashier, something more in keeping with the upbeat and chaotic staging of the band's performance. But Alistair had given them their orders. I was to remain stripped back and low key. A stark contrast to the four guys currently burning holes into the side of my face.

The crowd grew fractious, anticipation crackling in the air like lightning bolts. The lights were my cue. Until they blazed down on me, I was just a girl hiding in the shadows. It was impossible to make out anything other than the sea of Black Hearts fans. For those few seconds, I soaked up my last shreds of anonymity. Knowing I was standing on the precipice of something life-changing.

I adjusted my guitar and moved closer to the mic. Production had also wanted me to play something newer, but there was no way on Earth I was giving up my Gibson. She was a part of me. An extra limb I was lost without. The lights came up, blinding me, but it was nothing compared to the noise. A surge of adrenaline shot through me as I grabbed the mic and said, "Hello, Charlotte. I'm Eva Walker and I'm goin' to play some songs for you. I hope you like them."

I didn't think.

I didn't hesitate.

I just played.

My fingers swept over the frets as I closed my eyes and sang.

The days roll by and the clouds set in,
*   And it feels like I don't know where to begin*

The seconds tick by and time moves on
*   And it feels like I don't know who I've become*

I clutch my heart, I beg it to beat
*   I pray for a sign that I've got what it takes*
*   To be the girl I know I can be*
*   To dig deep inside and let myself be free*
*   'Cos I'm just a girl with the devil on her shoulder*
*   Don't know which road to choose but I'm not lookin' back*

Yeah, I'm not lookin' back... no, no, no

The arena fell into silence as my last note drifted into nothing. I felt breathless, and hot and sweaty as if I'd run a marathon. My lungs burned in the best kind of way and my skin hummed with adrenaline, every hair standing to attention. It almost didn't matter the audience was quiet.

Almost.

I frowned, the immense high slowly giving way to a soul-crushing sense of dread. But what did I expect? What had Alistair and the label expected? Fans of a band like Black Hearts Still Beat didn't want some country talent show contestant up on stage. They wanted dirty-mouthed, lawless rock stars.

Knowing I had no choice but to finish my set, I grabbed the mic just as I'd done earlier during sound check and took a deep breath. But I never got the first word out. The roar of the crowd hit me like a powerful wave.

They were applauding.

Seventeen thousand people were applauding... for me.

An involuntary smile tugged at my mouth as I scrambled to get my head around the fact they were cheering for me. "I know y'all came out here to see Black Hearts tonight," the noise hit another level, raising the roof on the Spectrum Center, "but I'd really like to play you a few more songs, if that's okay?

"This one is called *Look For Me* and it's about my best friend Molly. Love ya, Mols." I was going off script but I couldn't help it. It was like the audience's energy fueled me and I wanted more.

I wanted it all.

And for the next thirty-five minutes, I got it. With every song, I flourished. I became more confident interacting with the audience, almost floored when they sung the chorus back to me of my cover of *Sweet Child O' Mine*. By the time I bounced off stage, I was smiling so wide my cheeks hurt.

"Holy shit, Eva," Letty rushed over to me, "that was freakin' amazing." She pulled me into a hug. "You did it, girl, you really did it."

Laughter bubbled up inside me, spilling from my lips. She was right. I had done it, and it felt amazing. It felt more than I could have ever imagined.

It felt like I was supposed to be there, up on stage.

"Country, get over here." Levi crooked his finger at me, and Letty chuckled.

"They've been chomping at the bit for you to come off stage."

"Was I that bad?" I smirked, and Levi snorted.

"I fear we've created a monster." He closed the distance between us with his easy swagger. "You did good, Angel. Real fucking good."

"Yeah?" I grinned back at him.

"Yeah, just don't let it go to your head, not too much anyway."

"Great set, Eva," Damon added. "But now you get to watch how the pros do it." He winked.

"Get the hell out of here," Letty said.

"Hey, where's Rafe and Hudson?" I asked, noticing they weren't here.

"Already doing their thing." He pointed to the stage and I could see them helping the roadies get their instruments set up.

"Tell Hudson I said, 'break a leg'."

Damon roared with laughter and disappeared onto the stage. They had fifteen minutes until lights up. Fifteen minutes for me to catch my breath and watch their show. I needed to pee, get a drink, and catch my breath, in that order.

But first, I'd allow myself another minute to enjoy the high.

Because everyone knew after the high came the low.

CHAPTER TEN

RAFE

THE CROWD WAS ELECTRIC. I'd had my doubts about Eva opening for us, but I didn't need to worry. They had lapped up song after song. But it was when she sang her cover of *Sweet Child O' Mine* that things changed. Eva had held the fans in the palm of her hand for eight songs, but that was the moment they fell for the girl with pain in her eyes and music in her soul.

I'd watched her from the wings. Watched as she came alive and found her rhythm. She was a natural with the crowd, talking to them as if they were old friends. It was no surprise Alistair looked like the cat who got the cream. This was all part of his master plan, and step one had gone off without a hitch. Well, minus the story about Eva in the local paper this morning. But that would all be long forgotten when her name was splashed over every music and entertainment column across the country tomorrow.

"Hey, Charlotte, are you ready to rock?" My brother elongated the last word, letting it roll off his tongue slowly. Seductively. The crowd went wild as Hudson dropped the opening beat of one of our most popular songs *Blood Runs Thicker*.

I glanced off to the side, where our team stood. Eva was watching us, her eyes big and full of wonder. I wanted to tell her how amazing she'd been, how fucking proud I was of her. But I knew they were words I would never say. Not if I wanted the tour to go smoothly, for all of us. So I played. I strummed my guitar hard and fast letting out all the frustration and tension I felt. I played until sweat rolled down my back and my heart pounded in my chest. Until my breathing was ragged and my fingers were sore.

Yet, it still wasn't enough.

I felt like I was chasing a high I couldn't quite grasp.

After six songs, Levi took a breather, grabbing a bottle of water and chugging it down before emptying the rest over his head. He shook it out, sending water droplets spraying everywhere. Damon laughed, Hudson too. Even I managed a smile. It was hard not to when we were on stage together, doing something we all loved. Something that bound us together.

Something that had saved us.

"I think it's time to switch it up a little," Levi said over the mic. "You all met our good friend Evangeline earlier." The crowd exploded. "Well, how would you like to get her out here to perform with us?"

What. The. Actual. Fuck?

We hadn't discussed this.

We hadn't even contemplated having Eva join us on stage. It was one thing for Levi to get her on stage in some small downtown club, but to bring her on stage *now*... I searched for Alistair in the wings, half-expecting him to look shocked or pissed. But he didn't. He looked smug. There was no way he was in on this, was he?

I didn't know what the hell to think anymore.

Alistair looked like a man who was watching his greatest plan unfold while Eva looked ready to puke at any second.

"It would seem Eva's gone all shy on us." Levi smirked at her across the stage. "She might need a little persuasion. Can you help me out? Eva, Eva, Eva..." Levi's voice filled the air but soon it wasn't only my brother chanting, it was the whole arena.

"Get out here, Country," Levi chuckled. "We've got a show to get on with."

Eva stumbled on stage looking like a deer caught in the headlights, guitar cradled in her arms.

"Don't look so worried, Angel. I don't bite." Levi crooked his finger at her. I wanted to grab her arm and shield her from his madness, to protect her from his games and showboating. Or at least pull her to one side and ask her if she was okay with this. But Alistair was right. She'd signed on for this. She knew what my brother was capable of, and now she had to bear the consequences.

A stagehand ran on with a stool for Eva. Levi said something to her off mic and she nodded.

"Let me tell you something about this girl. The first time I met her, she had the balls to challenge me to a sing-off. Me. Levi fucking Hunter. Can you believe that?" The audience heckled but Levi continued, "So we sang. We sang and it was fucking magic. Some people say country and rock don't belong in the same sentence together. But to the skeptics I say, this is how it's done; and to the haters I say, go fuck yourselves. Because you're about to see magic happen. What d'ya say, Angel, ready to make magic with me?"

There was something about his words, the way he couldn't take his eyes off her that had my blood boiling. Eva was here to fix our reputation. She wasn't here to be Levi's personal plaything. But he was standing there, looking at her like she was his new favorite shiny toy.

And Eva?

Well, she was either a great actress, or she was falling for the Levi Hunter charm, hook, line, and sinker.

I watched on, not quite able to believe what was happening, as Levi indicated for someone to bring him a stool too, and the two of them sat there and sang another stripped back version of one of his favorite classics.

By the time they were done, Eva looked radiant and Alistair wasn't the only one who looked like the cat who'd got the cream.

———

FORTY MINUTES LATER, THE LIGHTS DIMMED, AND WE FINALLY jogged off stage. "Well done, everyone." Alistair was there to greet us. "That was fantastic."

"Fantastic, Ali boy?" Levi snorted. "It was fucking epic."

"It was good, Levi, but let's not get ahead of ourselves. And we need to talk about this thing with Eva."

"Yeah, yeah," my brother barged past our manager, "we can talk later. I need to eat."

Damon caught my eye and frowned. I shrugged. Eating was better than getting high or letting off steam inside a bottle of Jack.

"Hey, where's Letty and Eva?" Hudson asked Alistair who was shooting daggers at my brother's retreating form.

"They went back to the bus."

"Already?"

"Something about Eva feeling overwhelmed. I didn't ask."

That annoyed me for some reason. Alistair was supposed to be looking out for Eva.

"I need a shower and then I could eat, I guess." Hudson pulled his sweat-soaked t-shirt off his back and balled it up to wipe his face, taking off down the hall.

"Don't wander too far, we need to be on the road tonight."

"No problem," I said. Damon gave us a nod and disappeared down the hall leaving the two of us. "Levi's stunt could have backfired tonight."

"You saw the crowd, Rafe, they lapped it up." I saw the cogs turning in Alistair's expression. He didn't like that Levi had gone off script again, but he knew it had paid off.

We all did.

It didn't mean I had to like it though.

"Is there something you want to say?" His eyes narrowed.

"Nah, I'm good. I'll make sure the guys are on the bus within the hour." I took off toward the dressing rooms. I couldn't trust myself to be around Alistair right now, or my brother. But when I passed Eva's room and heard tears, I couldn't think about anything but checking she was okay.

Slipping inside, I closed the door and turned the lock. "Eva?"

"Oh, Rafe, I... uh..." She dried her eyes, avoiding looking directly at me. "I just needed a minute."

"You're supposed to be on the bus."

"I was but I couldn't find my cell phone."

"You could have sent Letty to look for it." She had to get used to using the people around us and letting them do their jobs.

"Confession. I wanted five minutes alone."

"I can..." I thumbed to the door.

"No, don't," she blurted out, her cheeks burning the second she realized what she'd said. "I mean, you don't have to leave, unless you want to." She finally gave me her big ocean eyes, and fuck, if I wanted nothing more than to drown in them.

She was so beautiful, even with tears rolling down her cheeks.

"Did something upset you? It wasn't my brother was it? I'm sorry he ambushed you like that again."

"It's okay. I actually really enjoy performin' with him." She might as well have stabbed me in the heart. "I mean, it's petrifyin' and surreal but it's kinda fun too."

"Well you rocked it. The crowd loved you."

"Yeah?" The smile lit up her whole face. "What did you think?"

"I..." I swallowed hard. She was no longer crying, her eyes glittering with something else entirely.

"I rendered you speechless, huh? I hope that's a good thing."

Eva's laugh was like my own personal lullaby. I wanted to bottle it. To keep it with me always.

"You were fucking amazing," I finally said, breaking the thick silence.

We'd moved closer, gravitating like magnets unable to resist the pull. "Why are you here, Rafe?" she whispered.

"I heard you crying." *I wanted to see you.*

"I'm not cryin' anymore, you should probably go."

"What if I don't want to go?" *What if I want to stay here, locked in this room with you for all eternity?*

"What *do* you want, Rafe?"

You, I just want you.

I inched closer, desperate to touch her, to feel her soft skin beneath my fingers again. I needed to leave, to turn around and get the hell out of here before things went too far. Before I did something I couldn't take back. But all I could see was her on stage smiling at my brother, singing with him. Laughing with him.

When it should have been me.

Everything was so messed up, and we were only a couple days into the tour. What would it be like in a month? Two? By the time the tour ended?

"Rafe?" Eva stared up at me with lust and longing in her eyes. "What is it? What's wrong?"

Jesus, she was too good, too pure, to be stuck in the middle of this mess. She wasn't supposed to be here and yet, there a part of me that was so fucking relieved she was.

"You shouldn't be here," I said, reiterating the same thing I'd said to her too many times before. Only, my conviction was no longer there.

Hurt flashed in her eyes but it quickly gave way to anger. "Stop pretendin' you don't feel it. I know you do," she rasped. "I feel it every time you look at me. I just wish you'd tell me what happened."

Her words reverberated through me. She saw through me. It was almost a relief to know Eva knew the truth; that she knew how hard it had been keeping her at arm's length. But it was bittersweet because it still changed nothing.

Then she said five little words that made me see red. "I think Levi likes me."

"Is that right?" I deadpanned, barely holding onto the thin line of control that kept me going off the deep end. "You think my brother is going to sweep you off your feet?"

"No, I didn't... that isn't what I meant."

I crowded Eva against the wall, pressing one of my hands at the side of her head. "You think just because Levi flirts with you, it means you're special?"

"Rafe," panic filled her voice, "that isn't what I meant."

"So what, *Angel?*" I threw his nickname for Eva at her, feeling anger zip up my spine. "What exactly did you mean?"

"It should have been you, okay?" she shrieked, her words like a jagged knife slicing me open. "It should have been you reassuring me and making me feel like I can do it. It should have been you, Rafe. But it was Levi. It wasn't you and I still don't know why."

"Because I can't have you!" The words tore from my throat, raw and painful. Eva gasped, jerking back against the wall. I dropped my head to the crook of her neck, breathing her in. It was the worst possible thing I could have done because all I could imagine was kissing her there. Tasting her salty-sweet skin.

"What do you mean you can't have me?" Eva's fingers slid under my jaw and tilted my face to hers. "I was yours, Rafe. I was yours and you cast me aside like I was nothing."

Even now I couldn't tell her the truth, so I did the only thing I could think of to distract her—the one thing I'd wanted to do since she walked into Razorsharp Records HQ.

I kissed her.

My hands drifted to either side of Eva's neck, teasing the soft curls there, as I brushed my lips over hers. She opened for me willingly, letting me push my tongue inside and swirl it with her own.

Eva tasted just like I remembered.

She tasted like a huge fucking mistake. But I couldn't stop myself. I needed this. Her. I needed one more kiss to remind me that what we shared in Camdena wasn't a figment of my imagination, that it was real.

Eva's hand slid against my chest, twisting into the damp material as our tongues danced together. I didn't care if I needed a shower or a change of clothes. In that moment, I only cared about this. I should have known it wouldn't be enough, should have known the second I kissed her lips I'd want more.

So much more.

I fitted my body against hers, pressing Eva into the wall. She moaned softly, rolling her hips into me. "Rafe..." My name was a prayer on her lips.

"We can't do this," I murmured unwilling to break the kiss, tracing my mouth over her jaw and down the column of her neck.

"We can..." Eva smothered a moan when I nipped the bare skin along her collarbone. One of her hands slipped between our bodies, palming me through my jeans. If my dick was hard before it was rock solid now and desperate to feel her. But we couldn't do this.

We couldn't fucking do this.

Sliding my hand to the base of Eva's neck, I held her there, brushing my nose featherlight over hers. "We can't."

"Because you don't want me?"

"Want you? I fucking..." I stopped myself dead, sucking in a harsh breath. "Because you're strictly off-limits and this will complicate things, and I don't want to do that to you."

"So you're doin' this for my benefit?" She levelled me with a gut-wrenching look.

"Alistair will have my balls if I touch you. If any of us touch you."

"I don't want anyone else to touch me, Rafe. I only want you." She tried to kiss me again, grazing my lips with her own. "You're really doin' this... again?"

My jaw clenched, my silence deafening.

"Fine. I get it. Just tell me one thing and we're done here." Her gaze turned icy, the lust that had been swirling there giving way to fiery anger. "Tell me you don't want me. Look me in the eye, Rafe. Look me in the eye and tell me I'm nothin' to you."

"Eva..."

"Say it," she seethed.

But I couldn't do it.

And that was the problem—Eva clouded my judgment.

"Coward." Eva shouldered past me, catching me off guard. I slumped against the wall. "Molly was right about you, Rafe Hunter." Glaring out at me, Eva's walls slammed up and pushed me out. "I should have kicked you in the balls the second I laid eyes on you again." She yanked the door open and stormed out of the room, leaving me alone.

I should have been relieved.

I wasn't.

CHAPTER ELEVEN

EVA

"You're sure something didn't happen?" Letty asked me for the third time since I dragged my exhausted body onto the bus. It was late, I was cranky, and there was no escaping the other four people on the bus with us. Thankfully, Riley had already retired to her bunk, so I wasn't forced to sit and look at her sour face.

"Nothin' happened. I just got overwhelmed. It isn't every day a rock star drags you onstage to perform with him."

"I already told you, you don't need to worry. Everyone loved it. It's all over social media. There's even a hashtag. #hunterwalkermagic." Letty's eyes lit up. She was loving this; the whole damn team was. By all accounts, as far as opening shows went, this one had been a roaring success. Alistair was already talking about making me a permanent feature of their set which was... un-freakin-believable.

But I had other things on my mind.

Other Rafe Hunter shaped things.

He'd felt so good pressed up against me. My walls had crumbled like sand and I'd pretty much thrown myself at him. But the second his lips touched mine, I felt it. The connection between us. The tether that had rooted itself deep inside me that weekend in Camdena. I was prepared to come here and be civil—to do what I needed to do to get through the tour.

I wasn't prepared to discover Rafe still cared.

Now I knew the truth though, and I couldn't just switch off my feelings. It didn't work like that. As I was quickly discovering, *I* didn't work like that. But I was treading unchartered waters. I knew he was worried about Alistair's rules about me being off-limits. But I couldn't help wonder if there was more to it. If his complicated relationship with Levi had anything to do with why he was fighting his feelings for me.

"You don't have to sit up with me," I said to Letty. "Get some sleep, it's late."

"You're sure?" She smothered a yawn, and I nodded.

"Go. I'll see you tomorrow."

"Congratulations on your first show, Eva. I know it still doesn't feel real, but it will. Give it time and don't listen to anyone who says you don't deserve to be here because tonight you more than proved you do." She traipsed down the bus to the bathroom. It was so quiet, with only the low rumble of the engine beneath my feet, that there was nothing to drown out my thoughts.

And there were many.

I was here for my parents—to repay them for everything they'd given up for me. But now that I was here, and I'd seen Rafe again, I couldn't help but wonder if my motivations were entirely selfless. Or if a small part of me, a part I'd locked away, was here because I'd clung onto the idea that there had been something real between me and Rafe.

Because I wanted it to be real.

I *needed* it to be.

I didn't want to be that girl, the girl pining over love lost and hearts broken, I didn't. But I also refused to accept that was it. I'd felt something with Rafe, not just inside me, but coming from him. A deep-seated need that transcended attraction and lust. I filled something inside him just as he filled a missing piece of me. But I wouldn't push. Not until I had answers.

Finally, unable to sit with my thoughts for a second longer, I made my way to my bunk and climbed inside, pulling across the curtain. Soft snores drifted over from Letty's bunk while Riley mumbled something in her sleep from the bunk above. I'd only ever had a sleepover with Molly and now I shared my nights with five other people; three of whom I'd barely had time to get to know thanks to their intense schedules. But when you were assistants to the production and road managers, the very people whose job it was to make sure the tour ran without a hitch, there was a lot to do.

My mind drifted to the other bus. I wondered if Rafe was already sleeping or if he was lying awake like me. I'd heard the stories about the bands crazy tour antics but had yet to witness any. There was plenty of time yet, I supposed. I knew from my brief visit onboard their bus that it was flashier, with not one, but two artist bedrooms. I'd even asked Letty how the guys agreed who got what room, but she'd simply smirked and told me not to ask questions I wouldn't like the answers to.

I guess I'd walked right into that one.

Maybe they weren't asleep at all. Maybe Levi had them all playing some crazy drinking game or Hudson was annoying them with his lame-assed jokes. Damon would be sitting there rolling his eyes like the dad-figure I sensed he was. But I would never know because although I was on tour with them, I wasn't *with* them. They were Black Hearts Still Beat, four friends bound together through more than just their music, and I was Evangeline Walker, a small-town girl swept up in their world. They could joke with me and make me feel welcome, invite me up on stage, and treat me like one of the guys, but they would always share something special.

Something no girl would ever come between.

And I was starting to wonder if maybe that was going to be a problem.

———

"Great, Eva, hold that, right there." The photographer, a flamboyant guy named Tobias, directed over the top of his camera. "Chin down a little, eyes right at me." The flash went off in a rapid succession of *click click clicks*. "Yes, that's it, that's the one."

I let out a quiet sigh, relaxing my shoulders. I'd been positioned and posed for the last thirty minutes. There had been no time to take in the sights of Orlando. Alistair had been contacted by *The Rock Report*. Following the press release, they wanted to run a double page spread article about my joining the Blood Runs Thicker tour. I hadn't even finished my first coffee when Riley breezed onto the bus looking every bit the assistant to a huge rock band and dropped the bombshell that a car would be picking me up to take me to a hotel downtown. She'd obviously forgotten to mention the band would be coming along because when I had stumbled into the car, still half-asleep, I'd landed half in Rafe's lap. Levi and Hudson had found it all very amusing while I'd scrambled off his lap quicker than you could say 'more coffee'.

I hadn't spoken to him since. When we'd arrived at the hotel, I was ushered off into one room while the band was taken somewhere else.

"You looked great." Letty said taking the guitar from me. It wasn't mine. I wasn't sure if it was even tuned, but they'd wanted the shoot to speak to my country roots.

"I felt ridiculous," I lowered my voice. "How much longer do we have to be here?"

"The band is just finishing up and then there's the—"

"Right," the photographer hollered, "if we can get the guys in here, we can do the group shoot."

"Group shoot?" I repeated, scowling at Letty.

"I just found out."

"Of course you did," I mumbled just as the door opened and the guys piled in, laughing and joking. Rafe's expression fell the second he saw me though, clouding with desire and regret.

My stomach tightened.

"Okay, Eva, let's get you in the middle with your guitar please. Boys fill in around her." Tobias began repositioning the lighting reflector. "Levi, Rafe, if you two stand either side and Damon and Hudson take a knee at the front."

"Take a knee, really?" Hudson muttered loud enough for everyone to hear.

"Just go with it," Tobias insisted.

The guys closed in around me. "Don't look so worried, Angel," Levi smirked.

"Okay, Levi, let's have your body angled toward Eva, but I want you to look at the camera. Move in closer." I felt his breath on my cheek and my own breath caught. "And now, Eva, if you lift your guitar a little and Rafe, slide you hand around the neck too so it looks like you're both holding it up."

Rafe let out a low hiss as his hand slid up the neck of the guitar and brushed my pinky finger. Nervous energy vibrated inside me, making me feel a little lightheaded. This was too close, too intimate.

"Good, good," Tobias cooed. But it didn't feel good. It felt downright awkward, standing there wedged firmly in between the Hunter brothers. Country's rose in the middle of two thorns.

I knew there were thousands of girls out there who would pay good money to find themselves in this position, but I was too tense to enjoy it.

I caught Letty's eye, but she was too busy smothering her amusement.

"Relax, Country," Levi whispered. "It's supposed to be fun."

Fun.

I shot him a hard stare and he howled with laughter. "Someone still has their panties in a—"

"Lev," Rafe all but growled his brother's name.

"Everyone needs to lighten the hell up. That shit this morning was funny. Come on, *Evangeline*," he taunted, "you know it was funny."

My eyes slid to Levi's, narrowing. I didn't expect him to cross his eyes and pull a silly face at me. The corner of my mouth lifted as I fought a smile, refocusing on the camera. Levi was like a child. A child who was always getting up to no good but in an endearing kind of way.

"Behave," I hissed.

"Right, if everyone can look at me on three, two, one." The flash went off. "Now Damon and Hudson look up at Eva. Rafe and Levi too."

My face burned with embarrassment.

"Looking good, Eva," Hudson tried to make light of the situation, but I felt ready to combust. As if that wasn't bad enough, I was sure I felt Rafe's fingers brushing back and forth over mine. I didn't look out of fear of giving him away, but I felt it.

I felt it all the way down to my soul.

I only wished I knew what it meant.

If it meant anything at all.

"Okay, now let's get a couple with just Levi and Eva."

Rafe went rigid beside me. I peeked over at him, expecting to see anger rolling off him, but his face was a mask of indifference.

"Just you and me, Angel." Levi grinned.

"Is this really necessary?" I blurted out.

"Alistair wanted a range of shots, and it makes sense to play up your relationship," Riley sauntered over to us, her saccharine-sweet smile hardly fooling me. She knew I was uncomfortable, but my feelings didn't enter the conversation.

"Yeah, come on, Country, we should give the fans what they want." Levi hooked his finger into my belt loop and pulled me closer, the air *whooshing* from my lungs.

"Yes!" Tobias gushed, letting out a little shriek of approval. "That's perfect." He took a bunch of shots before saying, "Eva, now drop the guitar in front of you and lean your hand on it."

I did as he instructed, wanting nothing more than for it to be over. "Perfect." Another bunch of flashes later and we were finally done. "We've got plenty to work with here."

"Alistair will want full approval of the final images." Riley marched over, her cell phone pressed to her ear.

"We know the drill." The two of them talked shop while I went to grab my things.

"Travis is waiting with the car. We have an hour before we have to be at the Amway Center. I thought you could use some... pizza, after that." Letty's eyes flicked over to where the guys were laughing and joking. Except Rafe; he was still brooding, but he didn't look at me.

"Actually, that sounds perfect."

"I'll just let Riley know our plans and we can go." Letty wandered over to her.

"Yo, Angel," Levi called, "we're going to get food. You in?"

"Actually, me and Letty are goin' to do our own thing."

Levi shrugged, his eyes darkening. "Fine, whatever," he clipped out as if my rejection had genuinely offended him. He gave me his back and my instant reaction was to say we'd go with them. But the truth was, after the photoshoot, I needed space.

"Okay, all set?" Letty came back.

"Yep, let's go." I motioned for her to lead the way. The sooner we got out of here, the better.

We said goodbye to everyone and slipped out into the hall where Travis was waiting. "Grayson is bringing the car around to the side entrance." He waited for us to move ahead of him and the three of us walked toward the hotel entrance. There had only been a small group of fans gathered when we'd arrived, but I was in no hurry to face them or the press.

"So are we going to talk about how tense things are between you and Rafe?" Letty whispered.

"Nope."

"Okay then, how about how weird Levi is around you?"

"Nope."

"So just to be clear, we're ignoring the fact that Rafe couldn't take his eyes off you... the same way Levi couldn't?"

"Yep."

"Good," she chuckled. "I'm glad we cleared that up. Now we can eat pizza and pretend like everything is okay."

I lifted my eyes to hers and said, "Sounds good to me."

———

FIVE HOURS LATER, I CAME OFF STAGE HIGHER THAN A KITE. IF I thought the crowd at Charlotte had welcomed me with open arms, it was nothing compared to the way Orlando greeted me.

"Great, show, Eva." Alistair came to check in with me. "Truly, you've surprised us all."

"Thanks." I graciously accepted a bottle of water from someone and drank it down.

"Hey," Letty appeared. "You killed it out there."

"Thanks."

"Do you need Eva to stick around?" she asked Alistair.

"No, the night is yours."

"I'm not performin' with the band tonight?" The words spilled out and I immediately wanted to take them back. No one had confirmed whether I would be invited on stage, but I'd assumed it would be a regular thing since everyone had responded so well and I'd heard Alistair tell Riley it was what the audience wanted to see.

From the tight expression on his face though, I knew I'd assumed wrong. "Not tonight," he said, "we want to keep the set fresh."

"Oh, okay." Dejection bounced around my stomach.

"Levi is... complicated, Eva. Don't take it personally."

"Come on, let's go raid the band's dressing room. They always get the best snacks." Letty found my hand and pulled me away. "Fucking Levi," she mumbled.

"I didn't dream it, right? I did hear Alistair tell Riley I was goin' on with them tonight?"

"Yeah," she sighed. "You heard right."

"So Levi changed his mind?"

"Levi is..."

"Complicated, yeah so everyone keeps tellin' me."

Letty pushed open the door to the bands dressing room and we slipped inside. She was right, they did get better snacks than me. There was a long table full of pizza and chips and dips and donuts and other sugary goods that looked too darn good to resist. I marched over to it and grabbed a Twinkie, stuffing it into my mouth.

"What did that Twinkie ever do to you?" Letty fought a laugh.

"Ugh, they're givin' me a serious case of whiplash, Letty, and it's only been a few days."

Three.

It had been three.

"It's because I turned him down when he asked me to go eat with them, isn't it? This his way of gettin' back at me?"

"Look, real talk." Letty dropped onto the couch while the opening notes of their set rambled overhead. I'd wanted to watch them perform, to see the magic Levi weaved on the stage. To watch Rafe as he came alive with the guitar in his hands. But it hurt knowing Levi had pulled a rock star sized tantrum and had me kicked off their set all because I needed space after the photoshoot.

"Levi is like a child. He's impulsive, reckless, and doesn't realize how hurtful his behavior can be at times. He doesn't let people in easily, Eva, and when he does, he's always just waiting for them to disappoint him. For Levi, attack is the best form of defense."

"What happened to him, Letty? What made him this way?" I'd sworn to myself I wouldn't ask, but if I was going to survive this tour, I needed something to work with.

"I don't know the whole story, no one does. That shit is sealed tighter than a declassified CIA dossier."

My brow quirked up and she chuckled. "What? I watch a lot of documentaries. My point is, if you truly want to be a part of Levi's life you have to be patient and you have to prove to him that you're not going anywhere just because he lashes out. But you can't let him walk all over you either."

"So you're sayin' I have to shower him with love and affection while being firm and fair? He really is like a child." I rolled my eyes.

"Whatever those brothers went through was bad, Eva, really bad. Just don't write him off too soon, that's all I'm saying."

I didn't know what to say to that—which question to ask first. So I opted for silence. There were still months of touring ahead of us which meant I had to find a way of dealing with Levi's tantrums.

"Let's go watch the band," I said, licking the sugar off my lips.

"Yeah?" Letty's eyes glittered with respect.

"Yeah," I mumbled, wondering just exactly what I'd gotten myself into with the Hunter brothers.

CHAPTER TWELVE

RAFE

W E W E R E a week into the tour when *The Rock Report* article landed.

"If that doesn't get people talking, I don't know what will," Hudson dropped the magazine on my lap and I fingered the glossy pages.

"Rose between two thorns," I laughed bitterly. They didn't know the half of it.

"Eva looks every bit the star, don't you think?" Hudson was probing, trying to get a rise from me. But I kept my thoughts to myself, grumbling some half-assed reply.

The truth was it hurt to look at her. She was damn beautiful, smiling at the camera. They'd gone with a shot of the five of us: me and Eva holding her guitar looking right at the reader. Hudson's smirk was enough to catch panties on fire up and down the country. But it was Levi who would be the talking point. He wasn't looking at the camera. His head was dropped slightly, his body turned into Eva, and he was looking at her. Longing and lust burning in his eyes.

Jesus. He was falling for her. My brother, the most important person in the world to me, was falling for the girl who already owned me.

And you let it happen.

"You noticed that, huh?" Hudson was watching me quietly.

"It's nothing."

"Doesn't look like nothing to me. Looks like she's about to go where no girl ever went."

"Hud..."

"Yeah, yeah." He wrapped his knuckles against the table before getting up. "Let's do what we always do, right? Pretend everything is fine and hope the truth goes away. Because that always works out so fucking well for us."

I stared at him in disbelief. Hudson was as bad as the rest of us. Hiding behind his wicked smirk and easy charm.

He let out an exasperated breath. "Look, man, I love you like a brother and I like Eva. I like her a lot. But you're lying to yourself if you think this,"—he jammed his finger at the magazine—"isn't a problem."

"Levi won't go after Eva," I said, hating how uncertain I sounded.

"That's your comeback? You know better than anyone that Levi does whatever the fuck he wants without consequence."

"Why is this so important to you?" I was clutching at straws now, picking a fight that I was bound to lose.

Hudson was right—Eva was a problem.

I'd walked away once because I didn't want her to come between me and Levi, but that was when I was never going to see her again. When I could push her to the recesses of my mind and keep her in my dreams.

But could I keep doing it?

Especially after kissing her again.

Fuck.

Everything was so fucking screwed up.

"Are you kidding me right now?" Hudson sneered. "The band is all I have, man, you know that. You, Levi, and Damon are my family, my brothers. You can't blame me for wanting to protect that."

Guilt snaked through me. He was right. Of course he was fucking right. We were all each other had; a fact that had kept our heads above water more than once.

"I'll figure it out."

"You'd better hurry the fuck up then before this thing goes sideways." His anger melted away, replaced with a look of longing. "She's just a girl, Rafe."

Eva wasn't just a girl to me though.

Just like I had a feeling Molly wasn't just a girl to him.

But neither of us were ready to own up to how we really felt.

He stalked off, the walls of the bus closing in around me as I sat there, staring at the article. I usually avoided reading whatever rumor and gossip they printed about us, but I found myself greedily absorbing the words. The article painted Eva as a girl who had found herself plucked out of small-town life and thrown into the lion's den. It even went as far as to suggest she might be the one to tame Levi's wild ways.

I scoffed at that—it had Alistair written all over it. He wanted to sell Eva as the band's salvation. But the article walked a fine line between making her sound like a new friend while hinting at her becoming something more. Or maybe I was just crazy jealous every time her name and Levi's came up in the same sentence.

"Yo, Rafe," Damon's voice filtered down the bus. "We have a meeting."

"Meeting?" No one had said anything about a meeting.

I dropped the magazine on the table and ran a hand through my hair. The last two days had been grueling. There had been back-to-back interviews yesterday and Alistair had arranged for us to visit a local youth center in Dallas the day before. That had been fun, rocking out with their band. Then we'd signed a bunch of merch and taken photos with the amped up kids. We always tried to build in at least a handful of visits to centers such as the Fannie C Harris Youth Center, like the one that brought us together when we were just kids.

Eva and Letty hadn't come with us. She had her own promotional stuff to do. Interviews. Appearances. The calls for Eva were coming in thick and fast, but she took it all in her stride. It had barely been a week since she joined us, but there was no denying fame looked good on her.

We hadn't talked about the kiss... in fact, we hadn't talked much at all. But when I stepped off the bus to find everyone waiting for me, including Eva and Letty, I sensed my attempts at us avoiding each other were over.

"What's up?" I asked no one in particular.

Levi wore a shit-eating grin while Hudson looked fit to burst. "Do you want to tell him or should I?" Levi looked at Alistair who also seemed unusually happy.

"You can do the honors." He gave my brother a nod.

"They want us." Levi looked so freaking happy it hurt.

"They?" I frowned and he mumbled something under his breath before saying, "Masterpiece."

"You're shitting me?"

"I'm not." He shook his head slowly. "It's the dream, little brother."

"I..." My head whipped around to Alistair. "It's true? They want us?"

"It's not a done deal yet, but yeah, it's looking pretty solid. So if we're not interrupting your little pity party for one," his brow went up and Hudson snickered. "Dowager wants to meet today."

"Hell yeah," I choked out.

Masterpiece was the crème de la crème of sound equipment, and the sponsorship deal me and Levi had dreamed of ever since we signed with Razorsharp Records. Over the years, Masterpiece had endorsed some of rock's biggest names: The Stones, Zeppelin, Ramones, and Pink Floyd but to name a few.

And now they wanted us.

My mind was officially blown. Until I realized Alistair wasn't done.

"What changed his mind?" I asked.

Tim Dowager, their MD, had been dragging his feet on sealing a deal all because of concerns over our reputation—or more to the point, Levi's instability. Alistair looked at Eva and I had my answer.

We all did.

"He only wants us if Eva's part of the deal?" Hudson gawked at him.

"We can discuss this later."

"That's some bullshit right there, Ali, and you know it."

"Hud," Damon interjected.

"Nah, man, and no offense, Eva, but you've been here for two seconds and now Dowager wants to sign us? We're not a package deal. People seem to be forgetting that Eva isn't in the fucking band."

She winced at that but held her ground. "If it makes you feel any better, I had no idea this was going to happen until just now." Her eyes burned into the side of Alistair's face.

"Dowager wants to talk. He's likely to make an offer, an offer we can negotiate. Let's at least go and see what he's willing to put on the table."

"We're doing it," Levi said. "We've wanted Masterpiece since the beginning. It's like the holy grail of endorsements, everyone knows that. Are you really going to dig in your heels because they might want Eva to use their stuff for the rest of the tour?"

"Fine, whatever." Hudson kicked the dirt with his boot. "Let's see what he has to say."

"Glad we got that settled." Alistair strolled toward the Mercedes Van and climbed upfront while Levi and Damon got in the back.

"You agree with this?" Hudson asked me, his eyes flicking to where Eva and Letty stood, deep in hushed conversation.

"I don't know, but Levi has a point, it's Masterpiece." Everything we'd always wanted.

"And if it ties us to her beyond the tour?"

Hudson's words gave me pause. I'd been so focused on what happened during the tour, I hadn't really stopped to consider what happened when it ended. Eva wasn't signed to the label. Once the tour was over so was her contract. That was unlikely to be the case though if Masterpiece wanted her too.

"We're still Black Hearts Still Beat, Hud, that's never going to change." But the second the words were out I felt the lie settle deep in my bones. Things were changing.

Eva was changing us.

And if we stayed on this road who only knew where we would end up.

———

The ride to Masterpiece's HQ in downtown LA was tense. Hudson sat beside me, his foot tapping the floor. Usually, I would have put it down to his drummer's mind, but today, I knew it was because he was agitated.

"Relax," I whispered, nudging his shoulder.

"Easy for you to say." His eyes flicked past me to where Eva sat on the other side of me. Letty had squeezed in beside Levi and Damon in the front row, giving me no choice but to sit in the back with Eva and Hudson.

"How are you holding up?" I asked her, when really all I wanted to do was apologize. For the kiss. For avoiding the huge fucking elephant in the room that was my brother.

For never calling her back.

"Honestly, I don't know. It's been a week, Rafe," she kept her voice low. "And everythin' is goin' at a million-miles-an-hour and I'm just tryin' to keep my head above water." The words tumbled out, her chest heaving.

Before I could stop myself, my hand slid against hers. Eva sucked in a shaky breath, keeping her eyes upfront. She wasn't the only one affected though; her touch was like kryptonite making my knees weak and my heart stutter. Her fingers slid precariously between mine, and I risked peeking over at her. The corner of her mouth lifted in a secretive smile.

Jesus, this girl.

How the hell was I supposed to stop?

Ever since kissing her, I'd dreamed of nothing else but doing it again. It was the reason I'd spent so much time avoiding her. I couldn't be near her without imagining crowding her against the nearest wall and pushing my body up against hers. If the heated looks I'd caught her sending in my direction more than once over the last couple of days were any indication, she felt the same.

We were a lit fuse racing toward its end, and only we could decide whether we exploded or flickered out to nothing.

Eva shifted on her seat, her arm brushing mine, sending shivers rolling up my spine. I hadn't even touched her, not properly, but I felt her everywhere. Could imagine her naked above me, the soft swell of her hips, the gentle curve of her waist, her perfect tits. I wanted to touch her and taste her and make her cry my name over and over.

It was my turn to shift uncomfortably, fully aware that I was sporting a raging hard on. Eva covered her mouth with her hand, smothering a laugh. Letty glanced back, a deep frown pinching her face. My hand shot down over my lap as I tried to conceal the evidence that I had zero fucking self-control around Eva.

Thankfully, Fenton announced we were almost at Masterpiece HQ. The sleek building loomed up ahead and I think we all breathed a sigh of relief when there was no sign of any Die Hearts. Travis came around and opened the door for Eva who hopped out. She glanced at me through her long lashes and smiled.

"Thank fuck," Levi groaned. "I was about to piss myself. Jake, shall we?" He jammed a hand into his pocket and swaggered over to his bodyguard, the two of them disappearing inside the building.

Alistair and Riley were busy discussing how to approach the meeting, while Hudson and Damon trailed in behind them. Leaving me with Eva and Letty.

"So, I'll be..." Letty thumbed to the door and took off after everyone while me and Eva walked casually inside with Travis and Fenton coming up behind us.

"I'm sorry," Eva whispered, "if I, you know..." She smothered another laugh, her eyes dropping to my jeans for the briefest of seconds.

My eyes narrowed, aware that we were no longer in the blacked-out van. "We should talk," I said. We had to figure out how to be around each other without me wanting to tear her clothes off at any given second.

"What, now?"

"No, later." I chuckled. "Tonight. After the show."

Eva nodded, fighting a smile. She seemed different. More confident and sure of herself. But there was something else—a determination in her eyes I'd never seen before.

A look that said, 'I'm here, all you have to do is take me'.

But if I crossed that line, if I put us both out of our misery... what then?

There was no time to dwell, we were herded into an elevator and directed to a huge meeting room overlooking downtown LA. Eva had made a beeline for the window, her eyes full of wonder. I could still remember what it was like, to see the world from new heights.

"Eva, Rafe," Alistair snapped, "if you'd care to join us, we can get started." I hadn't realized everyone was here, too busy watching Eva watch the city beyond the tinted glass.

Damon caught my eye, shooting me a concerned expression. I took the empty seat beside my brother while Eva sat with Letty. I hated these things, but they were a necessary evil for artists. An endorsement with the right sponsor could open up doors. For us, it meant Masterpiece, one of the industries most trusted brands, saw us as credible talent with a bright future. For Alistair and Riley and the label, it meant dollar signs.

"Ah, Alistair, good to see you again." Tim Dowager breezed into the room with a petite woman lapping at his heels. "This is Shelbie, my assistant."

"Shelbie," Alistair stood up and extended his hand, "it's always nice to put a face to a name." The woman blushed and shook his hand before greeting Riley with a warm smile.

Rumor in industry circles was that Dowager went through more secretaries than Hudson got through fan girls. Shelbie was his latest and from the way he watched her like a predator watched his prey, he wanted to bang her, if he wasn't already.

"I gotta say, Ali, I wasn't sure we'd ever get to this point."

"Come on, Tim." Alistair relaxed in his chair. "We all knew this was going to happen. It was just a case of when. Black Hearts can help bring Masterpiece into the new decade."

"Bold statement for the manager of a band who can't seem to control their lead vocalist." Dowager's eyes settled on my brother. "Levi, you're looking well."

"I'm in a good place, sir." Few people brought my brother to heel, but he knew what this deal meant, to us, to the band.

"Good to hear it, son. The tour's going well?"

"We'll let you be the judge of that." Levi flashed him a half-smirk, and Dowager roared with laughter.

"So damn cocky. You remind me a lot of Jagger back in the day."

"I'll take that as a compliment."

"You should. But even the greats aren't untouchable, kid."

Levi straightened at that. He despised being called 'kid'. Hated it with every fiber of his being. I pressed my boot down on his.

"We know that, Mr. Dowager," Damon cut in. "And we know what it means to represent a brand such as Masterpiece."

"Ms. Walker... can I call you Evangeline?" He turned his attention on Eva.

"Eva is fine, sir."

Dowager nodded. "Very well. I'd be keen to hear how you've found it being on the road with the band."

Alistair sat up and said, "Come on, Tim, that isn't—"

"It's fine. I don't mind answerin' his question." Eva smiled and we all saw Dowager soften under her spell. "The band have been nothin' but welcomin'."

"It was a bold move the label made adding you to the tour. Why do you think they picked you?"

"Tim," Alistair sounded pissed now, but Dowager waved him off, fully aware that he held all the cards.

"I was lucky enough to spend time with the band during the Jamesboro County Talent Showdown, and I guess you could say something clicked." She gave a half-shrug. "Besides, I had no idea who Black Hearts Still Beat was back then."

"You're shitting me?" Dowager was hanging on her every word. "And it's true, you challenged Levi to a sing-off?"

"It didn't quite happen like that, but yeah, there was some friendly competition."

He slammed his hand down. "I like you, Eva. I like you a lot. You've got your head screwed on straight. The fact you've survived a week on the road with these four speaks for itself. What you and Levi created on stage at Charlotte was music gold. Many artists have tried and failed to unite country and rock but you, missy, nailed it."

"Thank you, sir."

Tension rippled in the air. I was still physically restraining Levi underneath the table, while Damon and Hudson watched on, caution in their eyes as Dowager practically foamed at the mouth listening to Eva.

"Okay, let's get down to business. Masterpiece wants to be the official sponsor of Black Hearts Still Beat..." he paused, letting the information sink in. Levi relaxed into the chair, a long sigh leaving his lips. It was hard to put into words what this would mean for him. A guy who had been shunned by almost everyone in his life except for me and the guys.

"Fuck, yes." He scrubbed his face. "That's means everything to us, sir. Every damn thing."

"I'm glad to hear it, son. But we don't only want Black Hearts,"—he levelled his gaze on Eva again—"we want you too."

CHAPTER THIRTEEN

"WHAT DO you think he wants to talk about?" I asked Letty as we sat in the living area of our suite. The show wasn't until tomorrow which meant for one blissful night we got to sleep in an actual bed with fluffy covers and complete silence.

"I'm guessing it has something to do with Dowager's offer?"

The offer Alistair had said we needed time to consider. I still couldn't wrap my head around the fact there was an offer that included me.

Me.

The door swung open and Riley and Alistair marched into the room. "Sorry we kept you waiting, you must have a lot of questions."

"Actually," I said, "I don't really understand most of what just happened."

The second we'd left Masterpiece's building, Levi had wanted to celebrate, but then he and Hudson had gotten into it when the drummer voiced what I had no doubt everyone else was thinking—a deal with Masterpiece tied me to the band in ways no one had comprehended.

"I appreciate it's a lot to take in. When we signed you on for the tour, none of us could have predicted how quickly things would move. But that's the industry. Your life really can change overnight."

"You're tellin' me," I breathed.

"Riley, the papers, please." She handed Alistair a stack of official-looking documents, unable to disguise her annoyance. "This is an offer of representation, Eva."

"Representation?" I gulped over the giant lump in my throat.

"It supersedes the existing contract and means that Razorsharp Records becomes your official label."

"The label wants to sign me?" I wasn't a recording artist. I'd signed onto the tour to save my parents.

"You're whipping up a storm, Eva. If we want to capitalize on the interest, we need to act now. It's likely an extra leg will be added to the tour; an international leg."

"And you want me to be a part of that?"

"You're already a part of it, Eva," he chuckled. "You just need to say the word. We're only five shows in and ratings are already through the roof. People are responding, just as we'd hoped."

"Wow, I have no idea what to say."

"Don't talk, just listen," he said. "The label wants to drop an EP."

I looked to Letty and she clarified, "an extended play record."

"I know what an EP is," I murmured.

"Sorry." She leaned over and grabbed my hand. "This is a good thing, Eva. A really fucking good thing."

"They have already secured permission to record *Zombie* and I'm working on Axel's people to get permission for *Sweet Child O' Mine*. Then they'll want one of your original tracks."

My eyes almost bugged. This was... it was freakin' crazy. I was here as a favor to Alistair and the label. Here to help the band, and my parents. I wasn't here to sign with Razorsharp Records and become a recording artist.

"There was a poll—" Letty started, but I cut her off, shrieking, "A poll? I don't think I want to know."

She and Alistair shared a laugh, while Riley looked on with indifference. The band's sour-faced assistant was really starting to get under my skin.

"I know it's a lot," Alistair attempted to reassure me.

"The band—" I started, but he cut me off.

"The band will do whatever is in the best interests of the band, and right now, whether they like it or not, that's you. Dowager's offer doesn't require you to sign with the label, but you will need a manager; a job I am more than happy to continue. The fact he wants you in the first place speaks volumes about his trust in your talent and appeal."

"Okay, Ali, we get it." Letty held up her hands. "But maybe, give the girl some space to breathe."

"Of course. Nothing needs to be decided right now, although these things always have a limited shelf life. Take the night, talk to your parents, talk to your lawyer. Heck, even talk to God if it helps you arrive at an answer. But I will need an answer, Eva." Alistair checked his watch and stood up. "I have a meeting downtown, but Riley will be around to answer any questions that arise." Like I would be going to her for anything. "Letty's right, this is a good thing. The things dreams are made of. Together, me and Razorsharp Records can help you realize those dreams, Eva."

"Thank you," I choked out, still stuck on the part where the label was offering to sign me and put me in the studio to record an EP.

"We'll talk tomorrow. Enjoy a much-deserved night off."

I forced a smile, unsure if Alistair and I had the same idea about a night off. I'd hoped Letty would be able to show me some of the sights of downtown LA, but instead there was another party. This time it was a label party for one of their newly-signed artists, and the band was required to attend, which apparently meant, I was required to attend.

To my relief, once Alistair left, Riley didn't stick around.

"Holy shit, Eva, this is huge." Letty grinned. "I had a feeling it was heading this way but I didn't want to say anything in case it didn't."

"Did that really just happen?" I sank back into the couch, pulling a pillow into my chest.

"Oh, it happened. It so fucking happened. What are you going to do?"

"I have no idea. I mean, I signed on for the tour, that was it. I didn't really think about what happened after that." After being diagnosed with Non-Hodgkin, I'd learned not to make long-term plans and take every day as it came. I guess I still hadn't really broken that mindset. Because nothing was certain. No one could know what tomorrow would bring or the day after that. So I no longer looked far into the future. I couldn't.

"You should call your parents. This is a huge opportunity, but it will mean life as you know it is over."

Life as I knew it was already over.

It was over the second Molly entered me into the Talent Showdown.

Only, I was still figuring out if that was a good or bad thing.

I couldn't go back to being regular old Evangeline Walker now I'd performed for thousands of people; seen the sights of some of the country's biggest cities. But then, I hadn't been regular old Eva in a really long time. Cancer had changed me, and now this tour was changing me. And maybe, just maybe, there was a chance that among all the crazy I would find myself again.

Starting with Alistair's offer.

———

AFTER I'D HAD SOME TIME TO DIGEST THE LAST FEW HOURS, LETTY set me up on a conference call with my mom and dad. I'd spent five minutes chuckling as I watched the two of them try—and fail—to get the position of the webcam just right.

"Hi, baby."

"Hi, sweetheart." They both waved, Mom's eyes darting around the screen as if she was paranoid someone was watching her.

"It's just me, Mom," I said, fighting a smile. "My assistant thought it might be better if we could see each other."

Dad's brow pinched. "Did somethin' happen, sweetheart? You look like you've seen a ghost."

"Do you feel okay? You haven't been havin' any symptoms, have you?" The blood drained from Mom's face.

"No, no, I'm fine. I promise. Never felt better. But I do have some news."

"Okay, we're listenin'." Dad wrapped his arm around Mom's shoulder.

"Well, I... wow, this is a lot harder than I thought." I took a deep breath, trying to find the words. "Alistair, Mr. Portman, well, he said the label wants to sign me, officially." There was a pregnant pause while I let the news sink in. Mom's expression was unreadable, but Dad's frown melted away, being replaced with nothing but pride and happiness.

"Eva, sweetheart, that is... damn, baby, I'm so freakin' proud of you." He beamed "Aren't we proud of her, Jesse?" He nudged Mom's arm, but she didn't flinch.

"Mom?" My voice shook with trepidation.

"That's... it's a lot, Gavin. It's sounds like a very permanent thing, baby."

I got it, I did. She would always be my mom; the woman who had almost lost her only child. The idea of losing me again, after she just got me back, was a lot to process. But I couldn't deny it stung a little that she couldn't find it in herself to be happy for me.

"Jesse, this is Eva's dream. It's everythin' she ever wanted. Just think, our baby, the superstar."

"Oh, I don't know about that, Dad." Strangled laughter rumbled in my chest.

He made a clucking sound. "We've been followin' those Google alerts, sweetheart. By all accounts you're makin' quite the impression." There was a glint in his eye that had me wondering just what exactly they'd been reading. I knew *The Rock Report* article had stirred some speculation about the nature of the relationship between me and the band—specifically, me and Levi—but it was just that, speculation. It was tempting to read what people were saying about me all over social media, but I knew that stuff would only drive me crazy. Besides I had Molly sending me regular CliffsNotes of the latest rumors.

I was happy with my performances, and Alistair and the label were happy with the tour so far. That's all that mattered to me.

"You looked so grown up in that photoshoot, Eva. A little too grown up." He winked and I blushed profusely.

"I didn't realize it would be... like that," I mumbled, unable to meet his amused gaze.

"Sweetheart, you're a beautiful young woman. Those Black Hearted boys would be fools not to notice."

"Black Hearts, Dad. They're called Black Hearts Still Beat."

"Well, as long as they know they'll be dead hearts if they so much as lay a finger on my baby girl."

"*Dad!*" This was so not how I saw the conversation going, but I couldn't blame them after seeing the photoshoot. Even I'd blushed when I saw a copy, and I was in the darn shot.

"I'm only jokin'. I trust you to make good choices."

Rafe's face flashed into my head. What would my dad think if he knew the truth? If he knew I'd already given my heart to a Black Hearted boy. I liked to think he would trust my judgment; that he would have an open mind. But what did I really know about Rafe, about where he came from and what his childhood had been like?

Nothing.

I knew nothing.

Could you really feel so deeply for someone until you knew all the parts of them?

I was a fine one to talk though. I still hadn't come clean to the band. I didn't want it to change the dynamics between us—the way Damon always pulled me in for a hug after a show; or how Hudson liked to make some sarcastic remark about me stealing the show; or how Rafe and Levi both looked at me with such intensity I felt like I might combust at any second. If they knew the truth, all that would be replaced with pity and uncertainty and I didn't doubt they would start treating me like fragile glass.

"What do you want to do, sweetheart?" His expression softened as he gripped Mom's shoulder, probably urging her to give me something, anything.

"At first, I was so shocked, I didn't know what to think. The tour is one thing, but signing with the label... everythin' will change."

"What does it feel like when you're up there, on stage?" Dad went on.

"It feels... amazin', Dad. It feels like I'm free." I loved it, I did. On stage, with my guitar cradled in my hands, I felt alive. I felt at peace. Nothing else existed except me and the music and the lyrics. It was something I couldn't really put into words.

"You were born to perform, Eva. We didn't name you Star for nothin', you know." His lip curved.

"Your father is right," Mom finally spoke, tears pooling in the corners of her eyes. "You were always destined to be a star. I just... after everythin', I'm not ready to let go."

"I know, Mom. But this doesn't mean you'll lose me. I'll always be your little girl." *And I'll always owe you so much.*

"If you want this, baby, if you truly want a future in music, then you have to do it, Eva. You have to say yes."

Having Dad's support was something but having my mom's support was another thing entirely. A huge smile broke over my face, tears burning my throat. I swallowed them down, swiping at my eyes. "I love you both, so much. And if I do this, you'll never have to worry again." I could give them everything, make sure they never had to worry about another bill in their life.

"Oh, sweetheart, this isn't about us. This is about you, Eva. About you finally realizin' that you have a bright and successful future ahead of you. That's all we want, that's all we ever wanted."

I was finally getting that.

———

"I can't believe you didn't want to tell them," Letty whispered as we followed Travis into the swanky LA club.

"Tonight isn't about me," I replied through a tight smile. "It's about Nikki Denver."

Razorsharp Records' latest signing had just dropped her first album and we were all here to celebrate. Except, I had no idea who Nikki was or what she looked like.

"There she is." Letty pointed at a tall willowy girl wearing a skin-tight mini dress, long dark hair flowing down her back. She oozed sex appeal, and it was hard not to shrink into Letty's side as we passed her. There wasn't a single guy in the room not drooling in her direction, the band included. Hudson was practically panting as he stood with a group of people I didn't recognize. I rolled my eyes.

"Cocktail?" Letty asked as we approached the bar.

"Something not too strong."

"Sure thing." She flagged down a bartender and ordered for us. I let my eyes roam over the crowd. Unlike the club in Charlotte, most people here were younger, and I knew if Molly was here, she would have been able to pick out the latest pop stars, actors, and television personalities. But Molly wasn't here, and I didn't pay much attention to that kind of stuff. Which meant I had to rely on Letty to get me up to speed.

Handing me my drink, she hopped up onto a stool. "That's Alistair's sister," Letty pointed to a couple of girls at a booth, "and her friend, Skye Madison."

"Skye, who?" My expression was blank.

"That's it, tomorrow I'm buying you a copy of *OK!*, *Entertainment Weekly*, and *Rolling Stone*, it's time you got up to speed. Especially if you're going to be—"

"Oh, hey, Damon," I cut her off.

His brows bunched together as he studied Letty, then me. "What were you talking about?"

"Nothin'." A tight smile crossed my lips. "Cool party."

"Yeah." He let out a smooth chuckle. "I just wanted to come see how you're doing after the meeting today."

"I'm okay. Thanks for askin'."

"Don't worry about Hudson, he'll come around." He relaxed back against the bar. "It's nothing personal."

"He's just a grumpy motherfucker." Hudson appeared out of nowhere, grinning. "Sorry about earlier, Eva."

I gave a half-hearted shrug. "It's no biggie."

"Dance with me?" He pouted, offering me his hand. "My way of apologizing."

"I don't know." My eyes flicked to the dance floor.

"Ain't no one looking at you but me, Eva." His brows waggled. "One dance, come on."

"Oh, fine." I slapped my hand in his, shoving my cocktail at Letty.

"Atta girl," Letty gave me a thumbs up, sipping on her drink.

"Are the two of you goin' to be okay?"

"I... sorry, what?" Damon blinked, running a hand down his face.

"Is everythin' okay?" He looked pale.

"Fine, it's fine." I glanced to where he'd been looking but couldn't see anyone except Alistair's sister and her friend.

"Do you know them?"

"Who, Ruby?"

"Ruby, huh." I smiled. There was something telling in his voice.

"She's Alistair's sister. There was a thing, we met aaaand it's not important... go, show my boy how it's done."

"Like she could ever out dance me." Hudson yanked me toward the dance floor, and I swallowed all the questions I had for Damon. "Ready to make magic, Starshine?" He pulled me into his body, but I jerked back staring at him.

Nobody called me that except Rafe.

"If you could only see your face right now," he said. "Let's give my boy a little motivation, shall we?"

I didn't know what the hell he was talking about, but when Hudson spun me and my eyes found Rafe across the room, I knew I'd play along with whatever plan he was hatching. Because Rafe was standing with a female, dressed in even less clothes than Nikki Denver, and she was pressed up against him, hanging onto his every word.

And all I could think was, that was supposed to be me.

CHAPTER FOURTEEN

RAFE

"Just go over there and ask her to dance," Damon grumbled, nursing his sixth or seventh beer of the evening. I'd lost count, there had been so many, which wasn't like him at all.

"You know I can't do that." My eyes slid to his and I shook my head.

"Why not? She's spent the last hour dancing with Hud and Levi."

Didn't I fucking know it? I'd watched with jealousy swimming in my veins as they twirled her and hugged her, laughing and having fun with her. At one point, Eva had even tried to teach them a line dance. The crowd had loved it, whooping and cheering as my brother tripped over his own damn feet more times than he got the steps right.

"I just can't." I jammed my fingers in my hair. I wanted to. I wanted nothing more than to be the one twirling her around the dance floor, letting everyone know she was mine. But that wasn't our reality.

"What did you say to Hudson earlier?" Damon asked. "One minute he was ready to walk and then next he's apologizing to Eva and asking her to dance."

"I told him what he needed to hear." Hudson was never going to walk. He just couldn't handle the idea that something—or someone— might come between the band. But none of this was Eva's fault; it was mine. It wasn't fair for Hudson to resent Eva for things out of her control.

Things she didn't even understand.

"Looks like you've got an admirer." Damon tipped his head over to

255

where Kiki Felps stood, making no secret of the fact she was imagining all the very dirty and kinky things she wanted to do to me. I only knew because she'd whispered them to me earlier.

A shudder rolled through me. "Never going to happen."

"Does she know that? Because from the way she's watching you, it looks like she already staked her claim."

"Seriously, you think I'd go there?" I gave him a pointed look, and Damon held up his hands.

"Chill, I'm only messing with you. But between Riley and Kiki it isn't any wonder Eva's trying to make you jealous." His brow lifted and the asshole smirked.

"What the fuck are you..." Damn, he was right. "I don't blame her," I sighed.

"It's a dangerous game you're both playing. Push too hard and eventually one of you will detonate."

Maybe that's what we needed—to combust. Maybe then we could find a way to move forward.

Changing the subject, I asked, "What's with you and the wannabe actress anyway?"

"Who, Skye Madison? Hell to the no."

I reared back. "Well, I know you're not digging Ali's sister because he would hang you out to dry by your balls."

"I don't know what you're talking about."

"Damon," I lifted my head, "what the fuck did you do?" I'd seen him watching the two of them for most of the night. But he didn't seem interested... he seemed cagey.

"Nothing for you to worry about." He pressed his lips together, and it didn't surprise me in the least he had his own secrets. Damon was a dark horse who kept his private life locked down.

"I know it sounds weird, and don't hit me or anything, but I already can't imagine not having her around." He was looking at Eva now. It wasn't in a sexual way, but the kind of way a brother might watch his sister. Protective and caring.

His words hit me like a wrecking ball. I hadn't considered she might not stick around. We didn't need Alistair to confirm what came next, we all knew the drill. No way, the label wasn't going to try and sign her now Masterpiece wanted her.

"You know, I heard on the grapevine she only took the gig because of her parents," he said, eyeing me carefully. My expression must have said it all, because he let out a soft chuckle. "What, did you really think she said yes just to see your brooding ass again?"

"Fuck you," I nudged his shoulder. I'd assumed she'd said yes because this was her dream. A chance to make something of herself. Although she had hinted at having ulterior reasons.

"For real, you heard that?"

"Something about them needing money and Alistair making the offer too good to refuse."

My eyes went to Eva again. "She told me she was sick." The thought hit me out of left field. "Back in Camdena, she told me that. You think it has to do with that?"

He shrugged. "If it was something serious, medical bills would soon mount up. She never told you what was wrong?"

"No." But now he'd mentioned it, I couldn't stop imagining Eva sick, lying there in a hospital bed, the life draining from her eyes. The thought made my stomach churn. "She must be better," I said. "If it was something ongoing, Alistair would have told us."

"Whoa, I don't know where your head is at right now, but Eva is fine, man. Look at her, she's a picture of health."

He wasn't wrong there. I watched Eva as she waved my brother and Hudson off, making a beeline for the bar. Letty handed her a drink and Eva gulped it down, smiling, her eyes twinkling with happiness. My girl was flourishing.

My girl.

Jesus, it was impossible to think of her as anything else.

But we still needed to talk.

I still needed to figure out what the hell I was going to say.

One thing was certain though, I wasn't sure how much more of watching her with my brother, I could take.

———

"Rafe, there you are." Kiki Felps stepped in front of me, blocking my view of Eva. "I've been hoping to talk to you again." She laid her hand on my arm, curling her fingers around me possessively. "These parties are always fun but I prefer something a little quieter." Suggestion laced her words.

I got the message loud and clear, I just wasn't in the least bit interested.

"Actually, Kiki, I'm a little busy right now." I went to move around her, but she stepped into me, making out as if I'd stumbled into her, knocking her off balance.

"Oopsie." She gripped my shoulders to steady herself, making a show of laughing. "I really must be more careful." Kiki smiled up at me, hunger glittering in her eyes.

Just then, something caught my eye over her shoulder, and I saw

Eva's retreating form. "Not right now," I clipped out, removing Kiki's hands from me. "I need to be somewhere."

Eva.

I had to get to Eva.

She dashed by Travis, disappearing into a darkened hall. I knew this club pretty well, and I knew that area wasn't open to the public. I took off toward where Eva had disappeared into the shadows.

"Whoa there, Hunter," Travis growled. "Eva wants some space."

"I only want to make sure she's okay."

"You sure that's all you want?" His brow went up.

My jaw clenched. I didn't want to go head to head with Eva's bodyguard, but I was getting to her whether he liked it or not.

"Do me a solid, yeah, and let me see her. She needs me."

He hesitated for a second. I went to move around him, but his hand slammed into my chest at the last second. "I'm watching you."

"Wouldn't expect anything less." Understanding passed between us and Travis relented, letting me slip past. The hall was lined with doors, all locked, except for the last one which was slightly ajar. I slipped inside. The sound of the door clicking shut startled Eva. It was some kind of storage room, littered with broken chairs and tables, and other discarded stuff.

"Go away, Rafe, I want to be alone," she said, lifting her chin defiantly.

I prowled toward her, my heart pounding in my chest, eyes fixed on every bare inch of her skin. I didn't know where to look first, where to touch. "Are you sure about that?"

"I need space." She let out a weary sigh. "I need to catch my breath and I can't breathe with you here."

"That's tough luck, Eva, because I can't breathe without you." My eyes dropped to her lips.

"Rafe, the party..." Her wild gaze darted past me to the door.

"Can wait," My body collided with hers, pushing her against the wall. Eva's hand flew to my chest, but she didn't push me away. Instead, she stared up at me through her heavily made up eyes, her red pouty lips almost too good to kiss.

"If anyone finds us..."

I dipped my mouth to her ear and whispered, "No one is going to find us, Starshine." Travis might have let me through, but he knew to keep everyone else out, and he wouldn't disturb us unless it was important.

We were all alone.

Finally.

"The brunette," Eva said. "Who is she?"

"No one," I breathed, brushing the shell of her ear, unable to resist nipping the skin there. Eva shuddered, pressing my chest slightly, trying to put space between us.

"She wasn't no one. She was all over you." Her voice was tight.

"Did it make you jealous, seeing her touch me?" It had fucking disgusted me. But after watching Eva dance with my brother or best friend most of the night, I couldn't deny part of me wanted her jealous. I wanted her to feel what I felt every second of every day. Watching her and never being able to touch her.

"I wanted to rip her hands off." Eva's eyes flared, her fingers twisting into my shirt. She'd had a couple of drinks, the sugary sweet scent of strawberry liquor on her breath. I brushed my nose over her cheek, my lips hovering at the corner of her mouth. "Now you know how it feels. I watch him touch you and I want to hurt him, Eva." My body trembled with the weight of the words. "I have never wanted to harm my brother, ever. Do you get that? Do you see what you're doing to me?"

Her indignation melted away giving way to regret. It clouded her eyes making her seem so sad I wanted to spend my life trying to make her smile. "I didn't... that's not what I wanted to do. I never wanted to come between the two of you, Rafe."

Too late.

My eyes shuttered as I said, "You're already there."

"What are we going to do?" Her hands slid up my chest, tugging my collar, erasing the sliver of space left between us. I could feel Eva everywhere. She invaded my thoughts, my desires, my every fucking waking moment. But seeing Levi make her laugh, seeing him so at ease with her, so happy, it affected me in a way I wasn't prepared for.

Part of me wanted to step aside, to let him sweep her away with his misunderstood bad boy routine. She could fix him, or at least, she could be the Band Aid he so desperately needed. But for the first time in my life, I chose the selfish path.

I chose Eva.

I chose me.

And it was going to lead me straight to hell. But she was worth it.

What we shared was worth it.

"All I know, Starshine, is that I'm going to kiss you now," I whispered against her lips.

"Okay." The word was a gentle sigh I felt all the way down to my soul.

The second our lips touched, I felt it. The cosmic shift. This wasn't wrong; it wasn't some selfish mistake. It was two souls reuniting.

My hands slipped down to Eva's thighs and I hoisted her against me, pinning her to the wall. She wrapped her legs around my waist, the material of her skirt bunching up. "I thought we were going to talk," she chuckled, raining tiny kisses all over my lips, my jaw, down my neck.

We were impossibly close, only our clothes separating us, and yet, it still wasn't enough.

It would *never* be enough.

"We can talk later. I've missed you, Starshine. We've missed you." I rolled my hips into her, letting her feel just exactly what she did to me. Not that she needed any reminder after earlier in the van. "I've imagined that night so many times." My words fluttered over Eva's skin, making her shiver.

"Rafe..." she moaned, tipping her head back to let me trace my tongue over her skin.

"Tell me it's me you want, Eva, say it." *I need to hear you say it.*

"You, it's you."

A possessive growl rumbled deep in my chest as I smashed my mouth down on hers, stroking her tongue with mine. I didn't just kiss her, I devoured her. I wanted to bury myself inside her and never leave.

One of Eva's hands dropped between us, working my shirt up so she could feel my skin. Her touch burned me from the inside out.

Nothing else existed when it was like this—just me and Eva and the overpowering connection between us.

"I need you, Rafe," she whispered, her words shattering my chest wide open. "I need to know this is real."

"Eva, we shouldn't—"

"Don't you dare walk away from me again," she snapped, grabbing my jaw. "This, us, it's real. Tell me you know it's real, Rafe."

The desperation in her voice had me wavering. If we crossed this line, there would be no going back. It would only be a matter of time before the truth came out. But I was defenseless against her advances. Deep down, I knew the second I'd followed her in here, I'd already made my decision.

"It's real," I growled, plunging my tongue into her mouth as I rocked into her. Slow, precise thrusts, imagining it was real, that I was buried deep inside her.

"I need more," Eva panted, her breath warm against my lips as she fumbled with my belt and then my buttons. Her hand dipped inside my boxer briefs and wrapped around my hard length.

"Jesus, Eva," I hissed as she began to stroke me. "I didn't want our second time to be like this."

"I want it to be exactly like this," she murmured, clinging to me as she jacked me off.

"Easy..." I let out a tight chuckle as I felt myself begin to lose control. She felt too fucking good, and I didn't want it to be over too quickly.

Pulling her hand free, I pinned it against the wall beside her head. "My turn." I smirked, lowering her legs to the floor. Sinking to my knees, I trailed my hands down her waist and thighs, and then pushed them back up taking her skirt with them.

"Rafe, what are you—" she choked on the words as I nuzzled my face into her panties. Her hands went to my hair, tugging gently as I eased back to slowly inch the material down her legs. "I'm going to kiss you here." I pressed my lips to the soft skin on the inside of her leg. "And here." My fingers gently brushed her stomach as my mouth traced a path to the apex of her thighs. Darting my tongue out, I tasted her, brushing slow circles over her clit, making Eva writhe above me. Her fingers dug harder as I added a finger, pressing it inside her and curling it upward, sending her into a tailspin.

It was cruel and selfish, but I didn't want her to come, not like this, not when I couldn't see right into her eyes, into her soul. Tasting her one last time, I pulled away and stood up, kissing her hard and deep, letting her taste herself on me.

"You're a tease." Eva was flushed, her eyes glittering with desire.

"I need to be inside you when you come, Eva." It came out hoarse, my body shaking with need.

She slammed her hands against my chest and pushed me backward until the backs of my legs hit an abandoned chair. Eva worked my jeans down my legs before pushing me again. I dropped onto the chair, pulling her down with me. "Condom?" she said between kisses. Wet. Hot. Clumsy kisses.

I cupped her face, staring her dead in the eye. "I haven't been with anyone since you."

Eva's eyes fluttered closed, the weight of my confession wrapping around us both. When they opened again, I saw nothing but pure emotion. With no more words spoken between us, Eva leaned in to kiss me as she gently sank down on me, rocking her hips in a slow torturous rhythm.

"You feel perfect," I ground out, barely able to think, overloaded with sensation. Curving a hand around her back, I brought Eva closer. My lips traced letters of love over her skin, nipping and sucking while my other hand dug into the perfect swell of her hip.

This, her, it was everything. The way she gave herself to me and trusted me to love her. We hadn't said the words, but I knew what I felt and Evangeline Star Walker was put on Earth for me to love. No one would understand it though. Our business, the industry, didn't want a true love story. It wanted scandal and sex tapes, stories that sold records and movies and improved ratings.

Sliding my hand up her spine, I cupped the back of Eva's neck, pressing my forehead to hers. I wanted to be as close to her as possible, to go as deep as possible. She rolled her hips faster as I rocked against her, the sounds of our quiet moans filling the room.

"Rafe, I can feel you everywhere." Her words were choppy, her breaths coming in short sharp bursts, as we both raced toward the edge.

"Do you feel me here?" I dropped a hand to her breastbone, right where her heart lay. "Do you feel me in here?"

Eva gasped, her body trembling as she hurtled over the edge, crying my name in a soft symphony. She tried to melt against me, but I held her there, kissing her with everything that I had. Tongues and teeth and silent vows. It was enough to send me soaring into the atmosphere as white hot pleasure shot down my spine.

"Fuck," I moaned, slowing my movements to nothing. Eva caught her breath, pressing her cheek to mine.

"This changes everything, doesn't it?" she murmured.

"Yeah." Dread began to seep into my chest, blotting out the pure ecstasy I felt. "Yeah, it does."

CHAPTER FIFTEEN

EVA

RAFE HELD me against him tightly, as if he thought I might disappear at any second. As if he wanted to savor the moment, not knowing when we might get another.

"We should get back to the party." I stood up and straightened my skirt before trying to smooth my hair. I could still feel Rafe everywhere, and I wanted nothing more than to disappear to a hotel with him and spend all night wrapped in his arms. But I knew it was one dream that wouldn't come true, so I pushed the feelings down, focusing only on this moment.

"Wait a second." He pulled me back down, kissing me. "I wish things could be different, Eva. I wish I could walk out there with you and declare you mine for all to see."

"But you won't do that to your band, to Levi." Guilt flashed in Rafe's eyes and I knew I was right. Only I couldn't help but wonder who he felt most guilty toward—me, for choosing Levi; or Levi, for choosing me.

"Levi doesn't want me, Rafe, it's not like that between us."

"He'd still see it as a betrayal," Rafe let out a pained sigh. Tipping his head back, he closed his eyes, taking in a deep breath. I could feel his torment and all I wanted to do was take it away. To carry it as my own.

I leaned in, kissing just above his Adam's apple. "Tell me what to do, Rafe. Do you want me to walk away? To forget that this feels right." I pressed my hand to his chest, right where his heart lay, and his hand covered mine.

"I thought I could give you up." His eyes dropped to mine, dark, stormy, and full of so much emotion my breath caught. "I can't." Rafe leaned in, touching his head to mine, breathing me in. "I can't walk away."

"It's okay," I offered, bringing my hands to his face. "We'll figure it out."

"Eva, I—" A loud knock on the door startled me.

"It's Travis," Rafe said grimly. "We need to go."

"I'll go first?" My stomach knotted at the thought of leaving him, of going back out there and pretending I didn't care. But our time was up.

He gave me a tight nod, dropping a quick kiss on my lips. "See you soon."

I gave myself a second to calm my racing pulse and run a hand through my no-doubt disheveled curls, before hurrying to the door and slipping out of the room. I didn't look back. I couldn't. I didn't want to see Rafe's face in the darkness. The guilt and regret and longing.

"Eva," Travis said. "Ms. Castiel is looking for you."

"Thanks, Travis." I knew I was blushing, but Travis knew what we'd been doing. "And thank you for..."

He nodded, his face a mask of indifference. Then he cleared his throat. "It's probably not my place to say this, Eva—"

"So don't." I smiled. "I appreciate your concern, I do. But things with me and Rafe are complicated. I'm grateful for your discretion, Travis."

"Understood." Travis accompanied me back into the club where Letty ambushed me.

"Where the hell have you been?"

"I went to the restroom and then needed some air. Why, what happened?"

"Levi got into it with some guy."

"Is he okay?" Dread snaked through me.

"He'll live, but the other guy got a little bloodied up. Damon and Hudson left with him already, and Alistair is trying to smooth things over with the guy. We need to leave."

"Yeah, okay." My thoughts were running a mile a minute.

Letty scanned the club. "Have you seen Rafe? He wasn't with the guys. I thought he might be with—"

"Hey." He approached us. "What's up?"

"Levi threw a fit and now we all have to bail."

"Fuck," Rafe pressed the heel of his palm to his head. "They already left?"

Letty nodded but she seemed distracted, watching Rafe a little too closely. "Where were you?" she asked him.

"I... Kiki Felps. She wouldn't leave me alone, so I told her I had an emergency and went to get some air with Fenton."

"Air, huh." Her eyes slid to mine, glittering with suspicion.

"We should go," I pointed out.

As we left the club, Letty stopped to discuss something with Riley. She looked stressed, hovering behind Alistair as he dealt with the aftermath of Levi's meltdown. I peeked over at Rafe as we piled into the SUV, but his eyes were hard, focused only on the road. Dejection burned through me, but I knew he felt guilty for being with me when Levi had lost it, because part of me felt guilty too. I inched my fingers across the leather until they brushed Rafe's. His body sagged into the seat as he let his fingers graze mine right back.

"Shit." The sound of Letty's voice made me snatch my hand away and shove it underneath my thigh. "There's a grainy video."

"Already?"

"Someone posted it on social media. I need to call PR." Her fingers flew across the screen and then her cell blared to life.

"Is this bad?" I whispered to Rafe.

"It's not good, but it's nothing we haven't experienced a hundred times already. PR will kill the video and issue an apology and the world will keep on turning."

"What do you think happened?"

"Any number of things. My brother has a long list of triggers." He finally gave me his eyes. "I just need to get to him."

These brothers. These complicated confusing brothers.

The minutes seemed to drag on, but finally, the hotel came into view. Travis parked around the back and we slipped in through the service entrance. Letty was still talking to PR as security ushered us into the elevator. She covered the mouthpiece and said, "Go to the band's suite, and I'll be there soon, okay?"

"But—"

"We got it, Letty," Rafe said. "Go do your thing." They shared a look and my assistant took off down the hall and the doors closed.

The pit in my stomach grew and grew. But it wasn't until we stepped off the elevator that I knew something was wrong.

Really wrong.

I could hear screaming, glass shattering, and more raised voices.

"Maybe I should escort Eva back to her suite," Travis suggested, but Rafe let out an exasperated breath and said, "She comes with me."

He took my elbow and guided me down the hall. "I'm sorry you have to see this, Eva." The regret in his voice made my heart ache. I didn't want him to have to hide from me, to conceal the truth about Levi. But nothing could have prepared me for the devastation I found when we stepped into the suite.

"Stay right here," Rafe said before he moved deeper into the room. Shards of glass were littered over the floor like a blanket of fresh ice. Furniture was overturned, and cushions were strewn everywhere.

"CALM THE FUCK DOWN," someone yelled, startling me. Hudson, I think.

"You didn't fucking hear the things he said, so don't tell me to calm the fuck down. That fucker wanted to hurt her, he wanted to—" Something crashed against the wall, reverberating through the room.

"Levi," that was Rafe.

"You. Where the fuck were you, huh, little brother?" Levi sneered.

"I'm here now, talk to me, tell me what happened."

I didn't mean to, but I found myself moving through the suite, drawn to the desperation in Levi's voice. The pain.

"That fucking asshole pushed me, he started talking all this shit and I couldn't listen to it, I couldn't hear him saying those things."

"What things? What was he saying?"

"Eva." My name echoed around the room, hitting me right in my chest and stealing the air from my lungs.

Levi was like this because of... me?

"Eva," Rafe sounded wary. "What does Eva have to do with any of this?"

I'd reached the door to the bedroom they were all in. Inching closer, I peered inside. Damon saw me first, shaking his head gently, his eyes silently telling me to retreat. I froze, my eyes widening, when they landed on Levi. Blood splattered his shirt and his knuckles were split open. His gaze snapped to mine, and his nostrils flared. "You brought her here?" he spat at Rafe. "YOU FUCKING BROUGHT HER HERE?"

A mask of fury washed over him as he homed in on his brother. "Levi," I said calmly. "Look at me."

Damon moved slowly toward me, but I ignored him, focusing on Levi. "What happened tonight?"

"It doesn't concern you," he ground out. "You need to leave."

"I'm not leavin'." I took a step forward. "You're hurt."

His eyes dropped to his hand and he shrugged. "It's nothing."

"It doesn't look like nothin'. Why don't you let me clean it up and you can tell me what happened at the club?"

Levi looked like a caged animal ready to bolt. I had no idea what I was doing but I knew I couldn't just walk away and leave him. Not when he was in so much anguish.

"Is there a first aid kit around here?" I asked no one in particular.

"I'll get one," Damon said, obviously satisfied I had no intentions on leaving, or that Levi was stable enough for me to be around.

"Can I take a look?" I edged closer to Levi.

"You should go, Eva. I'm too amped up and I don't want to—"

"You won't hurt me." Reaching for him, I took his injured hand in mine. Levi flinched at the initial contact but soon relaxed into my touch. "Come sit on the bed," I said. "It'll be easier for me to clean it."

"I don't know about anyone else," Hudson said. "But I need a drink. You two good?" His eyes went to Levi, but I answered, "He's fine, aren't you?"

Levi's eyes narrowed with confusion, as if he couldn't understand why I was being like this, why I was trying to care for him. Whatever had happened to him growing up had left scars so deep I wasn't sure I'd ever understand.

"It doesn't look too deep." I inspected the wound. "Rafe, get me a clean damp towel?" Our eyes met and he swallowed. I knew this had to be hard for him, watching me attend to his brother, especially after everything he'd said earlier. But I had to do this.

I couldn't explain it, but something deep inside told me this was the right thing to do.

"You should see the other guy's face." Levi attempted to make a joke, but it came out strangled.

"He was pretty bloodied up. Did it make you feel better?"

He shrugged again. "For a second. I liked the feel of my knuckles crunching against his nose. But now, now it doesn't feel so good."

Rafe came back and handed me the towel. "Do you want me to stay?"

I wasn't sure if he was asking me or his brother, so I let Levi answer. "We're good," he said.

"I'll be in the living room." They shared a long look, and I wondered how many times they had done this routine. How often Rafe had to watch his brother lose his cool, and then try to pick up the pieces.

"This might sting." I pressed the towel to his hand but Levi didn't even flinch.

"I'm tired," he mumbled. "So fucking tired."

"It shouldn't take too long. Here, hold this a second." His hand brushed mine as he took over.

"Found it." Damon appeared holding up a first aid kit. "If you need anything else, I'll have to call down to reception.

"We should be good, thank you."

He gave me a small nod before backing up to give me some room. I dug out some gauze and tape. "Ready?"

Levi nodded, his eyes growing heavy. He'd been so wild when we'd gotten here, riding the crest of an angry wave, but now he was crashing toward the shore.

"What happened at the club, Levi?" I asked as I worked to wrap his knuckles.

"It doesn't matter."

"I think it does. I heard you say my name."

"You weren't supposed to hear that." He toyed with his lip piercings. On a regular day, Levi Hunter was a force to be reckoned with. Dark. Moody. Skin covered in metal and ink. But tonight, he seemed childlike. Vulnerable and volatile.

"I know what I signed on for." I went on. "I know sometimes people will say horrible things about me, and I'm okay with that. You can't go around hittin' people to defend my honor, Levi."

"It wasn't like," he scoffed but I saw the flash of regret in his eyes. "He wanted to bait me, and he used you to do it."

Silence settled over us as I finished bandaging his hand. My handiwork left a little to be desired but it would do. "There, all done." I patted his hand and then started cleaning up. Levi kicked off his boots and swung his legs up on the bed, scooting back against the headboard.

"Feelin' better?" I asked him with a smile.

"Will you hate me if I say I still want to pound the guy's face in?"

His words made me wince. Perching on the edge of the bed, I looked him right in the eye and said, "You were just startin' to grow on me; don't ruin it now."

Laughter rumbled in his chest as he folded his arms behind his head. "So, Miss Evangeline Star Walker, how's it feel being a big superstar now?"

"It's a work in progress." I kicked off my boots and joined Levi on the bed. It was king size so there was plenty of space between us. "It feels like I've been here forever, and yet, it's barely been a week."

"Don't tell the guys," he lowered his voice to a whisper. "But I think I like you the most."

My eyes flicked to the door where Rafe and the guys sat just on the other side. Guilt coiled around my heart. He was out there, and I was in here, with his brother. But I didn't feel like that toward Levi. Sure, I felt a strange desire to protect him and be there for him, but that's all it was. And despite his wicked smirks and innuendo and flirtations, Levi didn't give off the wrong vibes either.

"Sing to me, Angel."

"Levi, I can't sing to you."

"Sure you can. I need it to stop. I need it to fucking stop just for a second. Sing to me, please."

I had no idea what he was talking about, but I couldn't deny him.

"Any requests?" I looked over at him, but his eyes were closed, his brows drawn tight, as if he was trying to keep out unwanted thoughts.

"Anything, Country. Just need to hear your voice." His words were slow and quiet.

Pulling a pillow from beside me, I clutched it to my chest and sang the first thing that came into my head.

Woke up this morning, with tears on my pillow.
    And I cried.
    Went through the motions, the questions and anger.
    And I tried.
    Told myself I'd make it, would fight 'til the end.
    And I lied.

Because all it takes is a second for everything to change.

I woke with a start. My eyes strained against my unfamiliar surroundings. Where was I?

Oh.

Levi's room.

I was in Levi's room.

"He's been like that for hours." Rafe's voice was flat. I tried to sit up to better see him, but Levi had wrapped himself around me like a child.

Or a lover.

I pushed the unwanted thought out of my head.

Gently inching Levi's hand off my stomach, I sat up, pushing the hair from my face. "What time is it?"

"After three."

"Why didn't you wake me?"

Rafe let out a shaky breath. "I haven't seen him sleep so peacefully for years."

"He has nightmares?"

Rafe nodded.

"I should go." It had felt necessary to be here earlier but now it felt wrong.

Now it felt like a betrayal to Rafe.

"I didn't mean to fall asleep," I said, hoping he would understand.

"I know." He stood up and offered me his hand. I slid my palm into his and let him pull me to my feet. Levi stirred, mumbling something inaudible but quickly settled again.

Rafe leaned in, and I thought he was going to kiss me. Instead, he breathed in deeply and then moved away. "Come on, I'll walk you to your room."

The suite was quiet as we left Levi's room and headed for the door.

"I'm sorry," I blurted out. "I didn't mean to—"

"Eva," Rafe palmed my cheeks, "never be sorry for caring. Did I hate seeing you like that with him? Of course I did. But part of me is also so grateful that you were here. It doesn't usually end so well when Levi loses it, but you... he responds to you." Sadness washed over his expression, as if he already thought he'd lost me.

"This is very confusing," I admitted. Not because I felt for Levi what I felt for Rafe, I didn't. But I couldn't deny I did feel something. It wasn't as intense or as wrapped up in desire like the way my feelings for Rafe were, but it was there.

"It's you I want, Rafe."

"I know." He curved a hand around my neck and drew me close, pressing a kiss to my forehead. "You should go. It's late and we have a busy day tomorrow." But Rafe didn't move. There, in the cloak of darkness, he held me while I buried my face in his neck and silently wished things could be different. That things could be simple. That we could just be Rafe and Eva.

But we weren't just Rafe and Eva.

We were Eva and Black Hearts Still Beat.

We were Eva and Rafe... and Levi.

And nothing about that was simple.

CHAPTER SIXTEEN

RAFE

"LA, you're looking as sexy as fuck tonight," my brother yelled into the mic. He was high on the rush, bouncing on the balls of his feet, his inked skin on display. Our stylists had long given up trying to make him wear the outfits they used to carefully pick out for him every show. Levi Hunter did his own thing, and everyone else could either get on board or go fuck themselves.

Strutting across the stage, he ran a hand through his hair. "Are you ready to rock?"

The crowd's ferocious cheer almost blew me away. They were amped, anticipation rippling around the Staples Center. Eva and Letty were standing in the wings, and I couldn't resist glancing over at them. She grinned and I smiled back. It had been less than twenty-four hours since Levi had lost it. Less than twenty-four hours since I watched the girl who held my heart in the palm of her hand, comfort my brother. Seeing them lying there asleep, Levi curled into her body, had almost fucking killed me. I'd sat there in the shadows, watching for hours, my jaw clenched, my fist curled against my thigh. I wanted to pick her up and take her far, far away from him. But Eva was right.

It was confusing.

Because as much as I didn't want my brother to have her, I couldn't deny seeing how much she calmed him gave me a sense of peace. It was a mind fuck—wanting her but wanting him to have part of her too.

Damon dropped the opening beat to *Monsters in the Dark*, pulling me back into the moment as Levi howled the lyrics in the night.

Sun fades, darkness comes, and I don't want to be here,
  I don't want to see
  Shadows rein, nightmares live, and I don't want to move,
  I don't want to see

Beat me, berate me, but you can't break me.
  Beat me, berate me, but you can't break me.

The lights go off and I don't want to sleep. I can't let go, and I know I can't show
that I'm afraid... I'm afraid of monsters in the dark

Beat me, berate me, but you can't break me.
  Beat me, berate me, but you can't break me.

I'll fight, I'll resist, I won't give in... I won't give in to the monsters in the dark

HE DIDN'T JUST SING THE LYRICS, HE BLED THEM OUT ALL OVER THE stage. Every song we'd penned was personal: our story, the gritty details of our childhood weaved into every word. But we never publicly admitted it. Time and time again, we had been asked what our songs meant, about the dark and depraved meaning behind the lyrics. And time and time again we gave the same answer, they were just words.

Messed up words from four messed up guys.

We all knew the truth, but it was *our* truth, and we weren't ready to share that with the world.

Maybe we never would be.

It only added to the mystery, the intrigue and appeal.

It had been the four of us for so long, and now there was Eva. Sweet, compassionate, pure-hearted Eva. But she also carried a darkness, I'd seen it that weekend in Camdena. It had faded some since the tour commenced, but it was still there, deep inside her. Part of me wondered if that's why she'd so easily slipped into life on the road with us. If maybe, in some fucked-up cosmic way, she was right where she was supposed to be.

Levi jogged over to me, winking as he spun around and tipped his head back on my shoulder, belting out the lines, "The lights go off and I don't want to sleep. I can't let go, and I know I can't show that I'm afraid... I'm afraid of monsters in the dark."

All those people in the crowd and not a single one of them knew. They had no idea how close my brother had come to relapsing last night. That his past and present had collided and splintered his reality in a way he couldn't handle.

Usually, after such an incident, he woke up full of self-loathing and regret, reaching for a bottle or a chasing a high with whatever drug he could get his hands on.

Last night though, he'd reached for Eva.

To say his progress was bittersweet was a huge fucking understatement.

The knot in my stomach tightened. We hadn't talked about what happened and thanks to a busy day of interviews it had been easy to avoid Eva. But we couldn't avoid each other forever, and I didn't want to. She was so sure Levi didn't want her; yet, she didn't know him like I did. He was unpredictable and impulsive and he rarely gave a thought to how his actions might affect anyone else. He might not have wanted her now, but what happened when he decided he did?

By the time Levi invited Eva on stage with us, the atmosphere was electric. LA always turned out a good crowd, but tonight was a whole other level. As I watched my brother and Eva perform their stripped back version of *Running Up That Hill*, I knew it had something to do with him. He was revitalized.

Alive.

And I was pretty sure it was all thanks to Eva.

"WE'RE GOING OUT," LEVI ANNOUNCED ONCE WE WERE ALL BACK IN the dressing room. The show had been one of our best yet and everyone was still riding the high.

"No way," Alistair said. "No fucking way. After last night you're lucky you're not facing assault charges."

"It was a couple of punches." My brother shrugged in his usual arrogant way, running his busted knuckles across his jaw.

Ali straightened. "I mean it, Levi. Not tonight."

"This is bullshit." He leaped up. "We just killed it out there and you want to put us on lockdown? Well, newsflash, Portman, you can go fu—"

"*Levi!*" I snapped. "He's right. We can hang on the bus, order in, and play cards."

Or get some sleep, which was all I wanted to do.

"Fine, whatever," he grumbled, and relief spread through me that he wasn't going to fight me on this. "I only wanted to celebrate. She deserves it."

That had me frowning. Alistair shifted uncomfortably, clearing his throat. "It was supposed to be a need to know basis," he glowered at Levi, "but since he brought it up, I'm going to tell you. Eva has accepted the label's offer of representation. It isn't official yet, so I'd appreciate it if you can keep this between the four of you for now."

I felt so many things at once, I didn't know what to think.

I was happy, so fucking happy for Eva. She deserved this. But my happiness was tangled up in a web of fear and trepidation.

"Levi's right, we should celebrate," Hudson said, surprising everyone in the room. "What?" he added at our expressions of disbelief. "I'm over it. If anyone deserves it, it's Eva."

"No clubs, not tonight. Duke wants us on the road as soon as possible. Celebrations will have to wait."

"Actually, they don't." Hudson smirked. "I have an idea."

"I'm going to regret this, aren't I?" Alistair groaned, rubbing a hand over his face.

"Just hear me out, okay?"

For the next ten minutes, Hudson revealed his plans to us. To our surprise, Alistair had gone for it. If it meant us being on the bus and not roaming downtown LA causing trouble, he was all in.

"Do you think she'll go for it?" Damon asked me as we made our way back to the bus.

"Maybe." I went to grab the handrail, but he stopped me.

"About last night—"

"Let's not do this right now." I let out a heavy sigh. "He needed her, and she was there."

"Jesus, Rafe, you're a better man than me. I'm not sure I could have watched that." He made it sound like I'd walked in on them having sex. But I knew what he meant, and Damon was right. In some ways, seeing Levi curled into Eva hurt more.

"Tonight is about Eva, the rest can wait," I said before ducking onto the bus. If we were really doing this, time was against us.

———

"Oh my..." Eva covered her face with her hands as she moved into the bus. We all stood there like idiots, streamers everywhere and a few random balloons taped to the wall. Hudson and Levi had even scrawled 'congratulations' on a homemade banner.

"We're celebrating." Hudson slung his arm around her neck and dragged her closer to us. "Alistair told us the news, congratulations, Eva." He kissed her cheek and she blushed; a deep shade of pink that was so fucking adorable I wanted to see where else on her body I could turn that color.

"Congratulations, Eva." Damon pulled a party popper before pulling her in for a hug.

"I can't believe you guys did all this." Letty smiled, pride glittering in her eyes.

"If a few streamers and pizzas get you all excited, Let, I feel very sorry for the guy you end up with."

"Fuck you," she said, punching Hudson in the shoulder.

"There's cake," Levi added. "Don't forget about the cake."

Eva leaned in, inspecting the tray bake. "Does that say Happy Bar Mitzvah Kenny?"

"Do you have any idea how hard it is getting a cake at eleven thirty in downtown LA?" Hudson chuckled. "Pretty fucking hard. But the lovely lady at Cakes 'n' Shakes had this bad boy going to waste. Bar Mitzvah or no Bar Mitzvah, it tastes good." He stuck his finger in the frosting and dragged it along the edge before pushing it toward Eva's lips. She jerked back, fighting him off, but Hudson gave chase, her soft laughter filling the bus.

"I'll take your word for it. You guys, this is..." Her eyes found mine, silently telling me all the things I wouldn't get to hear, at least, not while we were with everyone.

"Did you bring your overnight stuff?" Damon asked Letty, and Eva frowned.

"Overnight—" Just then, the bus rumbled to life and her eyes widened. "We're moving, why are we moving?"

"Welcome to the party bus," Hudson winked. "You and Letty can take the second bedroom since we finally got rid of Alistair. We'd give you the first but well..."

"I've heard about that bedroom." Eva rose a brow at him. "The second one is fine."

"A drink for the lady." Damon handed Eva a plastic flute of champagne. We'd given Fenton and Jake a list of supplies to get from the twenty-four-hour gas station on the next block.

"Just when I think life can't get any stranger," Eva slid into the bench and everyone filed in around her. "I find myself on the tour bus with a rock band drinkin' champagne and eating pizza. Cheers, everyone." She lifted her flute, and we all followed suit.

"To Eva," Damon said.

"To Eva." Our voices echoed through the bus.

"And to livin' for the music," Eva added.

"Hear, fucking hear." Hudson downed his beer and slammed it on the counter. "Anyone for another?"

"I'll take another soda." Levi shook his empty. Our eyes connected and I gave him a reassuring nod. Every day he didn't reach for a bottle of liquor, a handful of pills, or a line of coke was progress. Even if his newest remedy was Eva.

We all dug into the pizza, eating like we'd never tasted tomato and cheese before. Eating on tour was a funny thing. You either wanted to devour everything in sight, or didn't have time, energy, or the stomach for food. Given how quickly we went through four large pizzas and various sides, it was safe to say we were all in the former camp tonight.

"That was so good." Eva rubbed her stomach. "I think I'm in a food coma."

"None of that. The night is still young and we have games to play," Hudson said.

"Games?" She smothered a yawn. "I'm not sure I have energy for games."

"Eva, Eva, Eva, you're killing me here. We wanted to take you out on the town but Alistair-Wouldn't-Know-What-Fun-Is-If-It-Hit-Him-In-The-Ass pulled the manager card and put us on lockdown, so here we are."

"Hey, give a girl some credit. Until a couple of months ago, I was just a high schooler tryin' to get through senior year."

"How'd your parents take it?" Damon asked. "It couldn't have been easy letting you quit senior year."

A sad expression washed over Eva. If anyone else noticed, they didn't say. I saw it though. "It's the dream, right? And I'm eighteen. Besides, I have a lifetime to get my GED."

Her words felt forced. Fake, even. Damon's words about her parents swam around my head. But it wasn't the time or place to ask her.

"I can't even remember what it was like to be in high school." Levi kicked his feet up onto an empty chair. "I can remember fucking hating that place with every breath though. Remember, Rafe, it should have been me keeping your ass in class, but it was always you dragging me there."

"It wasn't that long ago," Eva said, nibbling the last slice of pizza.

"Long enough, Angel." Levi used the nickname so easily now, but it was still like a punch to the gut every time it rolled off his tongue. Damon caught my eye. I dropped my gaze, unwilling to go there.

"School had its uses," Hudson added. "I learned a lot from the senior girls back in the day."

"Ugh, gross," Letty fake gagged, but it only spurred him on. He made a V with his fingers and licked the air. "Can it, Ryker. We don't know where that has been." She balled up a napkin and threw it at him.

"You're just jealous because it's never been on you," he teased.

"Yeah, that must be it." She rolled her eyes, murmuring, "I can't believe I ever thought you were the hottest member of the band. Pig."

"Lighten up, Letty. Sounds like you need a good hard—"

"Ryker," my brother hissed. "Shut the fuck up. If Eva doesn't want to play a game, we don't have to play a game. It's her night, her rules." Everyone's eyes slid to Eva and she shrank into the bench. "So, Angel, what would you like to do?"

She tapped the end of her nose and then pointed to the corner of the ceiling. "Does that work?"

Quiet laughter rumbled in my chest. Here she was, in the middle of a tour bus with four rock stars and Evangeline Star Walker wanted to watch a film.

"Do we even have any DVDs?" Hudson asked.

"I think there's a box in that overhead bin somewhere." Damon got up and went to find a movie.

"This has been great, you guys, truly, but I'm exhausted." Eva yawned again, stretching her arms high enough to make her Black Hearts t-shirt rise, revealing a sliver of skin. Fuck. This was like torture. Having her right there and not being able to touch her. But I would manage, the way I always did.

"Chick flick or action film?" Damon called. Letty and Eva shared a conspiratorial look.

"Chick flick." Eva grinned, returning her assistant's high-five.

"Never thought I'd see the day..." Hudson grumbled as he grabbed a cushion and stuffed it behind his head. We all spread out over the bench and chairs, getting comfortable. Eva was too far away for my liking but at least I wouldn't be tempted to do something stupid like reach for her hand.

"Okay, we should be good to go." Damon joined us.

"Before you hit play," Eva said, her voice turning serious. I sat a little straighter. "I just want to say..." She hesitated and alarm bells rang in my head. "I... well, thank you. For tonight, for makin' me so welcome. It means a lot. More than you'll probably ever know."

"Jesus, Walker, I thought you were about to tell us you and Hunter were having a secret love child or something." Hudson realized his error instantly, the color draining from his face. "Shit, I didn't... excuse me while I go bury myself in the giant fucking hole I just made."

Eva laughed it off, but I saw the tightness around her eyes. Letty and Damon watched the two us, trying to see past our façades. All while Levi sat there none the wiser, a wolfish grin plastered on his face, because he didn't think Hudson meant me.

He assumed the joke was on him.

And he didn't seem in the least bit bothered.

CHAPTER SEVENTEEN

EVA

I WOKE to the sound of the small television crackling. Sitting up, I rubbed my eyes and scanned the dimly lit bus.

"Hey," Rafe's whisper cut through the air and I found him across from me, relaxed back in a chair.

"I fell asleep?"

"You weren't the only one." His eyes went to Hudson and Levi who were both out cold, their gentle snores creating a strange symphony.

"Ugh, my neck," I tried to stretch out the sore muscle. "Damon and Letty?" I asked, and his eyes slid to the bunks further down the bus. "Together?" My brows hit my hairline.

"No." Rafe chuckled. "Letty took a spare bunk. Old habit, I guess. You can take the bedroom, get some sleep."

My eyes flicked to Hudson and Levi again. "Show me where it is?" I gingerly inched out from behind the table, careful not to knock Hudson.

"It's right down—"

"Show me," I reached Rafe, gazing down at him, "please."

His eyes shuttered as he drew in a harsh breath. I half-expected him to say no. We were on the band's tour bus, surrounded by his, albeit sleeping, bandmates. But Rafe didn't refuse me. Instead, he got up and moved down the bus, stopping outside a narrow door. "It isn't much, but it's private."

I slipped past him, the weight of his stare burning into my back. I glanced over my shoulder, ready to ask him to stay a minute, but he was already there. Rafe hooked his finger into my jeans and pulled me around, crowding me against the wall. "Do you have any idea how many times I've wanted to do this today?" His lips hovered over mine, teasing and tempting.

"Rafe." I slid my hands up his chest, pulling him closer. "We shouldn't..." The last thing I wanted was to get him in trouble but the tether between us snapped taut.

I needed him.

I needed to know we were okay.

"Don't move, Starshine, don't move an inch." Rafe kissed me, soft at first, slipping his tongue into my mouth with slow shallow licks. My body trembled, his touch almost too much to bear, but at the same time, nowhere near enough to douse the flames growing inside me. Rafe pressed his hand against the wall beside my head and leaned in, pushing his hard lines against my soft curves.

"Can you be quiet?" he whispered the words against my lips.

I nodded, smothering the moan building in my throat. Taking a step back, Rafe let his eyes move over me. He lingered on my lips, the curve of my breasts, the hem of my leggings.

"The things I want to do with you, Starshine." His voice was quiet, the words gruff. My tummy clenched, heat spreading through me. My eyes flicked to the door. It was ajar, a sliver of light shining inside. From my position, I could see just down the bus, but no one would be able to see inside the bedroom without coming much closer.

"Tell me you're mine." Rafe's eyes were as black as night, streaked with flashes of silver-gray. He looked deadly. Dark and dangerous.

He looked like he wanted to eat me alive.

"I'm yours," I breathed, gasping as he fluttered a single finger down the column of my neck. It lingered on the neckline of my t-shirt.

"I like seeing our name on you." Rafe's finger slipped to the printed heart and he slowly, painstakingly, traced each word.

Black.

Hearts.

Still.

Beat.

My heart crashed in my chest, overwhelming me in the best kind of way. I was trapped. Pinned in place by eyes so intense, so filled with torment and emotion, I could hardly breathe.

"You're mine, Starshine. Not his. Not the bands. *Mine*." Rafe's hand fanned out as he dragged it down my stomach, all the way to the apex of my thighs. He pressed his palm against me, eliciting a breathy moan from me.

"I shouldn't do this," he said, his voice thick with desire. "I shouldn't slip my hands inside and feel how wet you are for me. But I can't stop myself. You own me, Eva," his hand dipped inside my leggings, "you've owned me ever since the first day I laid eyes on you." His fingers found their way into my panties, sliding between my wetness.

I bit my lip to stifle the moan building. It felt too good. My legs quivered, but Rafe was right there to hold me up as he slowly worked two fingers inside me.

"More," I whisper-cried in the darkness, letting my head fall back against the wall. There was a gentle thud and both of us froze. A beat passed and another. Rafe watched me, his gaze hard and possessive as he began to move his fingers again. Curling and stroking. He didn't kiss me. He didn't speak or whisper dirty words into my ear. He showed me with his touch, communicated with his eyes, what he felt.

My skin grew hot, my breaths coming in short sharp bursts as Rafe took me to the brink. "I'm goin' to..." I smashed my lips together, trying to swallow the cries as heavy waves of pleasure washed over me.

Rafe leaned in, dragging his tongue up my neck and kissing me. "You look so fucking good like this." He bought his fingers to his lips and sucked them clean. "You taste good too."

My legs buckled again. He was so different like this. Dominant and dirty, and in complete control of me. My body.

I pressed my head to his shoulder, trying to catch my breath. "Is this the part where you leave me?" It was unfair of me to ask him, but the words spilled from my lips without warning.

"I wish it could be different." He sighed deeply.

"Rafe, I—"

"Dream of me, Eva. Dream of me right there beside you, holding you."

I nodded, swallowing over the lump in my throat.

Slowly, Rafe eased away from me, his eyes full of regret. "Sleep tight, Starshine." He pressed a kiss to my head before ducking out of the room.

As if he hadn't just rocked my world.

As if he hadn't just stolen the final piece of my heart and taken it with him.

———

THE SMELL OF BURNING WOKE ME UP. "WHAT THE...?" I PUSHED THE covers off, pulled on my leggings and went to see what on earth was happening.

"Morning, Angel." Hudson grinned as he pushed what I assumed was supposed to be bacon around a pan.

"What are you doin'?"

"Well, I was trying to make you breakfast, but I'm guessing from the way your lip is curled in disgust, I shouldn't have bothered."

"I think you killed the bacon." I smothered a laugh, moving closer. "Are there pancakes?"

"Of course there are... Damon, is there pancake mix?" he yelled over his shoulder, and Damon came padding out of the bathroom, a towel hanging low on his waist.

I quickly looked away, and they both chuckled. "We forget how sweet and innocent you are. Morning, Eva."

"Good mornin', Damon." I gave him a warm smile, keeping my eyes on his face. "Hudson killed the bacon."

"Nah," he reached into the pan plucking a piece out. "The crispier the better. Pancake mix should be in the cabinet." He motioned above our heads.

"Thanks. Where's Letty?"

"Morning briefing with the other assistants."

"So we're already in Nevada?"

"Crossed the border about an hour ago. Duke wanted to make a pit stop, refuel and stock up on supplies. We won't hit Vegas for another hour or so. This one," he nodded toward Hudson, "thought he'd try his hand at making breakfast."

"I think we can rustle up somethin' between the two of us."

"See, I knew you'd come in handy." Hudson smirked.

"Where are Levi and Rafe?"

"Levi is still sleeping and Rafe is... actually, I have no idea where Rafe is. He probably went to stretch his legs. Why do you ask?"

"No reason." I busied myself with searching for the pancake mix.

"How was the bed?"

"It was fine... better than the bunks." I felt their eyes burning into me, and heat spread up my neck.

Just then the door opened and Rafe appeared. "Hey," he said. "I thought I smelled bacon."

"We're makin' breakfast." I met his eyes, fighting a smile.

"How did you sleep?" It was an innocent enough question, but I knew he wasn't talking about whether I'd found the bed comfortable or not.

"Good, real good," I replied, my cheeks flushing.

"You two are—"

"What the fuck is that smell?" Levi came out of the other

bedroom, rubbing his face. His hair was sticking up at all angles, his eyelids heavy with sleep.

"We're makin' breakfast," I said for the second time. "Hungry?"

"Fuck, yes. I could eat a cow."

"We don't have cow, but we do have extra crispy bacon and I'm about to make pancakes."

"Hell, yeah." Levi slumped down on the bench. He seemed unusually tired, as if he was recovering from a big night out. But we'd stayed in and had all fallen asleep.

"Is Levi okay?" I whispered to Hudson as we worked side by side to make breakfast.

He glanced back to where his friend sat. "Sometimes he gets like this. One minute he can be as high as a kite and the next, he's barely awake. He'll be okay though."

"I hope there's enough for one more." Letty's voice filtered down the bus and seconds later she appeared, bright-eyed and well-rested.

"I have a surprise for you." She homed in on me.

"You have a fresh packet of bacon?" I asked earning me a nudge in the ribs from Hudson. Our laughter filled the bus.

"Nope. But how's this?" A slow grin spread over her face. "Molly is flying in to see the show tonight."

"She is? But how—"

"I'm not just the world's best assistant, you know. I have a few other tricks up my sleeve."

"Oh my gosh." I dropped the fork and launched myself at Letty. "You're the best, the world's best." I hugged her tightly.

She chuckled, hugging me back. "I thought you'd be happy."

Happy?

I couldn't believe it.

It had only been ten days since I'd seen her, but it felt like forever. Time moved differently in this world. The days were long, going from interview to interview; appearance to appearance; sound check to sound check. And the nights were surreal. The shows, the parties... it felt like I'd been gone ten hundred days, not less than two weeks.

"I was hoping your parents could come too, but they wanted to wait until they could drive."

"That sounds like Mom." She had a terrible fear of flying, and I couldn't imagine my parents in Vegas.

"Molly's flight gets in at two, so there'll be plenty of time to catch up before the show. I've got her a full backstage pass and then tonight, she'll be staying with us at the hotel."

"Thank you, this means everything to me." My eyes slid to Hudson. "Will you be okay seein' her again?"

"Wait, who's Molly again?"

I grabbed a towel and flicked it at him. He jerked back, trying to stop my attack. "Joke," he chuckled. "I was joking. This is your big moment, Eva. Of course you want your best friend there."

"You know, you're really not that bad sometimes."

"Only sometimes?" His brow quirked. "Sweetheart, I am fucking awesome."

"At everythin' except cookin' bacon it would seem."

Hudson's expression darkened. "It's a good thing I like you."

We didn't discuss Molly again. Instead, we ate breakfast while the guys told me about the last time they performed in Las Vegas. They had been at a smaller venue when a group of girls managed to break through security and storm the stage. It sounded terrifying, but they all laughed about it, reassuring me it had only ever happened a handful of times.

After breakfast, I went to get my cell and text Molly, only to find at least five messages from her.

Surprise!!! I'm on the way to the airport, I'll see you soon.

I packed a ton of outfits. You'll help me pick somethin out, right? I have to look incredible. I cannot see him again lookin anything less than a sexy goddess who is far too good for Hudson I'm-not-even-that-good-in-bed Ryker.

There was another sent straight after.

Crap, you're not with him right now, are you? Do not, I repeat DO NOT, ever let him see these messages. In fact, delete them. Delete them right now Evangeline Star Walker. Oh shoot, my flight is about to board. I'll see you soon xo

Holy shit, you should see the guy I'm sitting next to. Hello tall, dark, and handsome. Goodbye playboy rock star who will never get to see me naked again.

. . .

THE STEWARDESS JUST TOLD ME TO TURN OFF MY CELL FOR take-off. Tonight is goin to be epic, Eva. I can't wait to see you.

SHE'D SIGNED OFF WITH LITTLE GUITAR AND ROCK HORN EMOJIS. Typical Molly. Talking at a hundred miles an hour, thoughts shooting off in a hundred different directions. She talked a good talk, but I knew there was an underlying truth to her messages about Hudson. Molly was probably en route to Vegas armed with her favorite skin-tight mini dress armor and her secret weapon of choice: six-inch stiletto heels. It was a rock concert, but I didn't doubt my best friend would be dressed to kill with the specific mission of making the Black Hearts drummer as jealous as she possibly could.

Tonight was going to be very interesting indeed.

———

THE SECOND THE BLACK SUV ROLLED UP I SHRIEKED WITH excitement. Letty chuckled beside me. We were waiting in the basement garage of The Lyndham. It was reserved for VIP guests, lending us some privacy. Although my little entourage of one assistant and two bodyguards didn't quite have the same appeal.

Molly didn't even wait for the driver to cut the engine. She barreled out of the car and tackle hugged me. "Holy cow, Eva, this is the best day ever."

"I'm glad you think so." I hugged her tighter, relieved to have my best friend here. Just because there had barely been time to miss her, didn't mean I didn't feel the hole she left every minute of the day. We texted all the time and tried to FaceTime as much as we could, but it wasn't the same as seeing her in person.

"I missed you," I whispered, "so damn much."

"Oh no, superstar." She pulled back, holding me at arm's length. "None of that today. We are goin' to enjoy every second I'm here."

"Deal." My cheeks hurt from all the smiling.

"This is the life, babe. I mean look around."

"Hmm, Mol, we're standin' in a basement garage with my bodyguards."

"Exactly my point. This is higher level shit, Eva. I mean," she leaned in and whispered, "you have bodyguards now, and we're in Vegas. Vegas, baby! It's crazy."

The corner of Travis' lip tipped. Letty cleared her throat and I swung around to her. "Molly, this is my amazin' assistant Letty."

"We're acquainted." She smiled but it quickly turned into mask of disbelief as Molly pulled her in for a hug.

"Thank you so much for organizin' this. Any friend of Eva's is a friend of mine, and honestly, it's been a huge relief knowin' she has you."

"That's... fine." Letty politely untangled herself from Molly.

"You'll have to excuse Molly," I said, "she doesn't get out much."

"Damn right, I don't. I can't wait to see our room. Tell me we get the penthouse."

"Molly!"

"What, babe? This is a once in a lifetime opportunity. I plan on milkin' it for all it's worth."

"This is going to be fun," Letty said cryptically, and I couldn't help but wonder if she knew something I didn't.

But I'd find out soon enough.

Minutes later, we piled out of the elevator and made our way to our room on the thirty-fifth floor of the hotel. "Not quite the penthouse," Molly said as we entered the suite. "But it'll do."

"I'm sorry," I mouthed at Letty, but she seemed amused by the whole thing.

"The guys are right next door. They'll be along after they get done with the Rock Vegas FM interview."

Molly walked over to the window and peered over the city. "This is life, Eva. Hey, Letty, you don't happen to need an assistant, do you?" She waggled her brows, and the three of us burst into laughter. Then she said nine little words that sucked the fun right out of the moment.

"Is that a swarm of Die Hearts down there?"

CHAPTER EIGHTEEN

RAFE

"Aren't Riley and Alistair supposed to stop shit like this happening?" Hudson ground out as our SUV looped around the hotel for the second time. The Die Hearts were everywhere, waving their banners and sporting all kinds of Black Hearts merchandise.

"We have the all-clear from the hotel," Jake said from upfront. "We can enter via the service entrance."

"Eva and the girls are already inside, right?" Damon asked.

"Yeah, I just spoke to Travis. They've been inside about an hour."

Relief slammed into me. At least, they hadn't been down here to see this. It was crazy. There were already a handful of officers trying to contain the crowd. Eva had won over most of our fans. Show after show, their love for the new sweetheart of country only grew. But these fans were different; they truly believed they had some twisted ownership over us and it was only a matter of time before Eva got caught up in it. Damon had already showed me some of the stuff they were saying about her online.

The pure innocent little church girl letting a rock band dirty her up a little.

That shit made my blood boil. Thank fuck, Eva refused to fall down the social media rabbit hole, and I knew Letty screened what she shared with her, so she was oblivious to it for the most part. But there was no missing some of the Die Hearts more venomous banners aimed right at her.

It didn't matter if we were going all out to protect Eva from the dark side of the industry, we knew it was only a matter of time before someone said or did something to try to knock Eva off her new pedestal.

"Okay, let's move." Jake came around the side of the SUV and opened the door. "We need to be quick." His eyes remained on the alley leading around to the service entrance of the hotel.

We all climbed out and started toward the door, just as someone shrieked, "There they are. Oh my god, it's them, it's really them."

A wave of girls swept toward us, their voices blending into a loud crescendo as they drew closer. "Fucking hell," Damon breathed, as security scrambled to usher the four of us inside.

"Fenton, call for back up."

"On it," my bodyguard radioed through to the rest of the team.

"Levi, I love you."

"Fuck me hard, Hudson."

"Rafe, oh my god, look at him."

"Damon Donnelley owns my heart."

The catcalls and hollers rolled off us as we ducked inside, the door slamming shut behind us.

"You think Fenton will be okay?" someone asked.

He'd stayed behind to prevent any of them from trying to enter the hotel.

"Another team is almost here."

"We need to find out who the fuck is leaking our location to people. The hotel promised complete discretion."

"People talk," Jake grumbled. "It happens all the time."

And didn't we know it. But we hadn't even checked in yet, coming straight from the interview at Rock Vegas FM.

"The Die Hearts were already camped outside the hotel waiting," I said what we were all thinking. "They knew we would be here."

"Maybe someone saw Eva arrive."

"It's possible," Jake agreed but I saw the tightness around his eyes. He didn't wholly believe it.

Someone from hotel management met us at the service elevator. "On behalf of The Lyndham, I'd like to apologize—"

"Just keep them out and we'll be good," Levi waved him off.

"Of course. We have extra security posted at all entrances and we're liaising closely with the local PD. Your safety and privacy are our number one priorities, you have my word."

"Unless things change in the next hour, we'll need to adjust our plans for getting to Caesar's."

"Just tell us what you need." The guy practically tripped over himself at Jake's looming presence. He took Hotel Guy to one side and reeled off a list of demands before dismissing him and following us into the elevator.

"Caesar's," Hudson let out a long breath. "I fucking love that place."

"Dude, the last time we performed there you almost pissed your pants before we went on stage," Levi snickered.

"Fuck off, Hunter. It was a big deal." Las Vegas shows always were. "And now, Eva gets to experience it all for the first time."

"Alistair say anything about when they want to get her into the studio?"

"Not yet," Damon said. "But it won't be long. Our downloads are through the roof and we can't deny some of that is down to her."

"Don't give her too much credit," Levi said around a shit-eating smirk. "It'll go to her head."

"Not possible, she's one of the most grounded people I know."

"Excluding us, you know about five other people, Donnelley. It's not exactly a shining endorsement."

"Fuck off." Damon flipped Hudson the bird.

"I don't get paid enough to listen to your crap," Jake shook his head, stepping off the elevator and doing a quick sweep of the hall. I could see Travis and Grayson standing in position outside of Eva's room.

"Everything good up here?" Jake asked them.

"Nothing to report. Although the friend is very... excitable." Travis' brows pinched.

We all looked at Hudson and he balked, "What?"

"Nothing." I smirked, making a beeline for our room. "Nothing at all."

———

"I can't believe this, Eva. Caesar's Palace, Caesar's freakin' palace."

Me and Damon shared an amused look while Hudson grumbled beneath his breath.

"I mean it's Caesar's Pa—"

"Say it one more time for the people in the back why don't you?" He let out an exasperated breath, slumping back against the van's leather seat.

Security had vetoed us going to the venue in separate cars, deciding to put us all in the van with a security detail in front and behind us. Levi had thought it was all a little unnecessary until a group of Die Hearts rushed the van, clawing and banging the glass. I hadn't missed the way he'd moved closer to Eva, quietly asking her if she was okay.

If I wasn't so stunned, I probably would have turned green with envy.

My brother had a heart.

Who fucking knew?

"I'm sorry, did anyone hear somethin' just then?" Molly retorted, smirking at her best friend.

"Funny, Steinbeck, real damn funny."

She blew Hud a kiss. Jesus, she was out to push his buttons, not that I blamed her. Dressed to kill in a tight-fitting dress and shoes unworthy of one of our shows, Damon had pointed out she might want to rethink her wardrobe. But Molly had simply flicked her hair over one shoulder, looked right at Hudson, and said she was ready to enjoy the night.

I'd seen the flash of lust in his eyes, the way he'd greedily dragged his eyes down her body. He wanted her, which was hardly surprising. But I had a feeling she was going to put him through the wringer. It was hard to feel sorry for the guy. Hudson had a way of telling girls what they wanted to hear without ever really saying a thing. Even though he said he never made promises he had no intentions of keeping, it didn't stop the trail of broken hearts left in his wake.

"Oh my gosh, I see it, Eva. I see it." Molly pressed her face up against the tinted glass, awe lingering in her voice. "Best day ever."

Despite the simmering tension between her and Hudson, Molly's excitement was infectious and before long we all found ourselves smiling right alongside her.

"You think that's something, wait until you see us perform."

"Oh, I've seen your performance." Her eyes landed on Hudson again. "It didn't make a lastin' impression."

"Burn." Levi slapped his thigh, howling with laughter.

"Don't push me, Mols," Hudson's voice was low. "I never back down from a challenge."

"A challenge?" She gawked. "In your dreams."

"Oh you're in my dreams every night when I jack—"

"Okay, okay," Eva cut him off. "I think that's quite enough." She threw Hudson a scathing look.

He held up his hands. "She started it."

"Well, I'm finishin' it. Both of you play nice. We're in Las Vegas, about to perform at Caesar's freakin' Palace... can we please enjoy the rest of the night without all the sarcastic remarks?"

"Fuck yeah, we are." Levi agreed.

"What's gotten into you?" I quietly asked Hudson while Letty was doing her tour guide routine and pointing out all the famous landmarks on the strip.

"She's baiting me."

"And you're fucking rising to it."

"Seriously," he whisper-hissed, "you're trying to school me on women?" His eyes slid over to the girls.

"Fine, don't say I didn't warn you. That,"—I pointed a discreet finger at Molly—"has trouble written all over it."

"Rafe?" Hudson grimaced.

"Yeah?"

"Worry about your own dick and I'll worry about mine."

I didn't argue. From the way Eva kept catching my eye, I knew he was right.

He wasn't the only guy in trouble tonight.

———

THE COLOSSEUM WAS A SMALLER CROWD, BUT WHAT THEY LACKED IN size, they made up for in noise. By the time we came off stage, we were all soaked with sweat and high on adrenaline.

"We fucking rocked it." Levi bounced on the balls of his feet.

"Congratulations, guys." Alistair sauntered over to us. "That was really something. The manager wanted me to personally inform you they have reserved you a section on the balcony floor at Omnia. You'll have complete privacy."

"Nice!" Hudson said, grabbing a towel and running it down his face.

"Hey," Eva and Molly came over. "Great show," she said.

"Great show?" Molly rolled her eyes. "I almost had a heart attack, it was so freakin' good. Seriously, you blew my mind."

"Again," Hudson coughed, earning him a snicker from Levi. I didn't laugh though. I was too busy staring at Eva. She'd changed out of her performance outfit, into a black knitted sweater dress that finished just above her knee but scooped low on her shoulders. It looked sinful on her body, molding to her soft curves.

Jesus, she was pure fucking temptation.

Damon nudged me in the ribs and I managed to tear my hungry gaze off her. "So Ali was just telling us we have a VIP table at Omnia," he said to the girls. "If you would like to—"

"Yes, that would be an almighty hell yes." Molly grinned, swishing her hair off her shoulders.

"Another club?" Eva whispered and I knew what she was thinking. But this was different. This was a private party inside a club. If we didn't want to mingle or dance or join the masses, we didn't have to.

"It'll be different," Levi said, toying with his snake bite piercings. "There won't be any trouble."

"Come on, babe. I'm here for one night only. We need to make it count before I have to go back to life as a babysitter and general lackey."

"Fine, fine." Eva relented, her eyes flicking to mine. "We can go, but I need to call my parents first. My dad made me promise I'd call them after tonight's show."

"We need to get showered and changed anyway," Damon said.

"Okay, well I'm going to head back to the dressin' room and call them. Molly?" Eva asked.

"You go, I'm goin' to find Letty. She promised me a tour. I'll see you soon, okay?"

Eva nodded, taking off down the hall. I wanted to go after her, the magnetic pull almost impossible to resist.

"I'm going to shower on the bus," Hudson announced, his jaw clenched.

"Shower on the bus? Do you think we're all fucking blind?"

"Fuck off, Hunter," he growled at Levi.

"Just call it as it is. You're going back to the bus to rub one out because Molly has you all tied up in knots."

Hudson flipped him off. "I'll see you later."

"A hundred dollars says he's balls deep in her by the end of the night."

I shook my head and took off down the hall, but my brother raced past me. "Kiss it, I'm taking first shower."

Damon fell into step beside me. "Just say it," I said, sensing his mind working overtime.

"Actually, I was going to say I'll cover for you if you want to go see her."

My eyes snapped to his. "I don't... Yeah, fuck, okay. I owe you, man."

"Make it quick though and be fucking discreet."

With a small nod, I checked to make sure the coast was clear and slipped into Eva's dressing room. "Rafe?" she gasped. "What are you doin' here?"

Without words, I stalked toward her and curved my hand around her neck, fixing my mouth over hers. Eva's lips parted on a soft sigh, our tongues brushing. My fingers splayed either side of her head, burying deep into her curls as I tilted her face.

"Hi," I said, slowly withdrawing.

"Hi." She beamed at me. "What was that for?"

"Look at you." My gaze moved down her body. "You're trying to kill me, aren't you?"

"Molly made me wear it."

"I'll remember to thank her later."

Eva swatted my chest, quiet laughter filling the room. She fisted my t-shirt. "You're all sweaty."

"And you're mine, Starshine."

Her eyes fluttered closed. "Rafe..." My name formed on her lips. I knew she wanted to say more because I did too. The words were right there on the tip of my tongue. But something held me back.

"I should go before anyone catches us."

"Okay." She gave me a weak smile and I dropped a kiss on the end of her nose before backing up to the door.

"You were amazing out there tonight, Eva," I said as my hand curled around the handle. "It isn't any wonder our fans have fallen in love with you."

Just like I have.

CHAPTER NINETEEN

EVA

"Holy cow, Eva, that boy can't take his eyes off you." Molly leaned into me, slurping her cocktail. "I don't know how you do it."

"Do what?"

"Pretend you're not head over heels in love with him."

My eyes darted around and she chuckled. "Relax, we're all alone. I'm beginnin' to think it's me."

She had a point. We'd been in the club almost an hour and the guys had all deserted us. Even Letty was busy flirting with a guy she knew from another record label. Hudson was making a show of chatting up any girl who looked his way, and Damon had taken off after reading a text on his cell phone. Rafe and Levi were seated over by the bar, talking, pretending not to watch the two of us like hawks.

"It isn't you."

Okay, so maybe Hudson didn't stick around because he couldn't stand being around Molly, but I had a feeling that I was the reason the Hunter brothers were keeping their distance.

When Rafe had slipped into my dressing room earlier, I had been so close to telling him how I really felt. And I was almost certain he felt the same—it was in the way he held me, how his lips brushed over mine, the way his eyes saw straight into my soul.

I didn't blame him for keeping a safe distance because I was also struggling to rein in the urge to get up, go over, and finish what we started earlier.

Molly shrugged. "Who the hell cares? We're in a club in Las Vegas

294

sippin' drinks that cost more than my yearly allowance. And despite what you might think," Her expression softened, "I didn't come for them, I came for you."

"I love you too." I squeezed her hand. "And I'm so glad you're here. Bein' on tour has been more than I could ever have imagined, but it's been intense."

"I can totally imagine. Bein' stuck in the middle of a Hunter sandwich must be a terrible place to be." She teased.

"Molly," I warned. "It isn't like that."

"I know. I've known you your entire life, Eva, and I've never seen you the way you are with Rafe. I only have to say his name and you practically melt into a puddle."

"But what if it's doomed?" I peeked over at them. "There's somethin' between them, Mol. Something dark. Rafe feels this sense of responsibility to his brother and I think it stems from more than just Levi's addiction."

"Sometimes you just have to follow your heart and hope it leads you right. You're worth the risk, babe, and if he's worth your love, he'll see that."

Throwing my arms around her neck, I crushed Molly into me. "I've missed you."

"If I'd have known there was going to be tears," Letty said. "I would have thought twice before calling you."

"No tears." Molly said easing out of my arms.

"Maybe a few happy ones," I added, resting my head on her shoulder.

"Who's the hotty?"

"Someone I need to walk away from. Are you girls ready to hit the dance floor?"

"I'm not sure—"

"Yes, dear God, yes." Molly jumped up, shimmying down her dress. "Come on, Eva, we have to dance."

"They have to come too." I slid my eyes over to where Travis and Grayson stood.

"It's their job. I'll pretend they're not there if you will." My best friend pouted so I found myself saying, "Fine, lead the way."

The club was already packed, bodies crammed onto the dance floor underneath the huge kinetic chandelier. It was a far cry from the club in LA, and the even smaller one in Charlotte. The music was loud, thrumming through my chest. I grabbed Molly's hand as we followed Letty. Travis and Grayson blended in with the crowd but kept a close distance.

"I love this one." Letty yelled, throwing her arms up and rolling her hips. It was some popular dance hit, full of electro beats and heavy bass. I smiled weakly. This so wasn't my scene, but I didn't want to ruin Molly's big night out.

"You need to loosen up," she mouthed, dancing circles around me as I side-stepped awkwardly.

"Or she just needs her partner in crime." Hudson grabbed me and brought his mouth to my ear. "Will you hate me if I get with Molly tonight?"

"You care what I think?" I eased back to lock eyes with him.

"Of course I fucking care. You're one of us now, Eva. I just hope to God when the truth comes out, there's an *us* left to talk about."

"Hudson, I—"

"Don't you dare apologize. You can't help who you fall for, Angel." His gaze shifted and I wondered if he was looking at Molly.

"She talks a good talk, you know, but this: the dress, her attitude, it's just her way of keepin' the upper hand."

"I know." He swallowed.

"Just be careful with her heart, Hudson, that's all I ask."

"Shit, Eva, you can't ask that of me. I don't know how to..."

"Whoa, bitch, you need to back the hell up."

Our heads whipped over to find Molly facing off with some girl. "Fuck," Hudson muttered, grabbing my hand and leading me over to my best friend.

"Stay cool, Hud," Letty whispered. I spotted Travis and Grayson moving closer, Hudson's bodyguard too.

"I'm cool." He lifted his shoulders. "What's happening, Mol?"

The girl gasped, her eyes narrowing. "You really do know him? *You?*" Jealousy dripped from her words.

"I told you I did." Molly cocked her hip to the side. "Now move the hell on, you're ruinin' my vibe."

"Hey, Hudson, why don't you ditch these two country skanks and come party with some real girls?" She stepped closer to them, making a show of flicking her bottled blonde hair off her shoulder. It whipped straight into Molly's face.

"Oh hell no," she rolled back her shoulders. "You did not just—"

"Easy now." Hudson inched in front of Molly, stepping between the two of them. Another girl stepped up beside her friend and smirked.

"Yeah," she purred. "Ditch the skank, and we can have a private party all of our own."

"Like that's ever goin' to happen," Molly mumbled.

We were drawing an audience now, people trying to piece together who we were and what was happening. It wouldn't be long before people realized and started getting out their cell phones.

"Nobody asked you, bitch." The girl glared at my best friend. "Why don't you fuck off back to the ass crack of wherever the hell you came from and let Hudson hang with some real girls."

"We need to leave," Travis gently took my elbow, "Now."

"Is that Evangeline Walker?" someone said over the music. "Shit, it is."

"No fucking way," the girl choked on the words.

"Now, Eva."

"Sorry, girls, looks like we'll be leavin'... with Hudson." Molly flipped them off, but all hell broke loose as one of them lunged for Molly, grabbing a handful of her hair.

"Get off me, get the hell off of me." Molly managed to shove her off.

"That's our cue, baby," Hudson slipped his arm around Molly's shoulder and started leading her away.

"Dirty country skank," the girl yelled, "I bet she's fucking all four of them."

The blood drained from my face. "Ignore them," Letty said. But it was easier said than done. I knew there was a price to pay for my rising fame. Not everyone was going to like me or my music or my story. Only knowing it and having it shoved in your face were very different things.

"Screw 'em, babe," Molly said, still nestled into Hudson's arm, looking far too comfortable... and smug.

Travis led us back to the VIP area.

"What happened?" Alistair came over to us.

"There was an incident," Travis started but our manager cut him off. "Of course there was. Who do I need to pay off this time?"

"Actually," Hudson stepped forward, sliding his arm from around Molly's shoulder to take her hand instead. "Some girls came up to Eva and Molly. Die Hearts, I assume."

"Hey, what's going on?" Rafe and Levi appeared.

"We need to bail."

"What are we waiting for then?" Levi said, as if it was that simple.

"What, no third degree?"

"Nah," he said flatly. "It doesn't have the same appeal when you're sober."

"Fenton is bringing the van around to the side entrance," Travis said.

"Where's Damon?" I asked.

"He went to take a leak."

"I'll radio his guy and tell them to meet us."

I moved closer to Molly, aware Hudson still had her hand in a death grip. "Is it always like this?" her voice quivered as she smoothed her hair.

"Not always. Sometimes we stay in and watch movies."

"So rock-and-roll." We shared a nervous laugh. "I can't believe this is your life now. You can't even dance in some exclusive club in Las Vegas without bein' spotted."

"Kinda comes with the gig, Mol."

"I know," she said. "I just... wow."

"Should I be worried about that?" I whispered, dropping my gaze to where she held Hudson's hand.

"I want to be strong, Eva, I do, but..."

"It's okay, I get it."

No one would ever understand more than me. The only difference between me and Molly was she got to go back to the hotel and be with the guy consuming her every thought.

I didn't.

As if he heard my thoughts, Rafe approached us. "Are you both okay?"

"Yeah, it just made it real, you know? I'm not stupid. I know they're sayin' all kinds of things about me, but it was just white noise then."

He lifted his hand as if he was about to reach for me, but at the last second, he thrust it into his jean pocket, his stormy eyes silently saying all the things I wished he could say.

"You can't let them in, Eva," Hudson said. "That shit will drive you crazy."

I glanced over at Levi. He was quiet, his eyes cold and assessing. "Is he okay?" I asked Rafe.

"He's struggling a lot with his emotions right now."

"Because of me?" The second the words were out of my mouth, I regretted them. But Rafe—selfless, steadfast Rafe—didn't flinch.

"Yeah, but he's okay. If he wasn't, I'd be standing over there and not here with you."

My brow rose and Rafe let out an exasperated breath. "He wanted me to check on you."

"Oh."

"I see what you mean," Molly leaned in, whispering, "So intense."

Rafe frowned but our security team decided it was time to move. They escorted us through a network of closed access halls before a rush of cool air hit us.

"What happened?" Damon asked the second we reached him.

"Some Die Hearts started shit with the girls." Hudson didn't stick around, pulling Molly toward the minivan.

"Are you okay?" Damon asked me.

"Yeah, I'd just forgotten how cruel girls can be to one another."

"Jealousy is a powerful motivator, Eva."

"Probably didn't help that Hudson was down there dancing with her again." Levi brushed past us and got in the van.

"One thing is for sure, Eva," Damon smiled, "There hasn't been a dull moment since you joined the tour."

When he put it like that, I didn't know whether it was good thing or a bad thing.

———

I woke to the sound of voices. Sitting up, I tried to get my bearings. Molly was beside me, her dark hair fanned all over the crisp white linen. She must have crept in after her and Hudson got done *reacquainting*. After we'd arrived back at the hotel, I'd gone straight to bed. Part of me felt bad for cutting Molly's night in Vegas short, but Hudson had made it pretty clear he was more than willing to keep her company.

From the stream of sunlight pouring in through the window, I figured it was morning. "Wake her," someone said from outside the door.

"Let's not jump to conclusions," another voice said.

"Eva," Levi yelled, his voice fraught. I leaped out of bed and rushed to the door. It swung open and I came face to face with the eldest Hunter brother.

"Is it true?" he ground out.

"Is what true?" I treaded carefully, my mind immediately going to Rafe.

Me and Rafe.

We'd been super careful since the other night on the bus. Stealing glances here and there, and we'd barely even spoken last night.

"There's an article online about you, is it fucking true?"

"Levi, back up, let her have some space." Letty tried to usher him away, but he refused to move. I peered around them and found the whole band sitting there in our suite.

"I'll move," he gritted out, "when she tells me the truth. Is. It. True?"

He knew.

Levi knew about me and Rafe. It was the only explanation for his angry morning wake up call.

Steeling myself, I rolled back my shoulders and calmly said, "What did it say?"

Letty caught my eyes, her expression grim. But there was something else there, and it looked a lot like, 'I told you so'.

"They said you're sick," Levi choked out the words, his eyes wild and hands restless. "They said you're... dying."

The world went from under me and my hand shot out to steady myself on the wall.

"Eva?" Letty said. "Okay, Levi, back the hell up."

"It's true, isn't it? It's fucking true. You're just like the rest of them," he was agitated, pain and anger swirling around him like a dark vortex.

"Levi," someone said. "Come on, man, you need to calm down."

"Calm down," he roared. "You want me to calm the fuck down? She's fucking dying and you want me to calm—"

"I AM NOT DYIN'." My chest heaved, my heart galloping like a band of wild horses.

"Y- you're not?" Levi blinked at me.

"See, man, we told you to let her explain things, but, oh no, you had to go and jump off the deep end." Hudson threw up his hands and then jabbed a finger at me. "You've got some explaining to do, Angel."

"We should probably talk," I said quietly, stepping out of the bedroom and closing the door behind me. Molly was still sleeping, no doubt dreaming of Hudson. For as much as I wanted her to hold my hand, she didn't need to witness this.

Levi wouldn't look at me and when I found Rafe across the room, he refused to give me his eyes either.

Crap, I'd really screwed this one up.

I padded over to the couch, Letty following. Hudson was already seated with Damon, the two of them looking as somber as I felt, but Levi and Rafe remained where they were. I took a deep breath and Letty covered my hand with hers. "It's going to be okay," she said.

I gave her a little nod and started. "When I was sixteen, I was diagnosed with Non-Hodgkin Lymphoma."

"That's a type of cancer, right?" Damon asked and I nodded.

"It's a form of blood cancer, quite common in teenagers and has a high survival rate." I gave him a nervous smile. I didn't enjoy talking about cancer, who did? But it was public knowledge now, and Letty was right, they deserved to know the truth from me, not from some article based more on speculation than reality.

"Cancer can be at different stages. I was stage four."

"Shit, Eva," Hudson rasped. "That's... fuck."

"It's okay... I'm okay. The doctors didn't think I was goin' to make it, but after surgery and aggressive chemo, I made a full recovery." My smile grew but it was false. I already sensed the shift between us—the pity in their eyes, the questions running through their heads.

The betrayal.

Rafe couldn't even look at me, and Levi... well, Levi looked like I'd just told him his new puppy had died.

"So you're better?"

"I'm in remission, yes."

"But the cancer's gone?" Levi finally spoke. "You won't get sick again?"

"I..." I reminded myself he deserved the truth. Even if I knew he wouldn't handle it well, Levi deserved the facts. "The cancer is gone for now. It doesn't mean it won't come back one day."

The silence was deafening. Hudson cussed under his breath while Damon and Letty offered me soft smiles of reassurance. Rafe was still quiet, running a hand back and forth through his hair.

"So you could get sick again?" Levi asked, his eyes clouded with confusion. "You could get sick again and... die?" The word came out strangled, coiling around my heart like barbed wire.

"Levi!" Damon scolded him.

"It's fine," I said, keeping my eyes on Levi. "Yes, that's right. But anyone sittin' here could get sick at any time. That's life."

"Yeah, well life fucking sucks. I gotta get some air." Levi stalked away, the door slamming behind him.

"I should go after him," Damon said. "Hudson, a hand?"

"Yeah, of course." They got up and started to leave when Letty said, "I should probably come too. Strength in numbers and all that."

I released a quiet sigh, watching as they disappeared out of the room. Last night had been a blur. The show; the crowd; then the club with Molly, Letty, and the band. But the second things went sour, the guys were right there, putting us first.

Putting *me* first.

I hadn't realized just how much I'd integrated into their band until that moment.

And now everything was a mess again.

I should have known it was too good to be true. I should have known karma would be right around the corner waiting to rip the ground from beneath my feet.

I should have told them.

The thought rattled around my head, the guilt like a brick in my chest. But it was too late now.

My secret was out.

"You didn't tell me," Rafe's words cut like a knife.

"I... it's not somethin' I wanted to tell everyone."

"So I'm everyone now?" His expression was crestfallen, but his eyes were hard and cold, the truth like a vast cavern between us.

"That's not... I tried. I did. I was so close to tellin' you all the other night on the bus, but it was such a nice thing y'all did. I didn't want to ruin everythin'."

"You told me you were sick, but I didn't think..." Rafe swallowed, pain swimming in his eyes. "You almost died."

"But I didn't."

I didn't.

It was the first time the words took on a different meaning for me.

"I can't..." He stood up and panic flooded me.

"Rafe, please." Tears burned the backs of my eyes. "I never meant to hurt you. I was only protectin' myself."

"I can't do this right now, Eva, I need some air."

He left me.

Rafe walked away as if I'd broken his heart.

As if I'd broken us.

And maybe this time, I had.

CHAPTER TWENTY

RAFE

THE MINUTE I walked away from Eva, I regretted it. But a little voice in my head wouldn't stop whispering, *'she didn't tell you'*.

Eva had gone through something huge; the kind of thing that was bound to change a person. To leave its mark. I should have turned around and comforted her, but I needed time to clear my head. I also needed to figure out what the hell to do about Levi. The article had hit him hard, but then my brother had issues. Abandonment issues. Trust issues. Attachment issues. You name, he had it. It wasn't any surprise given everything he'd dealt with growing up.

I could only hope this didn't push him over the fine line he walked. He cared about Eva. I'd underestimated just how much she would affect him. But it was too late to wish things were different. Eva was here, stuck right in the middle of us, and there was no going back.

I tried our suite first, hoping to find my friends talking Levi out of one of his meltdowns, but there was no sign of them.

"Ah, Rafe, there you are." Riley breezed into the room. "I was hoping to talk to you about—"

"Now is not a good time," I said. "My brother is... well, you know how he gets. I need to go find him."

"Is it anything I can help with?" Her eyes softened but there was something about her tone that had alarm bells ringing in my head. I'd never been Riley's biggest fan, but the fact Damon and Eva had both pointed out she seemed to harbor a thing for me, made me feel uneasy.

"I don't think so." I brushed past her, but she stopped me dead, her hand curling around my wrist.

"What the fuck are you doing?" My hard gaze dropped to where she held me.

"I... hmm... sorry." Riley snatched her hand back and stepped back. "If something's going on with Levi, you can talk to me. I'm sure I can help."

"I can handle my brother, but thanks." I ducked out of the room just as my cell vibrated. I pulled it out and breathed a huge fucking sigh of relief.

Levi was okay.

For now.

———

I found Levi at the hotel bar exactly where Damon's text had said he would be. The three of them—Damon, Letty, and Hudson—had been hovering at the door when I'd arrived. They didn't want to spook him, but they didn't want to ambush him either. Thanks to our security team, the place was deserted. There was just Levi perched at the bar, running his finger around a glass, the bottle of vodka beside it.

The same vodka our mother used to drink.

"I haven't drunk any yet, in case you were wondering," he said without looking up at me.

He knew I'd find him.

I always did.

"I wouldn't blame you if you had." I slid onto a stool next to him.

"You know, I can still smell the vodka on her breath as she berated me. It used to make me sick to my stomach, still does."

"Where'd you get the bottle, Levi?"

"I've had it since I got out of rehab. A reminder of what I never want to become. But fuck, little brother, the voices are too loud sometimes." He spun the glass, staring into it as if it held all the secrets of the universe.

"Levi," I started, unsure how to approach this. There was no instruction manual here. No matter how many times I talked Levi off a cliff, I could never predict his response. But I also knew avoiding the elephant in the room wasn't going to help matters.

"Eva is fine."

"*Now*, she's fine now." Anguish clung to every syllable. "It isn't even that, it's that she lied."

"She didn't lie," I said. "She just didn't volunteer the truth. It's only what we do every single day of our lives."

"It isn't the same." He slammed his hand down on the bar, the glass rattling with its impact.

"So how is it? Talk to me, brother."

He let out a heavy sigh, running a brisk hand down his face. "She made me care. She made me fucking care and then I saw that headline and all I could think was she's going to leave me." A bitter chuckle rumbled in his chest. "Ironic isn't it? She's not even mine and I'm worried about losing her."

His words were like a knife to the stomach.

"It's okay to care, Levi," I choked out.

Sometimes the problem wasn't that my brother didn't care; it was that he cared too much. Me. Eva. Even the guys. His strong sense of attachment to us often got tangled up in his violent or angry outbursts. Bottom line was Levi was wired wrong and it was through absolutely no fault of his own. That was the cruelest thing about all of this. He didn't choose to be this way; it was just the shitty hand he'd been dealt.

"There's just something about her," he let out a frustrated breath, "I can't explain it."

"Yeah." *That makes two of us*, I swallowed the words, guilt snaking through me.

He deserved to know.

Levi deserved to know that I'd lied about my feelings for Eva. After the weekend in Camdena, when he'd asked me if I liked her, I'd looked my brother in the eye and lied. He had been spiraling. I'd seen it, the guys had seen it, we'd all fucking seen it. So instead of owning up to how I'd really felt about Eva and driving a huge wedge between us, I'd told him she was just a girl I'd had some fun with. I thought I was protecting him. I thought I was being the brother he needed me to be.

I was Levi's person—there was no room for Eva in that equation.

But here we were.

Rafe, Eva, and Levi.

And I still couldn't tell him the fucking truth because I knew once I did, it would be too much, and he'd snap.

"She's really going to be okay?" he asked, breaking the silence.

"Yeah, man, she's going to be okay." The knot in my stomach tightened. Then he said eighteen little words that blew my freaking mind.

"Eva is too fucking good for a guy like me," there was no pain in his voice, only resignation, "but she would have been good for you."

———

After calling in reinforcements, I left Levi at the bar. He wanted to hang out and play pool, to keep himself distracted from the dark and poisonous thoughts swimming around his mind. He also asked me, of all people, to go check on Eva.

That's how I found myself standing outside her room, Travis eyeing me from his position down the hall. I slipped inside only to come face to face with Molly.

"Oh, it's you," she sneered. "What do you want?"

"I just want to make sure she's okay."

Her eyes narrowed to deadly slits. "I like you, Rafe, I do, but I don't trust you. You broke her heart once, don't do it again. I'm going to find Letty and the guys. You're welcome." She shouldered past me and I closed the door.

"What do you want?" Eva asked coolly as she stepped out of her bedroom.

"I came to apologize. I didn't handle that well, I'm sorry."

Her eyes fluttered closed, tears rolling down her cheeks. "Don't cry." I rushed forward, pulling her into my arms. "Please don't cry."

"Everythin' is such a mess." She fisted my t-shirt.

"We all have secrets, Eva." Sliding my fingers underneath her jaw, I tilted her face to mine.

"Why are you really here, Rafe? You should be with Levi, he needs you."

"*You* need me. I'm right where I need to be."

Her eyes clouded over. "When I needed you, you walked away from me. Again."

"It wasn't like that, I swear." Panic twisted inside of me. "I was just so shocked. All I kept thinking was, 'what if I lose her?', 'what if she gets sick again?'. I got scared, okay? I know I screwed up and I'm sorry."

"You should go." Eva stared at me, defiance burning in her eyes.

My strong brave Starshine.

"Rafe, I mean it, you should—"

"Ssh," I slipped my thumb over her lips. "I'm right here." My mouth hovered over hers.

"Rafe, I..."

I kissed her. I couldn't help myself. She tasted of tears and torment. My hands slid into her hair, anchoring her to me.

"We shouldn't—"

"We should." I started walking Eva backward until we were in her bedroom. "Let me love you, Starshine. Let me make you smile again."

She pressed her lips together, giving me a small nod. It was the signal I needed to hook my hands under her t-shirt and drag it up her body. Her jeans went next, and then her bra. "You're perfect." I dipped my head, capturing a dusky bud in my mouth.

Eva moaned, shoving her fingers deep into my hair while her other hand slipped under my shirt. "I need to feel you," she whispered between kisses, our tongues stroking, teeth nipping.

Barely breaking the kiss, I managed to yank off my shirt and kick off my jeans. We took our time with our underwear, teasing and touching. By the time we were both naked, Eva's skin was flushed and damp. I hooked my arm around her waist and pulled her down onto the bed. We landed in a tangle of laughter and limbs.

Rolling Eva underneath me, I nestled between her legs. "No regrets," she said catching me off guard.

"No regrets." My chest tightened, but I was too high on her to let the lingering guilt dampen the moment.

Eva was it for me. I just had to come clean to Levi at the right moment and hope to hell he understood. Even if he didn't, I would find a way to make him see I needed her too. Besides, his words earlier gave me hope.

Hooking my hand under Eva's thigh, I hitched her leg around my hip as I slowly rocked into her. "Jesus," I groaned.

"More," she breathed, arching into me.

"Everything." I whispered against her lips. "I want to give you everything, Eva."

I only hoped it was a promise I could keep.

We lay side by side staring up at the ceiling. I hadn't planned to kiss her, to spend the last hour loving her. But the second I saw Eva, standing there, tears streaking down her cheeks, I knew I was a goner. I loved this girl. Fuck, I loved her so damn much. I wanted to carry her demons and shoulder her pain. I wanted to spend the rest of my days making her smile.

"I guess we should talk." My words pierced the silence.

"I think we were supposed to do that first." Eva's soft laughter washed over me like a warm blanket, and I never wanted this moment to end. But life wasn't a fairytale, it was cold and cruel and hard. And I knew just because we were here, together, didn't mean that out there would be as easy.

"Me and Levi had a rough childhood," I started, knowing if I didn't get this off my chest I might never do it. "We don't talk about it, ever. But it's always there."

Rolling onto her side, Eva brushed her fingers down my chest, staring down at me with so much love I felt winded.

"Our mom was... well, she was all messed up. She was a recovering alcoholic when she got pregnant with Levi."

"What about your dad?"

"We have different dads. Neither stuck around but I got the better deal. Levi's dad was a mean drunk. Used to beat her around. It only got worse when she got pregnant. And then he up and left. Said she was no good to him now she had a baby."

"That's awful." Eva lay her head on my chest and I ran my hand through her hair, loving how soft the strands felt against my fingers.

"It gets worse. She never bonded with Levi, blamed him for screwing everything up. Then she met my dad. He was good for her for a while. She fell pregnant with me and by all accounts, they were happy. But Levi was a difficult child. Always trying to get her attention and going about it the wrong way. She favored me and neglected him. It didn't help that she named him Leviathan and me Raphael."

Eva jerked back, her brows pinched in disbelief. "She called him that?"

I nodded, remembering the first time he told me what his name meant, what it represented. I barely understood what he was saying but I knew from the angry tears in his eyes, it wasn't good.

"I was her angel. Her gift from God. She used to say Levi was her damnation and I was her salvation."

"That's... I don't even know what to say."

"It's messed up and something we have to live with every day of our lives. We've been Rafe and Levi for a long time now."

"What happened to her?"

"My dad couldn't take anymore of her and Levi's strange relationship, so he left."

"Rafe, I–"

"It's okay. I took it hard at first but then she relapsed. Liquor, drugs, prostitution, anything she could do to escape her life. And Levi was such an angry kid, he had little in the way of self-preservation. I became his protector. His everything. There wasn't time to grieve for a guy who wasn't strong enough to stick around.

"Eventually, Mom had a complete mental breakdown when I was twelve and we were put into foster care. After four years of being shunted from home to home we finally decided to get our own place. We'd been playing small time gigs and had managed to save enough money to rent a room above a bar. It was a total dive, but it was ours and that's all that mattered."

"I had no idea." Tears glossed Eva's eyes as she looked up at me. "I mean, I knew somethin' bad must have happened, but I never imagined…" She swallowed, pity etched into her expression.

"It could have been worse." I shrugged. "We could have ended up being split up." Some kids weren't as lucky as us. They had no one.

We'd always had each other. Even when Levi hated me, and he had over the years, I'd been there for him.

"What happened to her?"

"She died when I was fifteen. Drug overdose."

"That's why you feel responsible for him," she whispered.

"It's not that I feel responsible for him, Eva, but Levi has only ever known abandonment. His dad left before he was born. Our mom treated him like he was the devil incarnate. Even my dad, who was a decent enough guy, didn't stick around. I'm the only person who has never left him." A beat passed as I let the truth sink in and then I said the words I never thought I'd say. "And then you came along."

"It isn't like that between us, Rafe."

"I know." I leaned up brushing Eva's cheek. "But he's attached to you. For the first time in years, Levi has formed a genuine attachment to someone, and it had to be the girl I've fallen hopelessly in love with."

"You love me?" Her soft ocean eyes widened, shining with emotion.

"I've loved you for a while now, Starshine."

"Oh yeah?" The corner of her mouth kicked up.

"Yeah." I craned my neck to kiss her. It was slow and deep, an acknowledgment of my confession.

"Well, it's a good thing really," she breathed against my lips before inching away to look at me. "Because I love you too. I love you, Rafe. *You.*" Eva dropped her head to mine, the weight of our words swirling around us.

"Do you have any idea how many times I've wanted to say that?" I asked her, and she smiled.

"Probably about as many times as me." We kissed again. Long and lingering, exploring each other's mouths as if it was the first time. And in many ways, it was. This was our first kiss with the truth all laid out before us.

Eva eventually broke away. "What do we do now? I'm not sure I can keep sneaking around. It's killin' me, Rafe. And Levi deserves to know the truth about us."

I sucked in a harsh breath. "He does. I'll talk to him. I wanted to tell him earlier, but he's too fragile right now. I'll also talk to Alistair."

"Do you think he'll understand?"

"What choice does he have? I've tried fighting it, Eva. I've tried to do the right thing. But for once, I want to be selfish. I want to follow my heart. And it's you, Evangeline Star Walker. You're my heart."

A stray tear rolled down her cheek, gutting me. "I'm scared," she admitted.

"Me too. But all I know is this is worth it, you're worth it."

"I'm worried about him," Eva whispered. "I don't want to be another person who breaks his heart."

"Levi will come around."

He had to.

Because the other option wasn't worth thinking about.

CHAPTER TWENTY-ONE

"What did your mom say?" I asked Molly as she flopped down beside me.

Rafe had left some time ago. There was an intimate gig tonight at a new club opening on the strip, and they needed to rehearse. I'd stayed behind wanting to give Levi some space. Rafe was adamant he would come around, but we agreed it should probably be on his terms.

"Just the usual. I have responsibilities, she needs to work, yada yada... as if those little brats are my kids, ya know?" Sadness clouded her eyes. "I love them dearly, but sometimes I just want to be a normal senior. I want to date and go on road trips and be reckless every once in a while."

"Well you're here now." I reached over and covered her hand with mine.

"I am." She beamed. "And I wouldn't be anywhere else."

In the aftermath of the article, Molly had decided to stay another night. Letty had already changed her flight home to tomorrow. Even though me and Rafe had cleared the air, it felt good knowing I had my best friend around for another night.

"I should have told them," I said quietly. "Then maybe it wouldn't have come to this."

The devastation and betrayal in Levi's eyes was something I wouldn't forget in a hurry, but it was nothing compared to the look of sheer desperation I'd witnessed in Rafe's eyes.

And all because of me.

"But you didn't," Molly's voice cut through my reverie. "Besides, those boys have more secrets than my old *Dear Diary*. Don't be fooled into thinkin' they don't."

"Rafe told me."

Her eyes bugged. "What do you mean?"

"He told me why Levi is like this."

"And?"

"I won't ever repeat their story, Molly, not even to you."

"I can respect that." She gave me a warm smile. "But maybe you should ask yourself why you didn't tell them." There was no judgment in her eyes, only gentle understanding.

I gave her a half-hearted shrug. "I guess I wanted them to see me for me, not for the girl who lived. That stuff changes things. Look how the kids at school acted when I came back. Just because I survived doesn't mean I don't live with cancer every day, Mol. I knew if I told them, things would be different."

"You were scared they would reject you?" My eyes dropped to the floor, but Molly reached over, taking my hand in hers.

"I was protectin' myself."

"I hate to tell you, babe, but I don't think it's you who needed protectin'. Those guys have all fallen completely in love with you."

"They don't love me."

Rafe loved me, but the others, the others had to like me given the circumstances.

"I'm not talkin' about hearts and flowers. I'm talkin' about the way a brother loves his sister. You saw how they were last night. They'd do anythin' for you."

Her words sank into me. When I'd first arrived, I was so adamant I wanted my survivor's story to stay out of the press to protect myself. But maybe Molly had a point. Maybe deep down, a part of me had done it to protect them. Something had happened that weekend in Camdena. Not only between me and Rafe but between me and the rest of the band. And the more I'd gotten to know them, the more I'd realized just how complicated they were. I didn't want to become another burden for them to shoulder.

"How do you think they found out?" She changed direction.

"I guess a journalist went home and asked around or someone tipped them off."

"Didn't Alistair say he'd taken precautions to prevent that?"

"Yeah, but I knew it could happen." *You knew and still didn't say anything.*

"Look, tough talk time." Molly folded her legs beneath her and faced me. "It's done. You can't change that, all you can do is find a way to move forward. You and Rafe, for as much as I want to kick his ass right now, are meant to be together. I know he's Levi's brother, I know they share some higher-level bond or somethin', but Rafe is also a person. He has hopes and dreams and desires all his own, and it's okay for him to go after them. It doesn't mean he's betrayin' his brother or abandonin' him."

"I know." I just wasn't sure Levi would see it that way.

"He loves you, babe, and you love him. You will find a way to make it work because I have to believe one of us is destined to be happy."

"Mol." I gave her a sad smile. "Don't say that."

"Don't worry about me. I'll figure my crap out one day. But today is not that day."

"But last night, you and Hudson seemed... *friendly*."

"Oh it was plenty friendly." She smirked. "But it's like between the sheets we've got it down and then it's over and we're both lyin' there and neither of us can think of a single thing to say. That's why I snuck out. I didn't want to do the whole awkward mornin' after."

"Has it occurred to you that maybe, just maybe, he likes you and doesn't know how to tell you?"

"Hudson Ryker doesn't like girls; he likes what girls can do for him."

"I wouldn't be so sure about that. He's been different."

"Different how?"

"I can't really put my finger on it, but I'm beginnin' to think there's a lot more to him than meets the eye."

"Oh there's definitely a lot more to him, if you know what I'm sayin'."

"Uh, gross." I threw a cushion at her, my nose scrunching in disgust.

"Made you laugh though." Molly grinned. "Just think, if I'd never entered you into that talent contest we wouldn't be sittin' here right now: me pinin' after a guy who is emotionally stunted and you head over heels in love with a guy who comes with enough baggage to fill an airplane."

"We're screwed."

"Certifiable," she added.

"But do you know what?" I said around a smile. "I wouldn't change a single thing."

We decided to stay in the suite for the rest of the day. I didn't feel like going out and Molly was more than happy watching trash TV and ordering room service. It wasn't exactly rock-and-roll but it was just what I needed after an emotional few hours.

"Hey," Letty breezed into the suite an hour later. "Where's Levi?"

"Levi?" My brows pinched.

"Yeah." She looked around. "He told the guys he wanted to clear the air with you. That was about an hour ago. I figured the two of you were still talking things through."

Panic flooded me. "I haven't seen him, Letty. Should I call him?" I asked, glancing at my cell.

Letty's expression fell. "No, I'm sure everything's fine. He perhaps needed some time to clear his head first." She pulled out her cell. "I'll text Rafe. I'm sure he's heard from him."

"How was he... earlier?" I knew she'd been with him down at the bar.

"He was okay. We didn't really talk about you but that's Levi's MO. He bottles stuff up. He did kick my ass at pool twice though, so he wasn't totally off his game."

We shared a smile. "Do you think he'll forgive me?"

"Eva, listen to me and listen good. There is nothing to forgive. What you went through, that's your business."

"Yeah, but—"

"I told her that three times already," Molly yelled from the bathroom.

"I'm glad she's here for you. Those Hunter boys can be intense, and I'm not in the middle of them like you are."

"I'm not... it isn't like that."

"I know. Rafe told me you two worked through things." A knowing smirk tugged at her lips. "I can't say I'm surprised. He's crazy about you. Alistair is going to have a nuclear meltdown when he finds out though."

My eyes widened to saucers. "Don't say that. Rafe said—"

"He's trying to protect you, Eva. It kind of comes with his boyfriend responsibilities."

I smothered a dreamy sigh. *Boyfriend.* I liked the sound of that.

"Alistair will get over it eventually, he'll have to. You're the label's next big thing. They won't want to lose you."

"See." Molly appeared. "There's nothin' to worry about."

I rolled my eyes. They were both so honest and yet, oddly reassuring. It was the kind of tough love a girl needed in her life.

———

Levi didn't show up at my suite. Neither did he show up for the gig at the club. Alistair had made up some excuse about him coming down with a stomach flu, cancelling the gig last minute, but rumors were already flying around as to the whereabouts of the Black Hearts frontman.

We waited and waited.

We waited until it was clear he wasn't coming back. The three of us sat in heavy silence. Every hour that passed was more painful than the last. Time offering no solace in the darkness of our hotel suite.

"He'll be okay," Molly said. "He's done this before, right?"

"Yeah." Letty grimaced. "But he's never slipped Jake like that before. Usually he hits a bar or finds a dealer, he doesn't go off the radar."

"I did this," I whispered.

"Eva, we don't know what happened yet. He was okay. He was coming to find you and clear the air, he told Rafe as much."

People lied all the time though. They looked you in the eye and told you what you wanted to hear, when really, on the inside, they were slowly drowning.

"We should be out there lookin' for him." I leaped up, wrapping my arms around my waist. "If I could just talk to him... explain..."

"Eva," Letty said forcefully and my eyes darted to hers. "We need to wait it out. Jake and his team can handle this. It needs to be professional and discreet."

Molly grabbed my hand and gently pulled me back down, wrapping her arm around me. "They'll find him."

Their attempts at reassuring me did little to ease the knot in my stomach. I felt sick; a sense of dread weighing me down. It was almost three in the morning and Levi had been missing for almost ten hours. Las Vegas was a big place full of vice and temptation; it wouldn't be hard for someone to remain lost if they didn't want to be found. Even someone as famous as Levi.

Burying my face in my hands, I smothered the tears threatening to fall. Crying didn't change anything.

"Maybe you should try to get some—"

The door swung open and Damon rushed inside. "They found him. He's a mess, but they found him."

Relief slammed into me as I rushed out, "Where is he?"

"He's here, they just brought him up to our suite. A doctor is on standby just in case, but it sounds like he's okay."

"A doctor?" I gasped.

"It's just a precaution, Eva. Rafe is pretty good at knowing how to care for Levi following one of his benders."

My stomach lurched as I stood up on shaky legs. "Where is Rafe?"

"He's heading back to our suite now."

"I'm comin'," I said.

Damon glanced at Letty, the two of them silently communicating. "I'm not sure that's a good idea." Letty gave me a sad smile. "Stay here and give them some space. Once we know—"

"I'm goin'." Defiance burned through me. I couldn't explain it, but I had to see Levi with my own eyes. I had to know he was okay.

"Fine, come on." Damon beckoned for me to go to him, wrapping his arm around me. "You two stay here for now."

"Of course," Letty said. "If you need anything..."

"Thanks."

We walked down the hall to the band's suite in silence. It wasn't until we reached their door, Damon dropped his arm and grasped mine. "You really don't need to be here to see this."

"Yes, I do, Damon."

"You really do care for him."

"Of course I do. He's Rafe's brother. He's important to me."

"I like you, Eva, I like you a lot, and I've rooted for you and Rafe from the start." He offered me a weak smile. "But you need to buckle down for the fact that this ride is about to get as bumpy as hell." Damon didn't offer any more of an explanation as he opened the door and slipped inside.

Leaving me standing there wondering how much worse it could possibly get.

As I stepped into their suite, the first thing I noticed was how quiet it was. The second thing I noticed was the smell. Hudson sat on the couch, his head buried in his hands. Damon went to him, sitting down. "Rafe?

"Already in there." Hudson's eyes flicked over to one of the bedroom doors.

"How is he?"

"Covered in his own puke, strung out on the fuck knows what."

"The doctor..."

"Not yet." Hudson shook his head. "He was barely conscious, but Rafe managed to get him to drink some water to try and flush that shit out of him. I've never... fuck." He slammed his fist down on the couch. "We let this happen, we fucking let this happen."

Hudson finally noticed me standing there, his eyes narrowing. "You shouldn't be here."

"I... I was worried."

"Seriously, Damon," he ignored me, "she shouldn't be here."

"She has a right to know exactly what he's dealing with."

The Black Hearts drummer looked ready to give me my marching orders, but instead he pressed his lips into a thin, disapproving line. Just then, Rafe came out of the bedroom, his expression broken. "I need some more towels and a bowl or some—Eva?"

That single word on his lips shattered me.

"She wouldn't be left behind."

"How is he?" I took a step forward.

"You should go." Rafe's mask slammed down, shutting me out.

"But I—"

An almighty crash rocked the suite and we all ran to the bedroom. Levi was rolling on the floor, the lamp smashed beside him, trying to clamber to his knees.

"Fuck!" someone grunted, but I could barely hear them, unable to take my eyes off the broken boy in front of me.

"Levi, bro, come on, work with me here." Rafe crouched down, helping his brother to his feet.

"OUT! He yelled in a strangled, distorted voice.

Damon took my elbow trying to lead me away, but I was rooted to the spot.

"Fuckin' bitch made me feel something, but it was all lies. Lies, lies, sweet fucking lies."

Tears sprang from my eyes. A rush of hot unstoppable tears. Levi's eyes were bloodshot, his pupils blown.

"Get her out of here," Rafe said without looking at me.

"But..."

"Don't fucking touch me, *little brother*." Levi sneered, trying to thrash out of Rafe's hold, the two of them stumbling into the wall. "No," I yelled just as Hudson dived for them. "Liars," Levi gritted out, spittle flying everywhere. "You're both fucking liars. Get off me, *Raphael*, get the hell off me."

Rafe staggered back, his face drained of blood, and let Hudson take over. I tore from Damon's grip and ran out of the room.

"Eva, wait," Rafe called after me. I ground to halt and turned slowly.

"He knows, doesn't he?"

He nodded, devastation clouding his gray eyes.

"How?"

"I don't know."

"I should go." Moving to the door, I grabbed the handle.

"Eva..."

I glanced back at Rafe and our eyes locked, saying all the things I knew we wouldn't ever say.

He wanted me.

He loved me.

He'd chosen me.

And in the process, we'd broken Levi.

"You should go be with your brother," I choked out the words. "He needs you."

"I'm so fucking sorry."

"Me too." The tears flowed freely now. He was saying goodbye. Barely a few hours after he'd told me I was worth it, that our love was worth it, Rafe was choosing Levi.

"Goodbye Rafe." It came out a strangled whisper as my heart splintered in two.

And the worst thing about the whole messed up situation was I didn't blame him. How could I when we'd created this mess?

We'd let it happen.

And now we had to pay the price.

———

I didn't sleep. Instead, I threw my few belongings in my duffel bag and sat curled into Molly's side until the sun finally peeked out from behind the high-rise skyline of the strip.

"Are you sure about this?" Letty asked. It was still early, the harsh light of day only reaffirming the decision I'd made after returning to my suite a few hours ago.

"Yeah, I think it's for the best, don't you?"

Sadness washed over her as she threw her arms around me. "Take some time, clear your head. Just don't make any hasty decisions. I'm sure things can—"

"I appreciate your kind words, Letty, but I think we both know I have to do this. I already broke Levi's heart. I can't stick around and destroy the group too. If I go now, maybe they can work things out. They've done it plenty of times before."

"This time is different, Eva. They need you. They *both* need you."

"I need some space." I needed to be away from the band. From Rafe and Levi and my intense feelings.

"All set?" Molly came out of our bedroom with her case.

"I think so."

"Are you absolutely sure about this?" she asked me.

Nodding, I swiped my eyes, drying the tears. "It's the right thing to do. Alistair agrees I should step back for now."

"Three days. He said take three days."

That had been one conversation I didn't want to relive in a hurry. Not only was I breaking the terms of my contract, and Alistair's golden rule about no fraternizing with band members, I was putting the entire tour in jeopardy. But if I stuck around, things would only get worse. I knew that and so did he. It's why, in the end, after a very heated discussion, he agreed to give me some time. I would miss the show in Seattle. But by the time the band hit Salt Lake City, he expected me to be back and ready to go. Whether or not I travelled with the band and continued performing with them was another thing entirely.

Something I couldn't even think about right now.

"Come on, the sooner we get out of here, the sooner you'll be able to think more clearly." Molly hugged Letty. "Thank you for everythin'. I got a little more than I expected with Vegas, but I appreciate you havin' my girl's back."

"Don't be a stranger," Letty hugged her back before settling her eyes on me. "Just promise me you won't hide. It's bad, yes, but whoever said love wasn't worth fighting for? You can be with Rafe and still be there for Levi. The two aren't mutually exclusive."

I gave her a small nod. It was all I could muster. Besides, I didn't want to make a promise I wasn't sure I could keep.

"Okay, get out of here before I get emotional." Letty pulled open the door and Travis greeted us. "The car is waiting."

"Thank you, Travis." I said, letting him take my bag. "For everythin'."

"The pleasure has been all mine, Eva." We shared a sad smile. "If you're ready?"

I nodded, glancing back one last time. It was just a hotel room; one I would probably never see again in my lifetime. But it didn't matter. I would take a little piece of the Lyndham with me always.

And in return, I was leaving a little part of my soul here.

Two days later...

"That is a sight for sore eyes," Mom breezed into the living room, a huge smile painted on her face.

"Hey, Mom. What's up?"

"Nothin' is up, baby. I'm just glad to have you home."

"Mom." I gave her a pointed look.

"I know, I know," she blew out an exasperated breath. "And this isn't me tryin' to sway you one way or another. I'm just happy you're safe and here, that's all."

To say my parents had been surprised when I'd turned up on their doorstep two days ago was an understatement. But they'd taken one look at my sore, puffy eyes and pulled me into their arms. I knew their judgment would come, their disproval and disbelief, but in that moment, I'd allowed myself to soak up their comfort and love.

"Has Mr. Portman—"

"His name is Alistair, Mom, and I thought we agreed no band talk yet, please."

"I'm sorry." She sat down opposite me. "I can't imagine how difficult this decision must be."

"It's the hardest thing I've ever done." And that was saying something.

"The brothers, they're..."

The brothers was her preferred name for the two guys we avoided talking about. I'd had to tell them something, cherry picking snippets of what had really gone on between the three of us.

"Workin' things out," I said.

I hadn't heard from Rafe. Nothing. Not one single text. Part of me wondered if Letty or Alistair had told him to give me space or whether he was too busy with Levi. Or whether he simply couldn't find the words. But I'd texted back and forth with Damon and Letty a lot. I'd texted Hudson too, but he was giving me the silent treatment after I'd left without saying goodbye. Letty liked to remind me not to check Google, or social media, or the papers. Of course, I couldn't avoid all the headlines. My favorite so far had been titled: *The Rise and Fall of Country's Newest Sweetheart*. It was chock full of speculation about my mysterious disappearance; connecting dots that weren't there to connect, and a few that were.

If only they knew the truth.

How not one, but three hearts had broken that night.

I knew I had to decide soon though. Alistair and the label were pressuring me for an answer tomorrow. There was nothing more I wanted than to go back and try to fix some of the mess I'd made. But how could I go back now everything was out in the open? Now that Levi knew we'd betrayed him?

It was ironic, but I realized now the issue was never Rafe and me, and me and Levi. It was Rafe and me, and Rafe and Levi. He was the one in the middle, forced to make an impossible choice.

A loud knock at the door startled me, and Mom chuckled. "I'll get it," she said, taking off toward the hall. "Eva, sweetheart, it's for you."

I got up and traipsed to the door, half-expecting to see Molly standing there.

"Hey, Starshine."

I sucked in a harsh breath, the ground ripped from beneath my feet. "Rafe? But what are you—"

"I choose you, Eva," he said with nothing but love and conviction in his eyes. "I choose you."

RULE

*"I don't believe in magic", said the young boy.
The old man smiled. "You will when you see her."*
- Atticus

CHAPTER ONE

EVA

"Does it hurt?" I ran my thumb over the tender skin along Rafe's cheekbone.

He covered my hand with his. "You should see the other guy." The smile fell from his lips, guilt flashing in his eyes. "Crap, Eva, I didn't..."

"Ssh." Leaning in, I touched my head to his. "I still can't believe you're here." I had questions, so many questions, but they could wait. Because this beautiful broken boy, the boy who had stolen my heart, was here.

He'd come... for me.

It was a lot to wrap my mind around.

"I'm done putting everyone else first." The words were a rough, pained whisper. "I want you, Evangeline Star Walker, more than I have ever wanted anything else. I can't do this without you." His other hand came around my waist, drawing me closer.

"Rafe, I—"

Someone cleared their throat behind me, and I jerked away. "Hey, Mom," I said, turning to her.

Her brow rose as she glanced from me to Rafe and back again. "I know you're eighteen now, sweetheart. But you're still my little girl." She glared at Rafe. "Please respect my boundaries."

"Mom," I hissed, embarrassment staining my cheeks.

"It's okay, Eva." Rafe's hand slipped to the small of my back, nudging me forward. "Your mom is right. I meant no disrespect, Mrs. Walker."

Her expression softened and she blew out a frustrated breath. "You may call me Jesse, Rafe. But you'll have to excuse my protectiveness. Eva is—"

"Mom," I groaned.

"She's important to you," he finished, standing up. I expected him to move away, but Rafe surprised me by taking my hand. "I get it, Mrs. Walker, I do. But you should know, she's important to me too."

"Yes, well," Mom pressed her lips together, "that doesn't excuse the fact my daughter fled the tour because of you and your brother." She gave him her best mom-stare.

Rafe's posture stiffened. I peeked up at him, smiling weakly. "I regret a lot of what happened," he said quietly.

"I'm pleased to hear it. How is your brother? The press has been quite brutal."

"Levi is... he'll be okay."

Something in Rafe's tone made my stomach knot. Levi wasn't okay. We both knew that. And given the mess of Rafe's face, I knew the Hunter brothers had come to blows.

Over me.

"So you did what exactly? Came here to beg Eva to return to the tour?"

"Actually, I didn't," he said with complete conviction. "I came because I love your daughter, Mrs. Walker. I love her so much, I couldn't leave things the way they ended. But if Eva decides not to re-join the tour, I won't try to persuade her otherwise."

"I see."

My eyes narrowed at my mom. Her coolness toward Rafe was justified, but it didn't make it any easier to watch it unfold.

"How long are you in town for?"

I felt his eyes burning into the top of my head. Slowly, I lifted my gaze to his. "That all depends on Eva," he said.

"We have a guest room. You can stay the night, but I expect my husband will want a word or two with you when he gets home."

Rafe didn't take his eyes off me. I saw every emotion right there in flecks of silver and gray. Love. Possessiveness. Anger. Pain. Regret. There was a storm raging inside him, and I was right at the center of it.

"Eva?"

I forced myself to look at Mom. She gave me a sad smile. "I'll give the two of you some space, but please respect—"

"Your boundaries. Got it, Mom."

She left and some of the tension dissipated. Rafe sank onto the stool and let out a low groan. That was when I noticed him holding his ribs. I reached for his t-shirt, pushing his hand away. Gently inching the material up, I gasped when I saw the ugly purple bruise marring his ribs.

"Rafe..." I cried.

I hated this.

Hated knowing that he and his brother had fought, all because of me.

"I'm so sorry," I said, unable to meet his heavy stare.

"Eva, look at me," he whispered. But I couldn't do it, the burden of the mess I'd created weighing too heavily on my shoulders.

"This isn't your fault." His hand slid against my cheek, tilting my face. I screwed my eyes closed, blinking away the tears building. "Starshine, look at me..."

I couldn't deny him. His voice called to me and I gravitated. Our eyes collided; Rafe's love wrapping around me like a warm blanket. "There she is." He smiled.

"What a mess," I sighed. "How are we supposed to fix this?"

"Ssh, come here." Rafe's hand curved around my neck as he leaned down and brushed his lips over mine. Once. Twice. And not nearly enough. My fingers twisted into his t-shirt pulling him closer. "We shouldn't," I breathed.

My mom would be lurking close by. I knew, and yet, I couldn't tear myself away. Because when I'd left Vegas, I hadn't known when—*or if*—I would see Rafe again. Sure, part of me hoped I would. But I left knowing I could never compete with Levi. With the bond the two of them shared.

But Rafe was here.

"Just give me this, please?" He kissed me again, harder. Deeper. Our tongues tangled together in soft, lazy licks and he cradled my face in his hands. "I love you," he murmured against my mouth, pushing me against the counter. "I love you, Eva."

The desperation in his voice shook me to my core, but I didn't break the kiss. I didn't ask him any of the questions running through my mind. I let him have this moment.

I let myself have this moment.

Because I wasn't the same naïve girl who had met Rafe at the Talent Showdown.

I had my eyes wide open now. I knew that even though Rafe was here, it didn't mean everything was fixed. We'd made a mess. We'd hurt Levi in a way I wasn't sure we could ever come back from.

And it was something we had to face up to.

———

"Fuck, Ali, I said I got it." Rafe paced back and forth in my parents' kitchen. "Yeah, yeah, Eva is," he glanced over at me. "She's okay. No, I don't know yet. We haven't... yeah, okay." He dragged a hand down his face, his expression weary. "How is he?"

I bristled at the mention of Levi. We still hadn't talked much about the events that led to Rafe being on my doorstep. But I knew we couldn't avoid it forever.

Dropping my gaze, I wrung my hands in my lap, trying to give Rafe some privacy. But then he was there, his hand curving around my neck, drawing me close as he said goodbye to Alistair.

"How bad is it?" I whispered.

"It isn't good." Rafe sighed, pressing a kiss to my hair. "But we'll figure it out."

"Ali asked about me?"

"They need an answer."

"I thought I knew what I was going to say... but now I'm not sure."

"Because of me?"

"Yes... no. I don't know. I thought walking away was the right thing to do. I never wanted to come between you and Levi." My lips curved into a sad smile. "He needs you."

"And I need you. I know I didn't handle any of this the right way. I thought I couldn't have you and keep Levi on the straight and narrow, but I realized something when you left."

"What?"

"I can't fix him, Eva. Not if he doesn't want to fix himself." He dropped his head to my shoulder and I looped my arms around his back.

"We'll figure it out."

"Yeah?" he mumbled. "Does that mean you're going to tell Alistair and the label you'll finish the tour?"

Did it?

I'd been almost certain leaving was the right thing to do. I had loved performing, loved the adrenaline pulsing through my veins night after night. But it had been more than that. I'd loved how accepted I felt with the band—like I'd found my place among a bunch of black hearted rock stars. Then there was Letty. She'd become a true friend; someone I knew I could count on no matter what.

But there was also the darker side of fame. The less than friendly fangirls. The constant press reports and rumors. The non-stop pace and pressure. It was a lot to handle, but part of me had thrived on it.

The reality was, being on tour with Black Hearts Still Beat had given me purpose again. And somewhere along the line, I'd come to care about Levi, there was no denying that. But I didn't care about him the same way as I cared about Rafe. Levi was a star. He walked out onto the stage and you couldn't help but be entranced. But Rafe... Rafe was the sun. I gravitated to his orbit, all too willing to burn if it meant I could get closer.

"What's going on in that head of yours?" He was staring at me and I hadn't even realized.

"If I come back, I need to know what happened between the two of you when I left." My finger ghosted over the bruise on his face. "No more secrets."

The sound of the front door slamming made me jerk away.

"Honey, I'm home," Dad's cheerful lilt drifted into the kitchen. "How was your day sweet—"

"Hey, Dad," I said, stepping far enough away from Rafe that it looked innocent, but staying close enough to feel him at my side. "This is—"

"I know who he is, Eva. What I don't understand is what he's doin' in my kitchen."

"Mr. Walker, I'm—"

"Save it. You broke my daughter's heart, rock star. That is not okay with me."

"Dad..."

"It's okay, Eva." Rafe touched my arm. "Your father is right."

"Darn right I am. So now would be a good time to tell me why the hell you're here." His eyes narrowed.

"I came for Eva." Rafe cleared his throat and my eyes flickered to him. He smiled weakly but his gaze was full of emotion. "I made a mistake, sir. I love your daughter. I love her more than anything, and I came to ask her... *beg* her, for another chance."

Heat flooded me, my cheeks burning as the two men who meant the most to me in the world, faced off against each other. Rafe rose from the stool, stepping forward. "I'll never forgive myself for hurting Eva, and I know I don't deserve your forgiveness, Mr. Walker, but I risked everything coming here. Because she's worth it. Eva is worth every damn thing. I love your daughter, sir, and I'll do whatever it takes to prove myself to you, if you'll just give me another chance."

The silence was deafening. My dad didn't blink, he didn't move. He just stared at Rafe as if he was trying to solve a puzzle.

"One chance," he said after what felt like an hour. "You get one more chance. I know my daughter, son, and she wouldn't just willingly hand her heart over to anyone. So I'm going to trust that you're a good man."

"Thank you, sir. You won't regret it, I promise."

"Yeah, well, you'd better hear me when I say if you hurt her again, I will hunt you down and—"

"Okay, Dad." I jumped between them, glaring at him. "I think Rafe gets it."

"He needs to know that you're my—"

"Dad," I snapped. "Trust me, he gets it. Now why don't you go find Mom. Or better yet, I'll give Rafe the tour, and we'll join you for dinner later." I grabbed Rafe's hand and pulled him toward the door.

"Hang on a minute, Eva," Dad protested. "I think we need to sit down and talk about this."

"And we will, later, over dinner." It would be less tense, less mortifying.

I hoped.

We slipped out of the kitchen and into the yard. It was drastic, escaping out of the back door, but I needed space. Between Mom's reaction and the look of complete horror in Dad's eyes when he spotted Rafe sitting there, I needed to regroup.

"So that was my dad," I said, finally releasing Rafe's hand and moving away. "I'm sorry he was—"

"Eva." Rafe stepped forward, rubbing his hands up my arms. "Don't do that. Don't apologize for his behavior. I deserve worse."

"I just... I want them to like you. You're not a bad guy, Rafe."

"No, but I made some shitty decisions."

"You're here now though."

"I am."

We moved closer, like magnets aligning. I craned my neck to look at him, letting my eyes absorb every detail of his face. Stormy gray eyes that looked right into my soul. A slightly crooked nose and perfectly chiseled jaw. The small ball of steel nestled perfectly against the pillow of his bottom lip.

"What happens now?" The words formed on my lips.

He leaned down, brushing his nose over mine, his fingers buried deep in my hair, and whispered, "Only you can decide, Eva."

CHAPTER TWO

RAFE

Mrs. Walker cooked a mean pot roast. I hadn't had a proper home cooked meal in forever. It was so fucking good I never wanted it to end. Even with Mr. Walker's heavy stare burning into me, I shoveled mouthful after mouthful in, savoring the rich flavor.

"That was really good, Mrs. Walker." As I rubbed my stomach, I could see Eva's mom knew my comment was genuine and not some lame attempt to win her over.

"Oh please, Rafe, call me Jesse." Eva's mom had warmed to me somewhat over dinner, but her husband was still looking at me like I was the devil incarnate.

Eva squeezed my hand under the table, coaxing my eyes to hers. She smiled and fuck, if it didn't do something to me.

Something primal.

When I'd realized Eva had left Vegas, it was like my world went dark. She was the light. My Starshine. She made the good days great, and the not so good days that much more bearable.

It wasn't until I saw Levi's fist driving toward my face that I realized just how bad I'd fucked up.

He blamed me for everything. Our past. The fact my mother loved me and loathed him. He blamed me for forcing him into rehab and for letting him disappear in Vegas and fall off the wagon again. For lying about my feelings for Eva.

Levi blamed me for all of it.

But I was done carrying that burden.

My whole life I'd been his protector, his family. I'd been the little voice on his shoulder urging him to make the right choices. But Levi was damaged. He was his own worst enemy. Always reaching for something—*anything*—to stop the voices that lived inside his mind. The voices whispering constantly that he wasn't good enough. Wasn't strong enough. Wasn't worthy enough.

Music saved him.

It had saved us all.

But it would never fix him.

Just like I couldn't fix him.

I got that now. I could be there for him, stand by his side, lift him up when he fell. But I couldn't fix him. I'd tried—I'd tried so fucking hard over the years that it had slowly chipped away at my soul. Caring for Levi had overshadowed *my* hopes and dreams.

And it had almost cost me Eva.

My fingers slid between Eva's, the simple touch anchoring me. I was going to marry this girl one day. It was the craziest notion I'd ever had, and when you were a world-famous musician, there were many, but I felt it all the way down to my soul.

Eva was it for me.

My salvation.

She was my shot at something real. Something good and pure and untainted by all the other bullshit.

"So what exactly does you bein' here mean, Rafe?" Mr. Walker dabbed his mouth with a napkin before throwing it down.

"Dad," Eva said at the same time as her mom grumbled, "Gavin."

"This is Eva's life. Our daughter's life, Jesse," Dad let out a weary sigh. "You saw how happy she was on the tour. It was like we were gettin' our girl back, and then she turned up on our doorstep heartbroken because of him." He looked right through me, but I didn't flinch.

I deserved his wrath.

I also respected the hell out of him for how much he cared about Eva.

"You're right, Dad." Eva shifted beside me. "It is my life. I love you and Mom so much, and I'll always be grateful for what you did for me. But I need to make my own choices now."

"Eva, sweetheart—"

"I love Rafe, Dad. I'm in love with him. He hurt me, yes, but there are things you don't understand. And honestly, I shouldn't have run the way I did." Her eyes flicked to mine. "I should have stayed. I'm sorry."

She held my gaze, silently telling me everything I wanted so desperately to hear.

"Eva, your father has a point."

"Not you too, Mom."

"Hear me out. It's clear you and Rafe share something very special, but I worry, baby. I worry about how your relationship will survive the limelight. Rafe's band is becomin' a worldwide phenomenon. That's a huge responsibility and look at Lev..." she trailed off.

"It's okay, Mrs... Jesse. I am fully aware of my brother's weaknesses."

"The truth is Rafe, you're all still young. I don't claim to know much about the music industry, but I can't imagine you have many adults guidin' you right."

"Alistair is—"

"Mr. Portman seems like a nice enough man, but he's a businessman. He wants to make money. He wants you to make him lots of money."

"Mom," Eva gasped.

"It's okay." I squeezed her hand. "Your mom is right. We've all had to grow up a lot faster than most kids and we've all been through things no kid should have to go through. But that doesn't mean we don't want to succeed, we do. Music is everything to us. Succeeding is everything to us."

"Rafe, I..." Mrs. Walker blanched, wringing her hands on the table as guilt glittered in her eyes.

"I know you think I'm just a selfish rock star with no sense of right or wrong, but with all due respect, you don't know the first thing about me." I pulled my hand free of Eva's, my body vibrating with frustration. "I'm really hoping you'll give me the chance to prove you both wrong. Thanks again for the meal." Shoving back from the table, I stood up and excused myself. It wasn't my house, and I knew I was making a scene, but I needed air.

I needed to be able to breathe for a second without Mr. Walker sitting there, judging me.

"Rafe, wait..." Eva's voice gave me pause, and I glanced back to look at her. I was already halfway to the back door, but she silently pleaded with me not to go.

"I need some air. I'll be okay, finish your meal."

I didn't wait around to hear her words as I made for the door and slipped out into the Walkers' yard.

———

"I think I owe you an apology." Mr. Walker looked over at me as I sat on one of their garden chairs, staring out at nothing.

"You don't owe me anything, sir."

He dropped in the chair beside me, stretching out his legs. "You know, me and Jesse always wanted two kids. That was the dream. Two kids, a quiet life in the country. But it took us a long time to get pregnant with Eva, and then she was born and we knew with one look into her big blue eyes that she was all we needed." He released a heavy breath, running a hand down his face.

His eyes caught mine and he grimaced. "You have to understand, Rafe, when we got the news Eva was sick, it was like... well, let me just say I've never felt so terrified. I'm her father. I'm supposed to be able to protect her."

"But you couldn't protect her from that."

"No, son, I couldn't. It changed her. Non-Hodgkin's took a piece of my daughter and I didn't ever think we'd ever get it back. Then Molly entered her into that talent contest and it was like gettin' a glimpse of her again, the girl who constantly sang around the house. Her and that guitar were inseparable from the moment I bought it for her. And after everythin', it was music that brought her back. That's why I encouraged her to go on the tour. I wanted her to live, to experience life and remember how good it could be. I sure didn't see you comin'."

"I never wanted to hurt her, Mr. Walker." The guilt was like a scab. Each one of his words picking at the wound until it was bloody and raw.

"She loves you, you know," he said, ignoring me. "It's the same way her mom used to look at me. Made me feel ten feet tall every time she pinned me with those sea-greens. My baby girl gave you her heart." He stood up, cutting me with a harsh look. "I'm trustin' you not to break it again." Shoving his hands in his pockets, he walked back into the house as if he hadn't just rocked my world.

It wasn't the blessing I would have liked, but something told me it was the best I was going to get.

"Hey." Eva peeked around the door. "You survived the Dad Talk. Sorry about that. I tried to beat him to it, but my mom held me down to give him a head start." Her smile made my heart pick up a beat. I reached for Eva's hand, threading our fingers together as I pulled her down beside me.

"I think he gave me his blessing."

"Yeah?" Her brow rose, a hint of amusement on her lips.

"Well, he didn't send me packing."

"My dad is super protective. They both are." Her voice dropped an octave.

"I can't imagine what your illness must have been like for them, for you." I leaned in, burying my face in her hair, breathing in vanilla and honeysuckle. Eva always smelled so good. Like hope and happiness.

Like home.

"I can't imagine a world without you in it," I whispered, the words cutting me open.

"Rafe..." Her breath caught. "I'm not goin' anywhere. I'm fine now, truly." Eva turned into me so we were nose to nose. "Besides, I have too much to live for."

"Yeah?" My pulse was like a steady beat beneath my skin as I let my hand glide up the side of her neck.

"I have my parents and music. Molly and Letty. The tour... You."

"You do, you know?" I inched closer until our faces were pressed together, our lips almost touching. "You have me, Eva. I'm yours."

She slid her hand up my chest, resting it right over my heart. "I'm sorry I ran."

"And I'm sorry I let you think you weren't my priority. You are. It's just..."

"Ssh." She kissed me. "You don't have to apologize for being an amazin' brother. What you've done for Levi over the years... I can't even begin to imagine."

"I will always feel responsible for him, but I want more, Eva." Music was a part of me, but it wasn't all of me. Between the band and Levi, I'd never stopped to think about the future.

About life *after* the band.

Now I had so many things running through my head, I had to stop myself from blurting them out.

"Eva, Rafe," Mrs. Walker's voice broke the spell that had fallen over us. "I made pie."

"Great timin', Mom," Eva grumbled, curling her fingers into my t-shirt.

"We have time," I said, kissing her forehead. "Come on, we should go inside."

"We could be a couple of minutes late." She batted her eyes at me, and I almost conceded. But just because Mr. Walker had given me his blessing didn't mean I was going to push my luck.

"Later," I said, standing up and pulling Eva with me. "I need to earn some brownie points with your father so I can sneak into your room later for a goodnight kiss."

Her cheeks turned an adorable shade of pink. "I think my father would actually kill you if he found you sneakin' into my bedroom."

I stopped before we reached the door and locked eyes with her. "I'll take my chances."

Eva was worth the risk.
She was worth every damn thing.

CHAPTER THREE

EVA

"He did what?" Molly shrieked over the line, and I chuckled, moving the phone away from my ear. "He's at your house, right now?"

"Yep."

"And your dad is okay with that?"

"He's not *un*happy with it. He's... dealin'."

"Wow," she let out a sigh, "I can't believe he came. Well, I mean, I totally can. He loves you, but what about Levi? What happened there?"

"We still haven't talked much about it. I know they got into a fight."

"Damn girl, you broke up one of the biggest, hottest rock bands in the world."

"Molly!"

"Relax, I'm jokin'. Mostly." Her soft laughter did little to ease the knot in my stomach. "Levi will come around. He'll have to, right? If you're all goin' to be tourin' together. I mean, you are goin' back on tour with them?"

"I think so. Alistair wants a decision tonight."

"I bet he almost shit a brick when he realized Rafe was gone."

"He's the least of our problems right now." The press was already speculating about my sudden disappearance and Levi's disappearing act at the Vegas club opening. Now Rafe was MIA and the band had cancelled their show in Salt Lake City, keeping up the excuse that the band had been struck down with a nasty stomach flu.

People weren't stupid though. They knew you didn't just cancel sell-out shows in huge arenas for a stomach flu. And I couldn't help but feel the weight of the consequences of the decisions Rafe and I had made. Consequences that had slowly begun to unravel his relationship with Levi, not to mention the band's stability.

"How are you holdin' up, really?"

"I'm okay, I guess. I ran, Mol. I left Rafe when he needed me most." I should have stayed; I knew that now. But I was a coward.

"You didn't run. You came home to regroup. It's not the same. Don't be so hard on yourself. This is new territory for you, and I think it shows how far you've come. You put yourself out there, Eva. You went on tour with Black freakin' Hearts. You did that. *You.* It isn't your fault you ended up havin' the Hunter brothers fallin' at your feet."

My eyes screwed shut as I inhaled a deep breath. Levi was so much more complicated than I ever realized, and I cared for him deeply, I did. But I'd have been lying if I said his attachment to me wasn't overwhelming. Levi had latched onto something he saw in me; placed me on a pedestal I didn't deserve.

And now he probably hated me.

"What if we can't get through this?"

"You and Rafe?" she tsked. "Of course you can. You're the music industry's next golden couple."

"I'm not just talkin' about me and Rafe, Mol. I'm talkin' about me, Rafe, and—"

"Levi."

"Yeah. He's a part of this whether we like it or not. He needs Rafe."

"And Rafe needs you. But what about you, babe, what do you need?"

I considered her words. I'd been so wrapped up in the tour, in finding myself again, and falling headfirst in love with Rafe, that there hadn't been much time to stop and catch my breath. But I knew I needed music. It was a vital part of me, as much as the blood flowing through my veins. Cradling my guitar in my hands and pouring my heart out on stage was more than fulfilling some childhood fantasy. It was a salve to my broken soul. I hadn't realized just how much performing meant to me... until I ran home and holed up at my parents' house.

"I want it, Mol," I breathed, a sense of clarity washing over me.

"Well, yeah, you do. You were so freakin' at home out there. You were born to do this, babe. With or without the band."

"I'm goin' to tell Alistair I'm in."

Her shrieks of approval filled the line and I flopped back onto my bed, laughing right along with her. Who knew what the future held? Maybe Rafe and I were destined for great things, or maybe we were meant to be nothing more than a lit match. Intense, hot, but something that burned out way too quickly.

I was the new Sweetheart of Country. A title I hadn't wanted, but one I now wore with pride. I couldn't throw that away because of a bunch of what ifs and maybes. Rafe and Levi had survived worse. They could survive this.

They could survive me.

And if they couldn't, I'd just have to figure out a way to prove them wrong.

———

THE SLIGHT KNOCK ON MY DOOR BARELY REGISTERED AS ALISTAIR barked down the line at me. "And you can tell Rafe that he better—"

Rafe's face appeared around the crack in the door. "You can tell him yourself." I held out the phone and he slipped inside, gently pushing the door closed behind him.

"Ali?" Rafe said, pressing my cell to his ear. "Yeah, yeah, tomorrow. We've got it. We know what's on the line... Yeah, I know. Fuck, Ali, come on." Rafe went silent and Ali's inaudible yells filled the air. "Yeah, yeah. Okay, bye."

"Do you think he's ever goin' to let us live this down?" I asked, the second Rafe hung up.

"Eventually. But I don't want you to worry about Alistair, okay?" Rafe placed my cell down on my dresser and swept me into his arms. "Hi." His lips curved into a warm smile, his lip piercing glittering as the stream of moonlight hit it.

"Hi."

Our lips met, soft and searching. Rafe's tongue slid against mine, sending a thousand bolts of lightning zipping through me. "I want you, Starshine." One of his hands found the curve of my butt, pressing my body closer to his. "I want you so fucking much."

I was about to tell him to break all my parents' rules, but my dad beat me to it. "Eva, sweetheart," he shouted. "It's gettin' late. I assume you're sayin' goodnight to Rafe before he retires to his own room?"

"Sure thing, Dad," I grumbled, Rafe's mouth curving against my skin as he kissed my neck.

"I guess this is goodnight." He lifted his head, his stormy gray eyes pinning me in place.

"What happens tomorrow, Rafe?" I asked, my heart galloping like a band of wild horses.

"The first day of the rest of our lives together."

No sooner had Rafe said the words, he'd slipped out of my room.

I was stunned. Rafe sounded so certain of things. So certain of us. I wanted to share his unwavering faith, but my faith had been tested once already. Since my miraculous recovery, I preferred to focus on the things I could control rather than the things I couldn't.

It was my decision to go back on tour with the band, but what happened when I got there was another matter entirely.

I couldn't control the outcome, but I couldn't let the fear of the outcome control me either.

"Miss Walk—" I rose a brow at Travis and his serious expression softened. "Eva," he said, "it's good to see you."

"It's only been a few days."

"True, but it's still good." Travis stepped closer, leaning down slightly. "Don't tell the band I said this, and definitely don't tell my boss, but things just haven't been the same without you."

"My lips are sealed." We shared a knowing smile, then I felt a hand on the small of my back. Not just any hand. Rafe's hand.

"Travis."

"Hunter. You have some damage control to run when we get to Denver."

"Don't remind me." Rafe focused on me. "Do you have everything?"

"I think so. I should probably go say goodbye." My eyes flicked over to where my parents stood huddled by the house. Mom was already crying.

"Go ahead. I need to talk to Travis for a second and then I'll come say my goodbyes too."

I left Rafe and Travis and went over to my parents. They pulled me into their arms, squishing me between their bodies. "Oh, sweetheart, I was hopin' I wouldn't have to say goodbye again."

"Mom..."

"I know, I know. But you're my baby, Eva, you'll always be my baby. I'm so proud of you. So proud. And you listen to me, don't let those boys walk all over you, okay?"

"Yes, Mom." I grumbled.

"Your mom's right, sweetheart." Dad's eyes were glassy as he levelled me with a hard look. "I won't hesitate to drive out to wherever you are and teach those black hearted boys some manners."

"*Dad!*"

"What?" His serious façade cracked a little. "You're precious goods, Eva. Besides, it's a father's prerogative."

"Your dad isn't wrong." I'd felt Rafe before I heard him. Slowly, I untangled myself from my parents and went to his side. He hooked his arm around my shoulder and pulled me close. "I'll take good care of her, Mr. and Mrs. Walker. I promise."

"I don't doubt it, son, because if you don't..." Dad let his warning hang in the air.

"I gave you my word, Mr. Walker." Rafe's grip on me tightened, his silent promise seeping into me.

We both knew we were walking into a storm. Rafe had told me he'd walked away from Levi after the fight and come straight here. He hadn't spoken to him since, although Hudson and Damon were constantly blowing up his cell phone. Part of me wondered if he had hoped I would refuse to go back. If Rafe wanted to stay here.

I'd only had a slice of fame. A couple of weeks of being on tour and performing night after night. Rafe had lived it for the last three years. I couldn't imagine what that must be like. The band were so close, like brothers really. But there was no space or place to catch your breath. There was always someone around, someone who needed or wanted something.

"Are you sure about this?" I asked him quietly.

He frowned. "Are you having second thoughts?"

My parents watched on as I turned into Rafe, curling my hands into his jacket. "I'm not, I promise. But do you need more time? We can stay here for another day or two. I can speak to Alistair and see if he'll—"

"You're amazing. You know that, right?" A wide smile split Rafe's lips.

"I just want you to be okay with this too. If you need more time..."

"I have everything I need."

We'd moved closer, like two lovers lost in their own little bubble.

Rafe tucked a strand of hair behind my ear. "Your dad is throwing me daggers right now, isn't he?"

I peeked over at my dad and smothered a giggle. "He's dealin'."

Dad cleared his throat. "He'd deal a lot more if you put a little distance between you and my daughter, son."

"Sorry, Mr. Walker."

"Tell me I'm not makin' a huge mistake, Jesse." He looked at my mom, who unsurprisingly had tears streaming down her cheeks.

"Oh, Gavin," she patted his chest, "I think we can trust Rafe." My jaw almost fell open at that. "Oh don't give me that look, Evangeline

Star Walker. I am allowed to have a change of heart, and now that I've met Rafe in person—"

"Okay, Mom." I pursed my lips. "We really need to get on the road. I'll call you when we reach Denver." Slipping out of Rafe's hold, I gave my parents one last hug. "Thank you, for trustin' me on this," I whispered to my dad. He nodded, swallowing thickly.

"Give 'em hell, sweetheart. And maybe I'll get your mom out to a show soon."

"I would love that."

"Mr. and Mrs. Walker." Rafe gave them a lingering look before guiding me toward the SUV.

"Ready?" Travis asked me, opening the door.

I could have told him my heart was like a runaway train and my palms were clammy, but instead, I held my head high, looked him straight in the eye and channeled my best inner Molly.

"I was born ready."

CHAPTER FOUR

RAFE

"We're almost there," Travis said from upfront. "You might want to wake her."

Eva was passed out, her head nestled in my lap. My hand was stroking her hair, her back. Anywhere I could reach. The ride to Denver had been long. So. Fucking. Long. But it had been uneventful enough. Travis and Fenton kept their conversations to a minimum, and I was content sitting next to Eva, soaking up her presence. She calmed me. Had ever since the first time we'd met, at the talent showdown regional in Ploughton. Of course, I hadn't realized then how important she would become to me. But by the end of our weekend together in Camdena, I knew she was special.

I knew Evangeline Star Walker had the power to make me want more.

To *be* more.

"Eva." I brushed her cheek and she murmured. "Starshine, we're almost here." Her eyes flickered open and I was pinned to the spot with two ocean blues that saw right inside me.

"I fell asleep?"

"Somewhere around St. Louis."

She sat up, taming unruly curls off her face. "I'm sorry."

"Never be sorry."

"Did you sleep at all?" The words were a muffled yawn.

"I got a few hours." I had a kink in my neck to prove it.

"Are the guys here?"

"Damon texted an hour ago. They're holed up in the hotel. Alistair wants us to head straight there. Well, after we grab some breakfast. I'm starving."

"Okay," she sounded cool, but I saw a flash of uncertainty in her eyes.

"I wish I could tell you that everything will be okay, but—"

"You don't want to lie to me?" Eva gave me a weak smile.

"As long as we have each other, we'll get through it, okay? You and me, Eva. I mean it. Alistair, the band, even Letty, no matter what they say or do, it's you and me." I needed her to know that.

"You think it'll be that bad?"

"I don't know what to expect, but we really fucked the tour and the label over."

She dropped her gaze, but I slid my finger under her jaw, tilting her face back to me. "Together, remember? What's done is done. We can only move forward now."

"You're right." Eva let out a weary sigh. "I can do this."

"*We* can do this. I'm right here."

"We're here." Travis called, his announcement dousing us with an icy blast of reality. "There's a small group of Die Hearts out front, so we're heading around back to the underground lot."

"Die Hearts," Eva grumbled. "I sure didn't miss them."

"Hey." I curled my hand around the back of her neck. "I know they can be a lot, but you can't let them get to you, okay?"

"Easy for you to say. You didn't just tear their beloved Black Hearts apart."

"Eva, you didn't..." I stopped myself. I didn't want to lie to her, and I didn't know what damage was done yet where the band was concerned.

"We'll figure it out."

It was fast becoming our motto, but it was the best I could offer her right now. Our relationship had started off based on secrets and lies. I didn't want it to continue that way. Even if the truth hurt.

WE TOOK LONGER THAN WE SHOULD EATING BREAKFAST. I DON'T think either of us were in any rush to face the music, but eventually, Travis had suggested we make a move.

The SUV came to an abrupt halt and Travis and Fenton jumped into action, climbing out and coming around to open our doors. I was used to the routine by now, but I knew Eva still found it overwhelming.

A pinch of guilt stabbed at my chest. Maybe I should have talked her out of coming back, fought harder for her to stay in Lyme. Eva was small-town, too pure and good for this life. But she deserved to shine. After everything she'd been through, she deserved to fulfil her dreams.

"What?" she asked as she slid her hand into mine and climbed out of the SUV.

"Nothing," I said. "Come on. The sooner we get this over with, the sooner we can get some sleep."

"We?" Hope lit up her face, a warm smile playing on her lips.

"Maybe... if you're lucky."

"If you can tear me away from Letty, you mean."

"Something like that," I mumbled, guiding her into the elevator. Travis entered last, giving us his back. The guy was a mean looking sonofabitch, but he was on our side, and I was fucking relieved Eva had him in her corner. I wasn't always going to be around to shield her from the inevitable storms that would blow our way.

We rode up to the penthouse in thick silence. Eva was nervous. It was in the way she tapped her finger against her thigh and chewed her lip. I snagged her hand and threaded our fingers together. Her eyes lifted to mine and pulled me under. She didn't release me until the doors pinged open and Fenton ushered us out.

Travis brought his wrist to his mouth, whispering something, and then said, "They're waiting for you." He flicked his head to where Johnson stood outside the door.

"Thank you, Travis, for everythin'."

"Just don't run out on me again, okay?" He winked at Eva before nodding sharply at me.

"Ready?"

Eva smiled. "As I'll ever be." She took a deep breath and grabbed the door handle. It opened with ease, the low rumble of voices falling silent.

"Eva?" Letty was first to reach us. "Thank God." She pulled my girl into her arms and hugged the ever-loving shit out of her.

"It's good to see you too, Let."

"Shit, sorry." Letty stepped back. "I'm supposed to be mad at you. And you..." She levelled me with a hard look. "I could beat you into next week. What the fuck were you thinking?"

"It's good to see you too," I grumbled, pushing past them both and moving into the living room.

"How nice of you to show up." Hudson kicked his legs up on the glass coffee table, folding his hands behind his head. "Oh wait, you're two days too late for that."

"Hud," Damon warned. "We said we wouldn't—"

"Fuck that, Damon. He screwed up; they both did. And look where it got us."

"I didn't mean to ruin things." Eva stepped forward. "I'm sorry."

"You think sorry is going to fix this? We had to cancel *another* show. Levi is... well, off doing whatever the fuck Levi wants. The label wants answers. And you..." His cool gaze landed on me. "You fucking bailed on us."

"It wasn't like that and you know it."

He leaped up, anger simmering in his hard gaze. "No. What I know is that nothing has been the same since she came onto the scene. I like you, Eva, I do, but you are the worst fucking thing to ever happen to us." He stomped off into one of the bedrooms, slamming the door behind him. The sound echoed around us, reverberating deep in my chest. Eva sucked in a harsh breath. She was pale beside me, tears streaming down her face.

"He'll come around," Letty said, as she took her hand and squeezed it. "He's just..."

"Concerned," Alistair finished. "We all are. Why don't we all sit?" He motioned to the huge sectional. Damon was sitting at one end, so we took the other. I pulled Eva into my side, rubbing her shoulder, wishing I could fix this. Letty perched on the arm on Damon's side, and Alistair sat on the loveseat opposite.

"We're glad you decided to return, Eva, but we need to address the huge elephant in the room. You and Rafe."

"We know we messed up, and we're sorry," she started. "But I won't apologize for fallin' in love with Rafe, Mr... Alistair. I can't do that."

"Jesus," he let out an exasperated breath. "You should have come to me with this. The second it became serious, I should have been informed."

"I'm sorry... we didn't..."

"He's not talking to you," I said. "He's talking to me."

Our manager cut me with a scathing look. "You messed up, Rafe."

"I was trying to do the right thing, for everyone."

"Well, you failed. Had I have been informed sooner, we could have spun it to our advantage."

"You think I wanted to put Eva through that?"

He slammed his hand down on the table. "Dammit, Rafe, she's in it whether you like it or not."

"Okay, why doesn't everyone just cool off?" Damon suggested. "Rafe knows he fucked up and Eva thought she was doing the right thing by leaving. We can't change any of that, but we do need to figure out what we do next. The fans are already talking, it's all over social media, the press. It's only a matter of time before they find out the truth, or a messed-up version of it."

"We should run an exclusive," Letty said.

"Absolutely not," Alistair said the same time as I grunted, "Hell, no."

"Hear me out, okay? If the two of you come out now, we can control the story. Country's sweetheart meets one of Rock's heartthrobs. The younger demographic will eat it up."

"And the Die Hearts?" I almost spat the words. We couldn't go public. It was a sure-fire way to hang Eva out to dry.

"Bigger picture. Eva has already won most fans over. Young girls relate to her. She's the perfect role model. Overcoming cancer to rise to fame and win the heart of a rock star." Pride shone in Letty's eyes as she looked at Eva. "What teenage girl wouldn't want to buy into that?"

"It could work."

"I'm not sure, Ali—" My girl wrung her hands in her lap.

"Consider it damage control." Alistair narrowed his eyes. "We need to sell you as the victim here or the fans will crucify you. You left to protect Rafe and Levi. You walked away for the greater good."

"Exactly." Letty's eyes lit up the way they did whenever she was scheming. "And Rafe went after her because he realized how much he needs her. How much the band needs her."

"Set it up," Alistair said. "I want a guaranteed exclusive with The Rock Report."

"A face-to-face interview would work better," Letty said. "We're in Kansas City tomorrow, they should be able to send someone."

"Do it."

"Wait a second," I rushed out, hyperaware of how Eva was shrinking in on herself. "We haven't agreed yet."

"Consider this your punishment. I think you're forgetting who owns you, Rafe. The label needs me to handle this, so I'm handling it. You don't like it? Then perhaps you should have thought about that before you went against the rules."

"Alistair's right," Eva whispered. I don't know who was more surprised. Me, Damon, or Alistair. Letty continued to look proud, grinning at Eva as if she expected nothing less from the quiet girl beside me.

"Eva," I said, looking at her. "We don't have to do this. There's time to figure out another way."

Alistair snorted at that. "I have calls to make. Letty, brief Eva on what to expect. Rafe, a word."

Reluctantly, I got up and followed him out of the suite. "Have you spoken to Levi?"

"No." I rubbed the back of my neck.

"He's okay but he's refusing to play ball. Given the circumstances, I think it's best you stay away, for now. We have less than thirty-six hours before the next show. Cancelling is not an option."

"Fuck," I breathed.

"I'm going to send Eva to talk to him."

"Like hell you are."

"Look, Rafe, I'm going to level with you. Levi is hurting bad right now and that's on you. I know Eva had a part to play too. But you're his brother. His family. His anger is all on you, and as difficult as it makes things, we need to keep it there. Eva is on the tour; she's in this whether you like it or not. I can't have him lashing out or making life difficult for her."

He had a point, but it was hard to think straight over the jealously coursing through me.

Alistair wanted to send Eva—*my Eva*—to try and comfort Levi. I didn't like it.

I didn't like it one fucking bit.

And yet, a part of me knew if anyone could reach him, it was her.

"Travis goes with her. He doesn't leave her side. I mean it, Ali. Levi is volatile. If he hurts..." I swallowed the words. I didn't believe Levi would ever hurt Eva. But I knew he couldn't always control himself, and I'd witnessed too many near misses where my brother was concerned.

"We'll let her settle first, but I'll let Travis know. We all knew going into this thing that having Eva here would be a complication." He didn't need to say anything else. I knew what he was getting at. I'd looked him in the eye and told him she wasn't going to be a problem.

"I never planned for it to go down like this, you know? I love my brother more than anything."

"More than her?" His eyes darted back to the door. "Women change things; it's the age-old tale of man." Ali clapped me on the shoulder, squeezing gently. "Let's just hope the band can survive this."

CHAPTER FIVE

"It's so good to see you." Letty came to my side as soon as Rafe stepped into the hall with Alistair. Her slim arms enclosed me, and I hugged her back. "It's all going to be okay," she whispered.

I wanted to believe her, but Damon caught my gaze over her shoulder and the knot in my stomach tightened.

"You messed up, Walker," he said, coolly.

"It's Walker now?" I asked as Letty released me.

"I'm not sure they'll come back from this. I've seen Levi all shades of fucked up, but that was something else."

"Damon," Letty chided.

"It's okay. He's only sayin' what everyone is thinkin'. I messed up." If I could rewind time, I would have gone back and chosen to stay. To give Rafe time and space to deal with Levi and wait until things blew over. It was too late though. I couldn't turn back time, and I had no choice but to own my mistakes.

"You're only human, Walker." Damon's frown melted away. "Just because you messed up doesn't mean I'm not happy to see you. Something tells me, we're going to need you over the next few weeks."

I didn't know what to say to that.

"Damon's right, we're glad you're here. Don't let anyone tell you any different, okay?"

Just then, the door swung open and Riley breezed into the room. "Oh, Eva, you're back."

Letty threw me a bemused look.

"Riley," I said tightly. She was the last person I wanted to see.

She pursed her lips. "Is Ali—"

"Right here." He beamed at her, quickly schooling his expression when he realized they had an audience.

"I was hoping we could go over tomorrow's schedule."

"Actually, I need to speak with Eva."

A flash of jealousy flared in her eyes. "I can wait."

"Why don't you head downstairs and order for us and I'll be there in ten?"

Letty smothered a snicker as Riley swished her hair and stormed out of the room. If Alistair noticed, he didn't let on as he came and sat down opposite me.

"We'll give you two some space. Let." Damon motioned for her to follow, but she hesitated.

"It's okay," I said. "Go. We'll catch up after."

They disappeared, leaving me with Alistair. He loosened the collar on his shirt and relaxed back in the chair. "I did not see this coming, Eva, and that doesn't sit right with me. It's my job to know."

"But tryin' to make it seem like there was somethin' between me and Levi... what about that?"

"It was good publicity."

"You told me I was here to tidy up the band's reputation. You never said anythin' about usin' me."

Alistair let out an exasperated sigh, running a hand down his face. "I omitted some of the facts, but I think we're both guilty of that."

"I agreed to do the tour for one reason: my parents. As far as I was concerned, Rafe wanted nothin' to do with me."

He regarded me for a second. "I'll cut to the chase. I need you to smooth things out with Levi. The band needs him."

"You want me to *what?*" Dread slithered through me.

"Rafe is Levi's anchor but he can't be that for him right now, so I need you to do it."

"I'm not sure he'll want to see me, not after—"

"You'll figure it out. Levi needs a friend right now, and that friend is you."

The air left my lungs. "I..."

Alistair stood up. "Travis will take you to him when you're ready. You'll be safe."

Safe?

What the hell did that mean?

"Does Rafe know about this?" I asked, and Alistair levelled me with a look that made me regret the question.

"Rafe is aware he doesn't get to call the shots, Eva. I do. Cancelling another show is *not* an option. So I'm asking you—no, I'm *telling* you—you need to do whatever it takes to get Levi on that stage tomorrow night. Got it?"

The weight of his words was heavy on my shoulders.

"Look," Alistair's expression softened, "I know this is a lot. But you're in this thing now, Eva. I have never seen Levi respond to anyone the way he responded to you. He trusts you."

He *had* trusted me. Before the truth came out about my cancer, and Rafe. Now I was just another person who had let him down.

"Eva. It has to be you."

"I... okay. I'll do it." Not that he was giving me much choice.

Alistair gave me a tight-lipped nod. "Good, Travis will be waiting whenever you're ready." He hesitated, his expression softening. "We have less than thirty-six hours before the lights go up. Time is something we don't have right now. I'm counting on you, Eva."

It was my turn to nod.

I'd ruined the band.

Now I had to fix them.

———

"So where are we going?" I asked Travis as we rode the elevator.

After my conversation with Alistair, I'd taken a shower and then fallen asleep on the huge bed. It wasn't until Letty came to wake me that everything came crashing back down around me.

I had to go see Levi.

Alistair was counting on me.

"Levi and Johnson are at The Radisson. We're meeting them there."

"Okay."

The doors pinged open and Travis hesitated, muttering under his breath. Then he stepped out and my eyes landed on Rafe.

"Two minutes," he said to my bodyguard, never once taking his eyes off me.

Rafe stepped inside, taking the air with him. "Shit, Eva, I'm so fucking sorry. I didn't know Ali would—"

"It's okay." I slid my hands up his arms. "I want to do this. I need to do this."

"Jesus," he sucked in harshly. "I fucking hate this. I hate that you're stuck in the middle of this. In the middle of us."

"There is no middle, Rafe. I'm yours. Nothing is goin' to change that. But right now, Levi needs someone."

"And that someone is you." He gave me a resigned smile.

"Apparently so."

Rafe dipped his head, brushing my jaw with his lips. "You can be there for him, Eva. Lift him up when he falls and be a shoulder to cry on when things get hard, but you can't save him. No one can."

The sadness in his voice made my heart ache. I couldn't even begin to imagine what the two of them had endured.

"Eva, we really should go," Travis interjected.

"Just a minute," I said, and he backed off, giving me and Rafe some space.

"Your heart is too pure for this life." He touched his head to mine, stormy eyes holding me hostage. "If he hurts you, I'm scared of what I might do."

"Ssh. Don't talk like that." I slipped a finger to his lips. "I'm a big girl, Rafe. I can handle Levi. Besides, Travis will be right there."

"Call me the second you get done."

"I will."

I felt the urgency in Rafe's voice, the sheer desperation. But I had to do this. Alistair was right—there was no other way.

"Promise me, Eva."

"I promise." My lips ghosted over his. "I should go. The sooner I leave, the sooner I'll be back."

"I'll be waiting." Rafe was rigid as I edged away, his eyes silently begging me to stay.

"I love you," I mouthed before forcing myself to turn around and head for the SUV.

"Eva," Travis said as he opened the door for me. I got in, catching a final glimpse of Rafe as the elevator doors closed.

Less than an hour of being back and Levi was already coming between us. But it was too late to worry now.

Another Hunter brother needed me.

———

THE RADISSON WAS A BEAUTIFUL HOTEL ON THE NEXT BLOCK OVER. It was hardly worth taking the SUV but, as Travis had pointed out, I could hardly walk it.

"He's in the bar," he said as we exited the elevator.

"Of course he is," I murmured, aware of the odd stare as Travis guided me across the foyer. The décor was opulent and a huge chandelier hung from the ceiling. It reminded me of something out of the nineteen-twenties.

"Johnson already cleared the clientele."

"At least we won't have an audience then." Sarcasm laced my words.

Travis paused at the double doors marked 'bar'. "Ready?"

"As I'll ever be." I motioned for him to lead the way.

We stepped inside, and the first thing I noticed was the quiet. The second thing was the lone figure seated at the bar. Levi glanced over at me and laughed bitterly. "Alistair is sending in the big guns. He must be really worried." He ran his finger around the rim of the glass in front of him.

"How are you?" I asked, inching closer. Travis remained by the door.

"Oh, you know how it is. My brother is a lying bastard and the girl I thought I could trust is also a liar... and as if that isn't bad enough, they're probably fucking each other all while laughing at poor little Leviathan."

His crass words made me flinch. "It isn't like that, and you know it. We made a mistake, Levi, a big one. But nobody is laughing at you."

"I know it, do I?" His eyes darkened. They looked almost black. Soulless.

I didn't like it.

A violent shiver worked its way up my spine.

"What?" An evil smirk tugged at the corner of his mouth. "Do I scare you, Country?"

He was baiting me. Trying to get me to play his game. But I wasn't here to spar with him.

"I'm not goin' to do this with you," I said, moving closer still.

Levi shifted on the stool, his dark expression clouding with something else. "And what's that, Angel? What are we doing? Because I can think of a whole list of things we can do. I'm game, if you are..." The wicked glint in his eye was one I'd seen enough times before.

This wasn't the real Levi. It was his front, his stage act. It was the person he hid behind when the truth got too much to bear.

"I'm sorry."

"What did you say?"

"I'm sorry," I spoke louder. "I should never have withheld the truth from you."

"I'm going to need a little clarification, Angel." He twirled the glass in the air. "Are we talking about the fact you lied about almost dying, or the fact you've been fucking my brother behind my back all this time?"

"I'm sorry I hurt you."

"Yeah, well you can save your apology. Once a liar, always a liar." Levi focused on the wall again, refusing to look at me.

"You don't really believe that?" I chose a stool, leaving one space between us. It was close, but not close enough to feel intimidating. At least, that's what I hoped.

"I know it." He scoffed. "The people in my life are nothing but a sore disappointment. I don't know why I thought you'd be any different."

"Levi, look at me..."

A beat passed.

And another.

Levi stared down at his glass as if it held the secrets of the universe. Then slowly, he lifted his face to mine. "You think you're special, Country? You think you're going to talk me off this ledge?"

"I'm not special," I whispered.

"He thinks you are. You're good for him, you know? Rafe deserves something good. He deserves more than a life sentence of dragging my sorry ass around."

"Rafe loves you. He'd do anything for you, you know that."

"Except give you up." His eyes locked on mine. He wasn't making much sense, contradicting himself at every turn. Part of me wondered if he was drunk or high, but he didn't seem out of control. Beneath all his anger he seemed... resigned. Sad, even.

"Is that what you really want? You want Rafe to walk away from me? I know you're hurtin', and that's on us. But I don't believe for a second that you'd rather Rafe be miserable and give up his shot at somethin' good, somethin' pure, because you can't bear losing him. I am not tryin' to come between you... why can't you see that?"

Levi paled, guilt and confusion clouding his eyes.

And my heart bled for the broken boy who had suffered so much.

"Look," I sighed. "We can't change the past, Levi. I know that better than most people. But we can choose how we walk into the future. You're Levi freakin' Hunter. You're one of the biggest rock stars on the planet right now."

"Alistair is good." He let out a low whistle. "I underestimated him; I'll give him that."

"This has nothing to do with Alistair, Levi. This is about you, me, and Rafe. He needs you, the band needs you. And somethin' tells me, you need the band. You and Rafe are brothers, family. Nothin', not even me, can come between that.

"Maybe I don't want it anymore. Maybe I'm sick of being everyone's puppet."

"Levi, you're not..."

"They don't get it. None of them get it." Shoving his fingers into his hair, he began to pull on the ends. "They don't know what it's like... nobody knows what it's like."

"So talk to me..." I got up and slid onto the next stool. Levi was breaking apart in front of me and it was a natural reaction to want to comfort him. I couldn't help it. It was who I was.

"I'm right here, Levi. I'm not goin' anywhere, I promise." I laid my hand gently on his hand.

"Don't make promises you can't keep, Angel." He smiled sadly, but I didn't miss the hint of warning in his words.

"That's not what this is." My voice was unwavering. "I want to help, truly."

"You think you can be who I need?"

Levi was still baiting me, still pushing. But I saw the defeat in his eyes. He was so close to losing it, to losing himself. He needed someone.

He needed me.

I looked him right in the eye and said, "Try me."

CHAPTER SIX

RAFE

THE SOUND of footsteps woke me. My eyes strained against the darkness as I searched for Eva. "Ssh, go back to sleep," she whispered. But I was awake now and she had my full attention.

Pushing up on my elbows, I watched as she undressed in the shadows, flecks of moonlight bouncing off her milky skin.

"What time is it?" I asked, a weird mix of jealousy and lust swirling in my chest. She'd been at The Radisson for hours. I'd wanted to go to her, to make sure she was okay. But Letty and Damon refused to let that happen, distracting me with beers and the promise that I could stay in Eva's room and wait for her.

If it wasn't for her text to say she would be back soon, I would have fallen asleep not knowing whether or not she was coming.

She pulled on an oversized band t-shirt and slipped in beside me. Silence stretched out before us as she curled up on her side, her eyes fixing right on mine. I mimicked her position, staring at the girl who owned my heart. The same girl who had spent the last three hours with my brother.

"Rafe, I—"

My mouth crashed down on hers as I rolled Eva beneath me, caging her body to the bed. Her hand slid up my chest, curling over my shoulders.

"You're mine," I rasped, running my lips down her jaw, sucking the slope of her neck. Eva arched into me, hitching her legs on either side of my hips.

"We should talk," she whispered.

"I don't want to talk, Starshine. I want to do anything but talk."

Eva guided my face back to hers. "Rafe, don't do this. Please."

"You think I like feeling like this? Imagine if it was me. Imagine if I'd just been with another girl, with your sister or best friend, talking to them, drinking with them..." My brow rose.

"I had one drink. One."

Fuck. I knew I could taste liquor on her lips.

My fucking brother was a bad influence on even the most innocent of souls.

I dipped my lips to her ear, nibbling the skin there. "I trust you, Eva, I do. But I don't trust Levi. He'll use you to hurt me. It's what he does best."

Her hands went to my chest, pushing slightly. "We hurt him, Rafe. *We* did that. The least we can do is try to fix it. And don't you dare throw that in my face. Do you think it's easy for me being around all your fangirls? The Die Hearts."

"Jealous, love?" It was a dick move. But I was angry and frustrated and so fucking powerless. Eva was the best thing ever to happen to me. The thought of losing her... it gutted me.

My eyes shuttered as I inhaled a ragged breath.

"Rafe, look at me." Eva slid her palm against my cheek. "I'm not goin' to do this with you. I love you, and I'm here for you, but I won't be your emotional punchin' bag. You have nothin' to worry about where me and Levi are concerned."

"Don't I?"

Disappointment washed over her. "You think I would ever..." She swallowed hard, pain glistening in her eyes. "I love you. *You.*"

A bolt of guilt shot through me, but I was drowning in doubt, struggling to keep afloat with the jealousy swimming in my veins. I dropped my head to her shoulder, but Eva slid her hand under my jaw, forcing me back to her. "Do you really think I would ever do that to you?"

"No, fuck, of course I don't. I don't know why I said it... everything's such a mess. I'm a mess and I don't know how to fix it." My body began to tremble.

"Ssh." Eva's lips found mine. Soft and gentle. The faintest of caresses. It wasn't enough though. I needed more.

I wanted to bury myself in her.

To lose myself completely.

"I need you, Starshine. I need you so fucking much." My body vibrated with need as I stared down at her, brushing the hair from her face.

"I'm right here, Rafe. You just have to let yourself believe it." Eva looked up at me through hooded eyes, one of her hands drifting down my body. Her touch was like fire, burning my soul.

Rocking back onto my haunches, I ran my eyes down Eva's body. She looked so fucking perfect, spread out before me, a halo of blonde hair surrounding her.

"What?" She smiled coyly.

"You. Just you." My hand gripped the hem of her t-shirt, pushing it up her body, revealing her black panties to me. I leaned in, swiping my tongue across her stomach. Eva sucked in a ragged breath, her fingers sliding into my hair as I continued a path up her body, pushing the t-shirt further and further until it was bunched around her shoulders.

I gently palmed one of her breasts, flicking my tongue across the peak. "Oh God," Eva breathed, her body restless beneath me.

I wanted to take my time, to worship every inch of her. But I wasn't sure I could wait.

"I need inside of you," I said, kissing the corner of my mouth.

Eva nodded, love and lust glittering in her ocean eyes.

Guiding her up, I pulled the t-shirt over her head, before climbing off Eva to rid myself of my boxer briefs. I sat down on the edge of the bed, reaching for her. She came willingly, crawling over me until she was straddling my lap. I loved that about her. My shy, quiet Eva trusted me implicitly, unafraid to let me love her.

She slipped her hand between us, grasped my dick, and guided me into position. One hand on her hip, I braced Eva as she sank down on me. Lips parted, skin flushed, she stilled as I fought every instinct not to move.

"You feel..." Both my hands gripped her hips as I rocked gently. "Fuck."

"Rafe," she cried out, pressing her body against mine, slowly rolling her hips.

Gliding one hand up her spine, I cupped the back of Eva's neck, pulling gently to reveal the creamy expanse of skin. "You're so fucking beautiful." I kissed her throat, running my tongue along her throat. Tasting. Teasing. Her body quivered, her movements growing faster.

But it wasn't enough.

"Slide your legs around me." I held Eva on top of me as she anchored herself around my waist, our bodies joined impossibly close.

"It's deeper," she breathed, rocking gently.

"It's everything." I kissed her, pushing my tongue into her mouth. I wanted to drown in her. To fall so deep I never resurfaced.

Being with Eva was like floating on air. She made me forget. She made me feel.

But most of all she made me feel worthy.

"Oh God," she panted, her skin flushed, damp and glistening. I ran my hand down her spine, over the curve of her hip, pulling her closer, harder.

"I love you," I whispered against her mouth. "I love you so much it freaks me the fuck out." Eva gripped me tighter, riding me like she was born to do it. I was so blinded by pleasure, it was hard to tell where I ended and she began.

"More," she cried. "More, Rafe."

Our bodies were slick with sweat, our hearts a frantic cacophony of beats. I grasped her hips as I shifted to the edge of the bed, thrusting upward.

"Rafe, oh God, I can't…" Eva's nails raked over my shoulders, as she shattered around me. Pure ecstasy shot down my spine as I came hard.

I fell back against the mattress, pulling Eva with me.

"That was…" Her small sigh of contentment tickled my jaw.

"It was you and me, Starshine."

"I like that." Her fingers trailed letters of love over my skin.

We lay there, sated and silent, until Eva whispered, "I don't want this to come between us, Rafe. Promise me." She leaned up to look at me.

"Me and Levi have always managed to find our way back, but this time… it's different," I confessed.

"You're family, that means something. You know it does." Silence enveloped us, and then, she added, "He's hurting too, Rafe."

My chest tightened. I knew Eva cared for him. She wouldn't have been the girl I'd fallen so hard for if she didn't. But I couldn't deny that a selfish part of me wished there was no Levi in the equation.

"It's late," I said gently edging her off my body. "We should sleep."

Hurt flashed in her eyes but she didn't argue, slipping between the sheets and giving me room to climb in beside her. "Tomorrow will be a better day," she said, pressing a single kiss to my lips.

I wanted to kiss her back, to reassure her that we were okay. I wanted to leave Levi at the bedroom door where he belonged. But he was back here with us now, wedged into the space between us, and I hated it.

"Rafe…"

"Get some sleep, Eva." I slipped an arm behind my head and closed my eyes.

Eva let out a soft sigh, rolling onto her side. I silently willed her to say something. To start a fight and call me out on my shitty behavior.

But she didn't, and that's how I fell asleep.

With Eva still and silent beside me and a million miles between us.

"You look like shit," Hudson greeted me as I walked into the suite. "Coffee's in the pot."

"Thanks, have you seen Eva?"

"She left with Letty about twenty minutes ago."

So that's why I'd woken up alone.

"How did she seem?"

"Pissed." He leveled me with a knowing look. "I take it you're the reason she slammed the door so hard she woke Damon?"

"I screwed up." I ran a hand down my face. "I really screwed up."

"Welcome to my world." Hud leaned back against the counter. He was shirtless, sweatpants hanging low on his hips, but it wasn't anything I hadn't already seen a hundred times before.

"I still can't believe you went after her."

"Come on, Hud, we've been over this. I love her."

"Yeah, but you fucking jeopardized everything for her. You just walked away."

"You know that's not how it happened. I just needed to get away. For once in my life, I needed to put myself first." He glared at me. "You don't get what it's like to be responsible for someone else."

"You're not respon—"

"It's always me, Hud. I pick him up when he falls. I nurse him when he's sick. I hold his fucking hair back when he's on detox, puking his guts up. Our relationship isn't healthy. I guess I just hadn't wanted to see it before Eva came along."

"Shit, I know, man." Guilt edged into Hudson's expression. "You're his person."

My head hung low as my best friend's word sank into me.

I *was* Levi's person.

Always had been.

"What are you going to do?"

"Fucked if I know. He won't even talk to me right now."

"But he talked to Eva." It wasn't a question. "She tell you what they talked about?"

I shook my head.

A faint smirk tugged the corner of his mouth. "Did you give her a chance to tell you?"

"We didn't exactly talk much."

"You're more alike than you realize."

"Who, me and Eva?"

"No, asshole, you and Levi. You're jealous of their relationship."

"I'm not... yeah, I am."

"And that's okay. You're only human. But she isn't in love with your brother, she's in love with you. What you need to figure out is, if you can deal with her being in both your lives. Because if I learned anything about Eva, it's that she has a huge fucking heart. She's going to fight for him, maybe as much as she'll fight for you."

"I know."

Fuck, I knew.

"So the way I see it is, you need to man the fuck up and do the right thing here. You love Eva and she loves you. Only you can decide if you let Levi come between that."

My brows furrowed. "Who are you right now?"

"Hey, I'm not just a pretty face."

"Maybe you should take some of your own advice sometime and call—"

"*Do not* finish that sentence."

"What?" I grinned, some of the tension in the room ebbing away. "I'm just saying, you sound like a guy in tune with his feelings, a guy ready to take the next step maybe?"

"Fuck you, Hunter. We're not talking about me, we're talking about you. And you're the one who has to play happy families with his girl and his brother. Good luck with that." He waved me off and stalked out of the room.

As if he hadn't just slapped me with a big dose of reality.

CHAPTER SEVEN

EVA

"I CAN'T BELIEVE you're makin' me do this," I grumbled, watching people rush around the studio, making the final preparations for our interview with The Rock Report.

"I will always support decisions I think are in your best interest, even if you hate me for it." Letty gave me a weak smile.

"I don't hate you. I just... Are you sure this will work?" The idea of going on TV and talking about my relationship with Rafe terrified me. It was the last thing I'd expected when I agreed to come back to the tour.

But here we were, with less than ten minutes until we went on.

"It's the best option we have right now. We need to control the story. You've seen some of the headlines."

I grimaced, looking out across the studio. Riley was busy talking to the production assistant, finalizing the approved question list. Alistair had granted The Rock Report the exclusive, but insisted his team had overall say over the direction of the interview.

"Have you spoken to Rafe yet? I saw him earlier; he didn't look good."

"It's been a busy mornin'. I haven't—" Drawing in a shaky breath, I turned slowly to find Rafe standing there.

"I'd better go check in with Riley." She squeezed my hand before disappearing.

"Hi," Rafe said, rubbing the back of his neck. "You were gone when I woke up."

"Letty needed me for something." My eyes darted off to the right, watching Letty. But Rafe stepped closer, putting himself in my line of sight.

"Eva, about last night... I was a jerk."

"You think?" My eyes cut to his. "You promised not to let him come between us and then right after we..." I stopped myself, lowering my voice. "We're supposed to be a team."

"We are." He reached for my hand, his touch melting some of my anger. "It's my issue to deal with. I can't promise I'll always handle things well, but it doesn't change how I feel about you."

"I just want you and Levi to—"

"Eva," his voice softened. "Not now, please. I know we need to talk about him, and we will. But not before we go on television and publicly announce our relationship."

"Are you scared?" I asked him.

"Scared?"

"It's a big pretty thing to go on TV and..." My voice trailed off as I dropped my gaze to the floor.

What we were doing?

Rafe cupped my face, forcing me to look at him. "You think I'm scared about telling the world I love you?"

"It's a big deal."

"I don't want to hide you, Eva. It was never about that. I just didn't want to drag you into the limelight before you were ready."

We'd moved closer. Without even realizing, my hands had ended up on Rafe's chest, and one of his arms was looped around my waist. "All I care about is you. If this makes things easier, after... everything, then I'm all in. Alistair and Letty know what they're doing. She prepped you, right?"

I nodded. We'd spent all morning going over my answers, over a mountain of pancakes and fresh fruit.

"Their host knows the drill, so none of the questions should throw us."

"And afterward?"

Rafe smiled. "Afterward, the whole world will know who you really belong to." The heat in his words was reflected in his intense gaze. There was no jealousy there this time. No torment.

Just raw possession.

He dropped a kiss on my head, lingering there. A camera flash went off and I glanced over to find Letty snapping photos of us.

"Eva, Rafe," someone from the studio approached us. "We need you on set now."

"Ready?" Rafe asked me, his gaze unwavering even with the assistant standing there, gawking at us.

I gave him a little nod. "Let's do it."

Maybe this wouldn't fix things with Levi, but it would go some way to fixing the damage caused to the band's reputation.

All I had to do was sit and answer a few questions.

And breathe.

———

The lights were blinding, making it difficult to see Kinney Gretchen, one of The Rock Report's most popular interviewers.

"So, Eva. Is it okay if I call you Eva?"

"Sure, everyone else does." *Smile. Don't forget to smile.*

Rafe squeezed my hand. They were wedged between our thighs, barely visible, but enough to hint at our intimacy.

Kinney chuckled. "Eva, it is. I have to say, I think we were all a little surprised when the news broke that you'd returned home to Tennessee. I hope everything's okay?"

"Everything's fine. I just needed some space."

"Being on tour with four guys will do that to a person," Rafe added. He looked so laid back, so at ease. While inside, I was a ball of nerves.

"It must get kind of crazy," she prompted.

"It has its moment. But honestly, it isn't as glamorous as it seems. Some of us just want the quiet life, you know?"

"You're trying to tell me, Rafe Hunter from Black Hearts Still Beat wants the quiet life?"

"One day, sure, why not?" He shrugged, and I had to force myself not to stare at him. But it was difficult. Usually Rafe was quiet, preferring the shadows to the spotlight, but today, he was so enigmatic. Radiant.

He was happy.

"A girl has to wonder, is there a reason for this new outlook?" Her smile grew as she glanced from Rafe to me and back again.

"What are you getting at, Kinney?"

"Oh, come on, Rafe. I'm sure I'm not the only one who has noticed how close you and Eva are sitting. Is there something you want to tell us?"

"I don't know," Rafe turned his attention on me. "Is there, Starshine?"

My heart stopped, my lips parting on a silent gasp.

"I think you rendered Eva speechless." Kinney's voice was drowned out by the roar of blood between my ears.

"I..." Concern flickered across Rafe's expression. No amount of Letty's pep talks or briefings from the production team could have prepared me for this moment. I was barely used to hearing Rafe say he loved me. Yet alone, ready to share it with the world.

"Eva gets a little gun-shy." He slipped his arm around my shoulder.

You can do this. You have to do this.

Sucking in a sharp breath, I smiled up at him "Eva, can speak for herself."

"Seriously, you guys are the cutest. I can hear hearts breaking all over the country." Kinney shifted.

"Yeah, well," I said, "you should try bein' on a tour bus with him."

"So the two of you..." She waggled her finger. "It's serious?"

"I can't speak for Eva, but I knew the first time I laid eyes on her." Rafe spoke with complete conviction.

"So it's official? Rafe Hunter is off the market?"

"Rafe Hunter was never *on* the market, Kinney, you know that." He winked at her.

"Touché. That can't be easy though, trying to navigate a new relationship whilst on tour... together. How are the rest of the guys taking it?"

Rafe stiffened slightly. We knew Kinney was going to bring up the guys, that was the whole point. But he was still hurting over his fight with Levi.

Running my hand along his leg, I rested it on his knee. "It's not like we're in each other's pockets twenty-four seven. I'm on the other tour bus. The band still have their space, and I have mine. I think that's important, you know?"

Kinney nodded. "And what about your relationship with Levi? There's been a lot of rumors flying around that maybe the two of you were getting close..."

"People see what they want to see. Me and Levi are friends. It's not easy bein' the only female artist on the tour, but all the guys have been really supportive and have made me feel nothing but at home."

"So Levi gave the two of you his blessing?"

"Come on, Kinney." Rafe let out a harsh breath. "His blessing? Really, what kind of question is that?"

"Don't shoot the messenger." She held up her hands. "But everyone out there will want to know what's really going on between the three of you."

Beads of sweat trailed down my back. She was pushing too hard, and Rafe was growing increasingly frustrated. It rippled off him, permeating the air around us.

"The last thing I want to do is come between Rafe and Levi, or Rafe and the band."

"I'm sure there are a lot of fans out there who wouldn't mind finding themselves in the middle of a Hunter brother sandwich."

"Wow, you went there," Rafe scoffed. My hand flattened against his thigh. Kinney had gone off script. It wasn't a total surprise—Letty had warned me she might try—but I felt a pang of disappointment all the same.

"Can I level with you, Kinney?" I said, rolling my shoulders back. "I might be a girl from a small town in Tennessee, but you think I don't know this kind of thing sells records? I thought we were here to set the record straight, and the truth is this... Rafe and Levi are brothers. I would never want to get between them. Ever. I know how important family is. I spent most of senior year in the hospital fightin' for my life. I wasn't supposed to survive." Nervous energy vibrated through me, my body trembling with every word. "But I did. I got a second chance when so many don't, and I want to make the most of it.

"I love makin' music and I love performin'. It's crazy and new, and I'm probably goin' to regret sayin' this the second I walk off stage, but I love Rafe and I'm excited to see where the future takes us." My eyes flicked to his, that same possessiveness I'd seen earlier, burning in his stormy gaze.

"You heard it here first people. The Sweetheart of Country has gone and won the heart of one of Rock's most beloved stars. So Rafe, what can we expect for the band in the coming months?" He blinked, breaking the simmering connection between us. "Is Levi over his stomach flu? Will he be at the Pepsi Center tonight?"

"We're feeling good. Eva's back where she belongs, and fans coming out to see us tonight can expect us to raise the roof off the place."

"Sounds like Black Hearts Still Beat fans can expect quite the show. Well, a huge thank you for coming on the show. I don't think I'm only one who will be rooting for the two of you."

"Thanks for having us."

"Thank you," I added, reality crashing down around me.

Kinney looked right at the camera as she wrapped up the interview. "Rafe Hunter is off the market, but with the three remaining Black Hearted boys still all single, there's hope for us yet." She winked. "I'm Kinney Gretchen, and this has been The Daily Rock Down."

"Cut," someone yelled. And Kinney began untangling her mic from her body. "Thanks guys, we appreciate it."

"What the fuck was that?" Rafe growled.

"Come on, Rafe," she gave him an easy smile. "You know how it is. I was only giving the fans what they wanted."

"Hanging us out to dry, more like." He leaped up, running a hand down his face.

"Rafe," Alistair boomed as he crossed the studio to us. "Kinney, couldn't stick to the script, I see."

"Look, I did you a favor. The fans are chomping at the bit for news on Eva and the band. Now they have it."

"We'll see about that." Alistair levelled her with a hard look. "You two, head back to the hotel with security. I'll see you there later."

"Good luck with the show tonight," Kinney said around a thin smile. "And no hard feelings, yeah."

I gave her a nod, and took Rafe's hand, gently pulling him toward where Travis and Fenton were standing. He took control though, dragging me back and caging me against his chest. "You were incredible," he whispered against my ear. "I'm sorry I lost my cool."

"You did fine." I twisted my face to look at him, but his lips were there, ready to brush over mine.

"Rafe," I breathed. "There's a lot of people here."

"Let them look." He smirked. "You're mine now, Evangeline Star Walker, and the whole world knows it."

CHAPTER EIGHT

RAFE

"How'd it go?" Damon asked the second we stepped into the suite.

"Eva rocked it," Letty beat me to the punch, breezing past us.

"Oh, I don't know about that." She buried her face against my arm, but I pulled it away, slipping it around Eva's shoulder.

"You were great."

"I still can't believe I did that."

"Did what?" Hudson padded out of one of the bedrooms and made a beeline for the refrigerator.

"Nothin', it doesn't matter." Eva blushed and I couldn't resist leaning in and kissing her. It felt so fucking good not to have to worry about getting caught.

"Ugh, gross," Hud grumbled. "That's like watching you kiss my sister."

"Oh, so you're my brother now?" Eva shrugged me off and stepped toward Hudson.

"Damn straight. I'm your older, wiser, much cooler brother, and I'm still pissed with you, little lady."

"*Little lady?*" She balked. "You did not just call me that."

Damon and Letty snickered. "Oh shit, Hud, you've done it now."

"I'm shakin' in ma boots." He put on his best southern drawl as he popped the cap on a beer and took a long pull.

"You're such an ass." Eva slipped passed me and joined Letty and Damon on the couch.

"What? That's it? I'm disappointed, Country." Hudson called.

"Knock it off." I punched him in the shoulder.

"We need to be at the arena in an hour." Letty looked up from her phone. "Levi is going to meet us there."

Awkward silence fell over us.

"Well, let's hope he shows because the label is going to be out for blood if he doesn't."

"He'll show," Eva said.

We still hadn't talked about what happened last night when she went to see Levi. But we needed to. I needed to know what he'd said. It was going to eat me up inside if I didn't.

"Can I get ten minutes with Eva?"

"That's what the bedroom is for." Hud smirked and I flipped him off.

"Don't you have to take a shower or something?"

"Come on," Damon stood up. "We should probably go over the set list."

"The set list that is the same as it—"

"Hudson, let's go."

"Fine, fine. I need some alone time anyway."

"Seriously, man?" Damon blew out an exasperated breath. "Do you think about anything other than your dick?"

"Hey, I think about other things." He roped Damon around the neck, leading him to the door.

"I'll make sure they don't get into any trouble." Letty threw me an apologetic glance. "But we do need to leave by three thirty, okay?"

I nodded. "It won't take long."

Letty trailed after the guys, the click of the door reverberating through me. "We need to talk," I said, settling my gaze on Eva.

"I know." She smiled sadly. "But are you sure you want to do this now? Before the show?"

I dropped my face into my hands.

"Rafe…"

"Just give me a minute." I inhaled a ragged breath. I'd seen Levi hit rock bottom more times than I could count. Strung out on drugs, higher than a kite, lying in pools of his own vomit, and everything in between. And every time, I'd picked him up, cleaned him off, and helped him get his head on straight.

I'd carried Levi since we were two kids who didn't know right from wrong.

"You know, I can't remember a time when it wasn't just the two of us. Even when I was just a child, I wanted to protect him."

"You're a good brother, Rafe." Eva slipped her hand up my arm and coaxed me out of my sanctuary.

"Look at me," she whispered, and I twisted my body to hers. "Levi is hurtin'. He's angry and frustrated and he feels betrayed, and do you know what? He's entitled to feel all of those things. But deep down, he loves you."

"The things he said to me..."

"We're all guilty of sayin' things we don't mean in the heat of the moment."

"He blames me."

"Because you're the only person he has. He's always goin' to reflect his emotions back at you. You're his person, Rafe."

"Not anymore." Tears pricked the corners of my eyes, but I swallowed them down. I didn't cry, and I wasn't about to start. Especially not in front of Eva.

"Give it time."

"And until then? I'm just supposed to stand by and watch him lean on you? Because I want to do the right thing; but fuck, Eva, I'm not sure I can be that guy."

She palmed my cheek. "You have to be."

"What did he say to you? Did he say he's going to be at the show?"

"He didn't give me an answer, but I know he'll do the right thing. Levi needs music, he needs the band."

"How can you be so sure?"

"Because I know how it feels to be so lost, you can't see a way out."

"Come here." I pulled Eva into my arms.

There had been so many times when I'd cleaned up Levi, got him into bed, and sat watching my older brother sleep off his demons. So many times, I'd felt alone. When I'd sat crumbling, wishing things could be different. People thought I was the strong one. The one holding things together. But they always failed to realize one vital thing.

Who held me together?

Who held together the person trying his fucking hardest to keep things going?

Then Eva came along. My sweet and innocent Starshine. For the first time in my life, I had someone to lean on.

"I love you." I angled her face to mine.

Eva smiled before kissing me. It would have been easy to lose myself in her, but if we were late getting to the Pepsi Center, I knew Alistair would blow his gasket.

"We should get ready."

"Now?" Eva's mouth curved against mine. "Now, you decide to grow a conscience?"

"Tonight, after the show."

"We'll be on the tour bus, or have you forgotten that?"

"Then you'll need to be quiet." I sucked Eva's tongue into my mouth, kissing her. "Very." Kiss. "Very." Kiss. "Quiet."

"Rafe…" She pressed her hand against my chest. For a second, I thought she was pushing me away, but then her fingers curled into my shirt.

"Ugh." I dropped my head to her shoulder. "I can't believe I'm saying this, but we really should stop."

"Tonight," she whispered.

"Tonight." After I figured a way to make sure we ended up on the same tour bus.

Just then voices sounded in the hall and Hudson, Damon, and Letty appeared. "I hope you're done because I do not need to see you and Eva doing that." He was covering his eyes with his hand.

"Were you guys standing right outside?" I asked.

"We went to raid the vending machine in the lobby." Letty held up a bag of chips.

"You could have just called room service."

"But where's the fun in that?"

"Damon and Hudson took some photos and signed some t-shirts. It's good publicity. But we really do need to get moving. Alistair wants us to do a full sound check."

"You're shitting me?" Hudson groaned. "We know the set inside out."

"Consider it part of your—"

"Punishment." I finished, feeling my spine stiffen.

"So now we're all being punished for Rafe's bad decisions. That's some fucking bullshit."

"Don't shoot the messenger, Hud. Alistair—"

"Yeah, yeah, save it. I'm going to take a shower." Hudson stalked off, his bad mood lingering in the air like the aftermath of a storm.

"This is going to be fun," Damon mumbled, giving me a serious look. He didn't say anything else; he didn't need to. Disappointment emanated from him.

"Come on, Eva." Letty broke the thick silence. "I have a few things to go over with you."

"Yeah, sure." She looked at me and I nodded.

"Go. I'll see you soon, okay?"

The girls disappeared, leaving me alone with Damon. "What?" I asked him, his heavy stare cutting me like tiny blades.

"I don't blame you for going after her, I don't. But..." He let out a heavy sigh. "Forget it, it doesn't matter. We have a show to prepare for."

Because that's what we did—we put on a show. Time and time again, we pasted on fake smirks and sex appeal and played it up for the fans, fulfilling their fantasies of us. But it was growing old, becoming a burden too heavy to shoulder.

It had always been the four of us. The band. Black Hearts Still Beat. We were all the others had. Levi, Rafe, Hudson, and Damon. We had our fair share of fallings out and arguments, but we always found our way back together. It's what we did. We fought and then we made up.

But I had Eva now.

Things were different.

I was different.

And I wasn't sure where that left us.

———

"Fuck me, he actually came," Hudson said through his teeth as we entered the arena. Levi was talking to Alistair and Riley while a dozen roadies pushed our kit into place, holding up wires, and rigging lighting. It was a well-oiled machine. One we were used to by now.

"Guys, Eva." Ali beckoned us over. I glanced at Eva, but she wore an easy smile as she approached them.

"Country, looking good." My brother smirked, making a bolt of anger zip up my spine. But then her hand was reaching for mine, grounding me.

"Levi," she said smoothly. "We're glad you're here."

"Where else would I be?" It was cocky and full of sarcasm.

"Okay, enough." Ali rubbed his temples. "I know this isn't... easy. But right now, you all need to focus on the show, nothing else. The label expects full cooperation. After the shitshow in Seattle and Salt Lake City, they want nothing but one-hundred and ten percent commitment. Am I clear?"

"Crystal, Ali boy." Levi dragged his snake bite piercings between his teeth, letting them pop. "I can't speak for the rest of the guys, but I'm ready to get out there and do my thing."

"Glad to hear it."

Damon shot me a wary look and I ran a hand down my face. "Shall we, then?"

"I can hardly wait." Hudson cut through the middle of us and headed to the stage.

"Problems in paradise?" Levi asked me.

"He's just pissed."

"What did you expect, little brother? You dropped the band and took off after Eva."

"Levi, this isn't helping." Alistair glanced between us.

He threw up his hands. "I'm just saying, you've got to wonder where Rafe's allegiance lies. I'm all in. Damon and Hudson are all in. But Rafe... he's got one foot in and the other pointed in Eva's direction."

"Levi..." Eva grimaced.

"It's all good, Angel." He moved closer, reaching for her. It took everything in me not to snatch his hand away as he brushed the hair from her face. "Ready to make some magic?"

"Fuck," Damon hissed beneath his breath.

"Come on." I slipped around them, needing to get away from Levi before I did something really fucking stupid.

Eva caught my eye, her soft expression silently asking if I was okay. I gave her a tight nod and kept on walking.

"Keep cool, yeah?" Damon fell into step beside me. "You know how he gets."

"He's baiting me."

"He's just wounded. Ignore him and keep your eye on the prize. If we can't get our shit together, we'll lose Masterpiece. And that doesn't just affect us, it affects Eva too."

Shit. He was right.

The endorsement deal with Masterpiece wasn't only for Black Hearts, it was for Eva too. A deal like that wouldn't only put her on the map, it could propel her career in ways nothing else would.

"You're right," I said as we climbed the stage ready to get into position.

"Of course I am. I'm the intelligent one of the group."

"Heard that, fucker," Hudson called out from behind his drum kit.

"Heard what?" Levi sauntered onto the stage as if he owned it. From his swagger and confidence, it was hard to believe that just two days ago we'd been fighting it out, trading insults and slinging fists.

"Damon fancies himself the intelligent one. I'm obviously the charming one."

"Oh yeah," my brother chuckled. "And Rafe's obviously the traitor, so what does that make me?"

I bit the inside of my cheek to avoid any of the insults spilling off my tongue.

"Why, you're our very own charismatic frontman." Hudson offered.

"Damn right I am." Levi locked eyes on mine. Things weren't okay between us, maybe they never would be. But right now, on stage, the music ruled.

It always had.

He gave me a swift nod and grabbed the mic. "Time to rock."

CHAPTER NINE

EVA

"Nervous?" Letty asked me as I watched Black Hearts from the wings. If it wasn't for all the media speculation, you would never have guessed there was a rift between Levi and Rafe. They performed flawlessly, Rafe's riffs and backing vocals blending with Levi's gravelly voice in a way that bewitched you.

I was completely and utterly enamored, right along with the twenty-thousand strong audience.

"A little," I sighed.

"You have that look." Letty nudged my shoulder.

"What look?" My gaze slid to hers.

"The look of love."

"I just keep pinching myself." Rafe was mine. He'd sat next to me in an interview that had aired across the nation and declared me his.

"I'm glad you came back, Eva. It was the right decision."

"Now you have that look."

"What look?" She pressed her lips into a thin smile.

"Like there's a 'but' coming..."

"I just hope you made the decision for you and not for Rafe." Letty faced the stage again and my eyes followed.

I could watch the band perform every day for the rest of my life and never grow tired of it. Their sound check had been immense. All their frustration and aggression and pain poured into every lyric, every note. It was palpable, and you couldn't help but be affected by it.

"They brought it tonight. The label will be pleased. The interview was a roaring success too. Now all we need is for Rafe and Levi to keep the peace."

"You really think they'll be able to do it?"

"If anyone can get the infamous Hunter brothers to kiss and make up, it's you, Eva."

"No pressure then." I frowned.

Letty chuckled. "I'm just saying, you're good for them. And I'm not just talking about Rafe and Levi. The whole band is better with you around. Hudson is less man whore. Damon smiles more. Even Alistair was less stressed with you around... until Vegas."

I flinched. I wanted to move past what had happened, not be reminded of it every two minutes.

"Look, I'm sorry. I don't mean to hurt your feelings, but you know you broke their trust when you left them, and I get why you did it. I do. But you've got to work to prove yourself again. I know you'll do it though, because you have to know how good you are for them. They're better with you around. You just need to show them you're not leaving again."

"You're right." I gave her a weak smile, "I'm just glad I have you in my corner." I stared out at the band once more. We'd already decided I wouldn't go on stage with them tonight. So when Levi looked over at us, a mischievous glint in his eye, and crooked his finger, I gasped.

"What is he doing?"

"Pulling a Levi Hunter, apparently." Letty grumbled something else, but I couldn't hear her over the roar of the crowd.

"Let me hear it, Denver. Who wants Miss Eva Walker to join us out on stage?"

The noise reverberated through me. Levi was grinning ear to ear, but Rafe looked murderous. Damon too. I couldn't see Hudson from behind his kit, but I knew he'd probably be pissed.

"What do I do?" I clutched Letty's arm. I'd performed with Levi before, but this felt different. It felt like he was putting me smack bang in the middle of his war with Rafe.

"You can't not go now. It'll look..." She trailed off as Levi called for me again.

"I think she needs a little encouragement. Eva, Eva, Eva."

"I'm goin' to kill him," I murmured as I ran my hands down my thighs before stepping out on stage. The crowd went wild, cheering and clapping, setting off a band of wild horses in my chest.

"Here she is, Denver. The girl who stole my brother's heart and did what no girl has ever managed to do before..."

My eyes widened with fear. Surely, he wasn't about to out me to twenty thousand avid fans. Not after today's interview.

He locked eyes on me, a flash of something there. He was going to do it; Levi was going to ruin everything... all because he was hurting and didn't know how to handle his emotions.

Before I could stop, Levi grabbed my hand and pulled me beside him, slipping his arm around my shoulder like we were old friends. "Let me tell you all something about Evangeline Star Walker," he said into the mic. "She isn't only a great musician, she's also a great person. She's everything I could wish for..." he paused, and the whole arena seemed to take a collective gasp, waiting for whatever he was about to say next.

Levi's tortured gaze dropped to mine. "I couldn't think of a better girl for my little brother, and I'm real happy you found each other." He squeezed my shoulder a little too tight. "Welcome to the family, Angel. Let's make some magic, shall we?"

Levi left me standing there while he jogged up to Hudson's kit. Someone rushed on stage with my guitar and a mic stand. I moved on autopilot, slipping the strap over my shoulder and positioning the mic right. Rafe was watching me, his intense gaze burning into the side of my face, demanding I look at him.

Slowly, I lifted my eyes to the storm in his. He was pissed, but pride was etched into his expression. I knew he didn't like that Levi had done this, but I also knew he wanted this for me. The stage. The spotlight. Rafe wanted all my dreams to come true. I smiled, mouthing, "I love you."

The faintest of smiles tugged at his lips. But then Hudson played the opening beat of *Nothing Else Matters* by Metallica. I only knew it because Levi often wove it into their set.

"Do you think you can pick up the riff?" he asked me off-mic, and I nodded.

The arena fell into eerie silence as Levi hit the opening lyrics. I waited, letting the band play the first verse. We hadn't rehearsed it, but the second we hit the chorus, it was as if we became a well-oiled machine. Damon and Rafe let me take the lead, the acoustic notes of my Gibson carrying over Levi's low growl. It was haunting. Full of pain and torment. The lyrics shouldn't have held any deep meaning, but I knew Levi well enough to know he hadn't picked the song at random.

I harmonized the rest of the song, letting my voice linger over his. As the final note trailed off, a smile played on my lips. It shouldn't have felt so good singing alongside him, given the circumstances. I couldn't deny it did though. Rafe had my heart, not a single part of me doubted that. But out here on stage, Levi and I connected in a way I'd never expected.

He bounded over to me and grabbed my hand, thrusting it into the air. "Eva Walker, everyone." Raucous applause filled the arena, sending another bolt of adrenaline shooting through me. I staggered off stage breathless and starry-eyed, drunk on the moment.

"When you two are like that..." Letty handed me a bottle of water while a stagehand took my guitar. "I don't know how Rafe does it."

"Does what?" I asked, even though I already knew the answer.

Letty gave me a knowing look. "You two were made to perform together. It shouldn't work, but by God, it does."

The high began to subside as I came back down to Earth. The band had launched into another song. I turned to watch them. Levi was alive on stage, holding the crowd captive in the palm of his hand. And Rafe—my strong and sturdy Rafe—was playing his Zemaitis like he was born to do it. His brow was furrowed with concentration, fingers moving up and down the frets at lightning speed. Music held these four boys together. It was in their blood, and I hoped it would be the thing that held them together no matter what was happening in their personal lives.

"I know it's probably not what you want to hear, but we're going out after the show."

My head snapped over to Letty. "Do I get a choice?" I didn't want to party, not tonight. Not with things how they were.

"I'm sorry, Eva. It's a label thing and they want you there. All of you."

"Do you think he's ready for it?" I flicked my head over to the stage; only this time, I wasn't looking at Rafe.

She let out a small sigh. "I guess we'll find out soon enough."

———

THE SOUND WAS A SWANKY CLUB DOWNTOWN. IT WAS PAST midnight by the time our SUVs pulled up outside the side entrance. A small group of paparazzi were hovering. The cameras started flashing before our bodyguards even got the doors open.

"Keep your head low and don't stop, okay?" Travis ushered me out of the vehicle, keeping me close as we hurried toward the door.

"Eva, Eva, over here."

"Eva, is it true Rafe and Levi came to blows over you?"

"Rafe, is it true you and Levi aren't speaking?

"Levi, Levi, can we get a statement on what you really think about Eva dating your brother?"

The barrage of questions was relentless.

"Just keep moving," Travis barked, keeping his hand on the small of my back. I was grateful he was here, to shield me from them.

A pretty brunette beckoned us inside, welcoming us to The Sound. "I'm Silla." She beamed. "We have the VIP section reserved for you. The fans are already lining up. We'll do the meet and greets in two sections, so you get to have a break. Once we're done with that, you can kick back and relax. Anything you need, just give me a shout."

Silla led us down a long hall and up a flight of stairs. It opened out into a mezzanine that overlooked the dance floor. The decor was sleek; dark and moody. The music was loud, pulsing through me like it had its own heartbeat.

"Sweet," Hudson pushed past me and made a beeline for the bar where they had a selection of drinks already lined up.

A frown crinkled my forehead. The guys had already been drinking. It had started pretty much straight after they came off stage. Even Rafe had joined them, which wasn't like him. And I knew the tension between him and Levi probably had something to do with it.

Everyone moved around me as I stood there, taking it all in.

"Hey." Strong arms slipped around me. "I missed you."

"It was only a ten-minute ride." I tilted my face up, and Rafe's lips brushed mine.

"Ten minutes too long." His lip piercing was cool against my skin as he kissed me harder, deeper.

"Get a fucking room," someone yelled.

"Rafe," I whispered, trying to untangle myself from his hold.

"I want you," he said against my lips.

"Are you drunk?" I could taste the liquor on his tongue, but it was more than that. He was acting... off.

"Seriously." He scowled. "You think I'm drunk?" His brow went up.

"Come on, let's go hang with the others." I took his hand and pulled him toward the plush leather booth.

Rafe flopped down, pulling me onto his lap.

"Drinks." Letty appeared with a tray in her hands. "I got beer, some mixers, and sugary cocktails for the lady." She winked at me.

"I'm not sure..." I held up my hand.

"One won't hurt you. Besides, we're celebrating. The interview was a hit. The show was killer. Everything is right in the Black Hearts world again."

I glanced over her shoulder. Levi was at the bar, knocking back a glass of what looked like whisky.

"Are you sure everythin's okay?" I asked her. She glanced back, watching Levi as he beckoned over a girl and slung his arm around her shoulder.

"Oh, hell no," she mumbled.

"Who is that?"

"Phoebe Halstead. She's the new intern at Razorsharp."

"But why is she here?" I asked. "Interns don't usually end up on the road, do they?"

"No, they don't. But apparently the big wigs thought it would do her good to learn on the job. She's going to be shadowing me."

"Maybe you should go rescue her then before Levi ruins everything," Rafe said, failing to disguise the bitterness in his words.

"Fuck's sake. I wanted to enjoy tonight, not play babysitter."

"You stay, I'll go." I slipped Rafe's hands off my hips and stood up.

"Are you sure?" Letty asked, and I nodded.

"Just keep your eye on him, okay?" I mouthed.

As I went to leave, Damon reached us. "I can't listen to Hudson for another second. He's like a dog in a heat. Great show tonight, Eva. Sorry about Levi going off script. I guess he's out to prove something." His eyes flickered to Rafe, but I didn't turn around. Instead, I excused myself and made a beeline for Levi and Phoebe.

"Hello," I said to the wide-eyed girl. "I'm Eva. You're Phoebe, right?"

She nodded, tucking a strand of hair behind her ear. "Hmm, hey." Her whole body was anchored to Levi's side, his arm now around her waist. She looked super uncomfortable but not as alarmed as I had expected.

"Levi." He was busy talking to someone else. "Levi," I snapped, and his eyes finally landed on mine.

"Oh, Angel, it's you. Great show tonight, right?" A wicked grin formed on his lips. We hadn't talked about what he did tonight, there had been no time. And honestly, I didn't really know what to say. I refused to be drawn into his games.

"Have you met my new... *friend?*" He turned his grin to Phoebe, but it quickly melted away.

"You can't remember my name, can you?" She quipped back without hesitation.

Well, okay then. I frowned, watching their strange exchange.

"Of course, I can... Penelope?"

"Cute, but no." She slipped out of his hold. "It's Phoebe."

"Aww, don't be like that, baby. I would have gotten it eventually, preferably when you were under me." Levi let his hooded gaze fall down the intern's body. She flushed under his scrutiny but didn't shrink.

Interesting.

"Phoebe works for the label, Levi." I arched my brow. "She's an intern."

"Sounds like a challenge to me."

"Behave," I mouthed. "Come on, Phoebe, you can come sit with us."

"Oh, Angel, you're no fun."

"Go on." I urged her. "I'll be right there."

She hesitated but then started toward Letty and the others.

"What are you doin', Levi?" I said the second she was out of earshot.

"Who, me?" He gave me a dismissive shrug. "I thought I was having some fun."

"Is that really a good idea?" My gaze went to the glass in his hand.

"Relax, I've got it under control."

"Have you?"

"Are you asking me as a friend or my brother's girl?"

"Levi... stop, please."

He stepped into my space, forcing me to crane my neck to look at him. "I appreciate your concern, Angel, but I don't need a babysitter. You all got your wish. I'm here, I did the show. What else do you want from me?" His intense eyes burned into me.

Words formed on the tip of my tongue, but nothing would come out.

Disappointment washed over him. "Didn't think so." With that, he brushed past me and stalked off, grabbing another drink on the way.

CHAPTER TEN

RAFE

"GOD, I'm glad that's over." I nuzzled Eva's neck, unable to keep my hands off her. It was the meet and greets. All the wandering hands and lovesick fangirls. I never liked that shit, but I knew it was part of the gig.

Tonight was different though. Tonight, was the first time I'd stood there playing up to their eager questions and over the top flirtations, with Eva close by. I knew she trusted me; it wasn't about that. It just felt wrong.

"Rafe," she chuckled. "Stop, we have an audience."

"Don't mind us," Hudson grumbled, taking a long pull on his beer. "There's nothing I enjoy more than watching Rafe's tongue down your throat."

"Dude." Damon frowned.

"I think it's cute." Phoebe glanced over at us but quickly ducked her head when I caught it her eye. She was a strange one. A new intern, here to shadow Letty, whatever the fuck that meant. It wasn't like we were the epitome of well-behaved clients. The label could have chosen another—any other band—but instead they'd sent her here, to shark-infested waters.

Poor girl.

"I need to pee." Eva leaned back and dropped a kiss on my cheek. "I'll be right back."

"Need company?" Letty asked.

"I think I can manage." My girl smiled. "Besides, Travis will be right there."

"Not right *there*, I hope." Hudson smirked at me and I flipped him off.

Eva tugged his hair as she walked by. He yelped like a little girl, rubbing his head.

"You deserved that." I pointed out. I had a nice buzz, more than usual. After watching Levi coax Eva on stage at the show tonight, I'd needed it. Needed something to take the edge off.

"Hey, you okay?" Damon nudged my knee with his.

"I'm okay. Not sure I can say the same thing about him though." I flicked my head over to where Levi was working the crowd.

"Johnson is keeping a close eye on him. It could be worse."

Yeah. He could be pounding his fist into my face.

"Have the two of you…"

"No."

"You did well, you know, holding it together on stage like that."

I kicked my legs out. "It's not like I have a choice."

"There's always a choice, Rafe." Damon gripped my shoulder, squeezing. "He'll come around. He just needs—"

"Time."

People kept saying that. Give him time. It was bullshit though. Levi didn't need time, he needed… fuck, I didn't know what he needed anymore.

Maybe I never had.

Conversations went on around me. Hudson entertained Letty and the new girl with his lame-ass jokes. Damon disappeared to talk to some industry people. And I sat there wondering when I could drag Eva back to the tour bus and bury myself deep inside her.

She was fast becoming my drug.

My high.

My dangerous addiction.

I'd never really understood it before, the craving. The permanent buzz underneath your skin. I wanted Eva all the time. I couldn't get enough of her: her kisses, her touch, even her eyes.

Her big ocean eyes.

"I'm going to look for Eva," I said after a few more minutes. She'd been gone too long, and Levi was nowhere to be seen either.

"Rafe, man, relax." Hudson rolled his eyes. "She's been gone like ten minutes."

Letty glanced over her shoulder and then settled her gaze back on me. "Want me to come with you?"

"I can handle it."

"Stay cool." She gave me a knowing look, and I nodded, slipping out of the booth. Fenton shadowed me as I cut across the VIP section towards the restrooms. Travis was waiting outside, as still as a statue.

"Is Eva still in there?" I craned my neck, looking over his shoulder.

"She's taking a call. It sounded like the friend. Miss Steinberg, I believe."

"So, she's okay?"

"You've got it bad, huh?" He chuckled.

"And Levi, is he—"

"Taking a piss." Travis nodded. "You need to relax. We've got this place locked down."

What I needed was to see Eva.

"I'm going to check on her." I started to move around Travis, but his arm shot out. "Take a breath, Hunter. Your girl is fine."

"What the hell are you doin'? I said no, get off me..."

I barreled past Travis and into the hall. It was dark, the strip lighting dimmed. At first, I couldn't see them, hidden by the shadows, but then I saw her.

Eva.

My Eva cornered by some asshole who was all up in her space, touching her hip intimately. As if she belonged to him.

"Get the fuck away from her," the words ripped from my lungs as I went to move, only to be torn away.

"Get him out of here," Travis yelled, storming past me, in full-bodyguard mode.

I thrashed against Fenton, but the fucker was too strong, dragging me out of there. Damon and Hudson were on me in a second. "What the fuck?

"Eva, someone get Eva," I yelled.

"Travis has her, relax." Fenton eased up. "You good?" he asked, giving me space.

I smoothed out my shirt and nodded. "I'm good." Anger vibrated through me, my body trembling. Damon inched closer, Hudson flanking my other side.

"I'm going to make sure they're okay." Fenton disappeared.

"He was... fuck," I roared, my body quivering with anger as I stared at the door leading to the restrooms. "What's taking them so long?"

"Our guys can handle it." Damon moved in front of me. "You need to calm down."

"I'll calm down when I see... *Eva*." I pushed my friends out the way and rushed over to her. "Are you okay?" My eyes scanned her face, her body.

"I'm... I'm okay." Her voice shook. "I told him I wasn't interested, but he didn't... he..."

"Ssh." I pulled her into my arms. "You're okay. Everything's okay."

Travis and Fenton appeared a second later, dragging the guy with them. His lip was busted open, blood trickling down his jaw as he hung limp between the two burly bodyguards.

What the fuck?

But it all made sense when my brother stalked out from behind them. He looked furious, his eyes wild and fists clenched at his side. Levi found me across the room and froze. Something passed between us. A momentary ceasefire. We weren't in a good place right now, but we could both agree on this.

On protecting the terrified girl in my arms.

I offered him an appreciative nod, and he returned it. Then he was gone, swamped by the rest of our security team.

"Come on." I said guiding Eva into my side. "We're getting out of here."

Travis stuck to us like glue as we exited the club. The SUVs were already waiting, the huddle of paparazzi smaller than when we'd arrived.

"Rafe, Rafe, over here. What happened?"

"Is Eva okay? Eva, Eva, did something happen?"

"Stay back." Travis shielded us as the camera flashes went off around us, lighting up the dark alley like July fourth.

"Hey man, back the fuck off." I glanced over my shoulder to find Hudson scuffling with an overeager journo.

"Travis," I yelled, trying to catch his eye. The last thing we needed was Hudson getting into it with the press.

"Stalter can handle it. Get Eva in the back." He yanked the door open and jogged around to the driver's side. Eva climbed in and I slid in after her. Letty and Phoebe came next.

"Crap, it's getting crazy out there. Hudson is—"

The door slammed shut and another bodyguard hopped in the passenger side. "Everyone good?" Travis asked, our eyes meeting in the rear-view.

Eva nodded, her fingers twisted into my shirt as she stared out the tinted window.

"Hey". I slipped my fingers underneath her jaw and gently angled her face to mine. "You're okay. I've got you, Starshine." Seeing that guy caging Eva against the wall, hearing her cry for help... it hadn't just sobered me, it had yanked me back to Earth with an almighty thud.

"I can't believe that happened," she breathed, blinking away the tears clinging to the corners of her eyes.

Letty's cell phone blared to life. "It's Ali," she mouthed, taking his call. The intern sat beside her, surprisingly calm considering the circumstances.

"Hey, you okay?" I asked her, and she nodded.

"Is it always so..."

"It gets easier." Eva sat up straighter. "I didn't think I could handle it at first, but you do. One day, it just all becomes less... intense."

"Are you sure you're okay?"

Eva glanced up at me, pressing close to my side. "I will be."

———

WHEN WE GOT BACK TO THE TOUR BUSES, ALISTAIR WAS WAITING for us. "What the hell happened?"

"Some guy cornered Eva," Hudson offered.

"Shit, are you okay?" His expression softened as he laid eyes on Eva.

"I'm fine, just a little shaken up."

"And you?" He looked to me. "You cool?" I knew what he was asking me. Did he need to bail me out of anything.

I shook my head. "I'm good. But Levi—"

Just then, my brother appeared. He stopped, frowning at us. "The asshole had it coming." He shrugged. "I'm only sorry I didn't get another couple of punches in."

Alistair hissed under his breath.

"Security handled it," Letty added. "There should be no blowback."

"Well since you're all here, we can get on the road. Duke will be glad to get ahead of schedule. Letty and Eva will remain on the second bus. Phoebe you'll also be with the girls."

My brow went up and Damon snickered.

"What?" Alistair gawked, his eyes shifting from me to Damon and back again.

"Eva's with me."

"Rafe, we've talked about this. She can't just—"

"I don't know about anyone else," Damon interjected. "But I need a drink. Why don't we all hang out on the Van Hool tonight and we can deal with the permanent sleeping arrangements tomorrow."

"Sounds good to me. We can initiate Pheebs into the fold." Hudson grinned.

"You'll do no such thing." Alistair glared at him. "Phoebe is—"

"Sounds good to me." All eyes fell on the new girl. "I mean," she stuttered, "if it's okay."

"Of course it's okay." Letty grabbed her hand and started pulling her away. "Come on, we'll grab some pillows and blankets from our bus."

"I don't like this." Alistair rubbed his temples.

"Relax, Ali, boy. It's one night," my brother said.

"You're telling me, you're okay with this?"

"I'm not going to be a dick about it, if that's what you mean." Levi caught my eye again. "Someone tried to hurt Eva. I think we'd all sleep better knowing where she is tonight." He stalked off, climbing aboard the bus like what he'd said was nothing.

It wasn't nothing though.

For someone like Levi it was every-fucking-thing.

"Did that really just happen?" Hudson asked.

But I was too busy staring at the door to the bus, wondering if maybe, just maybe, me and Levi were working toward peace.

Or if the only thing linking us anymore was the girl curled into my side.

"I don't think I can sleep yet." Eva let out a soft sigh.

"Sleep? Who said anything about sleeping? The night is still young, and we have a new recruit to toy with."

"Hudson, please don't traumatize the new intern before she's even had chance to settle in."

"That was you not so long ago." He quipped back as we moved toward the bus.

"I wasn't that bad, was I?"

"Nah. You were special. You were so freakin' shy, but you had this inner strength. We all saw it."

"Is that a compliment?" Eva smirked at him. Hudson pulled himself up, hanging half off and half on the bus.

"Don't let it go to your head, Country." He winked and disappeared inside.

"I'll see the two of you on board." Damon slipped around us.

"Are you okay?" Eva asked me.

"Isn't that supposed to be my line?"

She twisted to face me, curling her hands into my shirt. "He didn't hurt me, Rafe."

"I know." My jaw clenched as I tried to rein in my anger. "I just... fuck, I wanted to kill him."

"There's always going to be someone, Rafe. An overeager fan, a drunken guy at a bar. The band. Riley." Her brow rose.

"Riley? What the hell does she have to do with this?"

Eva let out a bitter chuckle. "She's made no effort to hide the fact she hates me, and I don't trust her."

"It's... complicated." I didn't trust her either, but she was banging Alistair. He got this starry-eyed look whenever she was around.

"Has she said something to you since you got back?"

"Nothing I can't handle." My eyes narrowed, and Eva let out a little sigh. "I just can't help but wonder what her endgame is. It's obvious she's ambitious, but what if she's prepared to do anything to get to the top?"

"She really bothers you?"

Eva looked at me, her eyes full of pain. "I just don't want anything else to come between us."

"Did something happen, because if it did—" Riley was our assistant, and Alistair's... well, what the fuck she was to him. But if she was making trouble for Eva, then I wouldn't hesitate to speak to Alistair.

"No, no. I don't want to make a big deal about it. It's just different now."

"Now what?"

"Now everyone knows I'm yours."

I pulled Eva into my chest, holding her there. She wasn't wrong. Going public was supposed to get the fans on our side, and to some degree, it had. But for everyone fan who supported us, there would be one who didn't like it. Eva was going places. People would want to knock her off the pedestal she'd found herself on.

I wanted to protect her. To shield her from ever having to witness the dark, ugly side of the industry. But the reality was, I couldn't.

And it was tearing me apart.

CHAPTER ELEVEN

EVA

"No FUCKING WAY. For real, you got a full house. I thought you said you never played Poker before?" Hudson gawked at me like I'd grown a second head.

It was late. But after what went down at the club, no one seemed in a hurry to go to sleep. Hudson had suggested strip poker to keep us all entertained, but we settled on regular poker. Rafe helped me the first couple of rounds, while Letty helped Phoebe.

Turned out, I was a quick learner.

"Pay up, Ryker." Everyone chuckled, as Hudson reluctantly pushed his piles of chips toward me.

"Another round?"

"Count me out." Rafe held up his hands. He glanced down the bus. Levi had declined to join us, holing up in the back bedroom instead. It had been awkward at first, but the lingering tension soon melted away as we got into the card game.

"I'll be right back," he said, sliding his hand across my knee.

"Do you think that's a good idea?" I whispered, knowing exactly where he was going.

"I just want to talk."

"I know but..." I let out a weary sigh. "Okay, if you're sure."

Rafe stood up and slipped out from the table. But before he got down the back end of the bus, Levi appeared. He'd changed out of his outfit into a pair of sweats that hung low on his waist. Phoebe's eyes grew to saucers as she took in his naked torso. I couldn't blame her. It was like a canvas, inked with a story of pain and passion.

"See something you like, New Girl?" Levi leaned back against the counter and uncapped a beer with his teeth.

"I... hmm..." Phoebe stuttered.

"Lay off her," Letty warned.

"Or what, Panem? You're not my keeper."

"No, but if I was, I'd tell you to put some fucking clothes on."

Levi ran a hand lazily down his lean body. "I don't see Eva or New Girl complaining."

Rafe glared at his brother, the air around us turning thick with tension.

"Levi, come on, man. You did a good thing tonight." That was Damon. "Don't ruin it, yeah?"

His eyes fixed on mine. Heated and intense. But it wasn't an expression of lust or longing, it was something else. Something akin to fear and anger.

"Listen," Rafe said quietly. Damon launched into telling Phoebe something to give the brothers a private moment, but I couldn't help eavesdropping.

"What you did at the club. Thanks, man. If anything had happened to Eva... fuck, I don't know what I would have done."

"It was nothing."

"It wasn't nothing, Levi." Rafe dragged a hand through his hair. "You and I both know that."

"Yeah, well don't make a big deal out of it. Things between you and me..."

"I know. I said a lot of things I regret. We both did." Rafe's eyes flickered to mine and I dropped my gaze.

"The thing is though, little brother, once they're out in the open, ain't no taking them back. I'm glad Eva's okay. Part of me is even glad you have each other. But honestly, I don't know where the fuck that leaves us."

"We're family, Levi. Nothing will ever change that."

For a second, I thought Levi might concede. I silently prayed he would drop his walls enough to let Rafe back inside. But he moved around him, grabbed another beer from the refrigerator and stalked off down the bus, disappearing into the bedroom again.

Rafe looked so sad. I wanted to fix it. I wanted to fix them. But this was one problem I couldn't fix. Not until Levi fully accepted the shift in their relationship, and Rafe accepted that he couldn't be everything to everyone all the time.

"Is he always so... rude?"

Hudson exploded with laughter at Phoebe's observation, slapping his hand down on the table. Bottles and glasses wobbled, cards and poker chips flying everywhere.

"Watch it, asshole." Damon started cleaning up. "You'll have to excuse Hudson, Phoebe, he isn't used to company."

"Fuck you, man. I'm not going to change who I am just because the label sent another little minion to spy on—"

"Excuse me?" Phoebe recoiled. "You think I'm here to *spy* on you?"

"Ignore him, girl. I do." Letty grinned, and Hudson flipped her off.

"I just don't understand what the label were thinking sending an intern on tour with us. Especially with..." he trailed off, glancing down the bus.

"What Hud is trying to say," Damon added. "Is that things have been a little tense lately."

"I get it, and I know you guys probably don't want me here. But I'm a quick learner and I promise not to get in the way."

"You really think you've got what it takes to tour with us?" Hudson climbed over Damon to go to the kitchenette. He pulled a bottle of liquor from one of the cabinets and found a couple of cups.

"Seriously, you're going to make her—"

"You think just because Levi is in his room sulking like a little bitch that tradition takes a backseat? Oh, hell no." He handed Phoebe a cup and poured her a generous shot.

"I'm not... I don't..." She sniffed the contents, blanching.

"You don't have to do it," I said.

"Sure, she does."

Phoebe ignored Hudson, asking me, "Did you do it?"

"I did. It's not my proudest moment." I grimaced. It felt so long ago, even though it was only a few weeks. So much had happened.

"It's not spiked or anything like that?"

"Jesus, what do you take me for? If I wanted to get you into bed, I wouldn't need to roofie you."

"I'm not..." Phoebe's cheeks burned. "You're a lot to handle."

"You haven't seen anything yet, darling." Hudson raised his cup. "Shall we?" He touched it to the edge of hers before raising it to his lips. Phoebe hesitated but then knocked it back in one.

"Wow, okay, I'd forgotten how badly that stuff burns," she breathed. "Water, I need water."

Everyone laughed while Hudson got her a bottle of water. "Congratulations, new girl, you're officially one of us now." He winked at her. "Welcome to the crazy."

"One of us and therefore, off limits." Letty gave him a pointed look.

"You think… me… and the new girl." His eyes widened. "No offense, but you're not my type."

"None taken." Phoebe shrugged. "You're not mine either."

"Ooh, burn." Letty slapped the table. "I like you already." She flashed Phoebe a grin.

"You have a type now?" Damon had kicked his feet up on the table and reclined back in the chair.

"Sure, he does. Her name starts with a M and ends with a—"

"Fuck you, traitor." Hudson balled up a chip packet and threw it at Rafe's head. "I think I'm going to call it a night. The party's dead and I need my beauty sleep."

"He's still hung up on Molly," Rafe whispered.

"I'll pretend I didn't hear that." Hudson yelled as he disappeared into the bathroom.

"Who's Molly?" Phoebe asked. She had that starstruck look, as if she couldn't quite believe she was sitting on a tour bus hanging out with Black Hearts Still Beat.

I knew the feeling well.

"She's my best friend. She and Hudson had… a thing." I turned in toward Rafe. "Am I allowed to say that?"

He chuckled. "She works for the label. She'll know all our secrets before the tour is over."

"I guess." I smiled around a yawn. "Sleep doesn't sound like a bad idea. I guess I'll be takin' one of the bunks…"

"Cute, Eva. Real cute." Damon smirked. "Like you didn't know the minute you stepped foot on the bus that you and Rafe would be stealing the other bedroom."

"I didn't want to presume." I fought a grin.

"Ladies," Damon addressed Letty and Phoebe. "I hope you brought earplugs."

"Hey," I cried. "You can't say stuff like that." My cheeks heated.

"Relax, Eva. I was talking about Hudson's snoring." Damon wore a knowing smile.

Rafe dipped his head and nuzzled my neck. "Don't worry, Starshine," he whispered, his words for my ears only. "I promise not to make you scream."

My breath caught, my stomach clenching, as I sat there wondering what the hell I'd let myself in for ever setting foot on this bus.

———

"THIS IS COZY." I BRUSHED MY NOSE OVER RAFE'S JAW. THE bedroom, if you could call it that, was steeped in darkness. I could just make out the lines of his face, guided by the glint of metal in his lip.

He let out a small breath, running his hand over my hip, dragging me closer. "I want to love you, Eva, I do..."

"It's okay." I kissed the corner of his mouth. "We have all the time in the world, right? I think all I want right now is for you to hold me." I was tired too. Emotionally drained from the events of the night, the dark Levi-shaped cloud still circling us.

"Always." I heard him swallow.

"Penny for your thoughts?"

"I just... Jesus, Eva. When I saw that guy with his hands on you..."

"Ssh." I touched my finger to his lips. "Don't do this, please."

Rafe hooked his arm around my body and crushed me against his chest. "What did I ever do to deserve you?"

"It's not about being deserving, Rafe. It's about finding the missing half of your soul."

"You think I'm your soulmate?" There was no humor in his words, but there was plenty of doubt.

"I'm not sayin' that... I'm just sayin' I like to think we came into each other's lives for a reason. I was in a dark place when I met you, Rafe. I was lost and you anchored me."

Silence enveloped us. Then Rafe started humming, his voice dancing over my skin like a warm breeze. "She's just a lost girl, drowning in space. Nowhere to run, nowhere to go. All she needs is an anchor, someone to reach out and pull. Take my hand, I'll be the one..."

"What is that?" I pushed up onto my elbow. "It's beautiful."

"It's nothing, just words." Rafe leaned up to kiss me.

I eased back, raising a brow. "It didn't sound like nothing; it sounded like something."

Even in the darkness, I could sense him shutting down. I knew things were different now. There was an us and them now. We'd done that. The band could make jokes and brush it under the rug, but it didn't change the fact we were all treading uncharted waters.

There was something else going on with Rafe though. I wanted to desperately push him to tell me, to talk it over. But I knew better than most people, that sometimes a person needed time and space to deal with things in their own way.

"Do you think Hudson and Molly will ever sort out their crap?" I asked, changing the subject.

Rafe tucked me back into the crook of his arm, so we were lying side by side, staring up at the ceiling. "Hudson isn't the settling down type."

"What happened to him?"

"That's not my story to tell, Eva. Even if he wanted to make a go of it with Molly, and I think a part of him does, he will screw it up. It's what he does."

"That's a little harsh, don't you think?"

"It's the truth. I've known Hudson a long time and the second things get too real, he bails. Foster carers, therapists, girls..."

"He's never bailed on you."

"That's different, we're the only family he has." Rafe ran his fingers up and down my arm as if he was playing the lines of my skin.

"I really swooped in and messed things up, didn't I?" A heavy weight settled in my chest. I wasn't sorry I'd met Rafe; how could I be when he'd had a hand in helping me find myself again? But I did hate that things with Levi and the band were so complicated.

"There are a lot of things I regret, Eva," he whispered, pain laced into every word. "But you're not one of them."

I fell asleep in his arms. Just a girl in love with a boy, wondering how they were going to survive the odds.

CHAPTER TWELVE

RAFE

THE NEXT THREE days were grueling. We had back to back shows in Kansas City, Minneapolis, and Chicago, followed by a smaller gig at the Grand Ballroom on Navy Pier tonight. This one was for official fan club contest winners, fans who were gifted tickets through non-profits like Wish Fairy, and friends and family. Except, none of us had friends and family, so it usually amounted to a bunch of industry types and clingers.

"We need to talk." Riley breezed into the suite we had at The Fairview. Two shows in the same city meant we had a hotel which, after being holed up on the bus for the last three nights with the guys, Eva, and Letty, was a welcomed thing. After that first night, Phoebe had decided to stay on the other bus, but Eva and Letty stuck around. Alistair didn't like it, but it was either that or I moved onto the other bus with Eva, which we both knew would only cause a bigger rift between the band.

For three days solid, we rehearsed, and we performed. Levi and I barely talked during the day, then at night on stage we found our common ground. Afterward, I dragged Eva back to our cramped bedroom and lost myself in her.

But tonight, there was no escaping. Tonight, we had to perform and then stick around and work the crowd.

"We have around fifty VIPs there tonight," Riley scanned her clipboard. "Three are terminal."

"Shit," Damon murmured beneath his breath. I glanced over at Eva; she had gone as white as a sheet.

"They're... terminal?" She choked out.

"Yes, why? Is that a problem?" Riley said, barely looking at her. "They're Wish Fairy recipients. It's a non-profit that—"

"I know what it is." Eva grimaced. "I just didn't realize... it doesn't matter." She got up and walked over to the window. It went from floor to ceiling with the best view of the city.

"What's her problem?" Riley let out an impatient huff, continuing to check her clipboard.

"Seriously, Riley, you went there?" Hudson grumbled.

I narrowed my eyes on her, feeling anger simmer in my veins. As a general rule, Riley kept her distance. I had kept my promise to Eva and hadn't said anything to Alistair. But every now and again she popped up, usually causing a stir.

"I'm sorry." She glanced up, batting her eyes. "Is there a problem?"

"Yeah, there's a problem..." I started but Levi shot up.

"You're a fucking cold-hearted bitch, that's the problem." He stalked off, not sparing her a second look.

"Did he just...?" Riley was flustered, color streaking her neck. "He... he can't call me that. And where is he going? The meeting isn't over yet. We still have to go over—"

"I think the meeting is done, Riles." Hudson kicked his feet up on the coffee table, fighting a smirk. He caught my eye, flicking his head over to Eva. I gave him an appreciative nod and got up to go to her. Not before I heard Damon say, "That was an insensitive thing to say, Riley. You know what Eva went through."

I didn't stick around to hear the rest.

"Hey." I moved behind Eva, rubbing her shoulders.

"Hey." She gave me a sad smile through the glass reflection.

"Ignore Riley, she just likes to—"

"Act like a cold-hearted bitch?" Eva smothered a grin.

"You heard that, huh? Seems like my brother is doing a fine job of defending you at every turn, when I kind of thought that was my role."

"He was protectin' you."

"How do you figure?"

"We both know Riley will complain to Alistair about Levi. If it wasn't him, it would have been you, and Alistair is still pissed at you."

"He's pissed at Levi too."

"He's always pissed at Levi. You're different." Eva turned in my arms. "I won't let her get to me anymore, if you don't."

"Deal." I sealed it with a kiss before groaning, "Do we have to go tonight?"

"If we don't want to get kicked off the tour, then yeah, we do."

"Maybe that wouldn't be such a bad thing."

Her eyes widened. "You don't mean that?"

Didn't I?

"Rafe?" Eva urged when I didn't answer.

"I'll be there, I promise."

"Of course you will, silly." She beamed at me. Jesus, that smile. It stopped my heart.

"Yeah, and why is that?"

"Because..." Eva pressed herself against me, pushing up on her tiptoes until her lips were brushing my ear, firing up every cell in my body. "I'm not lettin' you out of my sight. Wherever you go, Rafe Hunter, I go too."

Now that, I liked the sound of.

———

"Talk to me," Damon slid onto the stool beside me. I barely acknowledged him, too busy watching Eva. She had a group of young girls around her, all jostling for selfies and autographs.

"She's a natural with them," he added. "Did you see how some of them bypassed us and went straight to her? We must be losing our charm."

He was right. Eva was a natural. I'd worried how it might affect being with the fans from Wish Fairy, but Eva was as gracious and humble as ever, taking the time to talk to each of them and take photos. I'd had a lump in my throat the whole time, watching her, imagining what she must be thinking, feeling.

"Okay, spill..." Damon nudged my shoulder. "What is going on with you? You look like someone stole your favorite puppy."

"This thing with Levi, it has me all messed up," I admitted.

"I thought things were better there? Levi seems... together."

He did. He was at rehearsals on time, never missed a sound check, and every night, he gave one hundred and ten percent out on stage.

But there was still an ocean between us.

"It's not the same."

"Maybe it doesn't need to be the same. Maybe you need to find a new way forward."

"Yeah, maybe."

"Want to know what I think?"

"Not really," I side-eyed him, "but I'm guessing you're going to tell me anyway."

"I think you're waiting for him to screw up again. That way, you can justify leaving and going after Eva. You can justify choosing her."

"That's not... fuck," I breathed.

Was that it?

Was I really waiting for Levi to mess up again so I could alleviate some of the guilt I carried around in my chest?

"It's okay, Rafe. I've known you both a long time. He's always needed you and I think part of you has always needed to be needed by him. Your relationship is co-dependent, just not in the ways you might think. You're not only worried about what this will do to Levi long term, you're worried about what this will do to you."

I glanced at him out of the corner of my eye. "You know you're wasted in the band, right? You should have gone to college and studied psychology or something."

"Stop deflecting." Damon leaned his arms back against the bar.

"In all seriousness though, do you ever think about what comes after all this?"

"Do you?" His brow shot up.

"Maybe. Now and again."

"You mean, since Eva?"

"She makes me want things, Damon. Things I didn't ever let myself imagine I could have."

"And that's a bad thing?"

"This life..." I let out an exasperated sigh. "It chews you up and spits you out. We're barely adults and I already feel like an old man."

He regarded me for a second. "You're worried you won't survive the tour."

"I'm worried *we* won't survive the tour."

"Eva's strong, man. Stronger than we all give her credit for. I don't think her strength is the real issue here, I think it's yours."

I didn't answer, I didn't need to. Damon was right. Part of me had gone after Eva, and chased her back to Lyme, because I wasn't sure I could do this without her. And now she was here with me, I already felt her slipping through my fingers.

Jesus, I was more fucked up than I realized.

Damon shook his head, a faint smile playing on his lips. "You need to have a little faith. Because, and don't ask me how or why, but that girl is head over heels in love with you, and you're sitting here like the world is about to end when you could be over there, with her."

As if she heard us, Eva glanced over at us, her whole face lighting up at the sight of me.

"You're a lucky son of a gun, Hunter. Now stop moping and go be with your girl." The force of his hand against my shoulder had me stumbling off my stool. I righted myself and slowly made my way over to Eva. One of the girls in the huddle noticed, then another, and another, until their shrieks and giggles filled the air.

"I guess you all know Rafe?" Eva looked at me with such adoration.

I slipped my arm around her waist. "Ladies, did you enjoy the show?"

"Ohmigod, ohmigod, it's Rafe Hunter... I mean, yes... so good. Ohmigod." The girl was practically hyperventilating, her friends rubbing her arms as she tried to get out the words.

"Take a deep breath, Denver," Eva said around a smile. The girl inhaled deeply, running a hand through her long hair.

"Okay... I think I'm okay. I just... wow, I didn't think we'd actually get to hang out with you like this. It's..."

"Pretty mind blowin', huh?" Eva grinned. "I still pinch myself every day."

She nudged my shoulder gently, motioning to the girls.

"I... uh..." I mumbled, their expectant gazes like laser beams on me. "Is there anything you want to ask? Within reason?" I tagged on the end.

"So many questions," another girl spoke. "But I'll keep it simple. Where did you guys go on your first date?"

Shit. They were all looking at me expectantly, waiting to hear all about how I swept Eva off her feet with flowers and romantic gestures and all that stuff... I hadn't ever done.

"I... hmm..." My palms grew clammy.

Eva's hand flattened against my stomach as she let out a small laugh. "Dating is kind of hard when your boyfriend is the bassist for Black Hearts."

"So you mean he's never taken you out?"

Their crestfallen expressions made me wither and die inside.

"I don't need all that stuff," Eva said.

"If my boyfriend was Rafe Hunter, you'd better believe I'd want him to take me out," one of them said and a couple others nodded, their expressions clouded with confusion, as if I was killing their fantasy of me right before their eyes.

"I guess I'd better get my thinking cap on then." The words spilled out before I could stop them. Eva peeked up at me, frowning.

"Ohmigod, this is so exciting. We could totally help you plan it... I mean if you need some ideas".

"I think I've got it covered." A strangled laugh rumbled in my chest. "But thanks. Now do y'all mind if I borrow Eva for a little while?"

Their collective sighs made me chuckle; only this time it was a genuine hearty laugh. "Enjoy the rest of the party." I steered Eva away. "I'm never going to live that down, am I?"

"What do you mean?" she asked me.

"Being schooled on dating by a bunch of teenagers."

As I pulled her toward a quiet section of the club, the Bad Wolves cover version of *Zombie* started playing. I froze, lost in the memory. It felt like a lifetime ago since that weekend in Camdena, when I'd helped Eva with her arrangement for her audition.

"Rafe?"

"Come here, you." I gently tugged her into my arms, not sparing a thought for the room full of people all watching. The fan girls were right. I'd never taken Eva out on a proper date. I'd never danced with her, or watched her eyes light up with excitement and wonder as I picked her up from her house.

Burying my hand into her hair, I dipped my head and grazed the shell of her ear. "Go out with me?"

"W- what?" she breathed.

"On a date. Just you and me."

"Is this about what they said?" Eva eased back to look at me. "I don't need anything more from you Rafe. I have all I need."

"I know, but you deserve it. And I want it." Now that the seed was planted, I wanted it so fucking much.

A slow smile spread over her face. "You really want that?" I nodded. "Where will we go, though? And what about security?"

My other hand ran down Eva's spine, pressing her closer, as I swayed us to the haunting track. "I'll handle it." I lowered my face to hers. "So, what do you say, Starshine. Will you go out with me?"

Eva kissed me, murmuring against my lips, "Yes, I'll go out with you."

CHAPTER THIRTEEN

EVA

"ARE you sure I don't look... overdressed?" I looked myself over in the mirror again. Letty grinned over my shoulder.

"You look amazing. Rafe won't know what's hit him."

"He said wear something comfortable and warm, this is..." The denim mini skirt hugged my thighs and the pale pink blouse kissed the waistband. I'd teamed it with boots and a leather jacket. It wasn't my usual style, but as Letty had pointed out, this was unusual circumstances. Rafe was taking me on a date.

An honest-to-God date in Indianapolis.

I didn't know the ins and outs of how he'd managed to pull it off, and I didn't want to know. The guys had teased me about it all day as we rode from back-to-back interviews at the local radio stations. Except Levi. He had chosen to ride in the other SUV.

"Perfect. It's perfect, Eva. I'm so excited for you." I turned around and gave her a weak smile. "Oh no, not that look."

"What?" I chuckled. "It's normal to be nervous before a date, isn't it?"

"You're asking the wrong girl. I can't remember the last time I went out with a guy."

"I guess being at the beck and call of the band makes it difficult to meet people."

"Good job I'm only at your beck and call now." She winked at me, grabbing my purse off the table and thrusting it at me. "Promise me, you'll enjoy tonight."

"I will. What will you do?"

"Keep Phoebe away from Hudson's bad influence."

"You don't think he'd really try to..." My eyes widened. She was so quiet and naive. And deep down, a part of me was hoping he would sort out his crap and call Molly.

"I don't think it's Hudson we have to worry about."

My brows furrowed before realization dawned on me. "Levi would never... Besides, Phoebe isn't like that."

Or was she?

"You fell for the Hunter charm." She levelled me with a knowing look.

"You cannot let Levi seduce her, Letty. He'd eat her alive." Besides, it was a whole heap of drama we did not need right now.

"Jealous?"

"What? *No!* But I don't want her to get hurt and I don't want Levi to do something he'll regret."

"She's not the innocent girl you think, you know?"

"What's that supposed to mean?"

"It means... everyone has a story, Eva."

"I guess." Before I could ask Letty what she thought Phoebe's story was, there was a knock at the door. "Are you expecting someone?" I asked her. I wasn't supposed to meet Rafe for another twenty minutes.

"It's probably Phoebe, or the guys. Can you grab it? I need to..." She thumbed to the bedroom, a faint smirk playing on her lips.

"Letty." It was my turn to glare at her.

"Eva." Her smile grew. "Go, have fun. And don't do anything I wouldn't do."

I checked my reflection one last time, took a deep breath, and walked to the door.

"Hi." Rafe was standing there, arm propped against the jamb, looking every bit a gorgeous rock star. "You look beautiful, Starshine." He pulled his hand from behind his back and presented me with a bunch of pale pink roses.

"They're beautiful." Butterflies flapped furiously in my stomach as I took the flowers from him. "I thought we were meeting downstairs?"

"I want you to have the full date experience."

God, he looked good in black jeans and a black shirt peeking out of his leather jacket. His hair was damp, curling around his ears and hanging over his eyes a little. Eyes that lazily raked up and down my body.

"See somethin' you like?" I asked.

Rafe's gaze landed on mine again, and he swallowed. "If we don't leave soon, I'm not sure I can be held responsible for my actions."

"Give me a second to put these in some water and then we can leave." I backtracked into the suite.

Letty was hovering. "Boy did good." She eyed the roses. "Let me take them and you two lovebirds go."

"Thank you." I handed her the bouquet and made my way back to Rafe. He was in the hall talking to Travis, the two of them close, voices hushed.

"What are you two talkin' about?"

"Just discussing final arrangements." Rafe shot Travis a narrowed look, and my bodyguard let out a frustrated breath.

"Will you be joinin' us, Travis?" I tried to make light of the tension simmering between them.

He grunted some inaudible reply, ushering us into the elevator. Like most of the hotels we stayed in, it had a basement level parking lot. The sleek black SUV greeted us, its engine already purring. I spotted Fenton behind the wheel and waved at him. They were all so damn serious all the time.

Travis went to open the door, but Rafe cut him off. "I've got that," he said, yanking it open.

I stifled a giggle as I slipped inside and shuffled across the seat to give Rafe space. He climbed in beside me, tangling our hands together. "You should probably know I've never done this."

"You've never been on a date before?" I didn't know whether to be relieved or feel sorry for him.

"There's never been anyone like you before, Eva. I hope you know that."

My breath caught. Being with Rafe was intense, different to anything I'd ever experienced before. But I had underestimated just how new all of this was for him too.

"Do I get to find out where we're goin'?" I asked, nervous energy vibrating through me.

"It's a surprise."

———

WHEN WE PULLED INTO A CAR RENTAL PLACE TEN MINUTES LATER, I was no closer to guessing the location of our date. This time, Rafe let Travis open the door. He climbed out first, offering his hand to me. I frowned as I slid out.

"Okay... this wasn't quite what I had in mind." It was already dusk, the sun disappearing on the horizon. The place appeared deserted until a light went on inside and a guy appeared with a set of keys.

Travis beckoned him over and the two of them discussed something out of earshot.

"What are you up to?" I asked Rafe, who kept toying with his lip piercing.

"You'll see. Come on." He grabbed my hand and guided me over to where the two men stood.

"Mr. Hunter. Miss Walker." The guy greeted us. "Got a real beaut ready for you. She's got a full tank of gas and the... *special requests* all on board ready to go."

I shot Rafe a curious look, but he only smirked, accepting the keys from the man and leading me to a sleek black pickup truck.

"What is happenin' right now?" My brows bunched together as Rafe opened the door and motioned for me to get inside.

"Travis and Fenton will be right behind us."

I glanced back at my bodyguard and he nodded, despite the disapproval etched into his expression.

"Are you sure this is safe?" I whisper-hissed. I didn't want to be a Debbie Downer, but we weren't usually granted so much freedom.

"We've got it covered, I promise." Rafe helped me into the truck before jogging around to the driver's side. He climbed in, the click of the door taking the air with it. We were alone. No security. No bandmates. No Riley or Alistair.

Just the two of us.

A thrill shot through me.

"I thought we'd be goin' to have dinner in a shadowy corner of some fancy restaurant with Travis and Fenton standin' over us."

"You can thank the fangirls from last night. They made me realize something."

"Oh yeah?" I couldn't hide my smile if I tried.

Rafe fired up the truck, and the engine rumbled beneath us. "Yeah, now buckle up. We have somewhere to be."

It was a fifteen-minute ride out of the city. The familiar SUV tailed us, but the constant reminder that our lives were no longer our own didn't dampen the anticipation zipping through me.

When Rafe pulled off the main highway and down a darkened track, my heartbeat sped up.

"Nervous, Starshine?" He reached over and tangled our fingers together

"Are you?" My brow rose.

The truck rolled to a stop in what looked to be an empty field. My eyes strained against the darkness as I tried to figure out where we were. Rafe twisted around to me, demanding my attention. "Eva," he inhaled sharply. "I am always nervous where you're concerned."

"You are?" My voice was a quiet whisper.

"You're strong and passionate. Determined and humble. And you come from this good, solid family. A family who loves you and wants to follow your dreams. It's a little intimidating. "I didn't grow up around that kind of love. That kind of support. You want the truth?"

I nodded.

"I feel a little out of my league here, Starshine."

"Rafe, I—"

"Let me finish, okay?" He ran a hand through his hair. I loved watching him do that. Such a simple action but he did it with such care and precision as if the feel of each strand of hair soothed him.

"I love you, Eva. More than I have ever loved anyone else, and it terrifies me. *You* terrify me."

"I… I scare you?" Dread pooled in my stomach. There was so much pain in his words.

"You're going places, Starshine. You have this natural light that people gravitate toward. Me. The band. Masterpiece. People see something in you. I see something in you, and I don't want to screw this up. I don't want to lose you."

I shuffled along the seat so that I could touch him, resting my palm against his cheek. "You're not goin' to lose me, I promise. You think I care where you came from or how you were raised? I don't. You're a good person, Rafe. The way you have always looked out for Levi… you carry around the weight of the world on your shoulders and you ask for nothin' in return."

His silence fractured my heart. Leaning in, I touched my head to his. "Listen to me, and listen good, Rafe Hunter, you are worthy." He sucked in a harsh breath as I smoothed my thumb over his jaw. "You know you won over my mom, right? Molly too."

"Yeah?"

"It's true. She fell for you almost as hard as I did. Hard and fast and unconditionally. Your past doesn't define you, Rafe." I brushed my lips over his, slow and soft. If he wouldn't believe my words, then I'd show him.

I'd make him feel every single one of them.

My tongue darted out, tasting him, running over the ball of steel in his bottom lip. "I love you," I murmured. "*You.*"

I was halfway to climbing into his lap when the dark world lit up around us. "What the—" I looked out of the truck, speechless.

"We have the whole place to ourselves."

"The movies. You brought me to a drive-in movie?"

"I thought we'd have more privacy here and I requested your favorite movie."

The huge screen flickered to life, and the opening credits to *A Walk to Remember* began playing.

"But how did you—"

"Molly." That single word had me grinning from ear to ear. "She said you had a huge crush on Shane West back in the day."

"Oh, I did. He was just so stubborn, yet dreamy."

"We'd better hurry then." Rafe kissed the end of my nose before hopping out of the truck and coming around my side. He helped me out, leading me around to the back of the truck. "Give me two minutes."

Rafe dropped the tailgate and clambered up, moving around. I pretended not to notice the hamper, or the blankets and cushions hidden under some tarp.

"You're really pullin' out all the stops, huh?" I said, fighting a smile.

Nothing could have been more perfect.

A private viewing of one of my favorite movies ever, under the stars, with the guy who made my heart sing.

CHAPTER FOURTEEN

I HAD a long list of people to thank for tonight. The guy at the rental place had gone above and beyond. There were snacks, blankets—he'd even packed a cooler full of sodas. It was perfect.

Travis had reluctantly arranged everything with the security detail after scoping out the drive-in ahead of time. He'd handled the whole thing. I didn't want Eva to feel suffocated, I wanted her to feel normal. Just an eighteen-year-old girl on a date with her boyfriend. Then I'd had Letty call up Molly and ask her for a list of Eva's favorite movies.

It had been a lot of work, but it was worth it.

Eva was worth it.

I barely watched the movie, too entranced by her. We were stretched out in the truck bed, Eva tucked into the crook of my arm, a plaid blanket thrown over her body. She was a rainbow of emotion, living every high and low with the characters as she picked at the popcorn. My thumb swiped across her cheek, collecting the tears.

"We could have watched something else, but Molly said—"

"No, no. I love this one." She sniffled, sitting up and twisting her body toward me. "I used to think it was so sad, the way they had so little time together..."

"And now?" I palmed her neck. Throughout the whole movie I'd touched her. A gentle brush of my finger against her arm, our hands entwined between us. I couldn't get enough of her.

"Now, everythin's different." She smiled.

"I know exactly what you mean. You know, I was only fourteen the first time Levi got strung out. We'd been partying at this dive bar. The owner used to let us sneak in, so long as we promised not to cause any trouble. Well, this one night, a bunch of older guys showed up. Real hard looking guys. It was open mic night and the second they heard Levi up there, rocking his heart out, they started buying him drinks. He was so out of it, but he lapped up the attention. You've seen how he gets."

Eva nodded.

"One of them started cutting lines of coke, right there on the table. They were all doing it; so of course, when it got to Levi's turn, he didn't think twice. Anything for their validation."

I could still picture the look of shame in his eyes as he watched me watching him. He knew he was making the wrong choice, yet he did it anyway.

"I stuck around but kept my distance. I wasn't into any of that stuff. Levi played up to them, taking requests, then falling off the stage and doing more shots with them. He was completely out of control. It wasn't until he came stumbling out of the restroom with a couple of the guys, and I saw their pupils blown wide open, while they were laughing, off their faces, that I knew he was on something harder than coke."

"What happened?" Eva asked as I took a minute to collect myself.

"What always happens. They all left, and I was left to pick up the pieces. Our foster carer at the time was only in it for the paycheck. So I spent all night by his side while he came down. He was so fucking sick. It took me a long time to forget that smell. When he finally came around, he promised never to do that shit again and I stupidly believed him. Until the next time. After that, I realized Levi would always be chasing something."

"Has he ever seen a therapist?"

"He's tried. They have to do that kind of thing in rehab. It's like he gets so far, and his walls come up and there's no getting through to him. But you... you're different." The lump in my throat doubled. Even now, even with Eva right beside me, I couldn't help the small seed of doubt or guilt or whatever the fuck it was festering inside me.

"Not this again," Eva let out a frustrated breath. "Whatever me and Levi share, it isn't the same as what you and I share."

"I know it's irrational, but I can't help it. I can't help but wonder if I'd have stepped aside and let the two of you..." Fuck, what was I saying? I could never have watched my brother with Eva. She was mine. She had been ever since the first time I saw her.

"What do I have to do to get you to see that I'm right here? There was never a choice for me, Rafe. It was always you."

"Come here." I curved my hand around Eva's neck, drawing her close. I hadn't wanted to ruin the night with all the heavy talk, but it wasn't like we got chance to have these kinds of conversations on the road with a bunch of people always within earshot.

"I've been thinking, maybe I should talk to someone."

Eva's head bobbed up. "Like therapy?"

"Maybe." I shrugged. "I don't want to let my past relationship with Levi affect what we have."

"I think that's a great idea. Maybe Levi will... sorry."

"It's okay." I chuckled. "Your big heart is one of the reasons why it's so easy to love you."

"I just want you both to be happy."

"Tell me about you," I said, wanting nothing more than to turn the spotlight from me to her.

"What do you want to know?"

"Everything."

Eva smiled, her gentle laughter like a salve to my bruised heart. "That could take a while."

"Tell me about what you were like as a kid."

"You really want to know that stuff?"

I nodded.

"I was always so shy and uncertain about things. The total opposite to Molly. She was always so full of life and ideas. A lot of people didn't get our friendship, but it just worked. She's always been the gentle nudge I need to step out of my comfort zone, and I've always been the little voice of reason tellin' her not to do somethin' crazy."

"So, it's Molly I owe then?"

"What do you...?" Realization dawned on her face. "Yeah, I guess it is. You know, when I got sick, it was like being a celebrity at first. My friends all sent cards and posters, and they would come hang out at the house. But as time went on, the visits grew further and further apart. I couldn't go to school or hang out. Life kept movin' on around me while I stayed still. But Molly never stopped showin' up. Heck, she gave up most of junior year to be at my side. And if she went somewhere, she came and told me all about it the next day."

"She's a good friend," I said.

"She's the best. She doesn't have it easy. Her mom is a single parent working two jobs. Molly has to help around the house a lot and help take care of the twins whilst finishin' senior year and holdin' down a job."

"It sounds like she's got a lot on her plate."

"She has. She's this outgoin', impulsive girl who gives off a tough vibe, but inside, she's just cravin' someone to see her, really see her."

"Does she want to go to college?"

"She did, but since her dad left... I'm not sure how she'd pull off college and helpin' her mom with the twins. The University of Tennessee offered her a place, but she hasn't accepted it yet."

"Tell me about when you got sick..."

"You really want to know about that?"

I nodded. We'd talked about it a little, but I knew it was Eva's darkest part, just as my past was the darkest part of me.

"Scooch over." She laid down beside me, so we were shoulder to shoulder, under a blanket of stars. "I was a normal teenager, I guess. I hung out with Molly and our friends, cheered our football team on every Friday, played my guitar every chance I got. I was perfectly content with small-town life.

"I went to church every Sunday with my parents, made plans for the future. And then everything changed." She hesitated, taking a couple of deep breathes. I slipped my hand between us, threading our fingers together.

"I'm right here."

"Bein' told you're goin' to die is a funny thing." Eva sucked in a shaky breath. "It's like a dream. You know there's some element of truth to it, but you know you'll wake up at any second and everythin' will be okay again."

"I can't even imagine..." Except I could. Because I'd watched Levi push himself to the brink more times than I could count, wondering if he'd wake up after one of his blowouts.

"I was so angry and confused when I woke up in the hospital, Rafe. I couldn't understand why I'd been saved. My mom and dad kept callin' it a miracle, but it didn't feel like a miracle. It felt like a mistake."

Pain splintered through me at the honesty behind her words. To imagine a world without Eva was like imagining a world without the sun. Dark and desolate and somewhere I didn't ever want to be.

"I was supposed to die," she went on. "Yet I didn't. I had this pit in my stomach, guilt coiled in my chest. Why me? Why me and not one of the other kids?"

"Cody?" I asked, the pieces finally falling into place.

"How did you—"

"That night at Basement Vibes in Charlotte. You kept crying out his name in your sleep. At the time, I thought it was an ex maybe..."

"You never said anythin'?" Eva peeked over at me.

"I didn't want to pry, and then everything was happening so quickly with the tour and the band... Us."

"Cody was only a child, Rafe. He was just ten, but he was one of the strongest people I ever met." Tears rolled down Eva's cheeks. "He could draw almost anythin', his talent was... it was special. But cancer took him. After years of fightin', of not givin' up, it just took him." Her voice trembled. "Cody died and I lived, and I think I'll always carry a sliver of guilt over that."

"I'm sorry for your friend, Starshine, I am." I leaned in, putting us nose to nose, my hand gliding up her neck, slipping into her hair. "But I will never be sorry that you got a second chance. Never."

CHAPTER FIFTEEN

EVA

"Tell me this is real," I whispered against Rafe's lips. "Tell me this isn't all a dream."

I didn't think I would ever get used to this. To him being mine. Even after everything, it seemed impossible.

Only, it wasn't.

"I think that's my line." He inched away, his stormy gray eyes stripping me bare. The heat in his gaze turned my blood hot. I glanced around, searching for the familiar black SUV. We were in the middle of nowhere, in a deserted drive-in.

"We're all alone, Starshine." Rafe brushed the stray curls out of my eyes. "Peace at last". He smiled.

"Travis and Fenton are—"

"Close by. But not close enough that you have to worry."

"I don't think I'll ever get used to havin' a permanent shadow."

Rafe's hand dropped to my shoulder, pushing the jacket down my arms. "Ain't nobody watching you but me," he said, turning his attention to the neckline of my blouse. He popped one of the buttons, then another, revealing my lacy, pale-pink bra. His hooded gaze darkened, making my skin vibrate and stomach clench.

But Rafe waited... he waited for my permission.

"Touch me," I whispered. "I need you to touch me."

Eight months ago, I never would have done this. I never would have let Rafe undress me and lie me down against a pile of soft blankets, under the stars.

But I was alive.

Being with Rafe, on tour with the band, reminded me of that every second of every day. I got my second chance, and whether or not I deserved it, I knew now that I had to live it.

For my parents and Molly.

For Cody.

For myself.

"Love me, Rafe," I pleaded as he rolled me beneath him. My hands dipped under his shirt, tracing the lines of his chest. He managed to pull it over his head, his hands making quick work of his belt. I helped pop the button, helped him work his jeans down his legs, until we were nothing but skin on skin.

"I've waited so long for this". It came out thick. "Living your life in the spotlight isn't always what it's made out to be. But these moments, quiet moments with you, I live for them, Eva." His thumb brushed over my bottom lip as his mouth hovered near mine. "I always wondered what would happen after the band. What I would do when music is all I've ever known? But you changed all that. I look at you, and I want things, Starshine. Things I never thought I'd get to have."

His words stole the air from lungs. I was only eighteen. There was so much life left to live. Things left to experience.

"I love you, Rafe Hunter," I said, hitching my legs around his hips, pulling him closer into my body.

He kissed me, tracing his lips down the slope of my neck and nipping my collarbone. My soft moans filled the air, rising above the credits of the movie still playing in the background. Slipping a hand between us, Rafe pressed a finger inside me. The heat of his touch and the coolness of the breeze made me shiver.

"You're always so wet for me," he groaned the words as he circled his thumb over my clit while curling his finger deeper inside me.

"More," I panted, clutching onto his shoulder as I rode the waves building inside me.

"Take it." The words drifted over my lips. "Take everything, Eva." Rafe rocked into me, his hardness pressed up against my thigh. A bolt of pleasure shot through me.

"You, I want you." My words were choppy as I began to crash over the edge. Suddenly, Rafe's hand was gone. Hooking my panties to one side, he guided himself inside me, stealing the air from my lungs.

"Fuck, you feel... I need a second." Rafe stilled above me. His jaw was clenched, eyes closed as he looked to the stars. He looked so devastating, ribbons of ink running over his skin. Every tattoo a different story to his past. My hands traced down his body, curving over his slim hips.

"Rafe, I need you to—"

"Ssh." He leaned down and kissed me. Hard and deep and bruising. "I know what you need, Starshine." Rocking forward, Rafe filled me. Sliding a hand under my thigh, he went deeper, the gentle rocking motion making the truck buck and bronc.

But it didn't matter.

I was too lost in him to care. Too lost in the way he played my body, creating the perfect cacophony of racing heartbeats and soft moans.

"I want to feel you," he breathed against the shell of my ear, and my gaze slid to his in question. "Do you trust me?" he asked, and I nodded.

I trusted him implicitly.

"Hold on." Rafe took my hands and looped then around his back. Without warning, he flipped us over, leaning back on his elbows. My laughter filled the air. When I finally caught my breath again, Rafe was staring at me with such intensity, a shiver rolled up my spine.

"Ride me, Eva."

Rising on my knees, I grasped him in my hand, and gently inched down. It felt incredible.

He felt incredible.

"Look at you." Rafe swallowed, trailing his fingers down the valley of my breasts, down my stomach. He curved his hands around my hips and steadied my rhythm, making it as slow and deep as possible. I felt another wave cresting. It came out of nowhere, crashing over me with brutal force.

"Rafe," I cried, reaching out for him, to steady myself.

He sat up, crushing me to his chest, thrusting upwards, sending me soaring into the night's sky. "Fuck," he grunted. "I need to go harder."

"Take it," I barely got the words out. "Take everything, Rafe."

He was in control now, chasing his own end, using my body as his personal instrument. The truck rocked, our breathy moans rising higher and higher over the end credits. I was crashing, sated and sleepy, but I wanted to give Rafe what he needed.

I wanted to chase his demons away.

Stroking his hair away, I cupped his face and kissed him. Our bodies were impossibly close, slick with sweat and warm with love. He began to tremble, his hands clamped around my hips.

"Eva... Jesus..." Rafe jerked inside me, collapsing back against the side of the truck bed, pulling me with him. I could hear his heart beating in his chest. He stroked my spine, drawing out every last drop of pleasure.

Neither of us spoke, but we didn't need words. We knew what we shared was raw and intense. It was the darkest parts of our souls entwined together to create something beautiful. We were still so young. Too young to make big choices about the future.

So why did it feel like we had both just made a huge decision?

"You okay down there, Starshine?" Rafe finally broke the silence.

I peeked up at him. "I'm okay. Are you?"

"I'm... shit, Eva. I don't even have words to describe it. When I'm with you—"

"Ssh." I reached up, pressing a finger to his lips. I wasn't ready for whatever he was about to say. Not when things with the tour were finally calmer.

"No more serious talk. Not tonight. Not when everything has been so perfect."

I grabbed a blanket and pulled it around my shoulders. "What time do we have to leave?"

"We have time, Starshine."

"Good," I leaned up and kissed him. "Then let's make the most of it."

———

WE STAYED AT THE DRIVE-IN AND WATCHED ANOTHER MOVIE. THE whole night was perfect from start to finish. But I couldn't help but feel like I'd made a mistake shutting Rafe down when he'd been about to tell me whatever was on his mind. I just didn't want him to say something he couldn't take back.

And the truth was, I wasn't sure I would survive having my heart broken a third time by him.

Levi was his brother—his family. They would always be a part of one another's lives. Rafe felt like he'd made his choice now, but what happened down the line, when Levi needed him? Because that day would come. It would always come. I didn't want Rafe to make promises to me that he couldn't keep. And I didn't want him to think he had to choose.

"Penny for your thoughts?" he said as we pulled into the rental place.

"Tonight has been everythin' I could have wished for and more. I'll never forget it."

He cut the engine and shifted toward me, brushing my jaw. "It won't always be like this you know? After the tour, when the band has some downtime, we'll have more time."

"Rafe, it's okay." I smiled. "This is your life, I get it. I knew what I was gettin' into. Things are takin' off for the band in a big way, and

Letty says the label want to get me into the studio as soon as possible."

"They do?" A dark expression crossed his face, but then it was gone, replaced with a blinding smile. "That's amazing, Eva. I'm so fucking proud of you."

I still hadn't processed everything. I knew the label wanted to capitalize on my growing popularity, but I was focused on the tour, on getting through one day at a time.

"I just want you to know, we have time. I'm not goin' anywhere, Rafe, okay?"

"And if time isn't enough?" he said, lowering his voice. "If I want forever?"

My breath caught. But a loud rap on the glass startled me before I could get out a reply. Rafe grumbled something about my bodyguard's 'impeccable timing' before climbing out of the truck.

Travis opened my door and helped me out. "We need to go."

"You couldn't have waited five more minutes?" Rafe arched a brow.

Travis didn't reply, but I was sure I caught him smirking as he ushered me to the SUV. "Thank you," I said before climbing inside. "For helping Rafe pull this off."

"I'm not going to lie to you, Eva. What Rafe did tonight, it was a huge risk. But..." He let out a weary sigh. "You deserve a little slice of happiness. Just don't get too used to it." He nudged me inside and slammed the door, his warning a stark reminder that for as long as we were in this life, nothing about mine and Rafe's relationship would ever be normal.

CHAPTER SIXTEEN

RAFE

"What the fuck?" I grumbled as we stepped out of the elevator. Laughter drifted down the hall. Loud, raucous laughter.

"Relax," Eva said, flattening her hand against my stomach. "It's probably just Hudson foolin' around."

But it didn't sound like Hudson. It sounded like party central. Dread slithered up my spine as we reached Stalter.

"What's going on in there?" I asked him.

"Don't ask me. I only just got on shift an hour ago."

Eva rolled her eyes as she grabbed the handle and opened the door. "I'm sure it's—"

Music blasted out of the suite.

"The lovebirds are back," someone yelled, and everyone cheered, raising their cups in the air.

"I'll fucking kill him." I started scanning the room for Levi.

"Rafe." Eva touched my arm. "Don't make a scene. It's just a few roadies. Let them have their fun."

"You can't be serious?"

She stepped in front of me. "I just had the most amazin' date with my boyfriend. I'm not goin' to let anythin' ruin that, and neither should you."

"Fine," I conceded, my jaw clenching. "But I'm going to need a drink to survive this."

She leaned up, kissing the corner of my mouth. "Just don't have too many; I have big plans for you later."

"Shit, Eva." My hands ran over her ass, fitting her against me. "You can't say stuff like that to me and then expect me to behave."

"Wondered when you would show up." Hudson strolled over to us, handing me a beer.

"Let me guess, this was his idea." I still hadn't spotted my brother, which was weird considering he usually loved to be center of attention.

"Actually, it was mostly a group decision. You know, the ones we used to make together."

"Cheap shot," I grumbled.

"Play nice, Hudson."

"Sorry, Eva." His eyes clouded with regret. "I don't mean to be an asshole. It's just everything is different. It's messing with my Feng shui."

"You have Feng shui?" She chuckled.

"Hey, I'm a deep guy."

"Are you feeling okay?" I asked. "You're acting weird."

"And on that note, I'm goin' to find Letty and Phoebe. You two behave." Eva kissed me again before moving deeper into the suite.

"You struck gold with her, you know?" Hudson leaned back against the wall. "I want to hate her, but she makes it so damn hard."

Silence settled over us as we watched Letty pull Eva into her arms, the two of them smiling and laughing. Then Hudson said, "So, how'd it go tonight?"

"It was okay."

"Okay? What kind of bullshit reply is that?" He scoffed.

"What do you want me to say, man? I'm pretty sure you don't want to hear all about my date with Eva, just like I don't want to hear all about whatever girl you're hoping to bang tonight."

"Nah, man. I'm not feeling it."

"Has hell frozen over? Did you get a fever?" I leaned over and tried to touch his forehead to check his temperature.

"Get the fuck off me. I'm good. I just... fuck, I can't get her out of my head."

"Molly."

"She's in here." He tapped his temple. "I don't know when the fuck it happened, but after Vegas, things feel..."

"Different?"

He pressed his lips into a thin line, nodding. "But I don't do relationships, and despite all her bravado, something tells me Molly Steinberg isn't the kind of girl who will keep putting up my shit."

"Maybe you won't know if you don't try."

"Nah, man. I'm not that guy. I'm never gonna be that guy."

"Well, whatever you do, don't lead her on." I grabbed his shoulder. "She's Eva's best friend, and if you hurt her, it'll hurt my girl, and then, she'll want to hurt you. And that will get all kinds of awkward for me." I smirked.

"Fuck you, man." Hudson shucked me off. "I know where your loyalty lies, and it isn't with the band anymore."

"Jesus, are you ever going to let me off the hook? I needed to fix things with her, Hud. That's what you do when you love someone. You fight for them."

"Yeah, yeah, I get it. You love her more than you love the band."

"For fuck's sake will you—"

"Chill man, I'm busting your balls. She's good for you. I think she's good for all of us. It's just weird, you know. She's changing things."

I took a long pull on the beer Hudson had given me. Just then, one of the bedroom doors swung open and Levi staggered out, shirtless. "Look who decided to show up." His eyes landed on me, but then quickly swept the room for Eva. "Country, get over here and make some magic with me."

"Tell me he didn't take something," I ground out.

"He hasn't touched anything except liquor as far as I know."

It wasn't a saving grace. Drunk Levi could be just as much trouble as high Levi. Eva made her way over to my brother, but movement from the bedroom caught my eye. "Who the hell is that?"

"You know Levi and his magical ways," Hudson said, as we watched the random girl slip into the room unnoticed since all eyes were on Levi and Eva. Someone had found her a guitar, and she was busy tuning it.

"I'm not sure I can stick around and watch this."

"You're going to have to get used to that." He pointed a finger in their direction.

"Yeah, I know." Before I realized, I'd moved closer. Eva caught my eye, her gaze sparkling so much love, I couldn't turn and walk away even if I'd wanted to.

"I couldn't say no." She mouthed.

"It's okay," I replied. Moving closer, I dropped onto the sectional beside Letty.

"What do you think, Angel? Shall we play something dark and dirty?"

"Something off the album," someone yelled.

Levi's eyes lit up at the challenge. "What do you think, Country? You think you've got what it takes?"

"I think I can try."

Everyone cheered. "Show him who's boss, Eva," one of the roadies called.

"What do you fancy?" Levi grinned at her. He might not have been high on any substance, but he was high on the attention, the opportunity to stick it to me again.

My fist clenched at my thigh. Letty nudged my shoulder. "You cool?"

I nodded. "He's doing this to bait me."

"Is he? Or is he doing it because it's the only way he knows how to communicate?"

"What's that supposed to mean?"

Phoebe chose that exact moment to appear. She sat down on the other side of Letty, a cup of something in her hand.

"Where did you get to?"

"Nowhere." Her eyes flicked to mine, and she gave me a strange look, before sliding her gaze to my brother.

I knew that look... it was the look of longing.

Shit.

Phoebe and my brother... that was a huge fucking shitshow we didn't need.

Eva began strumming the opening notes to *The Ties That Bind*. Letty gasped a little. "She went there," she breathed.

I stared at her.

At them.

I didn't even know Eva knew the arrangement for one of our more mainstream songs. But it didn't surprise me. She had a gift, and she'd spent night after night watching us perform.

"I know what you're doing, Angel." Levi arched his brow at her, running a hand through his hair. "Someone get me a drink. I think I'm going to need it."

Two seconds later, a cup was thrust at him. Levi downed the contents in one, wiping his mouth with the back of his hand and throwing the cup over his shoulder with the other. "This one's for you, little brother."

"Damn, they sound good together." Damon joined us, offering me another beer. I drained my other one and took it.

"Thanks." It came out tight as I watched him sing about brotherhood and family. About how, no matter what was going on, you could always count on each other.

"How was it tonight?" Damon whispered, pulling me from my thoughts. Everyone was too captivated by my brother and Eva to be paying us any attention. But then, it was hard not to be.

"I'm in so fucking deep with her." I admitted.

His mouth curved. "I'm happy for you, truly."

"Thanks."

Eva harmonized the chorus, her tone softening Levi's jagged edges. Letty caught my eye and I noticed she was filming.

"This is perfect for your social media accounts," she mouthed. She lived for that shit; anything to bring us closer to our fans.

"You should go join them," Damon said, flicking his head to one of the other guitars propped up in the corner of the room.

"Yes!" Letty beamed.

"Nah, I'm not sure—"

"Get over here, brother." I don't know if Levi had heard Damon, or if it had been his plan all along, but I found myself standing up to a rumble of cheers.

I didn't pick up the other guitar though. Instead, I grabbed a stool and positioned it behind Eva, pulling her onto my knee and sliding my arms through hers. "Play with me, Starshine?" I moved my hands into position beneath hers.

"Any requests?" Levi asked the small crowd.

"Chasing Nirvana," Phoebe was first to answer.

A strange expression etched in Levi's face. "That's dark, New Girl."

She shrugged. "It's one of my favorites."

He sucked in a harsh breath, tilting his head slightly, his eyes fixed on hers, as if she was a puzzle he was trying to solve.

Jesus, what was happening right now?

"Chasing Nirvana, it is," I said, breaking the tension rippling between them. "Do you think you can pick it up?"

Eva nodded, stealing a quick kiss. Someone shrieked—Letty most likely—as I captured her face and slipped my tongue between her lips.

"Okay, okay, lovebirds, enough of that," Levi fake retched. "We have a song to sing." He downed another cup of liquor, swaying on his feet.

"Hey," I lowered my voice. "You good?"

"I'm good, little brother." A sloppy grin broke over his face. "Let's do this."

I ran my nose up Eva's spine before leaning around her and strumming the opening notes to the song. It was one of our darker tracks, full of pain and suffering. I'd woken up one morning, right after we'd been signed to the label, to find the coffee table covered in lyrics. Levi was asleep on the couch, the pen still in his hand, the floor around him littered with empty bottles.

"Late night?" I'd asked him, after getting him a glass of water and some Advil.

"The nightmares..." he'd said around a grimace. "But I wrote something. I think it's good. What do you think?"

I'd read the scattered lyrics, trying to make sense of his drunken ramblings. But I had quickly realized they weren't drunken ramblings at all, they were articulate feelings. Levi had bled his state of mind out all over the table.

Levi met my stare and nodded, and I saw another glimpse of my brother.

I hear the voices, inside my head
  Whispering things of sorrow and sin
  I hear the voices, inside my head
  They taunt me, telling me to just give in
  To succumb to the pain, to let go and fall
  But I don't wanna relent, I don't wanna fade

It feels so good, but it hurts so bad
  This high that I'm riding, don't want it to end
  I don't wanna come down, don't make me come down
  'Cos I'm chasing... I'm chasing nirvana

It feels so good, but it hurts so bad
  This high that I'm riding, don't want it to end
  I don't wanna come down, don't make me come down
  'Cos I'm chasing... I'm chasing nirvana

But I don't wanna die

As my fingers flew across the frets, I felt every word, every memory. This was his life laid bare. His vulnerability and weakness weaved into the fabric of every lyric. Eva was a statue, her lips parted, her eyes glossed with tears as she watched my brother sing his heart out.

Part of me wanted to ask Phoebe what the fuck she'd been

thinking requesting this song, but few people knew the truth behind the words. To them, Levi was nothing more than a privileged rock star with the world at his feet. Drugs, liquor, girls... it all came hand in hand with the gig. They didn't know what haunted him at night, what skeletons hid in his closet.

They didn't know.

Levi held the last note, his voice breaking. And then silence. No one said a word. His chest was heaving, his body was trembling, and I knew he was probably one second away from losing it.

"Fuck, yeah," One of the roadies slapped his leg. "That's how it's done."

Everyone began clapping, but Levi didn't look pleased... he looked gutted.

"Levi," Eva stood up, but Phoebe beat her to it.

"That was really something," she said to my brother.

He was jittery, eyes wild, scanning the room for a quick exit, or worse, a quick fix.

"Levi, look at me," she said calmly, gently laying her hand on his arm. He jerked up to meet her determined gaze. "You want to get some air?"

His eyes narrowed.

"Phoebe, I'm not sure that's—"

She flicked her eyes to us. "Relax, I've got this. Come on, rock star," Phoebe started to walk toward the balcony, "let's go get some fresh air."

And as if that wasn't fucking weird enough...

Levi followed her.

CHAPTER SEVENTEEN

EVA

"Did that really just happen?" Rafe and I watched after Levi as he followed Phoebe out onto the balcony.

"She's strange."

"She's not strange," I lifted the guitar over my head and placed it against the wall. "She's just new, but Levi seems to respond to her."

"He responded to you and look how that worked out for us."

"Rafe," I moved between his legs, "you need to let him find his own way." My fingers curled into the hair at the nape of his neck.

"I know, I just... we know nothing about her."

"Letty seems to think she can handle herself."

"Let's hope she's right." His fingers splayed around my waist possessively. "Can we kick everyone out now?"

"Just say the word." I smiled.

"Hey, fuckers," he yelled. "Party's over." There were a few grumbles, but people began filing out of the suite.

"We could have just gone downstairs." There were rooms reserved for us on the floor below, not that Rafe had any intention of letting me out of his sight.

"Not happening." He stood up, grazing his lips over mine. "I want you in my bed."

"Why don't you piss on her?" Hudson strolled over, "just to be sure."

"Jealous, Hud?" I said, expecting him blurt out some salty

comeback. But he didn't. Instead, he skulked off to his room, slamming the door. "Was it somethin' I said?"

"Don't worry about him. Come on." Rafe took my hand, guiding me toward our room. He paused as we passed Damon and Letty. "Will you two—"

"We've got you covered," Letty said. "Go get some sleep. Duke wants us on the road after breakfast."

"Thanks. See you in the morning."

I glanced back over to the balcony. I could just make out Phoebe and Levi's profiles in the shadows.

"Go," Damon insisted. "We'll keep an eye on them."

"Thanks, man, I appreciate it."

The two of them shared a lingering look, then Rafe started toward the bedroom again. When we were inside, he dropped down on the bed. I climbed on beside him, curling my body into his side. "Are you okay?"

"It's not me I'm worried about. That song..."

"It's about Levi, isn't it? His addiction?"

"It's more than that, Eva. It's all the pain, the hurt... it's every bad thing he ever went through."

"If you're worried he'll—"

"I'm not. Okay, maybe I am, I think I'll always be worried where he's concerned." Rafe tensed.

I slipped my hand under his shirt, tracing the ridges of his stomach muscles. "He wanted you to sing with us, you know?"

"He probably just overhead Damon and Letty. She was recording for social media."

"I don't think so. I think, in his own way, he's tryin' to make things right."

"I appreciate what you're trying to do, Starshine, I do. But it's going to take more than an impromptu performance to fix us."

"I know." I leaned up, kissing his jaw. "But you made baby steps tonight."

Kicking off my boots, I wrapped myself around Rafe and closed my eyes. "I'm proud of you," I murmured, sleep taking hold. "I just want you to know that."

———

WE ATE BREAKFAST TOGETHER. ALL SEVEN OF US. IT WAS THE FIRST time we'd all sat and eaten together since Rafe and I got back. Levi was calmer, but we all noticed the way he tracked Phoebe's movements as she made herself another coffee. No one mentioned last night. No one asked what the two of them had talked about out on the balcony. And no one brought up what, if anything, had happened after.

Despite all the elephants in the room, it was nice.

"What time does Duke want to head out?" Damon asked Letty as she finished her pain au chocolat.

"Soon." She checked her wristwatch.

"How are y'all feeling about the show in Detroit tonight?" Phoebe asked, taking a bite of an apple.

Something had shifted. She'd gone from quiet and shy new girl, to someone at total ease around us. I didn't know how to feel about that.

"It's always a good crowd. Although the Die Hearts are extra feisty in Rock City." Hudson snickered. "Remember last year, when we played the Fillmore, those two girls managed to sneak backstage and—"

"Okay, bro," Rafe interjected, "let's not put the girls off their food."

"Like anything you could say would surprise me. I've seen you all at your best... and worst." Letty smirked, and Hudson flipped her off.

"How are you finding things so far, Pheebs? Is everyone helping you settle in?" He fixed his eyes right on Levi who was staring at his hands.

"It's never easy being the new girl, but I'm not here to win any popularity contests so..." She shrugged.

"Are you here to win *other* things?" He smothered his amusement.

"Hud," Rafe warned. "Don't be a dick."

The scrape of Levi's chair across the tiles silenced everyone. "I need some air." He stalked out of the room, Phoebe staring after him.

"What's his problem?"

"Do you have to do that?" Damon scolded Hudson. "You know he's treading thin ice right now."

"What? I'm just trying to lighten the mood."

"More like stir the pot."

"You should cut him some slack." Phoebe got up and put her plate in the basin.

"Yeah, and what do you know about it?"

"More than you know." She gave Hudson a weak smile before making for the bathroom.

"So much for a nice breakfast." Letty let out an exasperated breath. "We should get cleaned up before Duke comes looking for us."

"Yeah, yeah, Letty. Crack the whip a little harder, why don't you?" Hudson and Damon got up.

"I need to go grab the rest of my stuff." Rafe kissed my cheek before following the guys.

"I'm going to check in with Duke and make sure everything's set." Letty grabbed her stuff. "I'll see you downstairs in twenty?"

I nodded.

"And then there were two," Phoebe offered me a smile. It seemed genuine, but I still couldn't get a good read on her. "You don't know what to make of me, do you?" She leaned back against the counter.

"Honestly, no. You seemed so unassuming at the club, but then last night you were... different."

"Trust me, it took me by surprise too. But Levi is—"

"Complicated." I'd heard that so many times before, and now I was the one saying it. But I felt protective of him, I always would.

"Oh, I get that. More than you know." She released a soft sigh. "He reminds me of someone I used to... it doesn't matter. I guess I just slipped back into old habits."

"Do you want to talk about it?"

"Not really. I'm here to 'put all that behind me', or at least, that's what my dad would say. He pulled some strings and got me this gig."

"He knows the band?"

"He knows someone high up at Razorsharp. I'm sure if he knew I'd landed this job, being on tour with the band, he'd flip. He probably thinks I'm filing papers and making coffees."

We shared a laugh, but it quickly turned to awkward silence. I stood up, ready to make my excuses, but Phoebe beat me to it.

"I know you probably think I'm in way over my head, but I can handle myself."

"It's not you I'm worried about. In case you haven't noticed, things are not okay between the guys right now."

"I picked up on the tension."

"Levi is hurtin'..."

"And when an animal is wounded it attacks. Message received loud and clear."

Lips pressed together, I nodded. "I'll see you on the bus."

———

HUDSON WASN'T WRONG ABOUT THE DIE HEARTS IN DETROIT. AS soon as the bus turned into Little Caesars Arena, we were flooded with a sea of girls all looking to get their glimpse of the guys.

"Holy crap, it's crazy out there." Hudson had his face pressed against the glass. "I see titties. Levi, get over here, this chick is flashing us."

"Nice, jackass." Letty sneered. "Real nice."

"Hey, I'm not discriminatory, Let. If you want to flash me your—"

"*Do not* finish that sentence, Ryker, or I'll beat your ass into next week."

"I love it when you get feisty with me." Hudson licked his lips, winking at her.

"So, what happens now?" Phoebe asked. She was scanning the schedule Letty had given her.

"Now, security try and get us through that in one piece." Levi strolled through the bus, heading for the bowl of chips on the counter.

"Letty said sometimes you stick around and sign some autographs and take some selfies, that kind of thing?"

"Sometimes we do, but not when the Die Hearts are extra crazy. And that," Damon jabbed his finger to the window, "is extra crazy."

"No meet and greet today, got it." She crossed out something on her list.

The bus jerked to a stop and the door opened. Alistair and Riley climbed aboard. "How are you all?"

"Better for seeing your face, Ali boy." Hudson grinned.

"There's something I wanted to talk to you about before we go in. Riley has brought it to my attention that some of you aren't treating her with the respect she deserves."

Silence fell over us. I glanced over at Levi who was stone-faced as he stared at her. Rafe had also gone rigid beside me.

This wasn't good.

"Riley is your assistant, not your plaything."

Hudson snickered, and Alistair let out a muffled groan. "Poor choice of words on my part. All I'm trying to say is, please work with her. She has your best interests at heart."

"Did you ask her?" Levi spoke up.

"Excuse me?"

"Did you ask her *why* I called her a cold-hearted bitch?"

"Well, no, I... Riley said you were being difficult."

Levi's gaze sharpened, burning into her. But she didn't shrink. She stood tall, glaring right back, the air crackling between them.

Damon got up and moved toward Levi, while Rafe vibrated with anger beside me. I reached for his hand, threading our fingers together.

"Respect begets respect," Damon said.

"Not you too," Alistair gaped at him, rubbing his temples.

"Sorry, Ali, but you went about this all wrong. You should have come to us and asked what happened before taking her side."

"Whoa now." His hands shot up. "I didn't... that's not what this is. Riley?" He glanced at the woman beside him.

"You heard what he called me. We were in the middle of a meeting and Levi—"

"You really want to do this?" Levi's brow shot up.

I shrunk into Rafe's side. I didn't want this. Not here, in front of everyone. But the lines had been drawn. Me and the guys on one side, and Alistair and Riley on the other.

"I'm sorry Ali, but Riley's out of line here." Damon shot me a reassuring smile. "She was rude to Eva and deliberately insensitive."

"I wasn't... that's not..." Riley huffed indignantly, narrowing her gaze on me. But this time, I didn't drop my gaze.

"Bullshit," Hudson added. "We all heard what you said. You upset Eva and then you didn't even bother to apologize. Not cool."

"Is this true?"

I looked up to find Alistair frowning.

"I'm not Eva's assistant. I didn't think—"

"Have you been living under a fucking rock?" Levi spat. "Eva went through something huge and you played it off as nothing."

"Okay, okay, I can see there's been some miscommunication here." Alistair looked flustered now, pulling at his collar. "I think we'll leave it there. Eva, I'm sure Riley is sorry if she offended you. While you're not Eva's assistant, Riley, she is a part of this tour. Let's get inside before the Die Hearts cause a security breach and we have to cancel another show." He stormed off the bus, Riley hurrying after him.

"Fucking snake." Levi hissed the second she was out of earshot.

"I can't believe she went to him over that." Damon rubbed his temples.

"Can't you?" Rafe finally spoke up. "She's made it clear she doesn't like Eva on more than one occasion."

"Rafe," I warned. "I'm not lookin' to cause—"

"Okay, why don't we all just calm down?" Letty stood up. "Whatever game Riley is playin' clearly backfired. I'm sure Alistair will set her straight."

"Yeah, he'll probably spank her for being a bad, bad girl."

"Not helping, Hud." Damon hit him upside the head.

"Whatever her problem, we've got your back, Eva." Hudson gave me a nod. "She might be banging the boss, but we can still—"

"Seriously?" Letty's eyes widened, warning glittering there. "I'll speak to Alistair. Let me handle it."

"Thank you," I said. "I don't want this to cause an issue for the band."

"So, we're not plotting revenge on the ice queen?" Hudson mumbled. "Shame."

No one said anymore about it as we grabbed our stuff and filed off the bus, flanked by our bodyguards. The frenzied catcalls filled the air, drowning out my thoughts. All except one.

The band had taken my side.

They had stood up for me against Riley.

They had declared their side.

I only hoped it didn't mean war.

CHAPTER EIGHTEEN

RAFE

"Oh Rafe, good," Riley smiled, darting in front of me and cutting off my exit. "I was hoping to talk to you. Listen," she tucked her hair behind her ear, flashing a sheepish smile at me. "I'm sorry about earlier, what happened with Alistair. I know how it looks—"

"What are you doing?"

"Excuse me?" Her smile fell.

"Why are you here, trying to apologize for acting like a bitch to Eva, when it's not me you need to apologize to?"

"Well, guess I thought you would—"

"You thought I'd be your middle guy? You thought wrong." My eyes narrowed. "I don't know what game you're playing, or what you're hoping to achieve here but it's not going to work. I'm with Eva. I *love* Eva. My allegiance will always be with her."

Her cheeks burned, but Riley rolled back her shoulders and met my stare head on. Geez, this lady had balls. Big ol' balls of steel. And I got it. The industry was as cutthroat as it came, but I still couldn't figure out her angle here.

"I see." Her whole demeanor turned cool. "I just wanted to apologize."

"Like I said, I'm not the one you should be apologizing to. Now, if you don't mind, I need to get back to it." I'd slipped out of the sound check to take a piss. Riley was the last person I'd expected to see.

I stalked off down the hall. The place was a maze, like so many of the arenas we performed in. As I drew closer to the main stage, I could hear Eva's voice. Soft. Sultry. That southern lilt that made my chest contract. God, I loved her voice. The way she sang right from her soul.

Eva was born to perform, to share her talent with the world. But I couldn't help but wonder where she saw her career going in a year... five... ten.

Three years in, and I was already tired—so fucking tired. And I knew there would come a time when our paths would split. Right now, Eva was on tour with us, but what happened when she got offered her own tour?

What then?

"Everything okay?" Damon sauntered over to me as I entered the arena.

"Fucking Riley. She cornered me in the hall, wanted to apologize."

"You're shitting me. What did you say?"

"I told her it wasn't me she needed to apologize to." I scrubbed my jaw. "I can't figure out her angle."

"You think she's really got it in for Eva?"

"I don't know. Part of me wants to believe it's just her ambition, but, I don't know, man. She acts... jealous."

"And we all know jealousy can send a woman crazy. You want me to talk to Alistair?"

"Not yet. He seemed pretty pissed earlier. Hopefully, he talked to her and she'll do the right thing."

"Well, you know we're behind Eva all the way. If Riley is becoming a liability, we can go around her and Alistair."

"Thanks, that means a lot."

"Of course." Damon nodded, staring over at Eva. She was busy talking to a set producer.

"Did Letty tell you the video of the three of you went viral?"

"You know I try to avoid all that shit."

"The fans went wild for it. They love her, man."

My brow rose, and he chuckled. "Okay, most of them love her. The Die Hearts were spouting their usual possessive bullshit, but it's nothing we haven't heard a hundred times before."

"Does their dedication to the cause ever freak you out?" I asked.

"I guess I've never really thought about it." He glanced back at me. "You're still waiting for the penny to drop, huh?"

"I just can't shake this feeling that everything's too good to be true. Eva's here, and we're stronger than ever. Levi seems to be handling things as best he can, and the tour is back on track."

"What happened to just enjoying the ride?" He clapped me on the back.

"Yeah, maybe you're right."

"I get it though. You have a lot to lose, I think it's only natural to feel a little on edge. But relax, man. You deserve this, you deserve her."

Damon really was the best of us.

"Hey," Phoebe appeared. "Are the two of you okay?"

"Yeah, we're good."

"Eva sounds great, doesn't she? I mean, I knew she was good, but seeing her stripped back like this... Anyway, Riley asked me to come tell you that you're back on in five."

"Riley couldn't tell us herself?"

Phoebe shrugged. "I'm only the messenger." She left us and went back over to where Letty was standing with a couple of the sound engineers.

"What do you think of her?" Damon asked.

"I can't get a read on her."

"Yeah, I know what you mean. She seems genuine, but there's a wall there."

"That or she's hiding something."

"Then she'll fit right in." He gave me a wry smile and murmured, "Because we all have secrets here."

———

"COME HERE, YOU." I PROWLED TOWARD EVA AS SHE HUNG OUT backstage with Letty and Phoebe.

"Don't you dare, Rafe. I just got done showering and you're all sweaty." She started to inch back.

"Too bad, Starshine. I need you." I lunged for her, hoisting her into my arms.

"Rafe, you're disgusting," she groaned as I rubbed my damp hair against her chest.

"Say cheese." We both glanced up and Letty took a photo.

"Letty!"

"What? It's for your Insta. It's really taken off."

"My what now?" I asked, frowning.

"Like you don't know what I'm talking about Mr-I-Have-Over-Eight-Million-Followers."

"Shit, it's that many? Wow, I had no idea." I really didn't because I let Letty and the team handle all that. "Now, where was I?" I began kissing Eva's neck as she tried to wiggle free. "You were amazing tonight," I whispered against the shell of her ear.

"What has gotten into you?" She grabbed my jaw, looking into my eyes.

"Do I need a reason to be happy now?"

"No, but... it's very disconcertin'."

"Thanks a lot," I grumbled.

"I gotta agree with Eva, Rafe. You do seem less broody."

"I do not brood."

They were all looking at me now.

So what, I was happy? The show had gone off without a hitch. Levi and I had shared a few moments on stage, especially during *The Ties That Bind*. Eva had performed with us, and tonight we didn't have to attend a party or do any meet or greets. We were heading straight for Philly, which meant in less than an hour, I would have Eva underneath me.

Everything was good.

Until Alistair delivered four little words that ruined my good mood.

"We've got a situation," he said around a grim expression. Beckoning the rest of the guys over, he waited for us all to gather. Travis and Fenton were close by with half a dozen other security.

"There's a situation in the parking lot. It seems the Die Hearts broke through the security barriers. The buses are swamped."

"So we're stuck here?"

"Local PD are en route, but honestly, this could turn into a media frenzy. Paparazzi are already gathering."

"Shit," Hudson muttered.

"I've spoken to security and we've agreed to make a break for it. The arena staff have their security guys trying to control the crowd, but I'm not going to sugarcoat it, it's mayhem out there."

Just then, a rather breathless Riley jogged up to us. "We should think about moving now," she said. "Security is concerned they may try to storm the building."

"You've got to be shitting me?" I hissed, tucking Eva into my side.

"What did I tell you, man. Rock City girls are a special kind of crazy." Hudson grimaced.

"Is everyone ready?" Alistair asked.

"We have some stuff in the dressing room still," Eva said.

"Leave it. I'll have someone make sure nothing gets left behind." Ali ran a hand down his face. "The most important thing right now is getting on those buses."

The hall became a hive of activity as bodyguards moved into position with their marks. I kept hold of Eva, forcing Travis and Fenton to flank us as we made our way down the long winding hall.

"Fuck me, are you hearing that?" Hudson let out a low whistle. The wail was blood curdling.

"We love you Levi. Rafe. Hudson. Damon. We love you."

"Stick with me or Travis, okay?" I said to Eva. Her eyes were wide with fear. She'd already faced her fair share of chaos since joining the tour, but this was different.

We all felt it.

It was in the way security flanked us a little too closely, and the way no one—except Hudson—was cracking a joke. We all knew what to expect when we burst out the doors, we'd lived it enough times. But no matter how many times you came face to face with a sea of overexcited and reckless fangirls—girls who would do anything for just one touch or one glance from the guys they worshipped—well, nothing could prepare you for that.

Johnson shouldered the door open and all hell broke loose. "Move, now!" he yelled, Travis and Fenton jostling me and Eva between them.

"Rafe, Rafe. Dump the country skank and come get yourself a real girl."

Eva inhaled a sharp breath, and I squeezed her hand. "Ignore them," I yelled over the noise.

"We need to keep moving," someone yelled. "Get back. Get the hell back."

Girls were everywhere: hands clawing, their screams piercing the air like a band of wild banshees. These were Die Hearts all right, their grit and determination to get close to us unwavering.

It was a strange thing, fan worship. The way rational thought flew out the window all because we played instruments and made music.

"Rafe, Levi, I'll let you..."

I blocked out the voices. The things they were offering. Dirty depraved things. A couple of years ago, when we were new to the scene, we would have high-fived at our newfound fame and attention. But it was wearing. I tried to search for Hudson among the crush, knowing he was probably lapping it up. But when I found him up ahead, even he looked worried.

"Back up. BACK THE FUCK UP!" Johnson roared, swatting away hand after hand. It was like an attack of bloodthirsty zombies and we were the hot-blooded snacks.

Travis looped his arm around Eva, drawing her away from me. I knew he was only trying to do his job, to protect her, but it went against everything I felt.

"Eva," I yelled.

She glanced back, her face pale and eyes wide. "Stay with Fenton," she mouthed.

"T's got her," my bodyguard said. "We're almost there."

But someone had seriously underestimated the strength of a few hundred girls. We were swamped and despite the tenacity of our security team and the arena's guys, it was a fucking shitshow.

"Rafe, Rafe, over here," someone yelled just as something hit me in the face. I grabbed the lace panties and threw them down in disgust. Fenton chuckled, and I shot him a scathing look.

"Come on, Casanova, we're almost there."

The rumble of the buses grew louder as we finally reached them. Fenton pushed me through the door, and I staggered up the steps. "Eva?"

"She's not here," Levi said through gritted teeth.

"What the fuck do you mean, she's not here?"

"She's on the other bus."

"The other... are you fucking with me?"

Damon shook his head over my brother's shoulder.

"I'm going to—"

"Holy crap, that was intense."

I spun around to find Riley standing there. She smoothed her hair down and gave us a weak smile. "Is everyone okay?" Her brows knitted.

"What the fuck are you doing here?" Levi barked.

"Levi," Damon warned.

"I'm going," I said. No way was I staying on the bus with Riley.

I went to move around her, but the bus jerked forward. "Rafe." A hand laid on my arm. My eyes snapped to Riley and she immediately snatched her hand away. "I'm sure Eva is fine. We'll stop just outside the city and you can—"

My cellphone began vibrating and I stalked into the bedroom, slamming the door. "Eva?"

"I'm okay," she breathed. "Before I knew what was happening Travis had me on the other bus. I didn't—"

"It's okay, I'm just relieved you're okay."

"That was crazy. I mean, I knew things could get... but not like that. They were wild. Is everyone okay?"

"Yeah, we're fine." I forced myself to calm down. Eva was fine. That's all that mattered. "What about you guys?"

"We're okay. Phoebe is a little shook up," she lowered her voice. "She got a couple of scratches."

"Fuck."

"She's fine. Letty already broke out the liquor."

"I'm so fucking relieved you're okay, Starshine. When I lost you in the crush, I almost—"

"Seriously, everythin' is fine."

I sank down on the mattress, raking a hand through my hair. "I'd feel a whole lot better if you were here right now."

"Me too. I hope everyone else is safe. Riley didn't make it on the bus. Do you think she and Alistair are takin' one of the SUV's?"

Fuck.

I hesitated.

"Rafe, what it is?"

"You should probably know Riley is here."

"What?" Her breath caught.

"Here, on our bus. I don't know why, but she's here."

"I see," Eva said coolly. "Well, she is your assistant. I guess it makes sense she'd want to check on you all."

"We'll stop outside the city and everyone can switch."

"Yeah." Her voice was tight.

"None of us want her here."

"I know, I just... It doesn't matter. Everyone's safe. I'll speak to you later. Goodni—"

"Eva?" I rushed out.

"Yeah, Rafe?"

"I love you, Starshine. Don't ever forget that."

CHAPTER NINETEEN

"I CAN'T BELIEVE she's on their bus."

"Hmm," I grumbled. My gut told me it wasn't a coincidence, but there was nothing anyone could do about it now. We were already on the highway out of Detroit, the bright city lights growing small in the distance behind us. "What's her deal, anyway?" Phoebe asked. She'd already changed into her pajamas and pulled her hair into a messy bun.

"Who, Riley?" Letty rolled her eyes. "Oh, just your usual over-ambitious shark willing to do whatever, or whoever, to climb her way to the top."

"Is it true she's sleeping with Alistair?"

"He's had a thing for her ever since she started at the label. But he was going through a messy separation and then there's the company policy about dating the people you work with." Letty looked at me, fighting a smirk.

"In my defense," I said, "I met Rafe before I knew who he was."

"I'm sorry, what?" Phoebe's brows bit her hairline. "You're telling me you didn't know who Rafe was?"

"I didn't know who any of the band was. Hudson was judgin' the talent contest I entered and if it wasn't for my best friend, Molly, I would have been none the wiser."

"That's... wow."

"Now you know why she's such a hit with the fans. Eva's the real deal."

I blushed as the two of them stared at me. "I'm exhausted, I think I'm goin' to call it a night."

"Are you sure?" Letty frowned. "I had all these plans to stay up and corrupt Phoebe."

"Hey, takes one to know one". She chuckled, sipping on her drink.

"I'm tired." And the last thing I wanted to do was sit and obsess over Riley.

"If we stop, I'll wake you."

I waved them off as I padded down the bus to the bunks. Thankfully, Letty was prepared and had an emergency supply of clothes and toiletries on board. Slipping into the bathroom, I washed my face and cleaned my teeth before changing into an oversized nightshirt. It felt weird being back in the bunks, but as soon as I lay down, exhaustion seeped into every inch of my muscles. I checked my cell phone, straining to see the screen. There were no messages, not that I expected any. Molly and my parents had texted me after the show, just like they did every other night.

Shoving it under my pillow, I closed my eyes, and let sleep claim me.

"Eva, Eva." The voice drifted on the edge of my consciousness. "We've made a pit stop. Do you want to switch to the other bus?"

"She's out cold, leave her be."

I pulled the thin sheet higher, falling back into a dreamless sleep. But then the rustle of the curtains gently coaxed me back to reality.

"Rafe?" I choked out as he climbed in beside me. There was barely any room, our bodies pressed impossibly close.

"Ssh, Starshine, go to sleep."

"But what are you—"

He nuzzled my neck, slipping his arm around me. "Sleep."

I started to drift again, comforted by the knowledge that Rafe was here.

"I love you," I murmured.

"I love you too," were the last words I heard before sleep claimed me.

I WOKE UNABLE TO MOVE, PLASTERED TO A WARM BODY.

Rafe's body.

"Morning," he drawled, smoothing his hand up my thigh, sending shivers skittering through me.

"Mornin'," I fought a smile. "These bunks really aren't made for two people." He had to be hanging off the thing.

"I didn't notice." He pulled me closer. The air was thick and suffocating, and I really needed a glass of water, but I couldn't find it in myself to move.

When life ran at a hundred miles an hour, it was nice to pause and soak up the little things. My fingers drew lazy circles on his bare chest. I never imagined myself falling in love with someone like Rafe. A tattooed rock star with a tainted past. But now I'd found him, I couldn't ever imagine loving anyone else.

"I can hear your thoughts from over here," he whispered, stroking my hair.

"I'm just thinkin' about how quickly things can change." I peeked up at him. "And I can't help but think if I'd never have gotten sick, I wouldn't be here right now... with you."

"Everything happens for a reason, Starshine."

"Do you truly believe that?"

Rafe smiled. It was such a rare and beautiful sight. I wanted to freeze frame it and keep it with me always. "I don't know." He chuckled. "But I do know this; you and me, Eva, it's not fleeting. It's real."

Taking my hand, he pressed it against his chest, right where his heart lay. "Feel that... it beats for you. I don't know where this thing with the band is going, or what lies ahead, but I do know one thing, Evangeline Star Walker, I don't want any of it without you by my side."

"Rafe..." I gasped, the weight of his words almost too much to bear. It wasn't that I didn't want it, I did. So much. But there wasn't only us to consider.

Just then, voices broke the silence, the smell of coffee drifting down the bus.

"Ugh. Letty is back which means our time is up." Rafe kissed my head.

"Damn right," she said, sounding closer now. "I have coffee."

Rafe slipped out of the bunk. "I need to go back to the other bus and clean up. I'll see you soon, okay?"

I nodded, fighting the urge to let my eyes run down his lean body.

"Hungry, love?" His gaze darkened.

"Go." I grabbed a pillow and stuffed it over my face, but he pulled it away.

"See you soon." He winked, and then took off down the bus. I heard him talk to Letty, their voices a low rumble. But one word stood out.

Riley.

"It's Molly," Letty handed me my cell phone. "You might want to take it." She winked.

"Mol?"

"Hey, babe. How's things in tourlandia?"

"Things are surprisingly good."

"Well, yeah they are. You get to perform every night with one of the world's hottest bands right now. And then you get to rub yourself all over their bassist."

"Did you really just say that?"

She let out a groan. "This dry spell is killin' me. I hate to say it..." Her hesitation was palpable. "But Hudson effin' Ryker has ruined me for all other guys."

I let out a quiet laugh. "He really got under your skin, huh?"

"You can never tell him. I mean it, Eva."

"Maybe *you* should tell him?"

"What?" She gasped. "Have you lost your freakin' mind? It's Hudson effin' Ryker."

"Yeah, yeah, you just said that, but—"

"No buts, Eva. Me and Hudson are destined to be nothin' more than a shootin' star. Burnin' bright and pretty to look at, but if you blink, you'll miss it."

"Nice visual, Mol," I said.

"Anyway, he is not the reason I called. My mom is takin' the twins to visit my grams next weekend, so I spoke to Letty and guess who will be comin' to your show in Louisville?" She sang the words.

"For real?"

"Real, aaand it won't be a fly by visit this time. I'm comin' for the entire weekend."

I let out a shriek of approval. "I'm so excited."

"Letty checked the schedule and you guys have a day off, so I was thinkin' we could hit up the city and do the whole tourist thing."

"Yes, yes, yes." Excitement blossomed in my chest. Leaving Molly and my parents behind was definitely the downside of touring.

"Have the guys said what they'll be doin' to celebrate Damon's birthday?"

"It's his birthday?" No one had said a thing. "How do you possibly know that?"

"It's called Google." She chuckled. "You should try Googling yourself, it's quite entertainin'."

"Please, don't." I covered my face with my hand, which was ridiculous given she couldn't see me.

"You should be so proud of yourself, babe. I saw the video of you singin' with Rafe and Levi. It has like a gazillion views."

Letty had told me it had been a hit, but I'd avoided it, like I tried to avoid everything else splashed all over the media. Even if it was a hit, I knew that for every compliment there would be a cruel comment.

"Okay, I got to go, the twins are—shit, the little brats are up to no good again. I'll text you soon."

"Bye." We hung up.

"Everything okay?" Letty reappeared.

"Thank you." I smiled, clutching my cell to my chest.

"Oh, it was nothing."

"What was nothing?" Phoebe breezed into the room, her hands full of coffee.

"Letty arranged for my best friend to come visit over the weekend."

"Awesome. Has Damon said what he wants to do to celebrate yet?"

I gawked at her. "Seriously, you know this stuff too?" Her and Molly were going to have no problem getting along.

"Well, yeah. Even before I joined the label, I knew... and that's totally weird."

"Don't let Hudson know you're *that* kind of fan, he'll never let you live it down."

Just then, Riley entered the room. "I need you to go over these." She thrust the papers at Letty.

"Hello to you too."

Riley's eyes cut to mine, but I pretended to be reading my phone.

"I think I'd be cranky too after spending a whole night on the bus with the band." Phoebe's tone was saccharine sweet.

I smothered a snicker with my hand. Letty was less obvious, coughing away her laughter.

"Actually, the guys all made me feel right at home." She spun around and marched out the room.

"I bet they did," Letty mumbled after her. "Is it me or is she becoming more and more hostile?"

"Oh, it's not you," I let out a weary sigh.

"Maybe Alistair finally put her in her place?" Letty said.

"Put who in their place?" The guys filed into the room. Hudson took a running leap, throwing himself over the couch, landing with a thud.

"Nothing," Letty answered. "What's in the bag?"

"Breakfast hoagies." He shook it. "We had security go out and buy us some."

"Ooh, gimme."

"For the ladies." Damon held out a bag and Letty snatched it up, opening it, and sticking her head inside.

"So. Good."

"Hey, Hud," I said. "Guess who's comin' to visit over the weekend?"

His smile fell. "Oh, hell no." He dropped his head back, running a hand over his face.

"Molly wants to know what your birthday plans are?" I rose a brow at Damon.

"I prefer not to celebrate."

"But you're twenty-one," Phoebe added. "You have to celebrate."

"Yeah, come on, Dame. We should do something. We have the day off Saturday." Hudson waggled his brows. "We could hit the clubs. Maybe check out a strip club—"

"Nice, real nice." Letty rolled her eyes.

"No strippers," Damon said. "Or clubs. But I wouldn't be totally against doing something low key and normal."

"But you're open to ideas?" I said around a smile. "It's your birthday, we have to celebrate."

"Fine, fine." He held up his hands. "But nothing illegal, or public, or risky." His glare snapped to Hudson. "I mean it, bro."

"Spoilsport."

Levi strolled into the room the exact moment I squeaked with approval. "What's got you so excited?"

"Damon's birthday," I said. "He says we can celebrate."

"For real?" Levi frowned at his bandmate. "But you never want to celebrate."

"What can I say? Eva's a bad influence; it's impossible to say no to her."

My heart swelled.

Molly and Letty were right. I was a part of this band. Somehow, some way, I had earned the friendship and trust of these four broken boys. And unlike Riley, the Die Hearts, or the label, it was something I would never take for granted.

CHAPTER TWENTY

RAFE

"Hey, can we talk?" I asked Levi as he walked off stage. We'd just finished sound check and had a couple hours to ourselves.

"What's up?" He wasn't hostile, but he wasn't friendly either. It was like we'd become strangers.

And I hated it.

"I just wanted to see how things are? You know... with stuff?" I ran a hand over my head, rubbing the back of my neck.

Fuck.

Why was this so hard?

It wasn't supposed to be hard. Levi was my brother, my blood. Nothing was ever supposed to come between us.

"I'm not going to head out and try to score, if that's what you mean?"

"Levi, I didn't... I just wanted to talk."

"So talk, little brother."

A beat passed.

And another.

I had all these things I wanted to say, things I'd spent hours stewing on. But now I was standing here, with him staring at me, and I had nothing.

"You and Eva are good?" he asked, breaking the silence.

My eyes went wide. "You're... you're asking me about..."

I didn't know what the hell to do with that.

"We're good."

He nodded. "You seem happy... with her, I mean." A faint smile played on his lips. "She's good for you. I mean that."

"Listen, maybe we can hang out? Just the two of us. I'd really like—"

"Honestly, this, us having some distance, it's working for me right now."

"Oh." My shoulders sagged.

Levi frowned. "This is just something I need to deal with, on my own."

"You're not alone though. You have the guys, Letty... Phoebe."

His eyes lit up, but quickly darkened. "The new girl? Is that a fucking joke?"

"You tell me. The two of you looked pretty close the other night."

"She's like me." He released a long breath.

"You mean she's an add—"

"Fuck, no. She's... it's not my story to tell."

"Just be careful, yeah?"

"You don't need to worry about me, bro."

But I did worry.

Even now, even after all the words and fists and distance, I worried. Levi walked his life on a tightrope. One slip up and he'd plummet into darkness.

He went to walk away, but I called after him. "Levi?"

"Yeah?"

"I know things aren't right between us, and I know that's on me, but I'll always be here for you. Always. I love you brother."

He regarded me for a second, processing my words, and then gave me a tight nod.

It wasn't quite what I'd hoped for when I approached him. But part of me couldn't help but feel proud, hopeful even. Levi wasn't spiraling out of control. If anything, he was more levelheaded than ever. But a little voice knocked at my conscience. Levi portrayed someone in control, but what if it was all a front? What if he was only showing me, and everyone else, what we wanted to see?

I wanted to go after him and make him talk to me, the way we had so many times before. Brother to brother. But I knew pushing him was not the way.

"There you are." Hands looped around my body from behind as Eva snuggled against me. "I wondered where you'd gotten to."

"I tried to talk to Levi." I pulled her around my side and into my arms.

"And?" Eva craned her neck to look at me.

"It could have been worse. Does he seem okay to you, really?"

"He definitely seems different. I don't know if that's a good or bad thing. But he's present, right? And he seems clearheaded. Why? Are you worried?"

"I'm always worried." I dipped my head, brushing my lips across hers. "Are you excited about the show?"

"Excited and nervous. I still pinch myself every mornin' to make sure this is real."

"Oh, it's real, Starshine. Do you need me to prove it?" My tongue licked the seam of her mouth, demanding entry. Eva let out a soft sigh, falling willingly into the kiss. She tasted of peppermint, taking my breath away.

"Have I told you lately that I love you? So fucking much."

Her soft laughter danced over my skin. "You're so goofy."

"I think the word you're lookin' for is whipped, at least according to Hudson."

"He really thinks that?" An adorable frown crinkled her brows.

"He's only jealous. What we have, it's the real deal. I don't think any of us ever thought we would find that."

"You're still all so young, you couldn't possibly know that..."

"I know that, and you know that, but when you've spent most of your life being told you're worthless or useless or an inconvenience, those labels, they start to stick."

"I hate that you all went through that."

I shrugged. "It is what it is. Besides, family isn't always blood; it's who you choose to let into your life."

"Well, I feel very lucky to know you all."

"Even Hudson?" I smothered a grin.

"Even Hudson." Eva nodded resolutely. "So, I was thinkin'... and I know Damon said he didn't want any fuss, but it doesn't seem right not celebratin' the fact he's turnin' twenty-one, so what if we throw him a surprise party?"

"A surprise party?" That sounded the opposite of low-key to me, but Eva looked so excited, I didn't have the heart to crush her idea.

"Nothin' excessive. Just you, me, the guys, Letty, Phoebe, and a few of the roadies. We can get him cake and decorate the hotel suite."

"Actually, that sounds pretty damn perfect." There would be no stress of having to arrange something, hoping our location wouldn't be leaked to the media.

"You know Hudson will probably want to get him a stripper or something."

"It's a good job Hudson isn't organizing it then."

I tightened my arms around Eva's waist. We weren't alone, with people coming and going around us incessantly, but it no longer mattered. We didn't have to hide our relationship from anyone. There was something so fucking freeing about that, being able to just be with Eva like this, in public.

"What?" She smiled up at me.

"Nothing." I kissed her again. Showing her that it wasn't nothing.

It was everything.

She was everything.

———

"G REAT SHOW, GUYS," A LISTAIR GREETED US AS WE FILED OFF STAGE. The crowd had been electric, a permanent buzz in the air. We were sweaty and high on adrenaline, and all I wanted was to find Eva and drag her into the nearest shadows and kiss her.

"Fuck yeah, it was," Hudson bounced on the balls of his feet, grinning.

"Listen, I need to speak with you all. Can you get cleaned up and meet me on the bus?"

Our good mood stalled. Damon's brows bunched together. "What is it? What's wrong?"

"Is Eva—"

"Eva is fine," Alistair said to me. "But some things have come to my attention that need dealing with. Get cleaned up and we'll talk." He turned and walked off, disappearing into the crowd of roadies gathered, waiting to dismantle the set.

"Well, that was fucking cheery." Levi stalked past us.

"What do you think he wants?" Hudson asked, the three of us following my brother.

"Nothing good." Dread slithered through me.

"Maybe he's going to finally own up to seeing Riley?"

"And break his own rule?" Hud shook his head. "Nah, I'm not buying it."

"Well, whatever it is," my brother stopped dead and turned to us, "we face it together." He stalked off down the hall, the three of us watching after him.

"Is anyone else starting to get freaked out by how calm he is lately?" Hudson remarked.

"Give him some credit," Damon scoffed. "He's trying."

"Yeah, I know. But what happens when trying gets to be too much? He's like a soda bottle, man. Shake him up and that thing's gonna blow."

"Hud." It was a low warning.

"Okay, okay." His hands went up. "Let's pretend everything is okay and ignore the fact our lead singer is acting like a Stepford wife."

"Come on." I moved between them. "Before Alistair busts our balls over being late."

We didn't speak another word about Levi, or Alistair, as we took it in turns showering and changing. I'd been so pumped coming off stage, eager to see Eva and celebrate another awesome show. But now I felt weary. Between Alistair's cryptic request, and Damon's and Hudson's comments about Levi, my good mood had all but disappeared.

By the time we got on the bus, Alistair was already waiting. Eva, Letty, and Phoebe too.

"Hey." Relief washed over Eva as I slid onto the bench beside her.

"Hey." I hooked my arm around her waist, pulling her closer. "I missed you."

Someone cleared their throat, muttering the word, 'whipped'.

I flipped Hudson off, causing everyone to laugh.

"Okay, children, settle down." Alistair pulled at his collar. "I know you're all probably wondering what's going on. Well, I wanted you to hear it from me first, Riley is off the tour."

"No fucking way." Hudson sat forward.

"What happened?" Damon asked.

"I'm not going to go into specifics, but let's just say, I'm not convinced she has the band's best interests at heart anymore." His eyes flickered to Eva.

"I'm sorry," she said. "I didn't want to cause any problems for the band or you."

"That is not the issue here."

Although the way he choked out the words would suggest it was part of the issue.

"I think we deserve to know what happened." Levi said coolly. He'd chosen to stand, towering over the rest of us like a dark, fallen angel.

Alistair stared at my brother, indecision etched into the lines of his forehead. Usually, he would have told Levi to back down, to leave management issues to management. But something had him hesitating.

Letting out a deep sigh, Alistair ran a hand down his face. "It came to my attention that Riley was working against us."

"What the fuck does that mean?" Hudson balked.

"It means I believe Riley was behind numerous leaks, including the article about Eva, as well as the location of numerous private events."

"No shit, Sherlock," Levi gritted out.

"Wait a second, you knew?" He ran his eyes over each of us. "You suspected Riley was... and you didn't come to me with it?"

"She's your woman," my brother said, as if it was nothing. "We knew who'd you believe." His hard stare found mine across the bus.

"I..." Alistair stumbled over his words. "You knew?"

"Everyone fucking knew."

"I see. Well, in that case then, you should probably know that, yes, me and Riley had been seeing one another for a while. She didn't just betray the band, she betrayed me."

"I'm really sorry, Ali," Eva said.

He gave her an appreciative nod. "What's done is done. Riley is off the team, and we're... over." He swallowed.

"Off the team? So she'll still be working for the label?" Alistair blanched and my brother straightened. "Tell me you're not protecting her?"

"It isn't like that, Levi. But I love... I loved her." Beads of sweat rolled down his forehead.

"That's some fucking—"

"Levi," I warned. "Let's all just take a breath. Do we need to be worried about backlash? She was privy to things.... information about our personal lives."

"She made a few bad judgment calls, Levi. She isn't—"

"Listen to yourself." Levi was furious now. "She fucked us over. She fucked Eva over, and you're sitting there defending her all because you were fucking her?"

Alistair shot up, the two of them glaring at one another. Tension crackled in the air, thick and suffocating.

"Levi," Damon moved beside him.

"I'm okay," his voice wavered.

After what felt like an eternity, Alistair finally edged away, slumping against the wall. "You're right, I'll talk to management first thing in the morning. Riley signed the NDA's like everyone else, but there's too much at stake. I give you my word, I'll fix this." He glanced at Eva again. "I'm sorry I didn't take it seriously enough when it first came to light."

"It's okay."

It wasn't, but nothing anyone said was going to change the fact the truth was out, and Riley was gone.

CHAPTER TWENTY-ONE

EVA

Something changed after Riley left.

No one saw her again. It was as if she disappeared into thin air. For a hot second, the guys had worried about who might take her place, but Alistair and the label decided that, with Phoebe's help, Letty could handle things for me as well as the band.

So that's how it went for the next four nights. We performed in city after city, and afterwards we all climbed aboard the Van Hool and played cards or watched a movie or just hung out, talking about everything and nothing. Levi still didn't participate much, locking himself away in the back bedroom, but there were rare occasions when he would sit with us.

Rafe was always more relaxed during those moments. I would feel the tension melt away from his body. I knew how hard it was on him, the distance between him and Levi, but I also knew he wouldn't stifle his brother. Not when everything seemed so calm.

Part of me wondered if me and Rafe were the only two reasons he stayed away, or if Phoebe stirred something inside him—something he wasn't ready to face. I'd caught him staring after her more than once. I even tried to talk to him about it, but every time he shot me down. I was a Tennessee girl through and through though, and we had enough tenacity to break through even the strongest of walls.

"You should go talk to her." I tipped my head toward Phoebe. We'd made a rare pitstop right outside of Cincinnati. It was early enough that the roadside diner was empty, save a couple of truckers who had no idea who we were. Even if they did, they weren't going to whip themselves into a frenzy like a teenage girl.

"You need to quit it, Angel." He levelled me with a hard look.

"She likes you too, you know."

"Nah." He kicked the ground with his boot, spraying dust into the air. "She doesn't like me. She looks at me and sees a project, something to fix. But there ain't no fixing something as broken as me."

The others were inside. I could see them through the windows, goofing around as they ordered breakfast. I reached for Levi's hand. "You're not broken, Levi. Maybe just a little damaged. But we all have dents and bruises. With enough love and attention and time, though, they start to fade."

Taking me surprise, Levi yanked me into his arms, hugging me tight. "You make it so hard to hate you, Eva."

"You want to hate me?" I eased back to look at him, really look at him. He was so intimidating with his piercings and tattoos and blacker-than-night eyes. But behind all the steel and ink was just a boy who had learned to expect disappointment. A boy who had been abandoned by his father and berated by his mother.

A boy who craved love and affection but had no idea how to handle his emotions.

"You need to let people in, Levi."

"I let you in and you hurt me."

Guilt flashed through me as I sucked in shaky breath. "I know, and I'm sorry. We thought we were protectin' you."

"I know," he said the words so quietly I would have missed them, if it wasn't for the fact I saw them form on his lips.

He was growing. Changing. And a small piece of me hoped it was seeing his brother find happiness that had done it. If Levi realized someone could love Rafe, then maybe, just maybe, he'd realize that one day, someone could love him too.

"You should talk to Rafe, Levi. I know he's hurtin' over this too. You've been through so much together, surely you're not goin' to let a small-town country girl come between you." Gentle laughter spilled from my lips.

"Just promise me, Angel," he said, ignoring my words. "Just promise me, that no matter what happens, no matter how far we go, you'll always be there for him."

My brows furrowed. "Levi, what's goin' on?"

"Nothing." He shook his head. "But Rafe always looked out for me. He was always there... and now, now I'm asking you to be there for him."

"I'm not plannin' on goin' anywhere," I said, feeling like I was missing some piece of the puzzle. He let me go and started to retreat, but I snagged his wrist. "Hey, are you sure you're okay?"

"Who, me?" He grinned, and just like that our moment was over, and Levi the showman was back.

"I hope you guys are hungry?" Phoebe approached us with a huge brown bag in her hands. "I got two of everything."

"I'll be on the bus." Levi spun on his heel and walked off, as if he couldn't get away quick enough.

"What's his problem?"

"Don't take it personally, he's..."

"Avoiding me?"

Phoebe had really found her feet around us. She was quick witted, and nothing the guys—especially Hudson—said or did seemed to faze her.

"You have to be patient with him," I said.

She arched a thin brow, smirking. "It just so happens patience is my superpower."

"Why does that not surprise me." I chuckled as we walked back to the bus together, but before I could follow her on board, someone caught me around the waist, pulling me backward.

"Got you," Rafe breathed against my ear, curving his body around mine.

"Seriously, you two," Hudson grumbled. "Do you really want me to puke over my breakfast?" He climbed onto the bus, leaving me with Rafe.

Turning me in his arms, he pushed me up against the side of the Van Hool. "Good morning."

"Good mornin' to you."

Rafe slid his hand into my hair, kissing me in that familiar way of his. "You taste good."

"I taste like I just got done brushin' my teeth." I smiled; I couldn't help it. He was different since Riley left. Sure, I knew he still carried a heap of guilt over Levi, but he was less tense.

We all were.

"Hey, are we all set for Saturday?"

He nodded, eyes sparkling with mischief. "Letty called ahead to the hotel and made the special requests."

"Do you think he'll like it?" The surprise party had been my idea, but now I wasn't so sure. It seemed a little dull for a world-famous rock star.

"He'll love it." Rafe dropped a kiss on my head. "I invited Alistair; I hope that's okay?"

"I guess he should be there, but I don't know if after the whole Riley thing, it's a good idea." I frowned.

"I know, but I feel sorry for the guy. And I know it's our night off, but he's our manager. He should be there."

"You're right. He's been... I don't know, sad, since Riley left."

"I guess she didn't only screw us over, she screwed him over too."

"I still can't believe they fired her." Letty had heard from a friend at the label that Riley hadn't taken too well to the news. She'd caused a huge scene before storming out of there.

"I'm just glad she's gone. We trust Letty implicitly and Phoebe seems genuine."

"You've changed your tune."

"What?" He shrugged, a faint smile playing on his lips.

"Wouldn't happen to have anythin' to do with the fact there seems to be somethin' there between her and Levi?"

Rafe's chest rumbled with laughter. "You need to stop trying to play matchmaker, Starshine. Levi's in a good place. At least, he seems like he is. Don't push for something he isn't ready for."

"Fine." I held up my hands, but Rafe pressed his palms against mine, pinning me against the bus and kissing me hard.

"Hey, fuckers, we'll leave without you," someone yelled from inside the bus. I chuckled, burying my face into Rafe's chest.

"One day," he said, tilting my face to his. "One day, it'll just be the two of us and no interruptions."

"I like the sound of that."

I liked it a whole lot.

Rafe tucked a piece of hair behind my ear. "Come on, before I drag you around the back and do very, very bad things to you."

Old Eva would have blushed at his words, but new Eva... new Eva pushed up on her tiptoes and brushed her lips against Rafe's ear, whispering, "Tonight, I want you to kiss every inch of me, Rafe. I want you to make my body sing." I slipped under his arm and walked away, his heated gaze following me every step of the way.

THE NEXT DAY, AFTER ANOTHER SELL-OUT PERFORMANCE, WE HAD finally arrived in Louisville, and I was eagerly awaiting the arrival of Molly.

"She should be here any second," Letty said. "Oh, I think that's them now."

One of the familiar black SUVs rolled into the underground parking lot. No sooner had it stopped, the door swung open. "Holy crap, Eva, look at you." Molly rushed over to me, pulling me into a tight hug. "Damn, I've missed you."

"It's only been a couple of weeks," I chuckled.

"It feels like forever. You have that superstar glow."

"Oh hush." My cheeks burned. "I'm still the same old me."

"Are you?" Her brow rose. "Because from the texts you've been sendin' me about... Rafe." She mouthed his name, mischief glittering in her eyes. "I need details. All the glorious and gory details."

"*Mol!*"

"It's like getting blood out of stone," Letty said from behind us.

"Letty, get over here and give this girl a hug."

I stepped aside, letting the two of them do their thing. Phoebe hovered beside me, chewing her thumb.

"You must be Phoebe." Molly smiled, stepping toward us. "It's great to meet you."

"Likewise. I love your hair."

Now that Phoebe mentioned it, Molly did look amazing.

"I may have dressed up for the occasion." She cast me a knowing look.

"Well your efforts are in vain, Mol. The guys aren't here."

"They're not?" Her smile dropped.

"Nope. They're on distract Damon duty." I checked the time. "We have around two hours to turn the suite into party central."

"Aren't there people you can pay to do that?" She arched a brow.

"There are, but this is way more fun."

"Turns out your girl is quite the party planner." Letty's words were laced with humor.

"I'm not *that* bad."

"You had Travis go to the store to buy balloons."

"And chips and dip," Phoebe added.

"Don't forget the piñata."

"You got a piñata?" Molly snickered.

"I may have gone a little overboard. I just want it to be fun."

"Oh, it'll be fun. Travis bought enough liquor to sink a ship."

"I didn't ask him to do that."

Letty rolled her eyes. "He's been around the band long enough to know how things usually go."

"It isn't supposed to be anythin' wild, Letty."

"Relax, Momma Bear," she teased. "Everything will be fine."

Nervous energy vibrated in my stomach. I really wanted Damon to enjoy his party. I wanted everyone to enjoy it. No fangirls or drama, no jealous assistants, and definitely no paparazzi.

Even world-famous rock stars deserved a little slice of normal every now and again.

"Come on, let's go up to the suite."

Travis followed us into the elevator, carrying Molly's bags and was as quiet as ever.

"It's good to you see again, T," Molly flashed him an eager grin.

"Miss Steinberg." He nodded.

"Miss Steinberg." She mouthed at me, waggling her brows. "You wouldn't believe how excited I was to get out of the house. I love those brats somethin' fierce, but there's only so much a girl can take, you know?"

"You have kids?" Phoebe gawked at her.

"Kids?" Molly's eyes grew to saucers, but then she roared with laughter. "Brothers. Twin brothers. A real pain in my ass too. My mom's at work a lot so I guess they might as well be mine. My dad, he left..." she trailed off, and I reached over, grabbing her hand.

"I'm so happy you're here."

"Me too, babe." We shared a knowing look. "Me too."

CHAPTER TWENTY-TWO

RAFE

"I STILL THINK we should have hit a strip club."

"What the fuck is wrong with you?" Damon clipped Hudson around the ear.

"I could ask you the same thing. When was the last time you got any, huh?"

"Fuck off."

"Yeah, that's what I thought. Girls are practically lining up to sit on your dick and—"

"Maybe I want more than a quick fuck with a girl I'll never see again. Ever stop to think about that, huh?" Damon's chest heaved with the weight of his words.

"Shit, D, I was only busting your balls."

"Forget it." He waved Hudson off.

"Don't do that..." Guilt shone in his eyes. "I was being a dick, sorry. You really want that though? To be whipped like Rafe?"

I gave him the finger.

"I don't know... maybe, one day."

"Shit, man. I didn't realize. I just thought you couldn't get it up or something."

Fenton and one of the other bodyguards smothered a snicker as we slipped into the back entrance of the hotel.

"Nice, dickhead. Real nice."

"What about you, Levi?"

"What about me?" My brother grunted.

"Are you looking to settle down?"

"What do you think?" He smirked. It was one of his trademark Levi Hunter smirks, the one reserved for fangirls and groupies.

Only it didn't quite reach his eyes.

And I couldn't help but wonder where his head was at.

We entered the service elevator. It had been strange spending the afternoon with the band, just the four of us. At first, it had been a little awkward, but we soon fell into old habits. Hudson had almost bailed when he found out we were going to watch a movie, and Damon moaned when we all stole his popcorn. It had been a welcomed reprieve from the fast-paced life of touring. Even if security had to arrange for the staff to let us sneak in through the emergency exit.

"So, tonight..." Hudson ran a hand through his hair. "Tell me your girl has something special planned."

He was going to have a big disappointment when we got to the suite and realized we weren't going out tonight.

"Molly's here. Are you ready to see her again?" I asked him.

He released a frustrated breath. "I know she's Eva's best friend, but she's really going to ruin my game tonight."

"You have game now?"

"Fuck off. How would you like it if you were on the prowl and your ex-fling was there?"

"First off, *prowl?* When the fuck did you become a lion? And second, ex-fling? Is that what we're calling it?"

Molly was more to him than just a fling. We both knew it. But if Hudson wanted to pretend different, then who was I to stop him?

I pretended to check my phone, texting Eva the signal. She had gone to so much effort for Damon, it only made me love her more. The way she'd accepted my friends without question. She didn't care where we came from or where we were going. She only cared about us: not the band, but the guys behind it.

"Do I get to know what that girl of yours has planned yet?" Damon jammed his hands into his jean pockets.

"You'll find out soon enough." I smirked.

"Hopefully it involves lots and lots of liquor and a night out. I'm feeling restless." Hudson's eyes went wide, guilt swirling there. "Sorry, Lev. That was—"

"Seriously, you guys," my brother let out a strained breath, "I'm okay. Are some days harder than others? Fuck, yes. But you don't have to tread on eggshells around me." He met my eyes in the mirrored walls of the elevator. "I've realized a few things lately."

"Yeah?" Hudson asked.

"Yeah. I'm trying to keep my shit together, I promise. There's too much on the line." His eyes burned into the glass, but he might as well have been looking right at me.

"Good to hear it, man," Damon said. "We're all proud of you, Levi. All of us."

The atmosphere turned tense, but then the doors pinged open and we filed out in the hall.

"It's quiet." Hudson's brows crinkled. "Are you sure they didn't leave without us?"

"They're probably still getting ready," Levi grunted. "You know how long girls take with that kind of stuff."

I hung in the back, letting the three of them go on ahead. Stalter shot me a knowing look as we approached him.

"Are the girls still here?"

"Yeah, they're inside," he said, giving nothing away.

Damon was first at the door. He opened it and stepped inside. "What the hell?" he mumbled as we all followed him. The place was silent, stepped in darkness, shadows dancing across the walls.

"They're not—"

"SURPRISE!" Someone hit the lights and Eva, the girls, and a couple dozen guests all cheered at Damon's arrival.

"Holy shit." Hudson let out a low whisper as he took in the suite.

Eva had gone all out. There were decorations, a homemade bar, snacks, and a... *piñata*. I smiled to myself. There was even a DJ set up in the corner of the room.

"Happy birthday." She reached us, enveloping Damon in a hug. "I hope this is okay?"

"Shit, Eva, I can't believe you did all this... for me."

"Hey now," Letty chimed in, "she had help."

"Thanks, seriously. This is..." Damon swallowed, cupping the back of his neck. "I'm speechless."

"Gifts, we need to do gifts." Eva grinned. She looked so fucking good in the denim mini skirt and off-the-shoulder plaid blouse. Her hair was a wild mass of curls framing her face, her smile painted bright red, and totally kissable.

"This is from me and Rafe."

"You got a couple's gift? Uh, whipped." Hudson coughed loudly, earning him a clip to the ear from Letty.

"I can't take any credit; this was all Eva."

"Open it." She handed Damon the box and he wasted no time tearing into it.

"Holy shit," he breathed. "Original Fender Patent prints. How the hell did you track these down?"

"I had a little help."

Damon flicked his eyes to me. "Don't look at me," I said.

"I'm not just a pretty face, you know." Letty scowled but it melted away seconds later. "Happy birthday, Damon."

"I'm blown away, thank you."

I reached for Eva, pulling her back against my chest. "Thank you." It was a whisper against her ear.

"What for?" She leaned back, tipping her face to mine, grazing my jaw with her lips.

"For being you. For loving me, and them." I flicked my head over to where Damon was busy opening more gifts.

"They're your family."

Family.

It was a word that had never held a simple definition for me before. There had never been family trips to the coast, or family meals and holidays spent with loved ones. There had been me and Levi, learning to survive after our family had chewed us up and spat us out. Then when we met Damon and Hudson at the music program, our family grew. We became four. Four guys who would go on to say 'fuck you' to the rules. A group of guys who would find themselves with the world at their feet and no one to guide them right.

And then came Eva.

Whether she realized it or not, whether they realized it, she was the glue. Meeting her hadn't been a coincidence. She came barreling into our lives at a time when things could have so easily spiraled out of control.

She changed us.

She made us better.

And there was no way I was ever letting her go.

I dropped my chin on her shoulders, watching as our friends celebrated. Someone started passing around drinks and we all toasted Damon before the DJ dropped a heavy beat and the place erupted.

"Where d'you find the DJ?" Hudson asked.

"You really have to ask?" Letty hip bumped him. "Don't worry, he knows the deal. Signed his NDA on the way in."

"We come bearing shooters." Phoebe appeared with Molly in tow.

"Guys, it's good to see you all again."

"Looking good, Molly. Phoebe."

The air turned thick as my brother barely looked at her.

"Here, pass them around." Molly started handing out the shooters, oblivious to the sudden tension.

"I thought we agreed nothing too wild?" Eva grimaced, reluctantly taking one.

"Just one, to toast the birthday boy?" Molly waggled her brows.

"I like your style, Steinberg." Hudson lifted his glass to hers.

"Too bad you won't be sampling the goods. Ever. Again." She smiled sweetly at him, but it was full of venom. And I realized Eva was right. Perhaps Molly was exactly the right girl to whip Hudson into shape.

"To Damon," she said, "on three."

"One... Two... Three. Damon."

We all knocked back our shooters, even Eva.

"Okay, wow, that was..."

"We need to toughen you up, Angel." Hudson hooked his arm around her neck and pulled her close. "If you're going to tour the world with us, you need to build up some resistance."

"W- world tour?" Her mouth fell open.

The party was in full swing now, people laughing and drinking. But the eight of us remained together, in our own little bubble.

Everyone was looking at Eva now. We hadn't talked about what happened after the US tour ended. We still had a leg left. But Letty had dropped it out that since the Masterpiece endorsement, a world tour was looking more and more likely.

"As in outside of the country?"

Hudson exploded with laughter, the rest of us following. She was still so damn sweet and innocent.

"Well, yeah, Country." Levi smiled, a real honest-to-god smile. "What do you say? Fancy spreading a little Hunter-Walker magic around the world?"

"I... wow." My girl stumbled over her words. "I have no idea what to say. Alistair hasn't said—"

"Because I was waiting for the right time to talk to you about this." He strolled over to us. "This is really something, Eva." He glanced over his shoulder to where everyone was having a good time.

"Oh, it was nothin' really." Her cheeks bloomed pink. I took her hand in mine, threading our fingers together.

"The details are still being finalized, but, yes, the label wants to take the tour global, and they want you too."

"Ohmigod," Molly's shrieks filled the air.

"I... I don't know what to say."

"Yes, obviously. The answer is yes."

"Molly has a point, Eva."

"Hold the phone. Did the arrogant Black Hearts drummer, the one and only Hudson Ryker, just agree with me?"

"Jesus," he said through gritted teeth, shaking his head.

"You don't have to decide anything yet," Alistair added. "It's a big decision and I'll sure you'll want to—"

"Yes," she breathed. "Yes, I want to do it."

"Holy shit, for real?" Hudson asked, and Eva nodded.

"Well, all right." My brother whispered something to Letty and she and Phoebe took off.

Seconds later they returned with a bottle of some expensive looking champagne and glasses. Alistair took the bottle from her, doing the honors. The cork popped spraying everywhere.

"Oh shit," Molly gasped. "Here." She held up her glass catching the spillage.

"Pass it around. This requires a toast with something other than whisky or those god-awful shooters you insist on drinking."

"Way to show your age, Ali." Levi snorted.

"Does everyone have one?"

We all nodded, waiting for our manager to start. "The day I saw you performing in that dive bar in Atlanta, I knew I'd found something great. You didn't just play your instruments; you became one with them. I'd never seen anything like it. And then Levi started singing and that was that. I knew I was staring at the next big thing.

"You don't always make it easy for me, and I know I give you a hard time more often than not, but it's only because I believe in you. Because I have every faith you can rule the industry for the next two... five... hell, even ten years."

"Hear fucking hear." Levi lifted his glass up and we all followed.

"You've got what it takes to go all the way. I see it, the label sees it, even Dowager sees it. But you're still young. Impressionable." He glanced at my brother. "You've got to keep your heads about this. Work with me. Take direction when it's suggested."

"Boooo," Hudson teased. "You had to go and ruin a perfectly good speech, didn't ya?"

"All right, all right, I'll save the TED talk for another day. But know that I'm proud of you. All of you, and Eva, I'm real happy you're here. I think I can speak for everyone when I say we all are." He raised his glass in the air.

"Hang on a second," Damon chimed in and Alistair stepped back. "Since it's my birthday I think I should get to say a few words. The last few months haven't been easy. In fact, at times, they have been downright shitty, but I couldn't think of a better bunch of guys to experience all the highs and lows with. And now we get to include Eva in that." His eyes settled on mine.

"I couldn't think of a better girl to come on tour with us. I mean, damn, if a girl gets you a piñata for your birthday, she's a keeper." He winked, raising his glass in the air. "To Eva and the band."

That was something I would never get tired of hearing.

Eva and the band.
It bound us together.
Made us one.
But most importantly, it meant I got to share every second of this crazy ride with her.

CHAPTER TWENTY-THREE

EVA

I WAS SO high I didn't want to come down.

A world tour... with the band.

With Rafe.

It seemed implausible, and yet, Alistair had stood there and said it —he'd even toasted to it.

The party was a sure-fire hit. I'd switched to soda after the first couple of celebratory drinks. I didn't want to embarrass myself. Besides, I didn't need a synthetic buzz, not with the amount of adrenaline coursing through my veins.

"I'm going to see if Johnson and Stalter will join us," I said to Rafe.

"You worry too much." He dipped his head, peppering my face with kisses. "You already took them cake."

"But it's late. Surely they can leave their posts for thirty minutes and come kick back with us."

"Kick back, huh?"

"Oh, hush." I kissed him, letting my tongue tangle lazily with his. Soft, deep licks that had my tummy clenching and my pulse racing.

"We get to do this all over the world..."

"I still can't believe it," I breathed.

"Believe it, Starshine." Rafe's hand cupped the back of my head as he deepened the kiss. "Is it time to call it a night yet?"

"Soon." I smiled against his mouth. "I love you." Untangling myself from his grasp, I grabbed two beers and headed for the hall. But movement in the shadows near the door stopped me in my tracks.

Phoebe was caged against the wall, Levi's body leaning over her, his hand pressed against the wall at the side of her head. They weren't doing anything besides talking, but it looked like a private moment.

An intimate moment I didn't want to disturb.

I'd gotten to know Phoebe over the last week or so and had quickly realized my snap judgment about her was all wrong. She was witty and organized. She didn't push or prod, and the guys all seemed to like her. Much like I had done, she'd slipped into the group with ease, and I already couldn't imagine not having her around.

Deciding to let them have their moment, I went to double back but Levi's gravelly voice gave me pause. "It's okay, Angel," he said. "It's safe to look." There was a hint of humor in his voice.

"Busted." I turned around and slowly approached them, feeling my cheeks heat. "Sorry, I didn't realize you were out here."

"It's okay." Phoebe sidestepped Levi, smoothing a hand down her dark locks. "We were just talking."

Levi frowned at that, brushing a thumb over his bottom lip as he watched her. I'd seen that look before—it was the classic Hunter gaze. Hot. Possessive. Levi wanted her. I just wasn't sure either of them were ready for that.

"I'm going to head back in." he motioned to the hall leading to the suite. "What you did for Damon, Eva, it was a real nice thing."

Levi left, leaving me with Phoebe. She let out a shaky breath. "You were right... he's intense."

"Is everythin' okay?" She looked a little shell shocked.

"I'm fine, I just didn't expect..." Pasting on a warm smile, she added, "It doesn't matter. Tonight is Damon's night. And yours. Congratulations, on the tour."

"Thank you. It still doesn't feel real." A beat passed. "Listen, are you sure you're okay?"

"Honestly? I'm not sure..."

"You're right. Levi is intense and complicated, but I think he likes you. I don't want to speak out of turn, but please don't—"

"Hurt him?" Phoebe didn't blanch or look offended, and I knew then, that she did understood Levi in a way most didn't. "I can't explain it, or maybe it's just my own screwed up issues, but I feel... something."

"Just promise me you'll be careful. Both of you."

"Oh, trust me, baby steps are all I have right now, for anyone."

"I'd really like to hear your story one day; if you ever want to tell me?"

She smiled. "I'd like that. Right, I guess I should go back inside."

"Okay, I won't be long."

I watched Phoebe head back inside. There was something about her... a sadness in her eyes I hadn't really noticed before. There had been no mistaking the chemistry between her and Levi, and although I knew not to get carried away, a little part of me couldn't help but hope she was exactly what he needed.

———

After persuading Johnson and Stalter to take a break and come hang out with everyone, I slipped back into the party, only to be ground to a halt by the sight before me.

"Look..." Molly rushed over to my side, sliding her arm through mine.

"They're..." The words dried on my lips as I watched Rafe and Levi serenade the room with a stripped back version of a song I hadn't heard before.

"Oh, Eva, you really love them, don't you?" Molly was staring at me.

I dabbed my eyes, swallowing down the rest of the tears. It was like a dream come true, watching these two damaged broken beautiful boys perform together. Sure, they did it night after night with the band, but this was different. This was acceptance. It was brotherhood.

It was unconditional love.

"They're so damn good," Molly swayed beside me.

"How did this happen?" I choked out the words.

"Levi asked Rafe to play with him."

"He did?"

"He did. Your Black Hearted boys are goin' to be okay, babe."

"They really are." Warmth spread through me as I watched them weave together a song so haunting and powerful the entire room had fallen under their spell.

Someone moved to my other side, and I glanced up to find Alistair standing there. "Now isn't that a sight to behold?"

I nodded over the lump in my throat.

"When I found out about you and Rafe, I honestly didn't know if they would survive it." He stared out at them, pride shining in his eyes. "I don't know what it is about you, Eva, but whatever it is, we need it. *They* need it."

Alistair squeezed my shoulder before slipping away, leaving me to ponder his words. I clutched my chest, completely enamored by the way Levi's voice blended with Rafe's backing vocals.

"Sweet baby Jesus," Molly whispered. "Can I get a job on the tour? You're a lucky, lucky lady, Eva Star Walker."

Wasn't I just?

The song finished and everyone gave them a standing ovation, but Rafe only had eyes for me. He didn't wait, striding across the room toward me.

"I'll give the two of you some space," Molly whispered, giving my hand a gentle squeeze before disappearing.

"Hi," I said when Rafe stopped in front of me.

"Hi." His eyes were clouded with disbelief, nervous energy rolling off him.

"That was unexpected."

"Tell me about it." He hooked his arm around my waist, pulling me close. "I was just standing there, watching everyone, and he strolled up to me and said, 'everything will work out, you know?'"

"He did?" My brows furrowed. That didn't sound like a very Levi thing to say. But no one could deny the change in him of late.

"I think he sensed my torment."

"Sensed your torment..."

"Yeah." Rafe dipped his head, brushing his lips over mine. "I was thinking about the future, about us. Thinking about how I don't know if I'm ready to share you with the world." His mouth curved. "A world tour, Starshine. Are you ready for that?"

"With you by my side, I'm ready for anythin'."

"God, I love you." Rafe kissed me again. But I still wanted to know one thing.

"So, what happened then, with you and Levi?"

"We talked a little, and then he asked me to sing with him. I think that's his way of saying we're going to be okay." Relief washed over his expression as he tightened his arms around me.

"Of course you're goin' to be okay." I hugged him back. "You're brothers, Rafe. Family. That doesn't just go away."

"I'm so fucking relieved." Rafe buried his face into the crook of my neck, kissing the soft skin there. "I thought... I thought I'd lost him. I thought—" His voice cracked.

"Ssh." I tightened my hold on him. "It's goin' to be okay. Everythin's goin' to be okay."

He lifted his face to mine, kissing me tenderly. "I know it is, because I've finally realized something."

"Oh, yeah?"

"I'm not alone anymore, I have you."

"You do, you know. Have me."

"I was so fucking worried about hurting him, about making an impossible choice between you and my brother, but I realize now, I can have both. You're my person, Starshine. You'll pick me up when I fall and hold me when things get too much."

"I will." My smile grew, his words taking root deep in my soul. "And know what else? I'll help you pick Levi up when he falls, and I'll hold him with you when things get too much. I am your person, Rafe, and together we can be Levi's people. Although,"—my eyes slid to where Levi and Phoebe were talking—"I'm not sure he's goin' to need us much longer."

Rafe trailed his fingers up the side of my neck, drawing my face to his. "If my brother finds someone to love him even half as much as you love me, he'll be a lucky guy."

I wrapped my arms around his neck, closing the distance between us and letting my lips hover over his. "You're right," I whispered against his mouth. "He will."

Rafe's laughter vibrated between us. Pure unadulterated laughter. "I'm never going to let you go, I hope you know that. Wherever this crazy ride takes us, whatever happens with the band, I need you, Eva. I want you, always."

"It's good thing I have no plan on leavin' you then."

"What's going on?" Hudson strolled up to us, pushing his face into ours.

"Just making sure Eva is clear that she can never leave."

"Damn right, she can't."

"Can't what?" Damon appeared, a goofy smile plastered on his face. I frowned.

"Are you drunk?"

"It's my birthday, getting wasted is the number one rule of birthdays. What's all this?" He motioned to the three of us.

"I was just telling Eva she can never leave us." Hudson puffed out his chest.

"*You* were telling me?" I smirked. "What happened to me being, 'the worst thing ever to happen to the band'?" My brow rose sardonically.

Guilt flashed in his eyes. "I was hurting. I say dumb shit when I'm upset."

"It's true." Levi barged into our crude circle. "Although you say a lot of dumb shit when you're not upset too."

"Fuck you, man."

"What's happening?" Levi asked Rafe.

"We were just discussing Eva never leaving the band."

"Fuck no, she can't leave. Who's going to keep us all from killing each other?"

"So, it's decided then." Hudson thrust his bottle forward. "Eva's staying."

"Guys, I never said I was leavin'."

"True, she didn't." Damon swayed on his feet. "But even if you wanted to, we wouldn't let you."

"Okay, birthday boy." I snagged the drink off him. "No more liquor for you."

"But it's my party." He lunged for me, but Levi and Hudson caught him, just before he went down, their howls of laughter like music to my ears.

"I think the party's almost over," I said.

"Oh, hell no, the power is already going to her head." Hudson rolled his eyes.

"Keeping talkin', Ryker and I'll have security remove you."

"Good luck with that, man." He gave Rafe a knowing look.

"Like Molly hasn't got you tied up in—"

We all fell silent as my best friend approached. "Why are you all lookin' at me like that?"

"We'll let you handle this one, bro." Levi clapped Hudson on the back before dragging Damon away.

"I, uh…" Hudson looked at us for help, but I pressed my lips together, fighting a smirk.

"We'll leave you two to… *talk*." Rafe grabbed my hand, pulling me toward the bedroom.

"Rafe," I giggled. "We can't just leave. The party is still—"

"Party's over," he yelled. "See yourselves out."

This time I didn't protest.

Because the truth was, I needed Rafe the way he needed me.

Unequivocally.

Unconditionally.

Always.

CHAPTER TWENTY-FOUR

RAFE

I RELISHED TIMES LIKE THIS. The quiet. The stillness. The beautiful angel sprawled out beside me, the sheet gathered around her body, giving me a hint of what lay underneath. Rolling onto my side, I slid my hand over the curve of Eva's hip, taking my time to trace the lines of her body.

After I'd announced the party was over, and dragged her back to our room, I'd loved her until the early hours of the morning. But it wasn't enough.

It would never be enough.

I knew a therapist would probably tell me my attachment to Eva was unhealthy. And there had been a time or two, where I'd questioned it myself. But that was before last night.

Before I realized that I wasn't alone.

Eva was here. She'd been here for a while now. But I was so consumed with guilt, with trying to find a way to protect everyone, to keep the band—my family—together while allowing myself to love Eva, I'd failed to see the truth.

Eva was all in.

She wasn't going to run again when things got too tough, and she wasn't going to make me choose. Because there wasn't a choice.

Levi was my brother, my family.

And Eva... well, she was my whole fucking world.

The two weren't mutually exclusive, our family was just growing.

"I can feelin' you watchin' me, you know." Eva peeked over at me.

"Can you feel me do this?" I let my hand drift down her stomach and between her legs.

"Mmm," it was a soft moan. "Good mornin'."

Leaning in, I captured Eva's lips, tasting her as I pressed a finger inside her. Her body quivered. "That feels..." She swallowed another moan as I added a second finger, curling them deep inside her.

Eva grasped the sheets, lifting her hips and riding my hand. She looked so fucking good like this. "Rafe, don't stop..."

"Never." I kissed the corner of her mouth, licking and nipping at her lips. Dragging my thumb across her clit, I kept my rhythm slow and steady, watching as she began to unravel around me.

"God, it's..." Eva gasped, her legs trembling, fighting against my touch.

"Let go, Starshine," I murmured against her lips. "Just let go."

"Rafe," Eva cried out, burying her face into my neck.

Waking up like this, being able to touch her this way, to make her lose control, it would never grow old.

"Good morning." I cupped the back of her head, gently coaxing her face to mine.

"That was... you know exactly how to play my body."

I brushed my lips over the shell of her ear. "I'm not ranked one of the best breakout guitar players of the decade for nothing."

"I guess I should count myself lucky then."

"See, that's where you're wrong, Starshine. I'm the lucky one."

"I don't think it's possible to love you any more than I already do... and then you go and land a line like that."

A loud knock on the door shattered our bubble. "Rise and shine, fuckers," Hudson yelled. "Breakfast is served."

"Do you think he and Molly...?"

"Do I really need to answer that question?" My brow rose. Hudson talked a good talk, but one look at Molly in her tight-fitting sweater dress last night and he'd been chomping at the bit.

"I would bet my Zemaitis on it."

Eva sat up. "You wouldn't bet the Zemaitis. You love that thing more than life."

"I've had a little talk with her and let her know there's a new lady in my life."

"If you ever want to get out of this bed, you really should stop bein' so swoony."

"You're totally right." I clambered out. "I wouldn't want to give the guys the wrong impression." Grabbing my jeans, I pulled them on. Pausing when I reached the door, I said, "You might want to take a cold shower and keep your hands to yourself today."

Eva's brows furrowed. "What do you mean?"

"You're not the only one pulling surprises."

"Rafe, what did you do?"

"Well I figured since we're in Louisville…"

"Yes?"

"And Kentucky is only a stone's throw from Tennessee…"

"They're comin'?" Her whole face lit up as she leaped off the end of the bed and ran at me. I caught her, the two of us crashing against the wall. "But how? I spoke to my dad and he told me they were goin' to wait for the Nashville show."

"They were. But I knew Alistair was probably going to bring up the world tour and I knew we'd be celebrating, and they're your parents, they should be here."

"Thank you." She planted a big kiss on my lips. "Thank you, thank you, thank you. But wait…" The color drained from her face. "They're comin' here, *now*?"

"And this is exactly why I didn't tell you yesterday. I knew you'd spend the day worrying."

Eva curled her fingers in the hair at the nape of my neck, staring into my eyes. "Have I told you lately how much I love you?"

"Maybe you should say it again." I fixed my mouth over hers and whispered, "Just to be sure."

———

MR. AND MRS. WALKER HAD LOOKED LIKE FISH OUT OF WATER, waiting backstage for the show to start. But the second Eva strummed her guitar, they were both spellbound.

"She's really something; you should both be very proud."

"I can't believe that's my baby." Eva's mom clutched my arm as we watched her daughter sing one of her original tracks. "Look at her, Gavin, just look."

"I never thought we'd get to see this day." His voice shook.

"She has a bright future ahead of her." Alistair breezed up beside us.

After Eva's parents had joined us for breakfast, Alistair had arranged for them to have a tour of the city. Molly tagged along, while the rest of us hung out at the hotel. They'd asked me to go but I'd declined, wanting Eva to have space to discuss the future with the people closest to her. She was an adult now. She didn't need their permission to come on tour with us, but I knew she'd want their blessing.

Of course, she'd got it.

"Mr. Portman, thank you, for everythin', truly." Gavin grabbed his hand, shaking it.

"You can be rest assured, we'll all take good care of her." Their eyes all found me.

"Rafe's still got a little way to prove himself yet, Mr. Portman." Gavin smothered a grin.

But I wasn't worried.

After what I planned later, there was no way they could doubt my intentions where Eva was concerned.

I only hoped she liked it.

Eva ended her set and the whole place went wild, the noise deafening. "Listen to that, Jesse," Mr. Walker hugged his wife, "that's all for our sweet girl."

Eva bounded off stage, her smile so wide it had to hurt. "I don't think I'll ever tire of hearin' that."

Her parents swamped her, the three of them crying and hugging. The lump in my throat doubled.

"Hey, you good?" Levi clapped me on the back. "Are they okay?" His expression turned hard as he watched Eva with her parents.

"I think it just hit them, you know?" I lifted my eyes to his.

"Yeah, I know. Listen, I've been meaning to ask you... are we good?"

"We're good."

His whole demeanor changed, as if a weight had been lifted. And I knew I was probably reflecting the same expression back at him.

"Are you ready for this?" he asked me.

"Ready as I'll ever be."

"Let's do it then."

"Give me a second." I cut past him, hovering near Eva and her parents. Mrs. Walker noticed me first, her smile full of so much acceptance I felt a little winded.

Eva glanced back, beaming at me. "Hi." We both moved, gravitating like magnets. I reached for her, pulling her into my arms.

"Before I go out there, I just want you to know one thing." Her parents backed off, giving us some space, but I felt Gavin's sharp gaze drilling holes in the side of my face.

"One day, in the future, I'm going to make you mine in every way possible. But until then, I hope you know that I love you with all that I am, and I hope it's enough, Starshine. I hope I'm enough." Pressing a quick kiss to her lips, I left her standing there, rosy-cheeked and breathless, and wondering what the hell I was up to.

EVA

My mom and dad were glued to my side as we watched the guys do their thing. I hadn't expected my parents to enjoy it so much, but both of them were tapping their feet and nodding their heads.

"Ooh, I like this one," Mom yelled over the heavy beat.

I rose a brow at Dad, and he chuckled. "She made a point of downloadin' their album." My eyes widened, and his chuckle turned into full on laughter. "She's become quite the fan."

"There's somethin' super sexy about them, don't you think, Gavin?"

"Okay, Mom. That's enough wine for you." I peeled the cup out of her hand and passed it off to a roadie.

"You should break out your old guitars, Gavin, and serenade me."

"Oh, dear lord," I mumbled under my breath.

Having my parents show up at the suite this morning, after I'd spent the night tangled in the sheets with my rock star boyfriend, was mortifying enough, but watching my mom lust after my rock star boyfriend and his bandmates was a whole other level.

"Behave, Jesse. You're embarrassin' Eva." He switched sides with me, wrapping his arm around Mom.

"Okay, Louisville, we're going to switch things up a little. This is where I'd usually bring Eva back out on stage and create a little magic. But tonight, my brother Rafe..." Twenty-thousand screams filled the arena. "He wanted to let you in on a little secret."

My heart sped up.

No one had told me about this.

Letty, Molly, and Phoebe appeared, surrounding me as if they thought I might pass out at any second.

"What is goin' on?" I asked.

"You're guess is as good as mine." Letty shrugged.

A couple of roadies ran on stage, moving around some of the equipment.

"Give it up for my little brother, Rafe, everyone."

"Oh my god," I breathed, reaching out for something to steady me.

"We've got you, babe," Molly said, wrapping her arm around me.

"Good evening, Louisville. You're looking pretty fine tonight," Rafe was a natural on the mic. He sat on a high stool, one foot on the floor, an acoustic guitar cradled in his hands. "Some of you might know this isn't my usual style. I let my brother have the spotlight because no one I know does it better than him. But you see, there's this girl..."

Blood roared in my ears as I tried to process what was happening.

"Evangeline Star Walker is one of the best people I know, and I don't know what I ever did to deserve her, but she's mine."

"Oh, sweet baby Jesus," Molly shrieked. "He wrote you a song."

Rafe cleared his throat. "People always say actions speak louder than words, but I didn't want to take any chances." His eyes flicked to mine. "Starshine, this one's for you."

She's just a lost girl, drowning in space.
Nowhere to run, nowhere to go.
All she needs is an anchor, someone to reach out and pull.
Take my hand, I'll be the one,

You saved me, but now it's my turn
To lift you up whenever you fall
Together we're stronger, I'm not letting go
Just give me your hand, and let me show you

I'll be your anchor, let me be your anchor.

She's just a lost girl, fighting through the dark.
Nowhere to run, nowhere to go.
All she needs is an anchor, someone to reach out and pull

I'll be your anchor, let me be your anchor.

I HAD NO WORDS.

None.

Rafe's song was so pure and honest, our love story woven into every lyric, every carefully thought out note.

"Wow, I think my ovaries just exploded." Phoebe smiled.

"Gosh, sweetheart." My parents made a beeline for me. "We knew that boy loved you, but we didn't realize it was quite so serious." She swiped away the tears staining her cheeks.

"I think me and that boy need to have another talk," my dad said around a half-smile. He leaned in. "But between you and me, he gets my blessin'. We'll make him work for it a little longer though." Dad winked.

"That's a good thing," my voice wobbled, even though I said the words with complete conviction. "Because one day, Daddy, I'm goin' to marry that boy."

EPILOGUE

EVA

I woke to an empty bed.

"Rafe?" Pushing up on one elbow, I rubbed the sleep from my eyes and scanned the room. There was a note on the pillow beside me.

Woke early but didn't want to wake you. Snuck out with Fenton to get breakfast.
Love you more than words,
R.

I flopped back onto the soft pillows, smiling at the memories of the night before.

After the show, we had all come back to the suite, my parents included. We ordered a bunch of room service and talked well into the night. There had been jokes and stories and laughter. So much laughter. Hudson always seemed to be laughing at something or other, but it had filled my heart hearing the guys joking around and genuinely enjoying themselves. Even Levi had embraced it, surprising us all with his very own rendition of *Jolene* for my mom, who had revealed she was a huge fan of Dolly Parton. Of course, he'd dragged me up with him, and the two of us had entertained everyone until the whole room had joined in with us.

It had been more than just a celebration. It had been a group of people bound together by love and friendship and family. And I couldn't think of a single place I would rather be.

It still all felt like a dream—Rafe, the tour, the future—except I knew it couldn't be because he had whispered the names of every city we would visit, every city he would kiss me in, as he made love to me.

A small knock at the door pulled me from my reverie. "Eva, can I come in?" Letty peeked her head around the door, her hand covering her eyes.

I chuckled. "It's okay, I'm decent."

"Thank God for that." She slipped into the room but didn't return my smile.

I instantly sat up. "What is it, what happened?"

"We have a problem." She came and perched on the edge of the bed, thrusting her phone at me. I frantically scanned the article.

"My drug-fueled night with a rock star... Mystery woman spills all on sordid night with Black Hearts Still Beat frontman Levi Hunter."

"What the hell is this?" My body trembled as I tried to read the article.

"It was posted this morning. It doesn't name the source and the details are pretty vague but social media chatter is already going wild."

"Oh God, I feel sick." I folded my legs underneath my body.

"Breathe. We've dealt with this kind of thing before. I checked the tabloids and it hasn't broken yet, but stories like this gain interest. PR is already on it... but there's something else." She took her cell phone from me and clicked a few buttons before holding it up for me to watch. "It's grainy; he's barely recognizable."

All the air left my lungs. This couldn't be happening. Not when things were finally good between everyone.

"Eva?"

"Is... is he doin' what I think he's doin'?" Letty was right. The video was grainy, but there was no mistaking Levi snorting a line of powder off a woman's stomach.

Bile rose up my throat.

"What do we do now?"

"We wait. The lack of clarity suggests the source is holding out for an exclusive. If we can figure out who is behind it before that happens, we may be able to stop them."

"I know exactly who's behind it," I said quietly, anger flooding me.

Just then voices filled the air, and heavy footsteps sounded outside the bedroom. "Eva?" Rafe sounded fraught.

"I'll let you two talk, okay? If you need me just call."

"Thank you."

"Eva?" Rafe burst into the bedroom, inhaling a ragged breath.

"I'll just be…" Letty thumbed to the door, slipping around Rafe. He stepped into the room, his eyes locked on mine, begging me to fix it.

"What are we going to do?" He stalked toward me, dropping to his knees at the side of the bed. "Things were finally looking up for him."

I nodded, shuffling to the edge and letting my legs fall on either side of him. "I know, but we'll figure it out, okay? Does Levi know?"

Rafe's expression darkened. "He spent the night with Phoebe. I haven't seen either of them yet."

"Crap," I muttered. "This is bad, real bad. You know who did this, right?"

He nodded. "There's only one explanation that makes sense."

Except it didn't make any sense. What the hell was Levi doing with Riley? But my gut told me I was right—that somehow, she was behind this.

"I can't believe she would stoop so low," I said. "What will happen if she gives the exclusive?" Riley, like all other employees at Razorsharp, would have signed an NDA.

"The label can seek damages. But it won't change the fact the video is out there. It's grainy, but if the exclusive interview breaks, the video will take on a life of its own."

A drug-fueled sex tape.

Just what the band didn't need.

Just what Levi didn't need.

And Phoebe… oh God, poor Phoebe.

The End.

RISK

An Eva & Rafe Bonus Story

"It's beautiful," I yelled across the helicopter. The bright lights of Music City twinkled beneath us. I could just make out the Country Music Hall of Fame and Fortune, and the AT & T building lit up in the distance. But Rafe wasn't watching the sights, he was staring intently at me.

"What?" My lips curved.

"Nothing," he smiled back.

It was two years to the day, that I met him in Ploughton at the Talent Showdown auditions.

My life had changed in ways I couldn't even comprehend back then. I'd gone on tour with the band. A world tour. We'd seen Paris and London, Munich and Barcelona. We'd had so many highs I couldn't even begin to list them all. Of course, touring with a world-famous rock band also came with its lows. But throughout it all, my one constant had been Rafe. He shared in my successes and held me when things got too much. He made me feel grounded, loved and cherished.

Rafe looked at me and my heart still skipped a beat.

It had been almost eighteen months since I first arrived in Atlanta ready to tour with Black Hearts Still Beat. Then, I hadn't realized how much those four broken boys would come to mean to me. They were my family. My best friends. And I couldn't imagine my life without them.

The helicopter did another loop around and I watched with awe as we rode along the Nashville skyline.

"Wow," I breathed. I felt weightless up here, so free and happy. "You're supposed to be watchin' the sights." My eyes slid to Rafe who was still watching me, and my brow lifted.

"My view is pretty good." He toyed with his lip piercing, heat simmering in his gray eyes.

"Rafe," I chuckled but it came out breathy.

He only had to look at me and my blood ran hot. We were supposed to be over the honeymoon stage, those first love flutters and butterflies. But our need for each other only intensified with time.

The helicopter began to descend, landing on the helipad of the Nashville Star Hotel. The rotors began to subside as Travis slid open the door. "Good trip?" He gave me a warm smile, offering me his hand.

"The best." I climbed out, waiting for Rafe, and our security flanked us as we headed inside.

We had the penthouse suite for the weekend. It was more than I needed but Rafe said he wanted to spoil me. It had the best view of the city, the river in the distance. It really was something.

"Are we all set?" I heard Rafe ask Travis.

"We are. The car is already outside."

"Outside?" I gawked at them. "But I thought we had reservations."

"We do." The corner of Rafe's lifted. "Just not at the hotel restaurant."

"What did you do?" My eyes narrowed.

"Don't you trust me?"

"You know I do." My heart fluttered wildly in my chest as we entered the private elevator that linked the penthouse suite with the helipad and the rest of the hotel.

Sometimes it was hard to believe this was my life. That I was Evangeline Star Walker, sweetheart of Country, and one of the biggest selling country musicians of the last decade.

I was also the girl that regularly performed with Black Hearts.

On tour, at charity events, for radio stations and television appearances, we often still worked together. It probably had something to do with the fact I had no desire to be away from Rafe, and he didn't like letting me out of his sight for more than a couple of days.

We were a package deal.

The golden couple of Rock and Country.

And the industry was all too willing to let us reign.

Security managed to get us out of the hotel and into the SUV without difficulty. the details of our trip we airtight, but no matter where we went, people usually spotted us. It was nice to be under the radar for once. Just a couple deeply, madly in love, taking in the sounds and sights of Music City.

My soul was at home here, among her kindred spirits.

Rafe slung his arm around my shoulder and tucked me into his side. "Hey," he said in that sexy low growl of his. The one that made my tummy clench and my breath hitch.

"Hi." I grinned up at him, sliding my hand along his jaw and leaning in. "What have you planned?"

"Wait and see." He winked, his eyes twinkling with mischief and promise. Rafe brushed his lips over mine and I couldn't resist fisting his t-shirt and pulling him closer. Our tongues tangled and heat exploded in my veins.

"Rafe," I breathed, inhaling sharply.

He touched his head to mine, chuckling. "God, I love you."

We rode like that across the city, stolen kisses and tender touches. By the time the car slowed to a stop, I was giddy on love.

"We're here." A faint smile traces Travis' lips. "Enjoy your evening, Eva."

I frowned. Was he in on this too?

Who was I kidding, of course he was. He and Rafe loved nothing more than surprising me.

Gazing up at the building I read the sign, "The Johnny Cash museum." Excitement began to unfurl in my stomach because right above the Johnny Cash museum was the Patsy Cline museum, my favorite country singer of all time.

"Tell me you didn't..."

"I know you've always wanted to see it so I've arranged a private tour."

"Rafe." I threw my arms around his shoulders and kissed him. "Thank you."

He chuckled, tucking me into his side. "Come on, they're waiting for us."

———

THE MUSEUM WAS EVERYTHING I KNEW IT WOULD BE AND MORE. As the tour guide took us around the collection of her personal items and memorabilia, I felt a chill run through me. Music had always settled my soul. It was a part of me, the way oxygen was a part of my blood. But being here, was something else.

"If you don't have any more questions, I'll let you have some time to peruse at your leisure."

"Thank you so much." I offered the tour guide a big smile.

Rafe moved behind and folded his body around mine, resting his chin on my shoulder. "So, what do you think?"

"I love it. It's like I can feel her here, ya know?"

We were in front of the timeline of her short life. "It's so sad she never got to live." My heart squeezed. "I can't help but think that could have been me. I could have so easily—"

"Don't." Rafe brushed his lips over my cheek and I tilted my face to kiss him back. "You lived Starshine. You were given a second chance because you have so much to share with the world."

"I love you," I whispered, blinking away the tears burning the backs of my eyes.

Rafe's expression grew serious. "And I thank the universe every day that Molly entered you in the Talent Showdown." He smiled down at me. I'd never felt as loved as I did right here, in this moment.

"Tonight has been perfect." A contented sigh slipped from my lips.

"Well, I have one more surprise, come on." Rafe took my hand began guiding me back through the museum to the stairwell leading to the exit. But we weren't met by Travis and the SUV, we were met with a horse drawn carriage.

"Seriously?" I fought a smile.

Rafe nodded. "No tour of Nashville is complete with a carriage ride."

"I can't believe you did all this."

He looped his arms round my waist and drew me close. "You're worth it Starshine, you're worth every damn thing."

As Rafe helped me into the carriage, I swooned. It was so romantic, so unexpected.

He tucked me into his side as the drive gave the horses the signal to go. We lurched forward and laughter rumbled in my chest. "I'm surprised Travis let you do this." He didn't usually like things that broke protocol.

"He isn't very far away." Rafe twisted around and pointed to the familiar SUV tailing us.

I rolled my eyes, but I didn't mind, not really. Having a security detail was part and parcel of my life now. Still, it was nice to enjoy one night of normalcy with the man I loved more than anything in the whole world.

ABOUT TEN MINUTES INTO THE RIDE, RAFE GREW ANTSY.

"Are you okay?" I asked him, noticing his fingers tapping rhythmically against his thigh.

When I'd first met Rafe, I'd thought it was habit, that he was playing a riff in his head. But as time went on, I realized it was his tell when he was nervous.

"Yeah, I'm fine."

My eyes narrowed. "You're lyin'."

He let out a strained breath, running his fingers through his hair. "I had this all planned out."

"Rafe, tonight was perfect."

"No, I'm not talking about that." He twisted around slightly and took my hands in his. "I didn't realize how hard this would be but then, Levi was always the one good with words."

"Rafe?" My heart beat wildly in my chest as he gazed at me with such reverence.

"Eva, I love you. I've loved you since the first time I saw you. I know loving me hasn't always been easy, I know our relationship is never going to be straightforward, but I would give it all up in a second if you asked me to. Because you're worth the risk, and all I want is a life with you, Starshine, whatever way I can get you."

I couldn't breathe, couldn't do anything but watch as Rafe pulled a small ring box out of his pocket and flipped the lid.

"I could write lyrics about this moment, turn our story into a song, but no love song will ever truly capture how I feel about you." He plucked the band from the box and took my hand in his. "Evangeline Star Walker, I don't just want right now, I want forever. Be mine. Marry me, Starshine? Make me the happiest guy on the planet."

"Yes," I cried. "Yes, yes, yes."

Rafe slid the perfect princess cut diamond ring onto my finger before cupping my face in his hand. "You and me, Eva. Always."

"Always." Tears rolled down my cheeks, my heart so full I thought it would burst.

Two years ago, I'd been a girl full of guilt and pain. I couldn't understand why I'd been given another chance... and then Rafe came into my life, and I knew.

I knew he was the boy sent to heal me.

All I had to do was take a giant leap of faith.

A risk.

Music saved me.

But Rafe, *loving* Rafe...

That gave me a reason to live.

RAFE

I can't stop looking at her.

My fiancé.

My Starshine.

The ring fit like a glove, all thanks to some sneaky sizing by Letty and Phoebe. I'd had it tucked away for almost three months, but the time never felt right. So when Alistair announced we had some time off at the end of the summer, I knew it was my opportunity.

The SUV rolled to a stop, and Travis came around to open the door.

"Thank you," Eva climbed out first and I marveled again at the ring on her finger.

My ring.

Fuck. That did all kinds of wild shit to my insides.

We entered the hotel through the side entrance, heading straight for the private elevator. But Travis didn't follow us inside.

"Rafe?" Eva asked as the doors began to slide closed. I gave him an appreciative nod. He wouldn't go far but I needed this time with her, alone.

"What is—"

I cut her off with my lips, my tongue sweeping into her mouth. Eva moaned, fisting my t-shirt as I backed her up against the mirrored wall. "I've wanted to do this all night," I breathed the words over her lips.

Eva's eyes sparkled with love and lust, hitting me right in the chest. "I'm so happy." A goofy grin spread over her face.

"You'll be happy in about ten minutes when I'm buried deep inside you," I whispered the words against her ear, and she shivered at my promise.

"How much longer?" Eva glanced over my shoulder at the elevator buttons.

"Almost there," I said, rolling my hips into her. Our quiet moans filled the small space.

The doors finally pinged open, and I picked Eva up, striding down the hall to our suite. "Rafe, put me down." She batted my chest.

"Never." I kissed her, curling my tongue around hers.

We passed security but they didn't bother me. Nothing was going to ruin this moment.

Not a damn thing.

Shouldering open the door, I walked inside and let Eva's body slide down mine. But I didn't let her go. Instead, I crowded her against the wall. "Do you know what you do to me?" I rasped.

"Show me." Eva's head fell back as I ground into her again.

"I'm not sure I can wait."

"So, don't. I need you, Rafe, so much." She began clawing at my t-shirt, my belt.

My hands dipped between us, pushing her skirt around her waist, and finding her panties.

"Oh god," she cried, as I rubbed her over the material. "More, Rafe... more."

"Ssh, Starshine," I drawled, high on the feel of her. Snapping my belt, I managed to shove my jeans down my hips. "Feel this," grabbing one of her hands, I closed it around my rock-hard dick, "it's all for you. Only ever you."

Pulling her panties aside, I lined up against her, letting Eva sink down slowly on me. "Jesus," I hissed, fighting the urge to move. I wanted to savor the moment, tattoo it on my bones and weave it into my soul.

Eva was made for me. Her talent and humility. The way she loved so completely. I loved her big heart and her strength. There wasn't a single thing I didn't love about this girl. And I couldn't wait to stand in front of our friends and family and make her mine.

Forever.

And always.

www.ingramcontent.com/pod-product-compliance
Lightning Source LLC
Chambersburg PA
CBHW070338170726

48291CB00001B/96